PRIZE STORIES OF THE SEVENTIES: FROM THE O. HENRY AWARDS

Over the past sixty years, the annual O. Henry Awards volume of *Prize Stories* has come to represent a standard of literary excellence unsurpassed in the field—one that is widely recognized by readers and aspired to by distinguished writers from every region of the country. Now, for the first time in paperback, twenty-three stories have been chosen from the ten volumes of *Prize Stories* that span the Seventies, with its diverse and talented writers and its stunning range of contemporary moods and modes.

Dramatic and romantic, comic and satiric, *Prize Stories of the Seventies* is a collection that is destined to become a literary milestone, treasured by lovers of the short story for decades to come.

PRIZE STORIES OF THE SEVENTIES: FROM THE O. HENRY AWARDS

Over the past sixty years, the annual O. Henry Awards volume of Prize Stories has come to represent a standard of literary excellence unsurpassed in the field—one that is widely recognized by readers and aspired to by distinguished writers from every region of the country. Now, for the first time in paperback, twenty-three stories have been chosen from the ten volumes of Prize Stories that span the Seventies, with its diverse and talented writers and its stunning range of contemporary moods and modes.

Dramatic and romantic, comic and satiric, Prize Stories of the Seventies is a collection that is destined to become a literary milestone, treasured by lovers of the short story for decades to come.

PRIZE STORIES OF THE SEVENTIES

FROM THE O. HENRY AWARDS

Selected and
with an Introduction by
William Abrahams

WASHINGTON SQUARE PRESS
PUBLISHED BY POCKET BOOKS NEW YORK

A Washington Square Press Publication of
POCKET BOOKS, a Simon & Schuster division of
GULF & WESTERN CORPORATION
1230 Avenue of the Americas, New York, N.Y. 10020

Published by arrangement with Doubleday & Company, Inc.
Library of Congress Catalog Card Number: 80-22790

ISBN: 0-671-41866-1

First Washington Square Press printing June, 1981

10 9 8 7 6 5 4 3 2 1

Printed in the U.S.A.

ACKNOWLEDGMENTS

"Robinson Crusoe Liebowitz," rewritten as "Reflections of a Wild Kid" in *I Would Have Saved Them If I Could* by Leonard Michaels. Copyright © 1970 by Leonard Michaels. Reprinted by permission of Farrar, Straus & Giroux, Inc. and International Creative Management.

"Small Sounds and Tilting Shadows," copyright © 1971 by Judith Rascoe, first appeared in *The Atlantic*, 1971 from *Yours and Mine: Novella and Stories* by Judith Rascoe. By permission of Little, Brown and Company in association with The Atlantic Monthly Press.

"The Destruction of the Goetheanum" by James Salter, first appeared in issue No. 51, winter 1971 of *The Paris Review*. Reprinted by permission.

"Subpoena" from *Sadness* by Donald Barthelme. Copyright © 1971 by Donald Barthelme. This story appeared originally in *The New Yorker*. Reprinted by permission of Farrar, Straus & Giroux, Inc. and International Creative Management.

"The Dead" by Joyce Carol Oates. Copyright © 1971 by Joyce Carol Oates. First published in *McCall's* as "The Death of Dreams." Reprinted by permission.

"Talking Horse" by Bernard Malamud. Copyright © 1972 by Bernard Malamud. Reprinted by permission.

"The Jewels of the Cabots" by John Cheever. Copyright © 1972 by John Cheever. Originally appeared in *Playboy* magazine. Reprinted by permission of the author.

"Brownstone" by Renata Adler. Copyright © 1973 The New Yorker Magazine, Inc. First published in *The New Yorker*. Reprinted by permission of the author.

"Alternatives" by Alice Adams. Copyright © 1973 by The Atlantic Monthly Company, Boston, Mass. Reprinted by permission of the author.

"The Faithful" by James Alan McPherson. Copyright © 1973 by The Atlantic Monthly Company, Boston, Mass. Reprinted by permission of the author.

"Usurpation (Other People's Stories)" from *Bloodshed and Three Novellas*, by Cynthia Ozick. Copyright © 1976 by Cynthia Ozick. Reprinted by permission of Alfred A. Knopf, Inc. and Campbell Thomson & McLaughlin Ltd.

"Are You a Doctor?" from *Will You Please Be Quiet, Please?* by Raymond Carver. Copyright © 1973, 1975, 1976 by Raymond Carver. Reprinted by permission of McGraw-Hill Book Company and Raymond Carver.

"His Son, in His Arms, in Light, Aloft," copyright © 1975 by Harold Brodkey. First appeared in *Esquire* magazine. Reprinted by permission.

"I-80 Nebraska, M.490-M.205" by John Sayles. Copyright © 1975 by The Atlantic Monthly Company, Boston, Mass. Reprinted by permission of the author.

"The Richard Nixon Freischütz Rag" from *Da Vinci's Bicycle* by Guy Davenport. Copyright © 1979 by The Johns Hopkins University Press. Reprinted by permission of the publisher.

"Night March," originally published in *Redbook* as "Where Have You Gone, Charming Billy?" from *Going After Cacciato* by Tim O'Brien. Copyright © 1975, 1976, 1977, 1978 by Tim O'Brien. Used by permission of the publisher, Delacorte Press/Seymour Lawrence and Jonathan Cape, Ltd.

"Separating," copyright © 1975 by John Updike. Reprinted from *Problems and Other Stories*, by John Updike, by permission of Alfred A. Knopf, Inc. and André Deutsch.

"Last Courtesies" from *Last Courtesies and Other Stories* by Ella Leffland. Copyright © 1976, 1980 by Ella Leffland. By permission of Harper & Row, Publishers, Inc. and Wallace & Sheil Agency, Inc.

"The Kugelmass Episode" from the book *Side Effects* by Woody Allen. Copyright © 1977 by Woody Allen. Reprinted by permission of Random House, Inc. First appeared in *The New Yorker*.

"The Schreuderspitze" by Mark Helprin. Copyright © 1977 by The New Yorker Magazine, Inc. First appeared in *The New Yorker*. Reprinted by permission of Julian Bach Literary Agency, Inc.

"My Father's Jokes" from *A Man of Middle Age* by Patricia Zelver. Copyright © 1970, 1971, 1973, 1976, 1978, 1979, 1980 by Patricia Zelver. Reprinted by permission of Holt, Rinehart and Winston Publishers and Wallace & Sheil Agency, Inc.

"Rough Strife" by Lynne Sharon Schwartz. Copyright © 1977 by The Ontario Review. First appeared in *The Ontario Review*. Reprinted by permission.

"A Silver Dish" by Saul Bellow. Copyright © 1978 by Saul Bellow. First appeared in *The New Yorker*. Reprinted by permission.

Contents

Introduction

From the 1970s come these twenty-three stories: all are the work of American writers, all were first published in magazines, and subsequently, having been chosen for O. Henry Awards, were included in an appropriate volume in the ongoing annual series of *Prize Stories*. The ten volumes that span the 1970s include a grand total of 187 stories, winnowed out from the approximately ten thousand eligible for consideration. Given these rather awesome statistics, I must emphasize at the outset that the twenty-three stories collected here are not offered as a further refining or pruning into a kind of "best of the best"—actually, it would not have been difficult to compile an alternative and equally impressive table of contents from among the 165 other O. Henry Award stories of the decade that for one reason or another have been reluctantly passed over.

But having begun on this note of caution, I don't hesitate to add that these twenty-three seem to me splendid exemplars of the quality and variety of the story in the 1970s. They repudiate altogether the notion—widely held in the previous decade—of the story as an endangered or outmoded species. The notion, it may be remembered, was fostered by practitioners of what was then known as the new journalism, and grew out of a palpable misconception: that the private "story" ought to mirror or illustrate in a quick, fictionalized way the public event or background contemporary with it. Surfaces accurately caught; details shrewdly observed; an event pinpointed; characters notated, so to speak, at a level of gossip—all this made for a high-colored, swinging reportage. It did not make for the life (or the view of life) that is the concern of the artist.

I think it fair to say that for most Americans there were two public political events of consuming importance in the 1970s. The first was the continuing, seemingly interminable war in Vietnam, its extension into Cambodia, along with public violence and protest at home, and its bleak, bitter, abrasive conclusion. The second was the criminal activity summed up in the word "Watergate," which led to the resignation (under threat of impeachment) of the President of the United States, and the imprisonment of a number of his aides and colleagues. Neither of these public events—the shame and scandal they have come to represent, the psychic wound they inflicted upon us all, the debasement of the language they encouraged at the time (a premature fulfillment of Orwell's grimmest foreboding in *1984)* and have encouraged since in the self-serving confessional "writings" of the ex-convicts—neither of these public events was dealt with in any extensive, overt way in the American short story. And indeed, since the journalists, new and old, along with the news-gathering and disseminating media, fulfilled the obligation for detail and more detail, there seemed nothing further required. Art could hardly better (or worsen) on a public level, the actual event; or imagine something more frightful than what we were shown on TV news broadcasts. (This truth would seem to be borne out by the frustrating experience of serious film makers attempting to come to terms with Vietnam.)

Not to treat a subject explicitly, however, is not the same as to ignore it, and writers don't live in a vacuum. The spirit of the age, the *zeitgeist,* is in their work—with the exception, possibly, of the rare fantast or historical fictionist who escapes into another age altogether. And the vast, generalized consequences of Vietnam and Watergate—the ever-widening gulf between public and private experience, between the language of politicians and the language of artists (not to say merely decent private individuals)—have formed a dominant theme, consciously or subliminally, in so many stories that it is a distinguishing characteristic of the literature of the 1970s. Again and again, however various the styles in which it is given form, we recognize it: alienation from others, a deep uncertainty in and of the self (who am I?), a tormenting awareness of alternatives, a distrust of accepted pieties. This is the emotional and psychological climate of the 1970s in which, unexpectedly, art thrived, perhaps because writers, turning to the privacy of individual experience for their subject, managed not to be bogged down in stereotypes of gloom and doom; perhaps because, unexpectedly again, comedy has been rediscovered as a means of expressing (and surviving) some of the bleaker truths about human experience.

This opposition between "private life" and "public event" has itself been made the subject of an odd, ironic, and memorable quasi-story—the author himself prefers to think of it as an "assemblage"—that I have included here: Guy Davenport's "The Richard Nixon Freischütz Rag." In it, Davenport introduces us, in a masterly set of juxtapositions, to Richard Nixon in China, on the occasion of his historic state visit; to Leonardo da Vinci in Florence, inverting the bicycle and beguiling a youthful admirer; to Gertrude Stein and Alice Toklas, as young women in love, in the fields below Assisi; and then, back to Mao's China again and public fatuity.

> On the Great Ten Thousand Li Wall, begun in the wars of the Spring and Autumn to keep the Mongols who had been camping nearer and nearer the Yan border from riding in hordes on their przhevalskis into the cobbled streets and ginger gardens of the Middle Flower Kingdom, Richard Nixon said:
> —I think you would have to conclude that this is a great wall.

Davenport remarks of his characters that they have "the instinct to forage," and Nixon, rather like a donkey, foraging in China, has his heehaw, setpiece interjections:

> —That's got to be a good poem, Richard Nixon said.
> —Poem by Chairman Mao, Comrade Tang offered.
> —He wrote that? Richard Nixon asked. Made it up?
> —At hard pass over Mountain Lu, Marshal Yeh said. Long March. February 1935.
> —My! but that's interesting, Richard Nixon said. Really, really interesting.

And in his final appearance—after the lyric outpouring that makes the private episode between Gertrude and Alice so magical—we hear the world's free-shooter (or the free world's shooter) in public with Chairman Mao:

—The world is watching us, Richard Nixon said.
—You mean Taiwan, Chairman Mao said.
—No, Richard Nixon said, beaming, the world out there, the whole world. They are watching their TV sets.
Chairman Mao grinned and leaned back in his comfortable armchair.
—Ah so, he said, the world.

Of such is the world of public events, so essentially remote from us, as far as China, awaiting the patient scrutiny of journalists and scholars. But there is another world we are all familiar with, where the lives of invented men, women, and children, our lives, in all their complexity and ordinariness and (borrowing a phrase of Harold Brodkey's) "an accidental glory," are brought close to us. That world is in these stories, "events" to be welcomed and returned to.

—WILLIAM ABRAHAMS

Robinson Crusoe Liebowitz

Leonard Michaels

LEONARD MICHAELS' first book, *Going Places,* was nominated for a National Book Award, and his stories have appeared in *Partisan Review, Paris Review, Esquire,* and elsewhere. This story, "Robinson Crusoe Liebowitz," appears in different form in his second book, *I Would Have Saved Them if I Could.*

Mandell asked if she had ever been celebrated.

She said, "Celebrated?"

"I mean your body, has your body ever been celebrated?" Then, as if to refine the question: "I mean like has your body like been celebrated?"

"My body has never been celebrated."

She laughed politely. A laugh qualified by her sense of Liebowitz in the bedroom. She was polite to both of them and good to neither. Certainly not to Liebowitz who, after all, wanted Mandell out of the apartment.

But did she care what he wanted? He was her past, a whimsical recrudescence, trapped in her bedroom. He had waited in there for an hour. He could wait another hour. As far as she knew he had cigarettes. But, in that hour, says Liebowitz, his bladder had become a cantaloupe. He strained against the window. The more he strained the more he felt his need.

"I mean really celebrated," said Mandell, as if she had answered nothing.

Perhaps, somehow, she urged him to go on; perhaps she wanted Liebowitz to hear Mandell's lovemaking. Liebowitz says her motives were irrelevant to him. His last cigarette was smoked. He wanted to hear nothing. He wanted to piss. He drew the point of a nail file down the sides of the window, trailing a thin peel, a tiny scream in the paint. Again he strained. The window wouldn't budge. And again. Nothing doing. At that moment, says Liebowitz, he noticed wall-to-wall carpeting. Why did he notice? Because he couldn't piss on it. "Amazing," he says, "how we perceive the world. Stand on a mountain and you think it's remarkable that you can't jump off." In our firm Liebowitz is considered brilliant. He should have done better in life. But there is no justice. He continues:

"My body," said Mandell, "has been celebrated."

Had that been his point all along? Liebowitz wondered why he hadn't been more direct, ripping off his shirt, flashing tits in her face: "Let's celebrate!" She was going to marry a feeb, but that wasn't his business. He had to piss, he had no other business.

"I mean, you know, like my body, like, has been celebrated," said Mandell, again refining his idea. It was impossible for Liebowitz, despite his pain, not to listen—the sniveling syntax, the whining diction—Liebowitz says he tasted every word, and, in that hour, while he increasingly had to piss, he came to know

Mandell, through the wall, palpably and spiritually to know him: "Some smell reached me, some look, even something about the way he combed his hair. . . . I'd never seen him, but I knew he had bad blood."

As for Joyce, a shoe, on its side, in the middle of the carpet—scuffed, bent, softened by the weight of her uncelebrated body—suffused the bedroom with her presence. He could see the walking foot, the strong, well-shaped ankle, peasant hips, elegant neck, and fleshy, boneless, Semitic face. A warm, receptive face until she spoke. Then she had personality. It made her seem taller, more robust. She was robust, heavy bones, big head, with dense yellow-brown hair, and her voice was a flying bird of personality. Years had passed. Seeing the hair again, and Joyce still fallow beneath it, saddened Liebowitz. But here was Mandell. There'd be time for them.

"Has it been five years?" asked Liebowitz, figuring seven. "You sound wonderful." She said he sounded "good." He regretted "wonderful," but noticed no other reserve in her voice, and, just as he remembered, she seemed to love telephone, to come at him much the thing, no later than yesterday.

"The thing," says Liebowitz, quoting one of his favorite authors, "is the thing that implies the greatest number of other things." If Liebowitz had finished his dissertation he'd have a Ph.D. He had too much to say, he says. Years ago his candidacy lapsed.

When his other phone rang he didn't reach for it, thus letting her understand how complete was his attention. She understood. She went on about some restaurant, insisting let's eat there. He didn't consider not. She had said, almost immediately, she was getting married to Hyam T. Mandell, "a professor."

Did Liebowitz feel jealousy? He didn't ask professor of what or where does he teach. Perhaps he felt jealousy, but, listening to her and nodding his compliments at the wall, he listened, he thinks, less to what she said than to how she spoke in echoes. Not of former times, but, approximately these things, in approximately the same way, he felt, had been said in grand rooms, by wonderful people. She brought him the authority of echoes, just the thing; and she delivered herself too, a hundred thirty-five pounds of shank and dazzle. Even in her questions: "Have you seen . . . ?" "Have you heard . . . ?" About plays, movies, restaurants, Jacqueline Kennedy; nothing about his wife, child, job, or spirits. Was she indifferent? embarrassed? a little hostile? In any case he liked her impetuosity. She poked, checked his senses. He liked her, Joyce Wolf, on the telephone; and he remembered that waiters and cabbies liked her, that she could make fast personal jokes with policemen and bellhops, that she tipped big, that a hundred nobodies knew her name, her style. Always *en passant*, very much here and not here at all. He liked her tremendously, he felt revived; not reliving a memory of younger days, but right now, on the phone, living a particular moment among them. For the first time, as it were, that he didn't have to live it. She has magic, he thought, art. She called him back to herself. Despite his grip on the phone, knees under the desk, feet on the floor, he was like a man slipping from a height, deliciously. He would meet her uptown in forty minutes. Did he once live this way? Liebowitz shakes his head. He smirks. He used to be crazy, he thinks.

On his desk lay a manuscript that had to be proofread, and a contract he had to work on; there was also an appointment with an author . . . but, in the toilet with electric razor and toothbrush, Liebowitz was purging his face and shortly thereafter he walked into a Hungarian restaurant on the East Side. She arrived twenty minutes later in a black, sleeveless dress; very smart.

He felt flattered. He took her hands. She squeezed his hands. He kissed her cheek, he said, "Joyce." The hair, the stretch of white smile, the hips . . . he remembered, he looked, looked and said, "It was good of you, so good of you to call me." And he looked into his head. She was there too. Joyce. Joyce Wolf who got them to the front of lines, to seats when the show was sold out, to tables, to tables near windows, to parties. . . .Sold out you say? At the box office, in her name, two tickets were waiting. But Liebowitz remembers, once, for a ballet, she failed to do better than standing room. "I didn't really want to go. I certainly didn't want to stand," he says. "Neither did she. But the tickets were sold out. Thousands wanted to go." She scratched phone numbers till her fingernail bled. That evening they stood with pelvises against a velvet rope and hundreds stood on either side and behind them, jammed into a narrow aisle. The effluvia of a dozen alimentary canals hung about their heads. Blindfolded, required to guess, Liebowitz would have sworn they were in a delicatessen. Lights dimmed. There was a sudden, thrilling hush. Joyce whispered, "How in God's name can anyone live outside New York?" She nudged him and pointed at a figure seated in the audience. He looked, nodding his head to show appreciation for her excitement and her ability to recognize anyone in New York in almost total darkness. "See! See!" He nodded greedily, his soul pouring toward a glint of skull floating among a thousand skulls, and he begged, "Who? Who is it?" He felt on the verge of extraordinary illumination when a voice wailed into his back: "I can't see. All year I waited for this performance and I can't see. I can*not* see." Liebowitz twisted about and glanced down. A short lady, staring up at him, pleaded with her whole face. He twisted frontward and said, "Move a little, Joyce. Let her up against the rope." Joyce whispered,

"This is the jungle, schmuck. Tell her to grow another head." He was impressed, says Liebowitz. During the ballet he stood with the velvet rope in his fists, the face between his shoulder blades. And now, going uptown in the cab, his mouth was so dry he couldn't smoke. After all these years, he was still impressed. Joyce got them tickets. She knew, she got what she wanted. Him, for example, virtually a bum in those days, but nice-looking, moody, a complement, he supposes, to her, though he doesn't really know why she cared for him. He was always miserable. "Perhaps a girl with so much needs a little misery." Not that she was entirely without it. She worked as private secretary to an investment broker, a shrewd, ugly Russian with a hunchback and a limp who wanted a "Collich girl" to kiss his ass. "Hey, Collich, make me a lousy phone call." After work, she used to meet Liebowitz and, hunching, dragging a foot, she would shout, "Hey, Collich. Hey, Collich." They laughed with relief and malice, but sometimes she met Liebowitz in tears. Her boss once slapped her across the mouth. "In a Longchamps. During lunch hour," she said, then screamed at Liebowitz, "Even if there had been a reason." Liebowitz stopped trying to justify such horror. He raged. The next morning he would go punch the man. The next morning, in chic Italian sunglasses, she left for the office. Alone. Five foot seven, she walked seven foot five, a Jewish girl passing for Jewish in tough financial circles. Liebowitz points out, "She made two hundred fifty a week in salary, and with insults and slaps, the Russian gave tips on the market." He, Liebowitz, then salesman in a shoe store, made eighty a week hunkering over corns. He had only rotten moods, a lapsed candidacy for the Ph.D. in philosophy, and her, a girl with access to the pleasures of Manhattan. Her chief pleasure was moody Liebowitz. She was twenty-four years old, a virgin when she met Liebowitz who took her, and what she represented to him, on their first date. "I don't know how it happened," she said. "Two minutes ago I was a virgin." Liebowitz coolly lied, "Normal." She had been surprised, confused. He had been merely cool, like a vulgar hoodlum. "Where's your shower?" he asked. Now he wonders if he hadn't been mean to her. He makes big eyes, he holds his palms up like a man asking for apples. "I had certain needs." The gesture is rabbinical, ancient, carried in his genes. "I descend," says Liebowitz, "from rabbis, deep readers of the Talmud and life." He had been mean, yet she was always good to him and, decently, had called him to announce her forthcoming marriage and ask him out to dinner. Walking into the restaurant Liebowitz acknowledges an erection, but, he asks, can that explain why he ran uptown with a dry mouth to meet her; then went strolling in the park, he asks; then went up to her apartment for a drink, he asks. Life is mystery, thinks Liebowitz. After the drink he was considering a hand on her knee, he says, to reach for solutions, when the doorbell rang. "Don't answer," he said. She pleaded the sweetness of Mandell, his wit, his conversational power. "Don't answer," said Liebowitz. "Maybe it's someone else," she said. It wasn't. Liebowitz opted for the bedroom, the shut door; finally, himself tearing at the window, wild to piss.

"Didn't you say you were going to work this evening?"

"Did I say that?"

Mandell had had a whimsy impulse. Here he was, body freak, father of her unborn children. She could have done better, thought Liebowitz. Consider himself, Liebowitz, for example. Seven years had passed, a girl begins to feel desperate, but still—her style, her hips—she could have done better than Mandell, he thinks, despite her strong conviction—in fact her boast—that Mandell wasn't just any professor of rhetoric. "He loves teaching—speech, creative writing, anything—and every summer at Fire Island he writes a novel of ideas. None are published yet, but Hyam doesn't care about publication. People say his novels are very good. I couldn't say, but he talks about his writing all the time, and he really cares about it."

"I can see Mandell," says Liebowitz, "curled over his typewriter. His forehead presses the keys. Sweat fills his bathing-suit jock. It's summertime at Fire Island. He is having an idea so he can stick it in one of his novels." To Joyce, Liebowitz said, "I wish our firm published novels. You know of course we only do textbooks." She said she knew, yet looked surprised and changed the subject. "He is terribly jealous of you. It was long ago, I was a kid, he wasn't even in the picture. But Hyam is the kind of man who wonders about a girl's former lovers. Not that he's weird or anything, just social. He's terrific in bed."

"Does he know I'm seeing you tonight?" His hand ached for her knee. It was getting late. Her voice had begun to cause brain damage, says Liebowitz; it had to be stopped. She laughed again. Marvelous sound, thought Liebowitz, just like laughter; and he was nearly convinced she deserved Mandell. But why didn't she send him away? Because Liebowitz's firm didn't do novels? Was he supposed to listen? to burn with jealousy? He burned to piss.

"Is something wrong, Joycie?"

Mandell didn't understand. Did she seem forbidding, too polite? Did she laugh too much?

"I wanted to talk to you about my writing, but, really Joycie, is there something like wrong?"

Liebowitz realized that Mandell was embarrassed, unable to leave. Of course. How could he leave with her behaving that way? He was just as trapped as Liebowitz, who, bent and drooling, gaped at a shoe, a dressing table, combs, brushes, cosmetics, a roll of insulation tape . . . and, says Liebowitz with rabbinical fire in his eyes, before he knew what he had in mind, he had seized the tape. He laid two strips, in an X, across a windowpane, smacked the nail file into the heart of the X, and, gently, pulled away the tape, carrying off sections of broken glass. Thus, a big, jagged hole in the pane.

"I was another Robinson Crusoe. Trapped, isolated, and yet I could make myself comfortable."

He felt proud. Mainly, he felt a searing release. Liebowitz pissed. Through the hole, across an echoing air shaft, a long, shining line. He listened to his flow—burning, arcing, resonant—as he listened to Mandell's. "I have a friend who says my novels are like writing, dig? He means they are *like* writing, but not real writing, you get it?" Liebowitz shook his head, thinking, "Some friend," as he splashed brick wall and a window on the other side of the air shaft, and, though he heard yelling, he heard nothing relevant to Robinson Crusoe, and, though he saw a man's face, he saw nothing relevant to his personal comfort, though he pissed on the man's face yelling from the window on the opposite side of the air shaft into which he pissed, says Liebowitz, as if it were his traditional and sovereign privilege to piss on the man's face.

"A very good neighborhood," says Liebowitz, with an appreciative mouth, puckered in the middle, curled down in the corners. "East Seventies, near the river. First-rate. The police wouldn't take long." He wondered what to say, how to say it, and he zipped up carefully. In the dressing-table mirror he saw a face bloated by pressure, trying not to cry. "According to my face," says Liebowitz, "a life was at stake." His life was at stake and he couldn't grab a cab. Mandell still whined about his writing. "Joyce couldn't interrupt and say go home. Writers are touchy. He might have gotten mad and called off the marriage." Liebowitz had no choice but to prepare a statement. "My name, officers, is Liebowitz." Thus, he planned to begin. Not brilliant. Appropriate. He'd chuckle perhaps in a jolly, personable way, like a regular fellow, not a drunk or a maniac. Mandell, meanwhile, was shrill and peevish: "Look here, look here, look here. My name is Hyam T. Mandell. I'm a professor of rhetoric at Bronx Community Institute, Moshalu Circle Campus. And a novelist. This is extremely ironic, but it is only a matter of circumstances and I have no idea what it means."

A strange voice said, "Don't worry, professor, we'll explain later."

Joyce said, "This is a silly mistake. I'm sure you chaps have a lot to do. . . ."

Mandell cut in, "Take your hands off me. And you shut up, Joyce. I've had enough of this crap. Like show me the lousy warrant or like get the hell out. No Nazis push me around. Joyce, call someone. I'm not without friends. Call someone."

Someone fell down. The strange voice said, "Hold the creep."

With something like hatred Mandell was now screaming, "No, no, no, don't come with me. I don't want you to come with me, you stupid bitch. Call someone. Get help." The hall door slammed shut. The bedroom door, suddenly, was open and Joyce was in it: "You hear what happened? Did you? How can you sit and stare at me? I've never felt this way in my life. Look at you. Lepers could be screwing at your feet. Do you actually realize what happened?"

Liebowitz shrugged yes mixed a little with no. "I never felt such clarity in her before," he says. He himself, he thinks, looked pale, sick with feeling. She said, "I see, I see. You're angry. You're furious because you had to sit in here. Well what could I do? What could I say? You're angry as hell, aren't you?" Liebowitz didn't answer. He felt a bitter strength in his position. She began pinching her thighs to express suffering and, unable to deal with herself alone, across the room from him, she came closer to the bed. "Are you angry? Do you know what just happened in that room?" Liebowitz said, "The cops took the putz away." His tone allowed her to sit down beside him. "It's horrible, it's humiliating," she said. "They think he pissed out the window." Then, "He called me a stupid bitch." Liebowitz said, "Joyce, you might be a stupid bitch, but I believe you look as good to me now as years ago. In some ways, better." He put his hand on her knee. It seemed to him a big hand, full of genius and goodness and power. Her mouth and eyes grew slow, as if the girl behind them stopped jumping. She glanced at his hand. "I must make a call," she said softly, a little urgently, and started to rise. Liebowitz pressed down. She sat. "It wouldn't be right," she said, and then, imploring, "Would you like to smoke a joint with me?"

"No."

She has middle-class habits, he thinks, a part of her style. "It wouldn't be right," she said, as if to remind him of the point, not to insist on it. But what's right, what's wrong to a genius? Liebowitz, forty years old, screwed her like a nineteen-year-old genius.

"My adventure," says Liebowitz, "gives me an idea for a novel. The theme is cloacal. A novel in the first person. For example: 'I was trapped in the bedroom. I had to piss.' How intimate. How immediate. Just like writing. But my trouble is I have no feeling for adventure. I was once the willing fool of chance, but now I despise adventure. It means chaos, evil. I'm a married man, I have a little child. I swim happily in the banal quotidian. I live in the West Nineties, I own a Dodge, a lot of furniture. Steal the Dodge, burn the furniture, give me skin disease. So? So I'm insured, mother, inside and out. Have you read the *Book of Job?* It's not about me. My name is Liebowitz," he says. "Liebowitz."

Small Sounds and Tilting Shadows

Judith Rascoe

JUDITH RASCOE was born in San Francisco in 1941, and grew up there and in Boise, Idaho. She studied at Stanford and at Harvard, and in 1969-70 she returned to Stanford as a Creative Writing Fellow. She is now living in California, working as a free-lance journalist and finishing a screenplay.

When I was twenty-one I was half-crazy—I spent myself on that, as if madness were entailed on my maturity. Perhaps it was: I am the youngest child of an elderly family, and when I came along they had already been confined in middle age, convalescing from the strenuous regime of pills, drink, and lawsuits that had cured them of youth.

When I was half-crazy I went to Paris, intending to be old. "Why do you have all these dark dresses?" my boyfriend said. "Look at them: dark green, dark blue, brown. Gray. Black." They lay folded on the bed, with black stockings, black leather shoes, black leather gloves, and handbags fitted with brass and secret locks. I had a diary bound in oilcloth and a letter folder that made a desk of one's lap and dispensed paper, envelopes, and stamps. I had a Swiss knife.

"I'll be with you in a month," my boyfriend said.

I thought he was lying, but now I think perhaps he meant to come, although I didn't want him to. I had a return passage on a ship and no companion; my family didn't even consider the hazards of my traveling alone—they had met no temptations in twenty years. They worried more about sickness and insisted I have all my teeth fixed before I left.

A week after I arrived in Paris I was sick and lay abed while the woman who managed my small hotel brought me broth and tea. I said *Merci,* echoing her voice that was lower and rustier than mine. The bellboy was a little Yugoslav who thought love would cure me. He came late at night and kissed me and brought magazines the guests had left in their rooms; he turned off the lamp and tried to get under the covers. "Ai ahm note ofraid," he said. At last the manageress called a doctor. He listened to my lungs and felt my pulse. "*Mademoiselle,*" he said, "*vous avez la grippe,*" and he ordered a vial of charcoal flavored with licorice.

When I could get out of the hotel again, I came to hate Paris. Although I wore a wrinkled coat, my hair was limp, and my face was spotty, I was followed in the streets and cafés by rat-faced men who usually claimed they had jobs with foreign consulates. When I yelled at them, *Allez!,* I humiliated myself more than them. I fixed on the idea of going to London, where people spoke English, for sometimes my head swam from listening too hard to French and finding words for my replies. *"J'irai, Madame, je voyage en Londres,"* I said to the manageress. *"L'addition, s'il vous plaît."*

In London I looked up all the names in my address book and went to "events." From a bed-and-breakfast hotel near Regent's Park I wrote letters home in my new italic handwriting to say that I was having a wonderful time. Air letters swiftly responded: why wasn't I in Italy? My aunts liked to talk about going to Italy: they took extension courses in the language and subscribed to travel magazines; but Wenona's husband hates airplanes and Vivian's husband, a diabetic, is convinced that there is no adequate medical care in Europe. "I hope you go to Rome," Wenona said in every letter.

But I was contentedly growing older: I bought walking shoes, mackintoshes, and tweed skirts, and with guidebooks and mystery magazines I went to Brighton and Horsham, Canterbury and Ely. The autumn came in languidly, filling the countryside with mists.

One evening in London I was walking out of Regent's Park when I realized that my stomach hurt and my face was hot. Mr. Wing at the hotel sent me to Doctor Evans, who asked me a good many questions—I had only one: was this *la grippe* again?—and touched me gently here and there and then prodded me until I squeaked. It was appendicitis—he suggested it had always been appendicitis—and the next morning my appendix was gone. Two or three of my new friends came to the hospital and seemed full of concern.

"I can't travel," I said. "They want to send me to a convalescent home."

Then by lucky chance somebody knew somebody else who knew of a flat.

"I can't afford a flat," I said.

"It's rent-free. You'd be caretaker. But you must be prepared to leave on a moment's notice."

"Well, that's no good," I said.

"It'll be weeks before you have to go."

"Then I'll take it," I said.

There are hundreds of squares in London that are indistinguishable from Canon Square, a meanly fenced little park surrounded by Georgian houses, each with its below-stairs rooms made into a "garden flat," with a flight of steps up from the street and staring big windows that the tenants must cover with heavy curtains to keep out the cold. Some of the houses on Canon Square were bed-and-breakfast places. One was a tenement full of Pakistani immigrants. Another (they said at the pub) was a brothel. "Which one?" I asked. Nobody was certain. On the side streets that did not command a view of the park there were cheap cafés and butcher shops, greengrocers, ironmongers. When I first moved to Canon Square, I hobbled, still bent double from my stitches, from shop to shop and satisfied the British taste for grotesquerie. "This is the lass what lost her appendix!" the greengrocer said to his other customers when I came into his shop. "When are you going to show us the stitches, love?"

"Here, look at this!" the butcher's wife said. She kicked off her shoe to show us a webbed toe. Everybody laughed but me.

Despite the discomforts of walking bent over, I stayed out much of the day. Partly it was the sheer inconvenience of the place, for the flat was at the very top of the house and there was no elevator, only steep, uncarpeted stairs. The rooms were low and had whitewashed walls and dark gray fitted carpeting. A tiny window in the kitchen looked down on Canon Square and the treetops that were losing their leaves by handfuls. Larger windows in the back rooms looked down into a wasted garden, across to other rooftops and chimneys. I bought flowers, several bunches at a time, but their color was lost in the dim white light of the rooms.

"Come back with me," I begged friends and acquaintances. "Let me fix you a meal. Let me fix you dinner." I turned on all the electric fires and kept the record player going all the time.

"It's a grim sort of place, isn't it," everybody said, sooner or later.

For a week I had an English boyfriend. "Don't mind my stitches," I said. "It doesn't hurt. Stay. Please stay." But as we lay side by side under cold sheets and rough blankets, the eye of the electric fire upon us, we were too much alone; the loneliness sifted between us, like falling snow. Silences blew into drifts and froze solid. At the end of the week he had to go up to Manchester, to see his family. His dad was ill.

The next week I went to a party where I met a big aggressive man who produced programs for the BBC. He sweated as he drank, and he wore a lot of rings. "What will you do with yourself, darling?" he asked, when he'd got my story out of me. "Will you go back to university? Or will you be an air host*ess?* Who are you, tell me that, will you, who are you?" I burst into angry tears. "Why do you want to know?" I said. "You don't care who I am."

"Come on," he said, aiming for a taxi, his flat, his bed. "Come on, darling, it's late."

"No," I said, though I wanted to go with him. It would be cozy in his flat: I imagined lots of magazines and whiskey. But I'll never know. He didn't find it worthwhile to argue with me.

I got into a taxi alone and said, "Canon Square, please," but then I pictured what the flat would look like when I got there. The light from any lamp I switched on would fall in a crisply drawn figure on the carpet; the bedroom had curtains of dark gray velvet, from the floor to the ceiling, and if I did not open them, I could not tell whether it was day or night. Sometimes I went into that room at noon and found myself staring at the shadow of the bed, the unchanging shadows in the curtains. I rapped on the taxi's partition. "Gloucester Terrace," I said. "I'm sorry. I've changed my mind."

A nice boy named Michael lived in Gloucester Terrace—a socialist who ran an office somewhere helping somebody. When I rang the bell, he came to the front door in robe and pajamas. "I'm sorry," I said, "but I couldn't stand to go home. Can I stay here tonight?" He looked at me as if he wanted to say no with all his heart, but he let me in anyway and gave me pajamas and tucked me into a far corner of his bed.

The moon came through the window and shone on the corner of the high-headed bed. It was silent and cold; Michael slept inaudibly, but I lay awake for a long time because I felt safe.

The next day, when I got back to Canon Square, I was obsessed by the big man who wore so many rings. He had asked who I was. I knew who I was, all right—so I said to myself: I am . . . and listening, I heard only water in the pipes, wind rapping on a window, my own sigh.

"Who lives here?" I said out loud.

The flat's leaseholder, the man with his name on the bell, was a Canadian journalist, I'd been told. The flat had come to me from a friend of his, who had been charged with its safekeeping and who had decided to go to Italy instead. I was to keep it clean, dusted, have the window washer in, and keep the cupboards stocked with tinned food. When I was given the key, I had asked: "Where is he? When will he be back?

"I think—but you mustn't tell anybody—I think he's in China," said the departing buddy.

"Then what should I do with the mail?"

"Keep it. Unless there's something that looks very urgent; you can send that to this address; let me write it down."

Finally a letter came that looked urgent. I telephoned the address I'd been given. "There's a letter here," I said, "that looks urgent. Can you . . . should I send it on to you? Where is he?"

"I suppose," said a woman who didn't sound as if she thought it urgent at all. "I don't know where he is, honestly I don't.'

"I don't mean to pry," I said.

"It's no secret," she said. "He's in Cuba."

Because I read mystery novels I began to wonder if my so-to-speak landlord was a genuine journalist, but when I looked up his name in a library, I found, to my disappointment, that every month or two he appeared in one magazine or another. He had been to Cuba before and had written three accounts of his visit, for *Maclean's*, the *Spectator,* and *Queen*. There were pieces on the theater in Prague, rural socialism in Yugoslavia, an academic dispute at the University of Toronto, and lots of reviews for English weeklies of books by Canadian writers. His style was distinguished for its impersonality, touched with a suggestion of "I would . . . if I could" and things unsaid but understood among friends. It was impossible to learn from his articles whether he was leftward or rightward in politics; whether he thought Canadian writing was comparable with contemporary stuff from France or America, or whether he thought it was a provincial disaster.

After reading his writings, I began to mention his name (these were the weeks of the boyfriend and the party), and everybody professed to know it, even to know him. "Oh, yes, Willie," was the typical response. "So that's where you're living, in Willie's flat."

One night I met a man who worked in a publishing house. Willie, he assured me, was in the American South, where he was writing about the civil rights movement.

A little more than three weeks after I had moved to Canon Square, I woke up late one morning and lay in bed, watching the sky for a bird or a change of hue upon the gray. Sometimes I dozed and the small noises of the house, pipes and drafts, filled my head so that I sank into sleep like a floating bottle that a wave tilts, and with a sigh is filled and sunk. And then I rose again. The clock said eleven, but it had stopped. I got out of bed and turned on the electric fire. I thought I heard footsteps.

"Who's there?" I said. "I'm coming."

The door of the flat opened upon a landing and a cascade of stairs, through darkness to the mat of light from the fanlight, three floors below. Walking downstairs, I saw that everybody's door was shut. In the mailbox there were two magazines for Willie Ferland and an advertising circular. I went upstairs again but hesitated on the threshold. "Is somebody there?" I said.

When there was no answer, I made myself go in and walk around the flat, from room to room. "Hello?" I said. "Hello, there?" Nobody was there.

Had there been somebody to ask me: "Do you think somebody got in the flat?" I would have said, No, I don't think so, because I did not think so in the ordinary way one thinks that, say, the telephone has rung or there's a strange noise from the garage. Rather it was as if a passing thought—"What if somebody darted into the flat while I went down for the mail?"—had lodged in my mind so tenaciously that it claimed a reality of its own and began to feed upon every sound and tilt of light. Or like a thought which, on the verge of sleep, becomes a dream.

I opened the closets. One held brooms and overshoes. Another held towels and a cigar box filled with prescription bottles. A third contained the immersion water heater and some stiff towels, left there to dry and forgotten. The closet in the bedroom was a big one with a rod at least six feet long. At one end hung my dresses and coats, with my suitcase open on the floor beneath them, spilling stockings, and at the other end of the rod were a few things that must have belonged to Willie: a green Irish sweater, a couple of jackets—one tweed and one corduroy—a Hudson's Bay wool shirt, and a dark blue woolen robe. I put on the robe and learned that Willie was a small man, for the robe almost fit me. In one pocket I found an expensive American ball-point pen, in the other a key on a piece of string. The warmth of the robe picked up my spirits; I went to the kitchen to make tea and then dialed the telephone to find out the time. It was almost three in the afternoon.

It began to rain. Straining over the sink, I could see the pavement round Canon Square darken, the only mother and child in the park hurry out of it, latching the iron gate behind them. I put Bach on the record player, ate toast with my tea, and chose one of Willie's books—he had stacks of them in the room that he used as a study, mostly Canadian novels. I read about a brave couple living alone in Saskatchewan. It grew dark. I switched on the lights and had sardines on toast for supper. The Bach record played over and over again until it began to sound comical, like a mechanical rainstorm. With Willie's ball-point pen I wrote a shopping list as an excuse to study my handwriting. It was nothing like Willie's. In the back of his books he had made notes for his reviews: his handwriting was small and upright, without ornament. I tried to copy it.

Willie Ferland, I wrote. My capitals were larger than his, my letters more florid.

Inaccuracies description p. 36 repeated later, I wrote, getting the knack of it: if I held the pen close to the tip, if I squeezed it tight and pressed each letter into the paper with a few hard strokes, I had the look of his writing. Yet only the look: the original was too small for me, done with an impulse of control I could not imitate. I essayed an independent sample:

Dear Mike: Sorry but my French isn't up to this. Who ever told you we were all bilingual? All my best, Willie.

Comparing it with a paragraph penciled in the back of a guidebook to Quebec I thought my forgery looked convincing at first glance. But forgery didn't interest me; the spirit of the writing did. I found a sheet of paper in the drawer of his desk and wrote the word *description* several times; then I decided to look for more examples. The desk had two drawers, one with stationery and the other full of manila envelopes marked Yugo Co., Chichester etc., Anthlgy, and *Blue Over and Under.* Peeping inside the envelopes I found typescripts, and put them back.

The only other objects in the study, besides desk and chair and stacks of books without shelves, were two pasteboard boxes. I opened one and found it full of letters addressed to Willie, all of them put back into their torn envelopes; the other box was full of manila folders holding typewritten manuscripts. I could imagine what would happen if I were to go through the letters and the manuscripts and then turn to find that somebody had been watching me.

I turned, saying, "Yes?"

There was nobody there.

I lifted out one manila folder and closed the box. There were no curtains on the window in the study: from the window I saw the raincloud lit up by the sodium lights and dabs of light on the curtained back windows of houses behind Number 12. I made myself a drink from the single bottle of whiskey that Willie had left behind and wrote *Scotch, Teacher's* in his handwriting on the back of an envelope addressed to me.

The next morning Michael called me. "Who's this?" he asked when I answered the phone.

"It's me," I said.

"I thought it was someone else for a minute. So you're still there in your gloomy great flat, are you? Do you ever leave it?"

"Most of the time," I said.

"Would you leave it for an excursion to the cinema?"

"Yes," I said. "Anytime."

I dusted and threw out dead flowers and changed the sheets. I wore Willie's robe because it kept me warm, and I carried on imaginary conversations with Willie because they kept me occupied. *Have you been in this country long?* I asked him.

Ten years, he said. *Five years.*

You don't want me to know.

I'm secretive, he said. *Why do you want to know?*

Do you like it here? Will you stay?

What do you think?

I don't know, I said.

In the cabinet in the living room I found a set of highball glasses wrapped in store tissue, a windup tin train engine, ornamental matchboxes, a spring device for exercising the arms, and a half-dozen big enlarged photographs of a handsome woman with windblown dark hair. She looked everywhere but at the camera, she favored her right side.

Michael came and said, "Christ, this is dreary."

When we left Canon Square and got to a main thoroughfare, I was surprised to find that London was full of people. They hurried along the pavements with their heads down and umbrellas up; the women's boots smashed through the puddles; their shopping bags bumped and swayed. The butcher was almost hidden by a crowd of heads in scarves; his wife wrestled with the goods in the window, elbowing hanging sides of beef out of her way as she went for the tray of kidneys. We had to wait in line for our fish and chips; we were pushed against the wall as we ate. The pub was noisy and steamy; not an empty table in the lounge, the dart board busy. There was even a queue for the movie. We bought chocolates and tickets for the middle stalls, and afterwards I said I'd had a super evening.

"Me too," Michael said.

We went to another pub, and in the closing-time uproar Michael said he was going to Bristol at the week's end; a job in social work had appeared; he didn't want to run the London office any longer.

"Why don't you come with me?" he said.

"Why?" I said.

"What's keeping you here?"

I was offended: "I have things to do."

"Oh, what?"

"I want to get a job teaching. I like London. I've been writing to the LCC—they might need somebody in the middle of the year. I expect I'll hear soon." It was a lie, but he had no reason to think so; instead he looked hurt and changed the subject.

The manuscript in the manila folder was a short story about a man who tries to get his wife into a lunatic asylum: he has taken a long train ride to the asylum so that he can talk to the doctors. They say that they have too many patients already, that they're understaffed. One doctor, a young Welshman, wants to talk only about what he could earn if he went into private practice. On the lawns of the asylum the patients take aimless walks or sit in the sun. An old man is lost and found again: the nurse comes to the psychiatrist's office to ask if he wants to see the old man. "Why shouldn't he try to escape?" the psychiatrist says. "It's the first sensible thing he's done. I don't want to see him." At last the visitor says he has to go back to London; the doctors advise him to care for his wife at home as long as he can manage it. The man leaves, and during the train ride back to the city, we learn he is not married.

"Who's there?" I said, when I finished it. I thought I'd heard a doorstep. I called the number of the woman who thought Willie was in Cuba. To a housekeeper I said, "It's about Willie Ferland." Then a man came to the telephone.

"Willie," he said. "Is that you?"

I hung up without answering.

That evening the telephone rang, and a man said, "Hello, Willie? I heard you were back."

I didn't answer that time, but when the telephone rang again within a minute I was scared he might call the police, and so I said, "Hello? Who is this?"

"Who's this? Is Willie there?"

"I'm afraid you have the wrong number."

"Is this EDGeware 4494?"

"This is EDGeware 3494."

"I'm sorry," he said.

He rang a couple of times but I didn't pick up the receiver. For the rest of the night, for the rest of the next day, I waited for the police, but nobody came. The telephone rang occasionally, but I would not answer it. Instead I went shopping for fresh flowers and Scotch, and I bought paper and envelopes—heavy, large cream sheets and large, stiff envelopes—to write to the London County Council.

"Dear Sirs," I wrote. "I am an American, just graduated from university, and having settled in London, I think I would like to teach.

"I have a B.A. degree in music and five credits of work in elementary education." But I hadn't. I had a B.A. in English and five or ten or fifteen credits in drama. I had signed for two courses in education and dropped them both; I could teach German expressionist drama, but that did not seem suitable for a London primary school. In the *New Statesman* I read of appointments vacant: librarians, scientists, lecturers in Anglo-African history at the University of Ibadan.

I twisted the heavy cream paper into spills and threw them into the basket. On a fresh sheet of paper I wrote in Willie's hand:

Dear Mike. No bloody luck with the jobs. I refuse to go to Malawi. Anything opening up at the magazine? Let me know soonest. Willie.

The mail brought a book from Jonathan Cape, Ltd., a collection of Canadian verse. I skipped about in it and thought it wasn't very good. On another piece of paper I composed a note to Willie: "This came October 2 and I opened it because I was curious. I look forward to your review." As I wrote I found myself trying to forge my own handwriting, but the letters were too carefully drawn, and some of Willie's mannerisms had crept in. So I copied the note again on the typewriter and put it in the book.

The telephone rang. "Willie, listen." I'd never heard the voice before. "I've got her in trouble, God help me. Do you understand? Do you know a doctor?"

"Willie's not here just now," I said.

"Who is this?"

"I'm just visiting."

"Leave a message for him, will you? Tell him to call John Webb. I don't suppose you know a doctor, do you?"

"No," I said. "Leave a number, and he'll call you."

"Tell him it's urgent."

"I will."

I called the fat man who worked for the BBC. "Listen," I said. "I'm sure you don't remember me, but I'm in an awful fix. I'm pregnant, and I'm really stuck."

"I don't see what I can do," he said. "Sorry, darling."

"Listen, I have nobody else to ask."

"Wait a mo'."

The receiver smashed against something, and there were voices in the distance, a woman's voice sounding querulous.

"You *might* . . ." he said. "You might give this girl a ring. Explain everything to her. Be absolutely frank. Do you understand me?"

"Thank you, oh, I can't thank you enough," I said.

"That's all right," he said. "I'm sorry to hear it."

I called the number, and when a girl answered, I was absolutely frank: my boyfriend was an American airman in Germany, I said, and I'd got knocked up by this man in London, a married man, and my boyfriend was coming and I was desperate.

"Love, that's terrible," the girl said. She had a nice alert voice. "Love, I can't help you much, I can only give you the number of this doctor in Maida Vale. Ring him and see if he can help. Otherwise, I dunno. It's been a couple of years."

"You've been a great help," I said.

"If he's not there, ring me again," she said. "I'll ask my girlfriend."

Then I called John Webb. "Willie had to go out again," I said. "But he asked me to give you this number. It's a doctor in Maida Vale. He doesn't know if it's still any good or not."

"Kiss him for me, love," John Webb said.

That same day a woman called who said that she had just arrived from Vancouver and that she loved his articles, she had read every one.

"He'll be happy to hear that," I said. "I'm sorry he's not in just now."

"I'll be in London for the rest of the week."

"Try later," I said. "I just can't say when he'll be back. But I'm glad you called. Lots of people don't realize that a writer doesn't get many compliments about his work. People think of writing to him and then they're shy. So I'll be sure to tell him you called."

"Thank you very much, Mrs. Ferland," she said.

I typed a note for Willie: "November 10, woman called to say she liked your articles, will call back."

The telephone didn't ring again that day, and I didn't leave the house. Wearing Willie's bathrobe I lay on the couch in the living room, reading Canadian verse and listening to Mozart. The clock stopped again and the rain started again. When my stomach ached I convinced myself I hadn't recovered from appendicitis. I went to bed early and drew the curtains in the bedroom and fell asleep with the light on. Sometime, I don't know when, I sat up in bed with my heart pounding.

"Who is it?" I said. "Hello?"

The rain trickled against the window, and I didn't know if it was day or night: I got up and opened the closet and looked at Willie's jackets. They were so frightening: what if I had to get up and put on Willie's clothes? Was that what I had to do? Then why was I frightened? That meaningless fancy seemed peculiarly horrible to me: what if I had to get up and dress in his clothes and do what he had to do? There was a smell of self-hatred in the flat. He kept no mirrors, no photographs of himself, no souvenirs to remind himself of who he was. He put his letters back in their envelopes, ready to be returned. On some days no letters came at all. If he held his breath, he would disappear. But when I held my breath I could hear voices chattering on in my head, like a dozen radios from neighboring houses: "The bears. You will. Don't. Can in glory, here give Gladys. Exactly. That's exactly right. Do you have any of the other? Shelves. I can get it for you! Don't lie!" They were not real voices, I knew; they were words caught in my head, scooped up like lint as I had been this place and that place; then they settled on certain rhythms of my mind. Hearing but not listening I had collected these voices. Now I listened. A voice called my name.

"Who is it?" I said. Perhaps it had been a real one.

Nobody answered. I looked at the bedroom door and tried to get myself to open it, but I couldn't. I had to sit down on the bed, and then I had to lie down, and at last I fell asleep. Sometime later I woke up because the doorbell was ringing. I put on Willie's robe and went as quietly as I could through the apartment until I could hear their voices:

"Ella said he was back."

"Did you ring up?"

"No, but I expect he's here, that is, if he's here."

"I thought I heard someone inside."

"I don't hear anything. Push the bell again."

"Let's go."

"He might not want company."

Their footsteps dwindled away down the stairs.

That night I went to an Italian restaurant on the next block. I was the only customer. When the manager-waiter finished cutting ravioli on a table in the back of the room, he sat down with me.

"Very good food," I said.

"Where you from? I don't see you round this place."

"I live on Canon Square."

"No you don'. I never see you there. Where you live?"

"Number twelve."

"Then why don' I never see you? I live just across."

He went back into the kitchen. Now and then a passerby put his face to the window and stared at me.

"Business is slow," the manager said, when I paid him. "Winter comes now."

He turned the lights out when I left.

The streets were full of water: it soaked through the seams of my shoes and chilled my feet, soaked my stockings. In the lamplight I saw black spots on my legs where drops had flown up as I walked. The light was confusing: black shot with bright lights and reflections, cracks from drawn curtains, the oddly unilluminating brilliance of the streetlights. A taxi crashed past, only its parking lights on. When I got to the newsagent's shop he was pulling down the shutter. "Wait," I said. "I'm closed, Miss," he said. "Sorry, I'm quarter of an hour late as it is. Sorry, Miss." So I went into a pub, where the drinkers stared as I entered the lounge. Then they started talking to each other again. A small table was free in the corner. "Whiskey, please," I said to the waiter; he brought whiskey and paper napkins and a dish of peanuts. I thought I heard somebody say "Whiskey" behind me, but when I turned my head, two middle-aged women were absorbed in a conversation. The sporting section of the *Telegraph* lay on the chair next to me, and so I read it and drank my whiskey and left. "Sorry," a man said, as we bumped at the door.

When I got to Canon Square I rang the doorbell, then

ran up the stairs and knocked on the door. I found the key, unlocked the door. "Hello," I said. "It's me. I'm here." In the bedroom I took off my clothes and put on Willie's blue robe. In the living room I put on the Bach record and made myself a drink. "Yoo-hoo, it's just me," I said. I went to the closet with the towels and the box of pills and I studied each little bottle in turn. "Just looking," I said; then I remembered the story in the manila folder, and hurriedly I returned it to its place in the study.

"Yes?" I said. "Yes."

A wind moved a door.

"I'm just in here," I said.

I thought of a voice saying, Why don't you like her? Well, she's, *you* know. I just don't. Don't ask me why. Who is she, after all?

Who's he?

"I'm in here," I said.

The telephone rang. "Is that you?" I said, and finally I picked it up. "Hello, who is this?"

"Who are you?"

"Who's this?" I said.

"Is Willie there?"

"Yes," I said. "Just a moment. Who shall I say is calling?"

"Tell him Joe Dolly."

"Can you hang on just a moment? Please?" I put the receiver gently on its side and walked from that room to the next and the next, calling, "Willie? Willie? It's Joe Dolly on the phone. Can you take it?" Then I went back to the phone and said to hold on, please.

"Willie?" I called. "Where are you? It's Joe Dolly."

"Oh, I'm awfully sorry," I said, at last. "He must have just stepped out. I don't know where. Down to the newsagent's, I guess. Is there a number he can call back?"

"Tomorrow'll do," he said. "Just remind him, would you? Tell him it's urgent."

"Right-o," I said.

By then I was convinced that he was coming back that night. I packed my suitcase, leaving only my raincoat on the rack, and I went over the bathroom looking for cosmetics and stray hairs. When the floor creaked, I said, "Yes? Hello?" On the bed I laid out a wool dress and undergarments and a pair of jade earrings; then, out of curiosity, I picked up the clothes and threw them across the room. They hit the velvet curtains almost soundlessly and dropped to the floor. Next I drew a bath and got in but got out soon because the shapes under the water were strange, my legs looked too long, my back hurt. "I'm in the bathroom," I said, putting on Willie's robe again. "I'm almost ready."

The question was, where should I go? And so I waited in the living room, listening and looking for an answer; and after a while I learned I had to go to the bedroom. "I don't want to," I said out loud, but I went anyway; I opened the door and stepped into the room and closed the door again. There were six things in the room, as far as I could make out: the velvet curtains, the bed, a black night table, a lamp, a clock, and the closet. Some clothes lay on the floor in front of the curtain, so I put them out of sight on a shelf in the closet. After listening a while longer I learned I had to sit down on the bed. "I don't want to," I said again. I imagined Willie saying, *But I want to meet you. I'm sorry,* I said. Something wicked was going to speak to me, and I trembled, waiting for its voice. If you sat in the room as I did, and as he did, the voice would speak after a while, when it was quiet.

Then the voice began to speak. I didn't hear its words—that is to say, the words were as usual: confused, entangled in other words: "Interest of, now, let's, my goodness! here you hand me, she's going. Give it up. That's. An elephant, isn't it? You don't, careful, if you don't follow, how can you?" But I understood now.

"No," I said, as each temptation came to me in turn, as bright in my mind's eye as Christmas cards: the window over Canon Square—open, a fresh cold vowel of air spoken to me; then the shady gas oven; the pills—medicinal allsorts; and at last the razor blades—they were thin and new: a matter of brightness, colors galore.

"No," I said. "Please don't. Oh, please don't. I beg of you."

I hung onto the blankets; I caught the belt of Willie's robe and then pushed it away as if it were a snake, or a rope.

"Wait," I said. "Not yet."

Somebody called my name.

"Who's there?" I said. "Who said that?"

Nobody, nobody, nobody.

I ran out of the bedroom and opened the front door and looked down the stairwell; there was nothing to be seen, nothing to be heard. When I went back to the bedroom, I took off the robe and put on my wool dress and my coat and picked up my suitcase. I dialed the time: it was almost two in the morning. So I opened all the curtains, made a jug of coffee, and sat up the rest of the night in the living room with my suitcase at my feet. It was not until dawn that I could make myself write a note:

"Thank you for letting me use your flat. Everything is as I found it. I hope you had a good trip. Here is the key I was given."

A little after six in the morning I left the building and found a taxi and went to Victoria Station. The Southern commuter trains were already disgorging men with bowler hats and umbrellas; moving against their tide, I caught the first train to Paris, and from Paris I went on to Florence.

"Having a wonderful time," I wrote, in any old handwriting at all. It was a lie, anyway. The beautiful *things* pierced my heart like hatpins, but there wasn't a drop of blood left. I bought one notebook and then another to solicit the expression of my new-made heart, but there was nothing to say. From my reflection in the wardrobe's mirror I photographed my face and learned what *pinched* meant. My eyes were too pale. In the evenings, after going round the churches and museums, I ate enormous suppers and drank lots of wine. Nobody seemed to see me; the Italians did not notice me. In the mornings, with cappuccino, I ate up American papers, but I might as well have been the charlady's daughter. So one morning I threw away all my clothes. It was hard to do, but quick, like a painful inoculation. I took the dark dresses, the walking shoes and tweed skirts, and made a bundle of them and tied them with string and left them in a public lavatory. From my spy-hole across the street, the window of a pastry shop, I saw the toilet-paper lady go in, come out, the bundle in her hands. She turned it around and around, as if it were a bomb.

The salesgirls fell on me like pigeons on bread-crumbs. They had lipsticks that tasted like icing; their boyfriends had magical scissors, and my hair fell to the floor in a pale brown wreath around the barber chair. "I was robbed," I said in Italian, and to please them I added that the thief was a German tourist.

Sometimes, at night, I looked in the wardrobe mirror at the unfamiliar head and caught a *familiar* look, a knowing glance. "Are you there?" I asked. The girl in the mirror ran her tongue over her icing-pink lips and lifted her curls with her fingers: she was terrible, worse than anybody I could imagine. In the daytime she wore tight skirts and stockings that hissed as she walked. She took to smoking cigarettes, left ashes all over the table, left behind air-mail editions of the London *Times,* but at last I decided she would not leave me, that nothing I could do would keep her away. She liked movies, after all, good food, strangers: at night, when I could feel the silence dissolve inside me like a pill in a glass of water, she got me out of the hotel, out to a café or a movie.

At Christmastime I went back to England. A girl I'd known at university had invited me to her house for Christmas, and she met me at Victoria.

"Gosh, look at you!" she said. Her look wasn't altogether happy. "Do you have any shopping to do before we go? I thought we'd take the six-forty train from Paddington."

"That's wonderful," I said. I began distributing money to porters, and my baskets and cases went into a taxi to Paddington; then from there I went in another taxi to Canon Square. A mean snowfall had left white streaks in the fenced park, and the lights were on in all the houses. At the top of Number 12 I seemed to see a light. The mailbox was empty, and I went up the stairs without ringing the bell downstairs. Only the bell beside the door. I could hear a new record on the Gramophone. Then it stopped. The door opened. Willie stood there in his blue bathrobe. His face was deathly white.

"I took care of the flat," I explained. "I wanted to thank you."

He looked me all over, but mildly, as if he didn't understand me. After a while he said, "Yes, you left a note. Do you want to come in?"

"I brought you something," I said.

It had not changed at all, except that there was a newspaper spread on the carpet in the front room and a tray of drinks on the record cabinet.

"This is it," I said. He opened the box and took out a bathrobe: it was white Italian wool, edged with cream-colored silk.

"This is a very expensive present," he said. "I thank you." Then he gave me a drink. "Who are you?" he said. "You're American, aren't you?"

"Yes," I said. "I'm American."

"You should lose your passport," he said, and laughed. Then he told me he had been in Quebec looking for a story about the Nationalists there. "I'm a Canuck," he said. "Didn't you know?"

"I thought of it," I said.

"I bet you did. But it's nothing. One wants to be something, but what is there to be? Now I wish I were an American, now that's something to be! Without a passport. Yes? Don't you feel it? It's worth traveling for, to *become* an American. Isn't that what's happened to you? How long have you been here? You were wrong to go to Italy, you should have stayed in London. Was everything all right here? What happened?"

"I just wanted to go to Italy," I said.

"Look at you," he said. "And this *present*. Do you understand what you've done?"

"What?" I said.

"I got the idea something had happened," he said.

"So did I," I said, and looked straight at him.

"Let me show you something," he said. He stood up and put his hands around my throat: they were as cold as glass.

"You'd better go," he said.

"Yes," I said. "I have to go. I have a lot to do."

"That's rich," he said. "Christ, you've become a crazy woman. You should try to control yourself." But he had the white bathrobe in his hands, and even as he spoke his hands explored the material; I could feel his interest fading like a breath on a cold window.

"You'll be back," he said.

But I never went back. That night Renata and I met at Paddington and got on the train stinking of perfume. We lighted cigarettes from my pack and drank gin from her picnic flask, and our laps and our coats were covered with fashion magazines. London disappeared into the dark; when we arrived at our destination, two boys were there to meet us. "Honey child," one of them said to me; and when he kissed me full on the mouth, I could taste fresh whiskey. "Who are you?" he said, after the kiss.

The Destruction of the Goetheanum

James Salter

JAMES SALTER'S novels are *A Sport and a Pastime* (newly reissued by Penguin) and *Light Years*.

In the garden, standing alone, he found the young woman who was a friend of the writer William Hedges, then unknown but even Kafka had lived in obscurity, she said, and so moreover had Mendel, perhaps she meant Mendeleyev. They were staying in a little hotel across the Rhine. No one could seem to find it, she said.

The river there flowed swiftly, the surface was alive. It carried things away, broken wood and branches. They turned, went under, emerged. Sometimes pieces of furniture passed, ladders, windows. Once, in the rain, a chair.

They were living in the same room, but it was completely platonic. Her hand bore no ring, no jewelry of any kind. Her wrists were bare.

"He doesn't like to be alone," she said. "He's struggling with his work." It was a novel, still far from finished though parts were extraordinary. A fragment had been published in Rome. "It's called *The Goetheanum,*" she said. "Do you know what that is?"

He tried to remember the curious word already dissolving in his mind. The lights inside the house had begun to appear in the blue evening.

"It's the one great act of his life."

The hotel she had spoken of was small with small rooms and letters in yellow across the facade. There were many buildings like it. From the cool flank of the cathedral it was visible among them, below and a little downstream. Also through the windows of antique shops and alleys.

Two days later he saw her from a distance. She was unmistakable. She moved with a kind of spent grace, like a dancer whose career is ended. The crowd ignored her.

"Oh," she said, "yes, hello."

Her voice seemed vague. He was sure she did not recognize him. He didn't know exactly what to say.

"I was thinking about some of the things you told me . . ." he began.

She stood with people pushing past her, her arms filled with packages. The street was hot. She did not understand who he was, he was certain of it. She was performing simple errands, those of a remote and saintly couple.

"Forgive me," she said, "I'm really not myself."

"We met at Sarren's," he explained.

"Yes, I know."

A silence followed. He wanted to say something quite simple to her but she was preventing it.

She had been to the museum. When Hedges worked

he had to be alone, sometimes she would find him asleep on the floor.

"He's crazy," she said. "Now he's sure there'll be a war. Everything's going to be destroyed."

Her own words seemed to disinterest her. The crowd was pulling her away.

"Can I walk with you for a minute?" he asked. "Are you going towards the bridge?"

She looked both ways.

"Yes," she decided.

They went down the narrow streets. She said nothing. She glanced in shop windows. She had a mouth which curved downwards, a serving girl's mouth, a girl from small towns.

"Are you interested in painting?" he heard her ask.

In the museum there were Holbein's and Hodler's, El Greco's, Max Ernst. The silence of long salons. In them one understood what it meant to be great.

"Do you want to go tomorrow?" she said. "No, tomorrow we're going somewhere. What about the day after?"

Thursday. He woke early, he was already nervous. The room seemed empty. The sky was yellow with light. The surface of the river, between stone banks, was incandescent. The water rushed in fragments white as fire, at their center one could not even look.

By nine the sky had faded, the river was broken into silver. At ten it was brown, the color of soup. Barges and old-fashioned steamers were working slowly upstream or going swiftly down. The piers of the bridges trailed small wakes.

A river is the soul of a city, only water and air can purify. At Basel, the Rhine lies between well-established, stone banks. The trees are carefully trimmed, the old houses hidden behind them.

He looked for her everywhere. He crossed the

Rheinbrucke and, watching faces, went to the open market through the crowds. He searched among the stalls. Women were buying flowers, they boarded streetcars and sat with the bunches in their laps. In the Borse restaurant fat men were eating, their ears were close to their heads.

She was nowhere to be found. He even entered the cathedral, expecting for a moment to find her waiting in the great, holy coolness. There was no one. The city was turning to stone. The pure hour of sunlight had passed, there was nothing left now but a raging afternoon that burned his feet. The clocks struck three. He gave up and returned to the hotel. There was an edge of white paper in his box. It was a note, she would meet him at four.

In excitement he lay down to think. She had not forgotten. He read it again. Were they really meeting in secret? He was not certain what that meant. Hedges was forty, he had almost no friends, his wife was somewhere in Connecticut, he had left her, he had renounced the past. If he was not great, he was following the path of greatness which is the same as disaster, and he had the power to make one devote oneself to his life. She was with him constantly. I'm never out of his sight, she complained. Nadine: it was a name she had chosen herself.

She was late. They ended up going to tea at five o'clock; Hedges was busy reading English newspapers. They sat at a table overlooking the river, the menus in their hands long and slim as airline tickets. She seemed very calm. He wanted to keep looking at her, he couldn't. *Hummersalat*, he was reading somehow, *rumpsteak*. She was very hungry, she announced. She had been at the museum, the paintings made her ravenous.

"Where were you?" she said.

Suddenly he realized she had expected him. There were young couples strolling the galleries, their legs washed in sunlight. She had wandered among them. She knew quite well what they were doing: they were preparing for love. His eyes slipped.

"I'm starving," she said.

She ate asparagus, then a goulash soup, and after that a cake she did not finish. The thought crossed his mind that perhaps they had no money, she and Hedges, that it was her only meal of the day.

"No," she said. "William has a sister who's married to a very rich man. He can get money there."

It seemed she had the faintest accent. Was it English?

"I was born in Genoa," she told him.

She quoted a few lines of Valery which he later found out were incorrect. *Afternoons torn by wind, the stinging sea* . . . She adored Valery. An anti-Semite, she said.

She described a trip to Dornach, it was forty minutes away by streetcar, then a long walk from the station where she had stood arguing with Hedges about which way to go, it always annoyed her that he had no sense of direction. It was uphill, he was soon out of breath.

Dornach had been chosen by the teacher Rudolf Steiner to be the center of his realm. There, not far from Basel, beyond the calm suburbs, he had dreamed of establishing a community with a great, central building to be named after Goethe, whose ideas had inspired it, and in 1913 the cornerstone for it was finally laid. The design was Steiner's own, as were all the details, techniques, the paintings, the specially engraved glass. He invented its construction just as he had its shape.

It was to be built entirely of wood, two enormous domes which intersected, the plot of that curve itself was a mathematical event. Steiner believed only in curves, there were no right angles anywhere. Small, tributary domes like helmets contained the windows and doors. Everything was wood, everything except the gleaming Norwegian slates that covered the roof. The earliest photographs showed it surrounded by scaffolding like some huge monument, in the foreground were groves of apple trees. The construction was carried on by people from all over the world, many of them abandoned professions and careers. By the spring of 1914 the roof timbers were in position, and while they were still laboring the war broke out. From the nearby provinces of France they could actually hear the rumble of cannon. It was the hottest month of summer.

She showed him a photograph of a vast, brooding structure.

"The Goetheanum," she said.

He was silent. The darkness of the picture, the resonance of the domes had begun to invade him. He submitted to it as to the mirror of a hypnotist. He could feel himself slipping from reality. He did not struggle. He longed to kiss the fingers which held the postcard, the lean arms, the skin which smelled like lemons. He felt himself trembling, he knew she could see it. They sat like that, her gaze was calm. He was entering the grey, the Wagnerian scene before him which she might close at any moment like a matchbox and replace in her bag. The windows resembled an old hotel somewhere in middle Europe. In Prague. The shapes sang to him. It was a fortification, a terminal, an observatory from which one could look into the soul.

"Who is Rudolf Steiner?" he said.

He hardly heard her explanation. He was beginning to have ecstasies. Steiner was a great teacher, a savant who believed deep insights could be revealed in art. He believed in movements and mystery plays, rhythms, creation, the stars. Of course. And somehow from this she had learned a scenario. She had become the illusionist of Hedges' life.

It was Hedges, the convict Joyce scholar, the rumpled ghost at literary parties, who had found her. He was distant at first, he barely spoke a word to her the night they met. She had not been in New York long then. She was living on Twelfth Street in a room with no furniture. The next day the phone rang. It was Hedges. He asked her to lunch. He had known from the first exactly who she was, he said. He was calling from a phone booth, the traffic was roaring past.

"Can you meet me at Haroot's?" he said.

His hair was uncombed, his fingers stained. He was sitting by the wall, too nervous to look at anything except his hands. She became his companion.

They spent long days together wandering in the city. He wore shirts the color of blue ink, he bought her clothes. He was wildly generous, he seemed to care nothing for money, it was crumpled in his pockets like waste paper, when he paid for things it would fall on the floor. He made her come to restaurants where he was dining with his wife and sit at the bar so he could watch her while they ate.

Slowly he began her introduction to another world, a world which scorned exposure, a world more rich than the one she knew, certain occult books, philosophies, even music. She discovered she had a talent for it, an instinct. She achieved a kind of power over herself. There were periods of deep affection, serenity. They sat in a friend's house and listened to Scriabin. They ate at the Russian Tea Room, the waiters knew his name. Hedges was performing an extraordinary act, he was fusing her life. He, too, had found a new existence: he was a criminal at last. At the end of a year they came to Europe.

"He's intelligent," she said. "You feel it immediately. He has a mind that touches everything."

"How long have you been with him?"

"Forever," she said.

They walked back towards her hotel in that one, dying hour which ends the day. The trees by the river were black as stone. *Wozzeck* was playing at the theater to be followed by *The Magic Flute*. In the print shops were maps of the city and drawings of the famous bridge as it looked in Napoleon's time. The banks were filled with newly minted coins. She was strangely silent. They stopped once, before a restaurant with a tank of fish, great speckled trout larger than a shoe lazing in green water, their mouths working slowly. Her face was visible in the glass like a woman's on a train, indifferent, alone. Her beauty was directed towards no one. She seemed not to see him, she was lost in her thoughts. Then, coldly, without a word, her eyes met his. They did not waver. In that moment he realized she was worth everything.

They had not had an easy time. Reason is unequal to man's problems, Hedges said. His wife had somehow gotten hold of his bank account, not that it was much, but she had a nose like a ferret, she found other earnings that might have come his way. Further, he was sure his letters to his children were not being delivered. He had to write them at school and in care of friends.

The question above all and always, however, was money. It was crushing them. He wrote articles but they were hard to sell, he was no good at anything topical. He did a piece about Giacometti with many haunting quotations which were entirely invented. He tried everything. Meanwhile, on every side it seemed, young men were writing filmscripts or selling things for enormous sums.

Hedges was alone. The men his age had made their reputations, everything was passing him by. Anyway he often felt it. He knew the lives of Cervantes, Stendhal, Italo Svevo, but none of them were as improbable as his own. And wherever they went there were his notebooks and papers to carry. Nothing is heavier than paper.

In Grasse he had trouble with his teeth, something went bad in the roots of old repairs. He was in misery, they had to pay a French dentist almost every penny they had. In Venice he was bitten by a cat. A terrible infection developed, his arm swelled to twice its size, it seemed the skin would burst. The *cameriera* told them cats had venom in their mouths like snakes, the same thing had happened to her son. Hedges was in agony, he could not sleep. The bites were always deep, she said, the poison entered the blood. It would have been much worse fifty years ago, the doctor told them. He touched a point up near his shoulder. Hedges was too weak to ask what it meant. Twice a day a woman came with a hypodermic in a battered tin box and gave him shots. He was growing more feverish. He could no longer read. He wanted to dictate some final things, Nadine took them down. He insisted on being buried with her photograph over his heart, he had made her promise to tear it from her passport.

"How will I get home?" she asked.

Beneath them in the sunlight the great river flowed, almost without a sound. The lives of artists seem beautiful at last, even the terrible arguments about money, the nights there is nothing to do. Besides, through it all, Hedges was never helpless. He lived one life and imagined ten others, he could always find refuge in one of them.

"But I'm tired of it," she said. "He's selfish. He's a child."

She did not look like a woman who had suffered. She drove very fast. Her teeth were white. On the far pathways couples were having lunch, the girls with their shoes off, their feet slanting down the bank. They were throwing bits of bread in the water.

The development of the individual had reached its apogee, Hedges believed, that was the essence of our time. A new direction must be found. He did not believe in collectivism, however. That was a blind road. He wasn't certain yet of what the path would be. His writing would reveal it, but he was working against time, against a tide of events, he was in exile, like Trotsky. Unfortunately, there was no one to kill him. It doesn't matter, my teeth will do it in the end, he said.

Nadine was staring into the water.

"There are nothing but eels down there," she said.

He followed her gaze. The surface was impenetrable. He tried to find a single, black shadow betrayed by its grace.

"When the time comes to mate," she told him, "they go to the sea."

She watched the water. When the time came they heard somehow, they slithered across meadows in the morning, shining like dew. She was fourteen years old, she told him, when her mother took her favorite doll down to the river and threw it in, the days of being a young girl were over.

"What shall I throw in?" he asked.

She seemed not to hear.

"Do you mean that?" she finally said.

It was arranged, they would all have dinner together, would Hedges sense something or not? He tried not to think about it or allow himself to be alarmed. There were scenes in every literature of this moment, but still he could not imagine what it would be like. A great writer might say, I know I cannot keep her, but would he dare give her up? Hedges, his teeth filled with cavities and all the years lying on top of his unwritten works?

"I owe him so much," she had said.

Still, it was difficult to face the evening calmly. By five o'clock he was in a state of nerves, playing solitaire in his room, re-reading articles in the paper. It seemed that he had forgotten how to speak about things, he was conscious of his facial expressions, nothing he did seemed natural. The person he had been had somehow vanished, it was impossible to create another. Everything was impossible, he imagined a dinner at which he would be humiliated, deceived.

At seven o'clock, afraid the telephone would ring at any moment, he went down in the elevator. The glimpse of himself in the mirror reassured him, he seemed ordinary, he seemed calm. He touched his hair. His heart was thundering. He looked at himself again. The door slid open. He stepped out, half expecting to find them there. There was no one. He turned the pages of the Zurich paper while keeping an eye on the door. Finally he managed to sit in one of the chairs. It was awkward. He moved. It was seven-ten. Twenty minutes later an old Citroën backed straight into the grille of a Mercedes parked in the street with a great smashing of glass. The concierge and desk clerk went running out. There were pieces everywhere. The driver of the Citroën was opening his door.

"Oh, Christ," he murmured, looking around.

It was William Hedges.

They all began to talk at once. The owner of the Mercedes, which was blinded, fortunately was not present. A policeman was making his way along the street.

"Well, it's not too serious," Hedges said. He was

inspecting his own car. The stoplights were shattered. There was a dent in the trunk.

After much discussion he was finally allowed to enter the hotel. He was wearing a striped cotton jacket and a shirt the color of ink. He had a white face, damp with sweat, the face of an unpopular schoolboy, high forehead, thinning hair, a soft beard touched with grey, the beard of an explorer, a man who washed his socks in the Amazon. He was alone.

"Nadine will be along a little later," he said.

When he reached for a drink, his hand was trembling.

"My foot slipped off the brake," he explained. He quickly lit a cigarette. "The insurance pays that, don't they? Probably not."

He seemed to have reached a stop, the first of many long, of enormous pauses during which he looked in his lap. Then, as if it were the thing he had been struggling to think of, he inquired painfully, "What do you . . . think of Basel?"

The headwaiter had placed them on opposite sides of the table, the empty chair between them. Its presence seemed to weigh on Hedges. He asked for another drink. Turning, he knocked over a glass. That act, somehow, relieved him. The waiter dabbed at the wet tablecloth with a napkin. Hedges spoke around him.

"I don't know exactly what Nadine has told you," he said softly. A long pause. "She sometimes tells . . . fantastic lies."

"Oh, yes?"

"She's from a little town in Pennsylvania," Hedges muttered. "Julesburg. She's never been . . . she was just a . . . an ordinary girl when we met."

They had come to Basel to visit certain institutions, he explained. It was an . . . interesting city. History has certain sites upon which whole epochs turn, and the village of Dornach gave evidence of a very . . . The sentence was never finished. Rudolf Steiner had been a student of Goethe . . .

"Yes, I know."

"Of course. Nadine's been telling you, hasn't she?"

"No."

"I see."

He finally began again, about Goethe. The range of that intellect, he said, had been so extraordinary that he was able, like Leonardo before him, to encompass all of what was then human knowledge.

"All of knowledge," he said distractedly.

That, in itself, implied an overall . . . coherence, and the fact that no man had been capable of it since could easily mean the coherence no longer existed, it was dissolved . . . The ocean of things known had burst its shores.

"We are on the verge," Hedges said, "of radical departures in the destiny of man. Those who reveal them . . ."

The words, coming with agonized slowness, seemed to take forever. They were a ruse, a feint. It was difficult to hear them out.

". . . will be torn to pieces like Galileo."

"Is that what you think?"

A long pause again.

"Oh, yes."

They had another drink.

"We are a little strange, I suppose, Nadine and I," Hedges said, as if to himself.

It was finally the time.

"I don't think she's a very happy woman."

There was a moment of silence, of indecision.

"Happy?" Hedges said. "No, she isn't happy. She isn't capable of being happy. Ecstasies. She is ecstatic. She tells me so every day," he said. He put his hand to his forehead, half covering his eyes. "You see, you don't know her at all."

She was not coming, suddenly that was clear. There was going to be no dinner.

Something should have been said, it ended too obscurely. Ten minutes after Hedges had gone, leaving behind an embarrassing expanse of white and three places set, the thought came of what he should have demanded: I want to talk to her.

All doors had closed. He was miserable, he could not imagine someone with weaknesses, incapacities like his own. He had intended to mutilate a man and it turned into monologue—probably they were laughing about it at that very moment. It had all been humiliating. The river was moving beneath his window, even in darkness the current showed. He stood looking down upon it. He walked about trying to calm himself. He lay on the bed, it seemed his limbs were trembling. He detested himself. Finally he was still.

He had just closed his eyes when the telephone rang in the emptiness of the room. It rang again. A third time. Of course! He had expected it. His heart was jumping as he picked it up. He attempted to say hello quite calmly. A man's voice answered. It was Hedges. He was humble.

"Is Nadine there?" he managed to say.

"Nadine?"

"Please, may I speak to her," Hedges said.

"She's not here."

There was a silence. He could hear Hedges' helpless breathing. It seemed to go on and on.

"Look," Hedges began, his voice was less brave, "I just want to talk to her for a moment, that's all . . . I beg you . . ."

She was somewhere in the town then, he hurried to find her. He didn't bother to decide where she might be. Somehow the night had turned in his direction, everything was changing. He walked, he ran through the streets, afraid to be late.

It was nearly midnight, people were coming out of the theaters, the café at the Casino was roaring. A sea of hidden and half-hidden faces with the waiters always standing so someone could be hidden behind them, he combed it slowly. Surely she was there. She was sitting at a table by herself, his eyes would find her in a second.

The same cars were turning through the streets, he stepped among them. People walked slowly, stopping at lighted windows. She would be looking at a display of expensive shoes, antique jewelry perhaps, gold necklaces, old watches with faces white as biscuits. At the corners he had a feeling of loss. He passed down interior arcades. He was leaving the more familiar section. The newsstands were locked, the cinemas dark.

Suddenly, like the first truth of illness, the certainty left him. Had she gone back to her hotel? Perhaps she was even at his, or had been there and gone. He knew she was capable of aimless, original acts. Instead of drifting in the darkness of the city, her somewhat languid footsteps existing only to be devoured by his, instead of choosing a place in which to be found as cleverly as she had drawn him to follow, she might have become discouraged and returned to Hedges to say only, I felt like a walk.

There is always one moment, he thought, it never comes again. He began going back, as if lost, along streets he had already seen. The excitement was gone, he was searching, he was no longer sure of his instincts but wondering instead what she might have decided to do.

On the stairway near the Heuwaage, he stopped. The square was empty. He was suddenly cold. A lone man was passing below. It was Hedges. He was wearing no tie, the collar of his jacket was turned up. He walked without direction, he was in search of his dreams. His pockets had blue bank notes crumpled in them, cigarettes bent in half. The whiteness of his skin was visible from afar. His hair was uncombed. He did not pretend to be young, he was past that, into the heart of his life, his failed work, a man who took commuter trains, who drank tea, hoping for something, some proof in the end that his talents had been as great as the others'. This world is giving birth to another, he said. We are nearing the galaxy's core. He was writing that, he was inventing it. His poems would become our history.

The streets were deserted, the restaurants had turned out their lights. Alone in a café in the repetition of empty tables, the chairs placed upon them upside down, his dark shirt, his doctor's beard, Hedges sat. He would never find her. He was like a man out of work, an invalid, there was no place to go. The cities of Europe were silent. He coughed a little in the chill.

The Goetheanum of the photograph, the one she had shown him, did not exist. It had burned on the night of December 31, 1922. There had been an evening lecture, the audience had gone home. The night watchman discovered smoke and soon afterwards the fire became visible. It spread with astonishing rapidity and the firemen battled without effect. At last the situation seemed beyond hope. An inferno was rising within the great windows. Steiner called everyone out of the building. Exactly at midnight the main dome was breached, the flames burst through and roared upwards. The windows with their special glass were glowing, they began to explode from the heat. A huge crowd had come from the nearby villages and even from Basel itself where, miles away, the fire was visible. Finally the dome collapsed, green and blue flames soaring from the metal organ pipes. The Goetheanum disappeared, its master, its priest, its lone creator walking slowly in the ashes at dawn.

A new structure made of concrete rose in its place. Of the old, only photos remained.

Subpoena

Donald Barthelme

DONALD BARTHELME was born in Philadelphia in 1931, raised in Texas, and now lives in New York City. His books include *Come Back, Dr. Caligari, Unspeakable Practices, Snow White, City Life, Sadness, Guilty Pleasures, Amateurs,* and *Great Days.*

And now in the mail a small white Subpoena from the Bureau of Compliance, Citizen Bergman there, he wants me to comply. *We command you that, all business and excuses being laid aside, you and each of you appear and attend* . . . The "We command you" in boldface, and a shiny red seal in the lower left corner. To get my attention.

I thought I had complied. I comply every year, sometimes oftener than necessary. Look at the record. Spotless list of compliances dating back to '48, when I was a pup. What can he mean, this Bergman, finding a freckle on my clean sheet?

I appeared and attended. Attempted to be reasonable. "Look here Bergman what is this business." Read him an essay I'd written about how the State should not muck about in the affairs of its vassals overmuch. Citizen Bergman unamused.

"It appears that you are the owner or proprietor perhaps of a monster going under the name of Charles Evans Hughes?"

"Yes but what has that to do with—"

"Said monster inhabiting quarters at 12 Tryst Lane?"

"That is correct."

"This monster being of humanoid appearance and characteristics, including ability to locomote, production of speech of a kind, ingestion of viands, and traffic with other beings?"

"Well, 'traffic' is hardly the word. Simple commands he can cope with. Nothing fancy. Sit. Eat. Speak. Roll over. Beg. That sort of thing."

"This monster being employed by you in the capacity, friend?"

"Well, employed is not quite right."

"He is remunerated is he not?"

"The odd bit of pocket money."

"On a regular basis."

"See here Bergman it's an allowance. For little things he needs. Cigarettes and handkerchiefs and the like. Nose drops."

"He is nevertheless in receipt of sums of money from you on a regular basis?"

"He is forty-four per cent metal, Officer."

"The metal content of said monster does not interest the Bureau. What we are interested in is compliance."

"Wherein have I failed to comply?"

"You have not submitted Form 244 which governs paid companionship, including liaisons with prostitutes and pushing of wheelchairs by hired orderlies not provided by the Bureau of Perpetual Help. You have also failed to remit the Paid Companionship Tax which amounts to one hundred twenty-two per cent of all moneys changing hands in any direction."

"One hundred twenty-two per cent!"

"That is the figure. There is also a penalty for noncompliance. The penalty is two hundred twelve per cent of one hundred twenty-two per cent of five dollars a week figured over five years, which I believe is the period at issue."

"What about depreciation?"

"Depreciation is not figurable in the case of monsters."

I went home feeling less than sunny.

He had a knowing look that I'd painted myself. One corner of the mouth curled upward and the other downward, when he smiled. There was no grave-robbing or anything of that sort. Plastic and metal did very nicely. You can get the most amazing things in drugstores. Fingernails and eyelashes and such. The actual construction was a matter of weeks. I considered sending the plans to *Popular Mechanics*. So everyone could have one.

He was calm—calm as a hat. Whereas I was nervous as a strobe light, had the shakes, Valium in the morning and J & B beginning at two o'clock in the afternoon.

Everything was all right with him.

"Crushed in an elevator at the welfare hotel!" some-one would say.

"It's a very serious problem," Charles would an-swer.

When I opened the door, he was sitting in the rocking chair reading *Life*.

"Charles," I said, "they've found out."

"Seventy-seven per cent of American high-school students declare that religion is important to them, according to a recent Louis Harris poll," Charles said, rocking gently.

"Charles," I said, "they want money. The Paid Companionship Tax. It's two hundred twelve per cent of one hundred twenty-two per cent of five dollars a week figured over five years, plus of course the basic one hundred twenty-two per cent."

"That's a lot of money," Charles said, smiling. "A pretty penny."

"I can't pay," I said. "It's too much."

"Well," he said, both smiling and rocking, "fine. What are you going to do?"

"Disassemble," I said.

"Interesting," he said, hitching his chair closer to mine, to demonstrate interest. "Where will you begin?"

"With the head, I suppose."

"Wonderful," Charles said. "You'll need the screw-driver, the pliers, and the Skil saw. I'll fetch them."

He got up to go to the basement. A thought struck him. "Who will take out the garbage?" he asked.

"Me. I'll take it out myself."

He smiled. One corner of his mouth turned upward and the other downward. "Well," he said, "right on."

I called him my friend and thought of him as my friend. In fact I kept him to instruct me in complacency. He sat there, the perfect noncombatant. He ate and drank and slept and awoke and did not change the world. Looking at him I said to myself, "See, it is possible to live in the world and not change the world." He read the newspapers and watched television and heard in the night screams under windows thank God not ours but down the block a bit, and did nothing. Without Charles, without his example, his exemplary quietude, I run the risk of acting, the risk of risk. I must leave the house and walk about.

The Dead

Joyce Carol Oates

JOYCE CAROL OATES' most recent novel is *Bellefleur* (E. P. Dutton & Co., Inc.). She was awarded the National Book Award in 1970 for her novel *them,* and was recently inducted into the American Academy and Institute of Arts and Letters. At the present time she is teaching at Princeton University.

Useful in acute and chronic depression, where accompanied by anxiety, insomnia, agitation; psychoneurotic states manifested by tension, apprehension, fatigue. . . . They were small yellow capsules, very expensive. She took them along with other capsules, green-and-aqua, that did not cost quite so much but were weaker. *Caution against hazardous occupations requiring complete mental alertness.* What did that mean, "complete mental alertness"? Since the decline of her marriage, a few years ago, Ilena thought it wisest to avoid complete mental alertness. That was an overrated American virtue.

For the relief of anxiety and the relief of the apprehension of anxiety: small pink pills. *Advise against ingestion of alcohol.* But she was in the habit of drinking anyway, always before meeting strangers and often before meeting friends, sometimes on perfectly ordinary, lonely days when she expected to meet no one at all. She was fascinated by the possibility that some of these drugs could cause paradoxical reactions—fatigue and intense rage, increase and decrease in libido. She liked paradox. She wondered how the paradoxical reactions could take place in the same body, at the same time. Or did they alternate days? *For the relief of chronic insomnia:* small harmless white barbiturates. In the morning, hurrying out somewhere, she took a handful of mood-elevating pills, swallowed with some hot water right from the faucet, or coffee, to bring about a curious hollow-headed sensation, exactly as if her head were a kind of drum. Elevation! She felt the very air breathed into her lungs suffused with a peculiar dazzling joy, worth every risk.

Adverse reactions were possible: *confusion, ataxia, skin eruptions, edema, nausea, constipation, blood dyscrasias, jaundice, hepatic dysfunction, hallucinations, tremor, slurred speech, hyperexcitement. . . .* But anything was possible, after all!

A young internist said to her, "These tests show that you are normal," and her heart had fallen, her stomach had sunk, her very intestines yearned downward, stricken with gravity. Normal? Could that be? She had stared at him, unbelieving. "The symptoms you mention—the insomnia, for instance—have no organic basis that we can determine," he said.

Then why the trembling hands, why the glitter to the eyes, why, why the static in the head? She felt that she had been cheated. This was not worth sixty dollars, news like this. As soon as she left the doctor's office she went to a water fountain in the corridor and took a few capsules of whatever was in her coat pocket, loose in the pocket along with tiny pieces of lint and something that looked like the flaky skins of peanuts, though she did not remember having put peanuts in any of her pockets. She swallowed one, two, three green-and-aqua tranquillizers, and a fairly large white pill that she didn't recognize, found in the bottom of her purse with a few stray hairs and paper clips. This helped a little. "So I'm normal!" she said.

She had been living at that time in Buffalo, New York, teaching part-time at the university. Buffalo was a compromise between going to California, as her ex-husband begged, and going to New York, where she was probably headed. Her brain burned dryly, urging her both westward and eastward, so she spent a year in this dismal Midwestern city in upstate New York, all blighted elms and dingy skies and angry politicians. The city was in a turmoil of excitement; daily and nightly the city police prowled the university campus in search of troublesome students, and the troublesome students hid in the bushes alongside buildings, eager to plant their homemade time bombs and run; so the campus was not safe for ordinary students or ordinary people at all. Even the "normal," like Ilena, long wearied of political activism, were in danger.

She taught twice a week and the rest of the time avoided the university. She drove a 1965 Mercedes an uncle had willed her, an uncle rakish and remote and selfish, like Ilena herself, who had taken a kind of proud pity on her because of her failed marriage and her guilty listlessness about family ties. The uncle, a judge, had died in St. Louis; she had had to fly there to get the car. The trip back had taken her nearly a week, she had felt so unaccountably lazy and sullen. But, once back in Buffalo, driving her stodgy silver car, its conservative shape protecting her heavily, she felt safe from the noxious street fumes and the darting, excitable eyes of the police and the local Buffalo taxpayers—in spite of her own untidy hair and clothes.

The mood-elevating pills elevated her several feet off the ground and made her stammer rapidly into the near, dim faces of her students, speaking faster and faster in the hope that the class period would end sooner. But the tranquillizers dragged her down, massaged her girlish heart to a dreamy condition, fingered the nerve ends lovingly, soothingly, wanted only to assure her that all was well. In her inherited car she alternately drove too fast, made nervous by the speedier pills, or too slowly, causing warlike sounds from the rear, the honking of other drivers in American cars.

In the last two years Ilena had been moving around constantly: packing up the same clothes and items and unpacking them again, always eager, ready to be surprised, flying from one coast to the other to speak at universities or organizations interested in "literature," hopeful and adventurous as she was met at various windy airports by strangers. Newly divorced, she had felt virginal again, years younger, truly childlike and American. Beginning again. Always beginning. She had written two quiet novels, each politely received and selling under one thousand copies, and then she had written a novel based on an anecdote overheard by her at the University of Michigan, in a girls' rest room in the library, about a suicide club and the "systematic deaths of our most valuable natural resource, our children"—as one national reviewer of the novel said gravely. It was her weakest novel, but it was widely acclaimed and landed her on the cover of a famous magazine, since her *Death Dance* had also coincided with a sudden public interest in the achievement of women in "male-dominated fields." Six magazines came out with cover stories on the women's liberation movement inside a three-month period; Ilena's photograph had been exceptionally good. She found herself famous, and fame made her mouth ironic and dry with a sleeplessness that was worse than ever, in spite of her being "normal."

The pills came and went in cycles—the yellow capsules favored for a while, then dropped for the small pink pills, tranquillizers big enough to nearly knock her out taken with some gin and lemon, late at night. These concoctions were sacred to her, always kept secret. Her eyes grew large with the prospect of all those "adverse reactions" that were threatened but somehow never arrived. She was lucky, she thought. Maybe nothing adverse would ever happen to her. She had been twenty-six years old at the start of the breakup of her marriage; it was then that most of the pills began, though she had always had a problem with insomnia. The only time she had truly passed out, her brain gone absolutely black, was the winter day—very late in the afternoon—when she had been in her office at a university in Detroit, with a man whom she had loved at that time, and a key had been thrust in the lock and the door opened—Ilena had screamed, "No! Go away!" It had been only a cleaning lady, frightened off without seeing anything, or so the man had assured Ilena. But she had fainted. Her skin had gone wet and cold; it had taken the terrified man half an hour to bring her back to normal again. "Ilena, I love you, don't die," he had begged. Finally she was calm enough to return to her own home, an apartment she shared with her husband in the northwestern corner of the city; she went home, fixed herself some gin and bitter lemon, and stood in the kitchen drinking it while her husband yelled questions at her. "Where were you? Why were you gone so long?" She had not answered him. The drink was mixed up in her memory with the intense relief of having escaped some humiliating danger, and the intense terror of the new, immediate danger of her husband's rage. Why was this man yelling at her? Whom had she married, that he could yell at her so viciously? The drinking of that gin was a celebration of her evil.

That was back in 1967; their marriage had ended with the school year; her husband spent three weeks in a hospital half a block from his mother's house in Oswego, New York, and Ilena had not gone to see him, not once, being hard of heart, like stone, and terrified of seeing him again. She feared his mother, too. The marriage had been dwindling all during the Detroit years—1965–1967—and they both left the city shortly before the riot, which seemed to Ilena, in her usual poetic, hyperbolic, pill-sweetened state, a cataclysmic flowering of their own hatred. She had thought herself good enough at hating, but her husband was much better. "Die. Why don't you die. *Die*," he had whispered hypnotically to her once, as she lay in bed weeping very early one morning, before dawn, too weary to continue their battle. Off and on she had spoken sentimentally about having children, but Bryan was wise enough to dismiss that scornfully—"You don't bring children into the world to fix up a rotten marriage," he said. She had not known it was rotten, exactly. She knew that he was jealous of her. A mutual friend, a psychiatrist, had told her gently that her having published two novels—unknown as they were, and financial failures—was "unmanning" to Bryan, who wanted to write but couldn't. Was that her fault? What could she do? "You could fail at something yourself," she was advised.

In the end she had fallen in love with another man.

She had set out to love someone in order to punish her husband, to revenge herself upon him; but the revenge was forgotten, she had really fallen in love in spite of all her troubles . . . in love with a man who turned out to be a disappointment himself, but another kind of disappointment.

Adverse reactions: *confusion, ataxia, skin eruptions, edema, nausea, constipation, blood dyscrasias, jaundice, hepatic dysfunction, hallucinations*. . . . Her eyes filmed over with brief ghostly uninspired hallucinations now and then, but she believed this had nothing to do with the barbiturates she took to sleep, or the amphetamines she took to speed herself up. It was love that wore her out. Love, and the air of Detroit, the gently wafting smoke from the manly smokestacks of factories. Love and smoke. The precise agitation of love in her body, what her lover and her husband did to her body; and the imprecise haze of the air, of her vision, filmed-over and hypnotized. She recalled having loved her husband very much at one time. Before their marriage in 1964. His name was Bryan Donohue, and as his wife she had been *Ilena Donohue*, legally; but a kind of maiden cunning had told her to publish her novels as *Ilena Williams*, chaste Ilena, the name musical with *l*'s. Her books were by that Ilena, while her nights of sleeplessness beside a sleeping, twitching, perspiring man were spent by the other Ilena. At that time she was not famous yet and not quite so nervous. A little insomnia, that wasn't so bad. Many people had insomnia. She feared sleep because she often dreamed of the assassination of Kennedy, which was run and rerun in her brain like old newsreels. Years after that November day she was still fresh with sorrow for him, scornful of her own sentimentality but unable to control it. How she had wept! Maybe she had been in love with Kennedy, a little. . . . So, sleeping brought him back to her not as a man: as a corpse. Therefore she feared sleep. She could lie awake beside a breathing, troubled corpse of her own, her partner in this puzzling marriage, and she rehearsed her final speech to him so many times that it became jaded and corny to her, out of date as a monologue in an Ibsen play.

"There is another man, of course," he said flatly.

"No. No one."

"Yes, another man."

"No."

"Another man, I know, but I'm not interested. Don't tell me his name."

"There is no other man."

"Obviously there is. Probably a professor at that third-rate school of yours."

"No."

Of course, when she was in the company of the *other man,* it was Bryan who became "the other" to him and Ilena—remote and masculine and dangerous, powerful as a nightmare figure, with every right to embrace Ilena in the domestic quiet of their apartment. He had every right to make love to her, and Gordon did not. They were adulterers, Ilena and Gordon. They lost weight with their guilt, which was finely wrought in them as music, precious and subtle and prized, talked over endlessly. Ilena could see Gordon's love for her in his face. She loved that face, she loved to stroke it, stare at it, trying to imagine it as the face of a man married to another woman. . . . He was not so handsome as her own husband, perhaps. She didn't know. She only knew, bewildered and stunned, that his face was the center of the universe for her, and she could no more talk herself out of this whimsy than she could talk herself out of her sorrow for Kennedy.

Her husband, Bryan Donohue: tall, abrupt, self-centered, amusing, an instructor in radiology at Wayne

Medical School, with an interest in jazz and a desire to write articles on science, science and sociology, jazz, jazz and sociology, anything. He was very verbal and he talked excellently, expertly. Ilena had always been proud of him in the presence of other people. He had a sharp, dissatisfied face, with very dark eyes. He dressed well and criticized Ilena when she let herself go, too rushed to bother with her appearance. In those days, disappointed by the low salary and the bad schedule she received as an instructor at a small university in Detroit, Ilena had arrived for early classes—she was given eight-o'clock classes every semester—with her hair barely combed, loose down to her shoulders, snarled and bestial from a night of insomnia, her stockings marred with snags or long disfiguring runs, her face glossy with the dry-mouthed euphoria of tranquillizers, so that, pious and sour, she led her classes in the prescribed ritual prayer—this was a Catholic university, and Ilena had been brought up as a Catholic—and felt freed, once the prayer was finished, of all restraint.

Bad as the eight-o'clock classes were, the late-afternoon classes (4:30–6:00) were worse: the ashes of the day, tired undergraduates who needed this course to fill out their schedules, high-school teachers—mainly nuns and "brothers"—who needed a few more credits for their Master's degrees, students who worked, tired unexplained strangers with rings around their eyes of fatigue and boredom and the degradation of many semesters as "special students." When she was fortunate enough to have one or two good students in these classes, Ilena charged around in excitement, wound up by the pills taken at noon with black coffee, eager to draw them out into a dialogue with her. They talked back and forth. They argued. The other students sat docile and perplexed, waiting for the class to end, glancing from Ilena to one of her articulate boys, back to Ilena again, taking notes only when Ilena seemed to be saying something important. What was so exciting about Conrad's *Heart of Darkness*, they wondered, that Mrs. Donohue could get this worked up?

Her copper-colored hair fell in a jumble about her face, and her skin sometimes took a radiant coppery beauty from the late afternoon sun as it sheered mistily through the campus trees, or from the excitement of a rare, good class, or from the thought of her love for Gordon, who would be waiting to see her after class. One of the boys in this late-afternoon class—Emmett Norlan—already wore his hair frizzy and long, though this was 1966 and a few years ahead of the style, and he himself was only a sophomore, a small precocious irritable argumentative boy with glasses. He was always charging up to Ilena after class, demanding that she explain herself—"You use words like 'emotions,' you bully us with your *emotions!*" he cried. "When I ask you a question in class, you distort it! You try to make everyone laugh at me! It's a womanly trick, a *female* trick, not worthy of you!" Emmett took everything seriously, as seriously as Ilena; he was always hanging around her office, in the doorway, refusing to come in and sit down because he was "in a hurry" and yet reluctant to go away, and Ilena could sense by a certain sullen alteration of his jaw that her lover was coming down the hall to her office. . . .

"See you," Emmett would say sourly, backing away.

Gordon was a professor in sociology, a decade or more older than Ilena, gentle and paternal; no match for her cunning. After a particularly ugly quarrel with her husband, one fall day, Ilena had looked upon this man and decided that he must become her lover. At the time she had not even known his name. *A lover. She would have a lover*. He was as tall as her own husband, with a married, uncomfortable look about his mouth—tense apologetic smiles, creases at the corners of his lips, bluish-purple veins on his forehead. A handsome man, but somehow a little gray. His complexion was both boyish and gray. He did not dress with the self-conscious care of her husband Bryan; his clothes were tweedy, not very new or very clean, baggy at the knees, smelling of tobacco and unaired closets. Ilena, determined to fall in love with him, had walked by his home near the university—an ordinary brick two-story house with white shutters. Her heart pounded with jealousy. She imagined his domestic life: a wife, four children, a Ford with a dented rear fender, a lawn that was balding, a street that was going bad—one handsome old Tudor home had already been converted into apartments for students, the sign of inevitable disaster. Meeting him, talking shyly with him, loving him at her finger tips was to be one of the gravest events in her life, for, pill-sweetened as she was, she had not seriously believed he might return her interest. He was Catholic. He was supposed to be happily married.

When it was over between them and she was teaching, for two quick, furtive semesters at the University of Buffalo, where most classes were canceled because of rioting and police harassment, Ilena thought back to her Detroit days and wondered how she had survived, even with the help of drugs and gin: the central nervous system could not take such abuse, not for long. She had written a novel out of her misery, her excitement, her guilt, typing ten or fifteen pages an evening until her head throbbed with pain that not even pills could ease. At times, lost in the story she was creating, she had felt an eerie longing to remain there permanently, to simply give up and go mad. *Adverse reactions: confusion, hallucinations, hyperexcitement*. . . . But she had not gone mad. She had kept on typing, working, and when she was finished it was possible to pick up, in her fingers, the essence of that shattering year: one slim book.

Death Dance. *The story of America's alienated youth . . . shocking revelations . . . suicide . . . drugs . . . waste . . . horror* . . . $5.98.

It had been at the top of the *New York Times* best-seller list for fifteen weeks.

Gordon had said to her, often, "I don't want to hurt you, Ilena. I'm afraid of ruining your life." She had assured him that her life was not that delicate. "I could go away if Bryan found out, alone. I could live alone," she had said lightly, airily, knowing by his grimness that he would not let her—surely he would not let her go? Gordon thought more about her husband than Ilena did, the "husband" he had met only once, at a large university reception, but with whom he now shared a woman. Two men, strangers, shared her body. Ilena wandered in a perpetual sodden daze, thinking of the . . . the madness of loving two men . . . the freakishness of it, which she could never really comprehend, could not assess, because everything in her recoiled from it: this could not be happening to her. Yet the fact of it was in her body, carried about in her body. She could not isolate it, could not comprehend it. Gazing at the girl students, at the nuns, she found herself thinking enviously that their lives were unsoiled and honest and open to any possibility, while hers had become fouled, complicated, criminal, snagged, somehow completed without her assent. She felt that she was going crazy.

Her teaching was either sluggish and uninspired, or hysterical. She was always wound up and ready to let go with a small speech on any subject—Vietnam, the oppression of blacks, religious hypocrisy, the censorship haggling over the student newspaper, any subject minor or massive—and while her few aggressive students appreciated this, the rest of her students were baffled and unenlightened. She sat in her darkened office, late in the afternoon, whispering to Gordon about her classes: "They aren't going well. I'm afraid. I'm not any good as a teacher. My hands shake when I come into the classroom . . . The sophomores are forced to take this course and they hate me, I know they hate me. . . ." Gordon stroked her hands, kissed her face, her uplifted face, and told her that he heard nothing but good reports about her teaching. He himself was a comfortable, moderately popular professor; he had been teaching for fifteen years. "You have some very enthusiastic students," he said. "Don't doubt yourself, Ilena, please; if you hear negative things it might be from other teachers who are jealous. . . ." Ilena pressed herself gratefully into this good man's embrace, hearing the echo of her mother's words of years ago, when Ilena would come home hurt from school for some minor girlish reason: "Don't mind them, they're just *jealous*."

A world of jealous people, like her husband: therefore, hateful, therefore dangerous. Out to destroy her. Therefore the pills, tiny round pills and large button-sized pills, and the multicolored capsules.

There were few places she and Gordon could meet. Sometimes they walked around the campus, sometimes they met for lunch downtown, but most of the time they simply sat in her office and talked. She told him everything about her life, reviewing all the snarls and joys she had reviewed, years before, with Bryan, noticing that she emphasized the same events and even used the same words to describe them. She told him everything, but she never mentioned the drugs. He would disapprove. Maybe he would be disgusted. Like many Catholic men of his social class, and of his generation, he would be frightened by weakness in women, though by his own admission he drank too much. If he commented on her dazed appearance, if he worried over her fatigue—"Does your husband do this to you? Put you in this state?"—she pretended not to understand. "What, do I look so awful? So ugly?" she would tease. That way she diverted his concern, she bullied him into loving her, because he was a man to whom female beauty was important—his own wife had been a beauty queen many years ago, at a teachers' college in Ohio. "No, you're beautiful. You're beautiful," he would whisper.

They teased each other to a state of anguish on those dark winter afternoons, never really safe in Ilena's office—she shared the office with a nun, who had an early teaching schedule but who might conceivably turn up at any time, and there was always the possibility of the cleaning lady or the janitor unlocking the door with a master key—nightmarish possibility! Gordon kissed her face, her body, she clasped her hands around him and gave herself up to him musically, dreamily, like a rose of rot with only a short while left to bloom, carrying the rot neatly hidden, deeply hidden. She loved him so that her mind went blank even of the euphoria of drugs or the stimulation of a good, exciting day of teaching; she felt herself falling back into a blankness like a white flawless wall, pure material, pure essence, a mysterious essence that was fleshly and spiritual at once. Over and over they declared their love for each other, they promised it, vowed it, repeated it in each other's grave accents, echoing and unconsciously imitating each other, Ilena carrying home to her apartment her lover's gentleness, his paternal listening manner. Maybe Bryan sensed Gordon's presence, his influence on her, long before the breakup. Maybe he could discern, with his scientist's keen heatless eye, the shadow of another personality, powerful and beloved, on the other side of his wife's consciousness.

Ilena vowed to Gordon, "I love you, only you," and she made him believe that she and Bryan no longer slept in the same bed. This was not true: she was so fearful of Bryan, of his guessing her secret, that she imitated with her husband the affection she gave to Gordon, in that way giving herself to two men, uniting them in her body. *Two men. Uniting them in her body.* Her body could not take all this. Her body threatened to break down. She hid from Bryan, spending an hour or more in the bathtub, gazing down through her lashes at her bluish, bruised body, wondering how long this phase of her life could last—the taunting of her sanity, the use of her rather delicate body by two normal men. *This is how a woman becomes prehistoric,* she thought. *Prehistoric. Before all personalized, civilized history. Men make love to her and she is reduced to protoplasm.*

She recalled her girlhood and her fear of men, her fear of someday having to marry—for all her female relatives urged marriage, marriage!—and now it seemed to her puzzling that the physical side of her life should be so trivial. It was not important, finally. She could have taken on any number of lovers, it was like shaking hands at a party, moving idly and absent-mindedly from one man to another; nothing serious about it at all. Why had she feared it so? And that was why the landscape of Detroit took on to her such neutral bleakness, its sidewalks and store windows and streets and trees, its spotted skies, its old people, its children—all unformed, unpersonalized, unhistoric. Everyone is protoplasm, she thought, easing together and easing apart. Some touch and remain stuck together; others touch and part. . . . But, though she told herself this, she sometimes felt her head weighed down with a terrible depression and she knew she would have to die, would have to kill her consciousness. She could not live with two men.

She could not live with one man.

Heated, hysterical, she allowed Gordon to make love to her in that office. The two of them lay exhausted and stunned on the cold floor—unbelieving lovers. Had this really happened? She felt the back of her mind dissolve. Now she was committed to him, she had been degraded, if anyone still believed in degradation; now something would happen, something must happen. She would divorce Bryan; he would divorce his wife. They must leave Detroit. They must marry. They must change their lives.

Nothing happened.

She sprang back to her feet, assisted by this man who seemed to love her so helplessly, her face framed by his large hands, her hair smoothed, corrected by his hands. She felt only a terrible chilly happiness, an elation that made no sense. And so she would put on her coat and run across the snowy, windswept campus to teach a class in freshman composition, her skin rosy, radiant, her body soiled and reeking beneath her clothes, everything secret and very lovely. Delirious and articulate, she lived out the winter. She thought, eying her students: *If they only knew* . . . . It was all very high, very nervous and close to hysteria; Gordon loved her, undressed her and dressed her, retreated to his home where he undressed and bathed his smallest children, and she carried his human heat with her everywhere on the coldest days, edgy from the pills of that noon and slightly hungover from the barbiturates of the night before, feeling that she was living her female life close to the limits, at the most extreme boundaries of health and reason. Her love for him burned inward, secretly, and she was dismayed to see how very soiled her clothes were, sometimes as if mocking her. Was this love, was it a stain like any other? But her love for him burned outward, making her more confident of herself, so that she did not hesitate to argue with her colleagues. She took part in a feeble anti-Vietnam demonstration on campus, which was jeered at by most of the students who bothered to watch, and which seemed to embarrass Gordon, who was not "political." She did not hesitate to argue with hard-to-manage students during class, sensing herself unladylike and impudent and reckless in their middle-class Catholic eyes, a *woman* who dared to say such things!—"I believe in birth control, obviously, and in death control. Suicide must be recognized as a natural human right." This, at a Catholic school; she had thought herself daring in those days.

Emmett Norlan and his friends, scrawny, intense kids who were probably taking drugs themselves, at least smoking marijuana, clustered around Ilena and tried to draw her into their circle. They complained that they could not talk to the other professors. They complained about the "religious chauvinism" of the university, though Ilena asked them what they expected—it was a Catholic school, wasn't it? "Most professors here are just closed circuits, they don't create anything, they don't communicate anything," Emmett declared contemptuously. He was no taller than Ilena herself, and she was a petite woman. He wore sloppy, soiled clothes, and even on freezing days he tried to go without a heavy coat; his perpetual grimy fatigue jacket became so familiar to Ilena that she was to think of him, sharply and nostalgically, whenever she saw such a jacket in the years to come. The boy's face was surprisingly handsome, in spite of all the frizzy hair and beard and the constant squinting and grimacing; but it was small and boyish. He had to fight that boyishness by being tough. His glasses were heavy, black-rimmed, and made marks on either side of his nose—he often snatched them off and rubbed the bridge of his nose, squinting nearsightedly at Ilena, never faltering in his argument. Finally Ilena would say, "Emmett, I have to go home. Can't we talk about this some other time?"—wondering anxiously if Godon had already left school. She was always backing away from even the students she liked, always edging away from her fellow teachers; she was always in a hurry, literally running from her office to a classroom or to the library, her head ducked against the wind and her eyes narrowed so that she need not see the faces of anyone she knew. In that university she was friendly with only a few people, among them the head of her department, a middle-aged priest with a degree from Harvard. He was neat, graying, gentlemanly, but a little corrupt in his academic standards: the Harvard years had been eclipsed long ago by the stern daily realities of Detroit.

The end for Ilena at this school came suddenly, in Father Hoffman's office.

Flushed with excitement, having spent a hour with Gordon in which they embraced and exchanged confidences—about his wife's sourness, her husband's iciness—Ilena had rushed to a committee that was to examine a Master's degree candidate in English. She had never sat on one of these committees before. The candidate was a monk, Brother Ronald, a pale, rather obese, pleasant man in his thirties. His lips were more womanish than Ilena's. The examination began with a question by a professor named O'Brien: "Please give us a brief outline of English literature." Brother Ronald began slowly, speaking in a gentle, faltering voice—this question was always asked by this particular professor, so the candidate had memorized an answer, perfectly—and O'Brien worked at lighting his pipe, nodding vaguely from time to time. Brother Ronald came to a kind of conclusion some fifteen minutes later, with the "twentieth century," mentioning the names of Joyce, Lawrence, and T. S. Eliot. "Very good," said O'Brien. The second examiner, Mr. Honig, asked nervously: "Will you describe tragedy and give us an example, please?" Brother Ronald frowned. After a moment he said, "There is *Hamlet* . . . and *Macbeth*. . . ." He seemed to panic then. He could think of nothing more to say. Honig, himself an obese good-natured little man of about fifty, with a Master's degree from a local university and no publications, smiled encouragingly at Brother Ronald; but Brother Ronald could only stammer, "Tragedy has a plot . . . a climax and a conclusion. . . . It has a moment of revelation . . . and comic relief. . . ." After several minutes of painful silence, during which the only sounds were of O'Brien's sucking at his pipe, Brother Ronald smiled shakily and said that he did not know any more about tragedy.

Now it was Ilena's turn. She was astonished. She kept glancing at O'Brien and Honig, trying to catch their eyes, but they did not appear to notice. Was it possible that this candidate was considered good enough for an advanced degree, was it possible that anyone would allow him to teach English anywhere? She could not believe it. She said, sitting up very straight, "Brother Ronald, please define the term 'Gothicism' for us." Silence. Brother Ronald stared at his hands. He tried to smile. "Then could you define the term 'heroic couplet' for us," Ilena said. Her heart pounded combatively. The monk gazed at her, sorrowful and soft, his eyes watery; he shook his head *no*, he didn't know. "Have you read any of Shakespeare's sonnets?" Ilena asked. Brother Ronald nodded gravely, *yes*. "Could you discuss one of them?" Ilena asked. Again, silence. Brother Ronald appeared to be thinking. Finally he said, "I guess I don't remember any of them. . . ." "Could you tell us what a sonnet is, then?" Ilena asked. "A short poem," said Brother Ronald uncertainly. "Could you give us an example of any sonnet?" said Ilena. He stared at his hands, which were now clasped together. They were pudgy and very clean. After a while Ilena saw that he could not think of a sonnet, so she said sharply, having become quite nervous herself, "Could you talk to us about any poem at all? One of your favorite poems?" He sat in silence for several seconds. Finally Ilena said, "Could you give us the *title* of a poem?"

A miserable half minute. But the examination was nearly over: Ilena saw the monk glance at his wrist watch.

"I've been teaching math at St. Rose's for the last five years . . ." Brother Ronald said softly. "It wasn't really my idea to get a Master's degree in English . . . my order sent me out. . . ."

"Don't you know any poems at all? Not even any titles?" Ilena asked.

"Of course he does. We studied Browning last year, didn't we, Brother Ronald?" O'Brien said. "You remember. You received a B in the course. I was quite satisfied with your work. Couldn't you tell us the title of a work of Browning's?"

Brother Ronald stared at his hands and smiled nervously.

"That's my last duchess up there on the wall. . . ." O'Brien said coaxingly.

Brother Ronald was breathing deeply. After a few seconds he said, in a voice so soft they could almost not hear it, *"My last duchess? . . ."*

"Yes, that is a poem," Ilena said.

"Now it's my turn to ask another question," O'Brien said briskly. He asked the monk a very long, conversational question about the place of literature in education—did it have a place? How would he teach a class of high-school sophomores a Shakespearean play, for instance?

The examination ended before Brother Ronald was able to answer.

They dismissed him. O'Brien, who was the chairman of the examining committee, said without glancing at Ilena, "We will give him a B."

"Yes, a B seems about right," the other professor said quickly.

Ilena, whose head was ringing with outrage and shame, put her hand down flat on the table. "No," she said.

"What do you mean, no?"

"I won't pass him."

They stared at her. O'Brien said irritably, "Then I'll give him an A, to balance out your C."

"But I'm not giving him a C. I'm not giving him anything. How can he receive any other grade than F? I won't sign that paper. I can't sign it," Ilena said.

"I'll give him an A also," the other professor said doubtfully. "Then . . . then maybe he could still pass . . . if we averaged it out. . . ."

"But I won't sign the paper at all," Ilena said.

"You have to sign it."

"I won't sign it."

"It is one of your duties as a member of this examining board to give a grade and to sign your name."

"I won't sign it," Ilena said. She got shakily to her feet and walked out. In the corridor, ghostly and terrified, Brother Ronald hovered. Ilena passed by him in silence.

But the next morning she was summoned to Father Hoffman's office.

The story got out that she had been fired, but really she had had enough sense to resign—to write a quick resignation note on Father Hoffman's memo pad. They did not part friends. The following year, when her best-selling novel was published, Father Hoffman sent her a letter of congratulations on university stationery, charmingly worded: "I wish only the very best for you. We were wrong to lose you. Pity us." By then she had moved out of Detroit, her husband was in San Diego, she was living in a flat in Buffalo, near Delaware Avenue, afraid of being recognized when she went out to the drugstore or the supermarket. *Death Dance* had become a selection of the Book-of-the-Month Club; it had been sold for $150,000 to a movie producer famous for his plodding, "socially significant" films, and for the first time in her life Ilena was sleepless because of money—rabid jangling thoughts about money. She was ashamed of having done so well financially. She was terrified of her ability to survive all this noise, this publicity, this national good fortune. For, truly, *Death Dance* was not her best novel: a hectic narrative about college students and their preoccupation with sex and drugs and death, in a prose she had tried to make "poetic." Her more abrasive colleagues at the University of Buffalo cautioned her against believing the praise that was being heaped upon her, that she would destroy her small but unique talent if she took all this seriously, etc. Even her new lover, a critic, separated from his wife and several children, a fifty-year-old ex-child prodigy, warned her against success: "They want to make you believe you're a genius, so they can draw back and laugh at you. First they hypnotize you, then they destroy you. Believe nothing."

The flow of barbiturates and amphetamines gave her eyes a certain wild sheen, her copper hair a frantic wasteful curl, made her voice go shrill at the many Buffalo parties. She wondered if she did not have the talent, after all, for being a spectacle. Someone to stare at. The magazine cover had flattered her wonderfully: taken by a Greenwich Village photographer as dreamily hungover as Ilena herself, the two of them moving about in slow motion in his studio, adjusting her hair, her lips, her eyelashes, the tip of her chin, adjusting the light, altering the light, bringing out a fantastic ethereal glow in her eyes and cheeks and forehead that Ilena had never seen in herself. The cover had been in full color and Ilena had looked really beautiful, a pre-Raphaelite virgin. Below her photograph was a caption in high alarmed black letters: ARE AMERICAN WOMEN AVENGING CENTURIES OF OPPRESSION?

Revenge!

Death Dance was nominated for a National Book Award, but lost out to a long, tedious, naturalistic novel; someone at Buffalo who knew the judges told Ilena that this was just because the female member of the committee had been jealous of her. Ilena, whose head seemed to be swimming all the time now, and who did not dare to drive around in her Mercedes for fear of having an accident, accepted all opinions, listened desperately to everyone, pressed herself against her lover, and wept at the thought of her disintegrating brain.

This lover wanted to marry her, as soon as his divorce was final; his name was Lyle Myer. He was the author of twelve books of criticism and a columnist for a weekly left-wing magazine; a New Yorker, he had never lived outside New York until coming to Buffalo, which terrified him. He was afraid of being beaten up by militant students on campus, and he was afraid of being beaten up by the police. Hesitant, sweet, and as easily moved to sentimental tears as Ilena herself, he was always telephoning her or dropping in at her flat. Because he was, or had been, an alcoholic, Ilena felt it was safe to tell him about the pills she took. He seemed pleased by this confidence, this admission of her weakness, as if it bound her more hopelessly to him—just as his teen-aged daughter, whose snapshot Ilena had seen, was bound to be a perpetual daughter to him because of her acne and rounded shoulders, unable to escape his love. "Drugs are suicidal, yes, but if they forestall the actual act of suicide they are obviously beneficial," he told her.

With him, she felt nothing except a clumsy domestic affection: no physical love at all.

She was so tired most of the time that she did not even pretend to feel anything. With Gordon, in those hurried steep moments back in Detroit, the two of them always fearful of being discovered, her body had been keyed up to hysteria and love had made her delirious; with Bryan, near the end of their marriage, she had sometimes felt a tinge of love, a nagging doubtful rush that she often let fade away again, but with Lyle her body was dead, worn out, it could not respond to his most tender caresses. She felt how intellectualized she had become, her entire body passive and observant and cynical.

"Oh, I have to get my head straight. I have to get my head straight," Ilena wept.

Lyle undressed her gently, lovingly. She felt panic, seeing in his eyes that compassionate look that had meant Gordon was thinking of his children: how she had flinched from that look!

The end had come with Gordon just as abruptly as it had come with Father Hoffman, and only a week later. They had met by accident out on the street one day, Gordon with his wife and the two smallest children, Ilena in a trench coat, bareheaded, a leather purse with a frayed strap slung over her shoulder. "Hello, Ilena," Gordon said guiltily. He was really frightened. His wife, still a handsome woman, though looking older than her thirty-seven years, smiled stiffly at Ilena and let her gaze travel down to Ilena's watermarked boots. "How are you, Ilena?" Gordon said. His eyes grabbed at her, blue and intimidated. His wife, tugging at one of the little boys, turned a sour, ironic smile upon Ilena and said, "Are you one of my husband's students?" Ilena guessed that this was meant to insult Gordon, to make him feel old. But she explained politely that she was an instructor in the English Department, "but I'm leaving after this semester," and she noticed covertly that Gordon was not insulted, not irritated by his wife's nastiness, but only watchful, cautious, his smile strained with the fear that Ilena would give him away.

"In fact, I'm leaving in a few weeks," Ilena said.

His wife nodded stiffly, not bothering to show much regret. Gordon smiled nervously, apologetically. With relief, Ilena thought. He was smiling with relief because now he would be rid of her.

And so that had ended.

They met several times after this, but Ilena was now in a constant state of excitement or drowsiness; she was working out the beginning chapters of *Death Dance*—now living alone in the apartment, since her husband had moved out to a hotel. Her life was a confusion of days and nights, sleepless nights, headachey days, classes she taught in a dream and classes she failed to meet; she spent long periods in the bathtub while the hot water turned tepid and finally cold, her mind racing. She thought of her marriage and its failure. Marriage was the deepest, most mysterious, most profound exploration open to man: she had always believed that, and she believed it now. Because she had failed did not change that belief. This plunging into another's soul, this pressure of bodies together, so brutally intimate, was the closest one could come to a sacred adventure; she still believed that. But she had failed. So she forced herself to think of her work. She thought of the novel she was writing—about a "suicide club" that had apparently existed in Ann Arbor, Michigan—projecting her confusion and her misery into the heads of those late-adolescent girls, trying not to think of her own personal misery, the way love had soured in her life. Her husband. Gordon. Well, yes, men failed at being men; but maybe she had failed at being a woman. She had been unfaithful to two men at the same time. She deserved whatever she got.

Still, she found it difficult to resist swallowing a handful of sleeping pills. . . . Why not? Why not empty the whole container? There were moments when she looked at herself in the bathroom mirror and raised one eyebrow flirtatiously. *How about it? . . . Why not die?* . . . Only the empty apartment awaited her.

But she kept living because the novel obsessed her. She had to write it. She had to solve its problems, had to finish it, send it away from her completed. And, anyway, if she had taken sleeping pills and did not wake up, Gordon or Bryan would probably discover her before she had time to die. They often telephoned, and would have been alarmed if she hadn't answered. Gordon called her every evening, usually from a drugstore, always guiltily, so that she began to take pity on his cowardice. Did he fear her committing suicide and leaving a note that would drag him in? Or did he really love her? . . . Ilena kept assuring him that she was all right, that she would be packing soon, yes, yes, she would always remember him with affection; no, she would probably not write to him, it would be better not to write. They talked quickly, sadly. Already the frantic hours of love-making in that office had become history, outlandish and improbable. Sometimes Ilena thought, *My God, I really love this man,* but her voice kept on with the usual conversation—what she had done that day, what he had done, what the state of her relationship with Bryan was, what his children were doing, the plans his wife had for that summer.

So it had ended, feebly; she had not even seen him the last week she was in Detroit.

Bryan called her too, impulsively. Sometimes to argue, sometimes to check plans, dates. He knew about the pills she took, though not about their quantity, and if she failed to answer the telephone for long he would have come over at once. Ilena would have been revived, wakened by a stomach pump, an ultimate masculine attack upon her body, sucking out her insides in great gasping shuddering gulps . . . So she took only a double dose of sleeping pills before bed, along with the gin, and most of the time she slept soundly enough, without dreams. The wonderful thing about pills was that dreams were not possible. No dreams. The death of dreams. What could be more lovely than a dreamless sleep? . . .

In late April, Bryan had a collapse of some kind and was admitted to a local clinic; then he flew to his mother's, in Oswego. Ilena learned from a mutual friend at Wayne Medical School that Gordon had had a general nervous collapse, aggravated by a sudden malfunctioning of the liver brought on by malnutrition—he had been starving himself, evidently, to punish Ilena. But she worked on her novel, incorporating this latest catastrophe into the plot; she finished it in January of 1968, in Buffalo, where she was teaching a writing seminar; it was published in early 1969, and changed her life.

Lyle Myer pretended jealousy of her—all this acclaim, all this fuss! He insisted that she agree to marry him. He never mentioned, seemed deliberately to overlook, the embarrassing fact that she could love him only tepidly, that her mind was always elsewhere in their dry, fateful struggles, strung out with drugs or the memory of some other man, someone she half remembered, or the letters she had to answer from her agent and a dozen other people, so many people inviting her to give talks, to accept awards, to teach at their universities, to be interviewed by them, begging and demanding her time, her intense interest, like a hundred lovers tugging and pulling at her body, engaging it in a kind of love-making to which she could make only the feeblest of responses, her face locked now in a perpetual feminine smile. . . . With so much publicity and money, she felt an obligation to be feminine and gracious to everyone; when she was interviewed she spoke enthusiastically of the place of art in life, the place of beauty in this modern technological culture—she seemed to stress, on one national late-night television show, the tragedy of small trees stripped bare by vandals in city parks as much as the tragedy of the country's current foreign policy in Vietnam. At least it turned out that way. It was no wonder people could not take her seriously: one of the other writers at Buffalo, himself famous though more *avant-garde* than Ilena, shrugged her off as that girl who was always "licking her lips to make them glisten."

She did not sign on for another year at Buffalo, partly because of the political strife there and partly because she was restless, agitated, ready to move on. She sold the Mercedes and gave to the Salvation Army the furniture and other possessions Bryan had so cavalierly—indifferently—given her, and took an apartment in New York. She began writing stories that were to appear in fashion magazines, Ilena's slick, graceful prose an easy complement to the dreamlike faces and bodies of models whose photographs appeared in those same magazines, everything muted and slightly distorted as if by a drunken lens, the "very poetry of hallucination"—as one reviewer had said of

Death Dance. Lyle flew down to see her nearly every weekend; on other weekends he was with his "separated" family. She loved him, yes, and she agreed to marry him, though she felt no hurry—in fact, she felt no real interest in men at all, her body shrinking when it was touched even accidentally, not out of fear but out of a kind of chaste boredom. So much, she had had so much of men, so much loving, so much mauling, so much passion. . . .

What, she was only twenty-nine years old?

She noted, with a small pang of vanity, how surprised audiences were when she rose to speak. *Ilena Williams looks so young!* They could not see the fine vibrations of her knees and hands, already viciously toned down by Librium. They could not see the colorless glop she vomited up in motel bathrooms, or in rest rooms down the hall from the auditorium in which she was speaking—she was always "speaking," invited out all over the country for fees ranging from $500 to a colossal $2000, speaking on "current trends in literature" or "current mores in America" or answering questions about her "writing habits" or reading sections from her latest work, a series of short stories in honor of certain dead writers with whom she felt a kinship. "I don't exist as an individual but only as a completion of a tradition, the end of something, not the best part of it but only the end," she explained, wondering if she was telling the truth or if this was all nonsense, "and I want to honor the dead by reimagining their works, by reimagining their obsessions . . . in a way marrying them, joining them as a woman joins a man . . . spiritually and erotically. . . ." She spoke so softly, so hesitantly, that audiences often could not hear her. Whereupon an energetic young man sitting in the first row, or onstage with her, would spring to his feet and adjust the microphone. "Is that better? Can you all hear now?" he would ask. Ilena saw the faces in the audience waver and blur and fade away, sheer protoplasm, and panic began in her stomach—what if she should vomit right in front of everyone? on this tidy little lectern propped up on dictionaries for her benefit? But she kept on talking. Sometimes she talked about the future of the short story, sometimes about the future of civilization—she heard the familiar, dead, deadened word *Vietnam* uttered often in her own voice, a word that had once meant something; she heard her voice echoing from the farthest corners of the auditorium as if from the corners of all those heads, her own head hollow as a drum, occasionally seeing herself at a distance—a woman with long but rather listless copper-red hair, thin cheeks, eyes that looked unnaturally enlarged. *Adverse reactions: confusion, edema, nausea, constipation, jaundice, hallucinations. . . .* Did that qualify as a legitimate hallucination, seeing herself from a distance, hearing herself from a distance? Did that qualify as a sign of madness?

During ths fall and winter of 1969 and the spring of 1970 she traveled everywhere, giving talks, being met at airports by interested strangers, driven to neat disinfected motel rooms. She had time to write only a few stories, which had to be edited with care before they could be published. Her blood pounded barbarously, while her voice went on and on in that gentle precise way, her body withdrawing from any man's touch, demure with a dread that could not show through her clothes. She had been losing weight gradually for three years, and now she had the angular, light-boned, but very intense look of a precocious child. People wanted to protect her. Women mothered her, men were always taking her arm, helping her through doorways; the editor of a famous men's magazine took her to lunch and warned her of Lyle Myer's habit of marrying young, artistic women and then ruining them—after all, he had been married three times already, and the pattern was established. Wasn't it? When people were most gentle with her, Ilena thought of the tough days when she'd run across that wind-tortured campus in Detroit, her coat flapping about her, her body still dazzled by Gordon's love, damp and sweaty from him, and she had dared run into the classroom, five minutes late, had dared to take off her coat and begin the lesson. . . . The radiators in that old building had knocked as if they might explode; like colossal arteries, like her thudding arteries, overwhelmed with life.

In the fall of 1970 she was invited back to Detroit to give a talk before the local Phi Beta Kappa chapter; she accepted, and a few days later she received a letter from the new dean of the School of Arts—new since she had left—of her old university, inviting her to a reception in her honor, as their "most esteemed ex-staff member." It was all very diplomatic, very charming. She had escaped them, they had gotten rid of her, and now they could all meet together for a few hours. . . . Father Hoffman sent a note to her also, underscoring the dean's invitation, hoping that she was well and as attractive as ever. So she accepted.

Father Hoffman and another priest came to pick her up at the Sheraton Cadillac Hotel; she was startled to see that Father Hoffman had let his hair grow a little long, that he had noble, graying sideburns, and that the young priest with him was even shaggier. After the first awkward seconds—Father Hoffman forgot and called her "Mrs. Donohue"—they got along very well. Ilena was optimistic about the evening; her stomach seemed settled. As soon as they arrived at the dean's home she saw that Gordon was not there; she felt immensely relieved, though she had known he would not come, would not want to see her again . . . she felt immensely relieved and accepted a drink at once from Father Hoffman, who was behaving in an exceptionally gallant manner. "Ilena is looking better than ever," he said as people crowded around her, some of them with copies of her novel to sign, "better even than all her photographs. . . . But we don't want to tire her out, you know. We don't want to exhaust her." He kept refreshing her drink, like a lover or a husband. In the old days everyone at this place had ignored Ilena's novels, even the fact of her being a "writer," but now they were all smiles and congratulations—even the wives of her ex-colleagues, sturdy, dowdy women who had never seemed to like her. Ilena was too shaky to make any sarcastic observations about this to Father Hoffman, who might have appreciated them. He did say, "Times have changed, eh, Ilena?" and winked at her roguishly. "For one thing, you're not quite as excitable as you used to be. You were a very *young* woman around here." She could sense, beneath his gallantry, a barely disguised contempt for her—for all women—and this knowledge made her go cold. She mumbled something about fighting off the flu. Time to take a "cold tablet." She fished in her purse and came out with a large yellow capsule, a tranquillizer, and swallowed it down with a mouthful of Scotch.

Father Hoffman and Dr. O'Brien and a new, young assistant professor—a poet whose first book would be published next spring—talked to Ilena in a kind of chorus, telling her about all the changes in the university. It was much more "community-oriented" now. Its buildings—its "physical plant"—were to be open to the neighborhood on certain evenings and on Saturdays. The young poet, whose blond hair was very long and who wore a suede outfit and a black silk turtleneck shirt, kept interrupting the older men with brief explosions of mirth. "Christ, all this is a decade out of date—integration and all that crap— the NAACP and good old Martin Luther King and all that crap—the blacks don't want it and I agree with them one hundred percent! King is dead and so is Civil Rights—just another white middle-class week-night activity the blacks saw through long ago! I agree with them one hundred percent!" He seemed to be trying to make an impression on Ilena, not quite looking at her, but leaning toward her with his knees slightly bent, as if to exaggerate his youth. Ilena sipped at her drink, trying to hide the panic that was beginning. Yes, the NAACP was dead, all that was dead, but she didn't want to think about it—after all, it had been at a civil-rights rally that she and Bryan had met, years ago in Madison, Wisconsin. . . . "I haven't gotten around to reading your novel yet," the poet said, bringing his gaze sideways to Ilena.

Ilena excused herself and searched for a bathroom. The dean's wife took her upstairs, kindly. Left alone, she waited to be sick, then lost interest in being sick; she had only to get through a few more hours of this and she would be safe. And Gordon wasn't there. She looked at herself in the mirror and should have been pleased to see that she looked so pretty—not beautiful tonight but pretty, delicate—she had worked hard enough at it, spending an hour in a hotel bathroom steaming her face and patting astringent on it, hoping for the best. She dreaded the cracks in her brain somehow working their way out to her skin. What then, what then? . . . But beauty did no good for anyone; it conferred no blessing upon the beautiful woman. Nervously, Ilena opened the medicine cabinet and peered at the array of things inside. She was interested mainly in prescription containers. Here were some small green pills prescribed for the dean's wife, for "tension." Tension, good! She took two of the pills. On another shelf there were some yellow capsules, perhaps the same as her own, though slightly smaller; she checked, yes, hers was 5 mg. and these were only 2. So she didn't bother with them. But she did discover an interesting white pill for "muscular tension," Dean Sprigg's prescription; she took one of these.

She descended the stairs, her hand firm on the bannister.

Before she could return safely to Father Hoffman, she was waylaid by someone's wife—the apple-cheeked Mrs. Honig, a very short woman with white hair who looked older than her husband, who looked, in fact, like Mrs. Santa Claus, motherly and dwarfed; Mrs. Honig asked her to sign a copy of *Death Dance*. "We all think it's so wonderful, just so wonderful for you," she said. Another woman joined them. Ilena had met her once, years before, but she could not remember her name. Mr. Honig hurried over. The conversation seemed to be about the tragedy of America—"All these young people dying in a senseless war," Mrs. Honig said, shaking her white hair; Mr. Honig agreed mournfully. "Vietnam is a shameful tragedy," he said. The dean's wife came by with a tray of cheese and crackers; everyone took something, even Ilena, though she doubted her ability to eat. She doubted everything. It seemed to her that Mrs. Honig and these other people were talking about Vietnam, and about drugs and death—could this be true?—or was it another hallucination? "Why, you know, a young man was killed here last spring, he took part in a demonstration against the Cambodian business," Mrs. Honig said vaguely; "they say a policeman clubbed him to death. . . ." "No, Ida, he had a concussion and died afterward," Mr. Honig said. He wiped his mouth of cracker crumbs and stared sadly at Ilena. "I think you knew him . . . Emmett Norlan?"

Emmett Norlan?

"You mean—Emmett is dead? He died? He died?" Ilena asked shrilly.

The blond poet came to join their group. He had known Emmett, yes, a brilliant young man, a martyr to the Cause—yes, yes—he knew everything. While Ilena stared into space he told them all about Emmett. *He* had been an intimate friend of Emmett's.

Ilena happened to be staring toward the front of the hall, and she saw Gordon enter. The dean's wife was showing him in. Flakes of snow had settled upon the shoulders of his old gray coat. Ilena started, seeing him so suddenly. She had forgotten all about him. She stared across the room in dismay, wondering at his appearance—he wore his hair longer, his sideburns were long and a little curly, he even had a small wiry brown beard— But he did not look youthful, he looked weary and drawn.

Now began half an hour of Ilena's awareness of him and his awareness of her. They had lived through events like this in the past, at other parties, meeting in other groups at the university; a dangerous, nervous sensation about their playing this game, not wanting to rush together. Ilena accepted a drink from a forty-year-old who looked zestful and adolescent, a priest who did not wear his Roman collar but, instead, a black nylon sweater and a medallion on a leather strap; Ilena's brain whirled at such surprises. What had happened? In the past there had been three categories: men, women, and priests. She had known how to conduct herself discreetly around these priests, who were masculine but undangerous; now she wasn't so sure. She kept thinking of Emmett dead. Had Emmett really been killed by the police? Little Emmett? She kept thinking of Gordon, aware of him circling her at a distance of some yards. She kept thinking of these people talking so casually of Vietnam, of drugs, of the death of little Emmett Norlan—these people—the very words they used turning flat and banal and safe in their mouths. "The waste of youth in this country is a tragedy," the priest with the sweater and the medallion said, shaking his head sadly.

Ilena eased away from them to stare at a Chagall lithograph, "Summer Night." Two lovers embraced, in repose; yet a nightmarish dream blossomed out of their heads, an intricate maze of dark depthless foliage, a lighted window, faces ghastly-white and perhaps a little grotesque. . . . Staring at these lovers, she sensed Gordon approaching her. She turned to him, wanting to be casual. But she was shaking. Gordon stared at her and she saw that old helplessness in his eyes—what, did he still love her? Wasn't she free of him yet? She began talking swiftly, nervously. "Tell me about Emmett. Tell me what happened." Gordon, who seemed heavier than she recalled, whose tired face disappointed her sharply, spoke as always in his gentle, rather paternal voice; she tried to listen. She tried to listen but she kept recalling that office, the two of them lying on the floor together, helpless in an embrace, so hasty, so reckless, grinding their bodies together in anguish. . . . They had been so close, so intimate, that their blood had flowed freely in each other's veins; on the coldest days they had gone about blood-warmed, love-warmed. Tears filled Ilena's eyes. Gordon was saying, "The story was that he died of a concussion, but actually he died of liver failure. Once he got in the hospital he just disintegrated . . . he had hepatitis . . . he'd been taking heroin. . . . It was a hell of a thing, Ilena. . . ."

She pressed her fingers hard against her eyes.

"Don't cry, please," Gordon said, stricken.

A pause of several seconds: the two of them in a kind of equilibrium, two lovers.

"Would you like me to drive you back to your hotel?" Gordon said.

She went at once to get her coat. Backing away, always backing away . . . she stammered a few words to Father Hoffman, to the dean and his wife, words of gratitude, confusion. Good-by to Detroit! *Good-by, good-by.* She shook hands. She finished her drink. Gordon helped her on with her coat—a stylish black coat with a black mink collar, nothing like the clothes she had worn in the old days. Out on the walk, in the soft falling snow, Gordon said nervously: "I know you're going to be married. Lyle Myer. I know all about it. I'm very happy. I'm happy for you. You're looking very well."

Ilena closed her eyes, waiting for her mind to straighten itself out. Yes, she was normal; she had gone to an internist in Buffalo and had been declared normal. *You are too young to be experiencing menopause,* the doctor had said thoughtfully; *the cessation of menstrual periods must be related to the Pill or to an emotional condition.* She thought it better not to tell Gordon all that. "Thank you," she said simply.

"I'm sorry they told you about Emmett," Gordon said. "There was no reason to tell you. He liked you so much, Ilena; he hung around my office after you left and all but confessed he was in love with you . . . he kept asking if you wrote to me and I said no, but he didn't believe me . . . he was always asking about you. . . ."

"When did he die?"

"Last spring. His liver gave out. Evidently it was just shot. Someone said his skin was bright yellow."

"He was taking heroin? . . ."

"God, yes. He was a wreck. The poor kid just disintegrated, it was a hell of a shame. . . ."

He drove her back downtown. They were suddenly very comfortable together, sadly comfortable. Ilena had been in this car only two or three times in the past. "Where is your wife?" she asked shyly. She watched him as he answered—his wife was visiting her mother in Ohio, she'd taken the children—no, things were no better between them—always the same, always the same—Ilena thought in dismay that he was trivialized by these words: men were trivialized by love and by their need for women.

"I've missed you so much . . ." Gordon said suddenly.

They walked through the tufts of falling snow, to the hotel. A gigantic hotel, all lights and people. Ilena felt brazen and anonymous here. Gordon kept glancing at her, as if unable to believe in her. He was nervous, eager, a little drunk; an uncertain adolescent smile hovered about his face. "I love you, I still love you," he whispered. In the elevator he embraced her. Ilena did not resist. She felt her body warming to him as toward an old friend, a brother. She did love him. Tears of love stung her eyes. If only she could get her head straight, if only she could think of what she was supposed to think of . . . someone she was supposed to remember. . . . In the overheated room they embraced gently. Gently. Ilena did not want to start this love again, it was a mistake, but she caught sight of Gordon's stricken face and could not resist. She began to cry. Gordon clutched her around the hips, kneeling before her. He pressed his hot face against her.

"Ilena, I'm so sorry . . ." he said.

She thought of planets: sun-warmed planets revolving around a molten star. Revolving around a glob of light. And the planets rotated on their own, private axes. But now the planets were accelerating their speed, they wobbled on their axes and the strain of their movement threatened to tear them apart. She began to sob. Ugly, gasping, painful sobs. . . . "Don't cry, please, I'm so sorry," Gordon said. They lay down together. The room was hot, too hot. They had not bothered to put on a light. Only the light from the window, a dull glazed wintry light; Ilena allowed him to kiss her, to undress her, to move his hands wildly about her body as she wept. What should she be thinking of? Whom should she remember? When she was with Lyle she thought back to Gordon . . . now, with Gordon, she thought back to someone else, someone else, half-remembered, indistinct, perhaps dead. . . . He began to make love to her. He was eager, breathing as sharply and as painfully as Ilena herself. She clasped her arms around him. That firm hard back she remembered. Or did she remember? . . . Her mind wandered and she thought suddenly of Bryan, her husband. He was her ex-husband now. She thought of their meeting at that civil-rights rally, introduced by mutual friends, she thought of the little tavern they had gone to, on State Street in Madison, she thought of the first meal she'd made for Bryan and that other couple . . . proud of herself as a cook, baking them an Italian dish with shrimp and crabmeat and mushrooms . . . yes, she had been proud of her cooking, she had loved to cook for years. For years. She had loved Bryan. But suddenly she was not thinking of him; her mind gave way to a sharper thought and she saw Emmett's face; his scorn, his disapproval.

She stifled a scream.

Gordon slid from her, frightened. "Did I hurt you? Ilena?"

She began to weep uncontrollably. Their bodies, so

warm, now shivered and seemed to sting each other. Their hairs seemed to catch at each other painfully.

"Did I hurt you? . . ." he whispered.

She remembered the afternoon she had fainted. Passed out cold. And then she had come to her senses and she had cried, like this, hiding her face from her lover because crying made it ugly, so swollen. . . . Gordon tried to comfort her. But the bed was crowded with people. A din of people. A mob. Lovers were kissing her on every inch of her body and trying to suck up her tepid blood, prodding, poking inspecting her like that doctor in Buffalo—up on the table, naked beneath an oversized white robe, her feet in the stirrups, being examined with a cold sharp metal device and then with the doctor's fingers in his slick rubber gloves—checking her ovaries, so casually—*You are too young for menopause,* he had said. Was it the pills, then? The birth-control pills? *This kind of sterility is not necessarily related to the Pill,* the doctor had conceded, and his subtlety of language had enchanted Ilena. . . .

"Don't cry," Gordon begged.

She had frightened him off and he would not make love to her. He only clutched at her, embraced her. She felt that he was heavier, yes, than she remembered. Heavier. Older. But she could not concentrate on him: she kept seeing Emmett's face. His frizzy hair, his big glasses, his continual whine. Far inside her, too deep for any man to reach and stir into sensation, a dull, dim lust began for Emmett, hardly more than a faint throbbing. Emmett, who was dead. She wanted to hold him, now, instead of this man—Emmett in her arms, his irritation calmed, his glasses off and set on the night table beside the bed, everything silent, silent. Gordon was whispering to her. *Love. Love.* She did not remember that short scratchy beard. But she was lying in bed with an anxious, perspiring, bearded man, evidently someone she knew. They were so close that their blood might flow easily back and forth between their bodies, sluggish and warm and loving.

She recalled her husband's face: a look of surprise, shock. She had betrayed him. His face blended with the face of her student, who was dead, and Gordon's face, pressed so close to her in the dark that she could not see it. The bed was crammed with people. Their identities flowed sluggishly, haltingly, from vein to vein. One by one they were all becoming each other. Becoming protoplasm. They were protoplasm that had the sticky pale formlessness of semen. They were all turning into each other, into protoplasm. . . . Ilena was conscious of something fading in her, in the pit of her belly. Fading. Dying. *The central sexual organ is the brain,* she had read, and now her brain was drawing away, fading, dissolving.

"Do you want me to leave?" Gordon asked.

She did not answer. Against the hotel window: soft, shapeless clumps of snow. She must remember something, she must remember someone . . . there was an important truth she must understand. . . . But she could not get it into focus. Her brain seemed to swoon backward, in an elation of fatigue, and she heard beyond this man's hoarse, strained breathing the gentle breathing of the snow, falling shapelessly upon them all.

"Do you want me to leave?" Gordon asked.

She could not speak.

Talking Horse

Bernard Malamud

BERNARD MALAMUD was born in Brooklyn and attended City College and Columbia University. He has taught at Oregon State University and Harvard and is now teaching at Bennington College. He has published seven novels, and three collections of short stories. For *The Magic Barrel* he received a National Book Award, and for *The Fixer,* a National Book Award and the Pulitzer Prize. His latest novel, *Dubin's Lives,* was published in 1979.

Q. Am I a man in a horse or a horse that talks like a man? If the first, then Jonah had it better in the whale; more room all around; also he knew who he was and how he had got there. About myself I make guesses. Anyway, after three days and nights the big fish stopped at Nineveh and Jonah took his valise and got off. Not Abramowitz, still at hand, or on board, after years; he's no prophet. On the contrary, he works in a circus sideshow full of freaks—though recently advanced, on Goldberg's insistence, to the center ring inside the big tent in an act with his deaf-mute master—Goldberg himself—may the Almighty forgive him. All I know is I've been here for years and still don't understand the nature of my fate; in short, if I'm Abramowitz, a horse; or a horse including Abramowitz. Why is anybody's guess. Understanding goes so far and no further, especially if Goldberg blocks the way. Maybe it's because of something I said or thought or did, or didn't do, in my life. It's easy to make mistakes. As I say, I have my theories, glimmers, guesses, but can't prove a thing.

When Abramowitz stands in his stall, his hoofs booming nervously on the battered wooden planks as he chews in his bag of hard yellow oats, sometimes he has thoughts, far-off recollections, they seem to be, of young horses racing, playing, nipping at each other's flanks in green fields; and other disquieting images that resemble memories; so who's to say what's really the truth?

I've tried asking Goldberg, but save yourself the trouble. He gets green in the face at questions, very uptight. I can understand—he's a deaf-mute from way back; he doesn't like interference with his plans, or thoughts, or the way he lives, and no surprises except those he invents. He talks to me when he feels like it, which isn't so often—his little patience has worn thin. Lately he relies too much on his bamboo cane—whoosh across the rump. There's plenty of oats, and straw, and water, and once in a while a joke to make me relax; but usually it's one threat or another followed by a flash of pain if I don't do something or other right, or something I say gets on his nerves. It's not necessarily this cane that slashes like a sword; his threats have the same effect, like a zong of lightning through the flesh; in fact the blow hurts less than the threat—the blow is momentary, the threat you worry about. But the true pain, at least to me, is when you don't know what you wish to.

Which doesn't mean we don't communicate. Goldberg taps out Morse code messages on my head with his big knuckle—crack crack crack; I feel the vibrations go through the bones to the tip of my tail—when he tells me what to do next or he threatens how many lashes for the last offense. His first message, I remember, was NO QUESTIONS. UNDERSTOOD? I shook my head and a little bell jingled on a strap under the forelock. That was the first I knew it was there.

TALK, he knocked on my head, "You're a talking horse."

"Yes, master." What else could I say?

My voice surprised me when it came out high through the tunnel of a horse's neck. I don't exactly remember the occasion—go remember beginnings. My memory I have to fight to get an early remembrance out of. Maybe I fell and hurt my head on a rock or was otherwise stunted? Goldberg is my deaf-mute owner; he reads my lips. Once when he was drunk and looking for company he tapped me that I used to carry goods on my back to fairs and markets before we joined the circus; before that I thought I was born there.

"On a rainy, snowy, crappy night," Goldberg Morse-coded me on my skull.

"What happened then?"

He stopped talking. I should know better but don't.

I try to remember that night, and certain hazy thoughts cross my mind, which might be some sort of story I dream up when I have nothing to do but chew my oats. It's easier than remembering. The one that comes to me most is about two men, or horses, or men on horses, though which might be me I can't say except that Goldberg rides on my back every night in the act. Anyway two strangers meet, somebody asks the other a question, and the next thing you know they're locked in a fight, either hacking at each other's head with their swords or braying wildly as they tear their flesh; or both at the same time. If riders, or horses, one is thin and poetic, the other a fat stranger wearing a black crown. They meet in a stone pit on a rainy, snowy, crappy night, one wearing his cracked metal crown that weighs heavy on his head and makes his movements slow, and the other has his ragged colored cap; all night they wrestle by weird light in the slippery stone pit.

Q. "What's to be done?"

A. "None of those accursed questions."

In the morning one of us wakes with a terrible pain. It feels like a wound in the neck but maybe like a headache. He remembers a blow he can't attest to. Abramowitz, in his dream story, suspects Goldberg stuffed him into a horse because he needed a talking one for his act and there was no such thing. I wish I knew for sure.

NO QUESTIONS. WHEN ARE YOU GOING TO LEARN?

That's his nature; he's a lout, though not without a little consideration when he's depressed and drinking from his bottle. That's when he taps me out a teasing anecdote or two. He has no friends. Family neither of us talks about. When he laughs he cries.

It must frustrate the owner that all he can say aloud is four-letter words like geee, gooo, gaaa, gaaw, and the circus manager who doubles as ringmaster, in for a snifter, looks embarrassed at the floor. At those who don't know the Morse code Goldberg grimaces, glares, and grinds his teeth. He has his mysteries. He keeps a mildewed three-prong spear haning on the wall over a stuffed pony's head. Sometimes he goes down in the cellar with an old candle and comes up with a new one, yet we have electric lights. Though he doesn't complain about his life, he worries and cracks his knuckles. Maybe he's a widower, who knows? He doesn't seem interested in women but he sees to it that Abramowitz gets his chance at a mare in heat, if available. Abramowitz engages to satisfy his physical nature, a fact is a fact, otherwise it's no big deal; the mare has no interest in a talking courtship. Furthermore, Goldberg applauds when Abramowitz mounts her, which is humiliating.

And when they're in their winter quarters the owner once a week or so dresses up and goes out on the town. When he puts on his broadcloth suit, diamond stickpin, and yellow gloves, he preens before the full-length mirror. He pretends to fence, jabs the bamboo cane at the figure in the glass, twirls it around one finger. Where he goes when he goes, he doesn't inform Abramowitz. But when he returns he's usually melancholic, sometimes anguished, didn't have much of a good time; and in this mood may hand out a few loving lashes with that nasty cane. Or worse, make threats. Nothing serious but who needs it? Usually he prefers to stay home and watch television. He is fascinated by astronomy, and when they have such programs on the educational channel he's there night after night, staring at pictures of stars, galaxies, infinite space. He also likes to read the *Daily News* but tears it up once he's done. Sometimes he reads this book he hides on a shelf in the closet under some old hats. If the book doesn't make him laugh outright it makes him cry. When he gets excited over something he's reading in his fat book, his eyes roll, his mouth gets wet, and he tries to talk through his thick tongue; but all Abramowitz hears is geee gooo gaaa gaaw. Always these words, whatever they mean, and sometimes gool goon geek gonk, in various combinations, usually gool with gonk, which Abramowitz thinks means Goldberg. And in such states he had been known to kick Abramowitz in the belly with his heavy boot. Ooof.

When he laughs he sounds like a horse, or maybe it's the way I hear him with these ears. And though he laughs once in a while, it doesn't make my life easier, because of my condition. I mean I think here I am in this horse. This is my theory though I have my doubts. Otherwise, Goldberg is a small stocky figure with a thick neck, heavy black brows, each like a small moustache, and big feet that swell up in his shapeless boots. He washes his feet in the kitchen sink and hangs up his yellowed white socks to dry on the whitewashed walls of my stall.

In winter they live in the South in a small, messy, one-floor house with a horse's stall attached that Goldberg can approach, down a few steps, from the kitchen of the house. To get Abramowitz in he is led up a plank from the outside, and the door shuts on his rear end. To keep him from wandering all over the house there's a slatted gate to just under his head. Furthermore the stall is next to the toilet and the broken water closet runs all night. It's a boring life with a deaf-mute except when Goldberg changes the act a little. Abramowitz enjoys it when they rehearse a new routine, although Goldberg hardly ever alters the lines, only the order of answer and question. That's better than nothing. Sometimes when Abramowitz gets tired of talking to himself, asking unanswered questions, he complains, shouts, calls the owner dirty names. He snorts, brays, whinnies shrilly. In his frustration he rears, rocks, gallops in his stall; but what good is a gallop if there's no place to go, and Goldberg can't, or won't, hear complaints, pleas, protest?

Q. "Answer me this, if it's a sentence I'm serving, how long?"

A.

Once in a while Goldberg seems to sense somebody else's needs and is momentarily considerate of Abramowitz—combs and curries him, even rubs his bushy head against the horse's. He also shows interest in his diet and whether his bowel movements are regular and sufficient; but if Abramowitz gets sentimentally careless when the owner is close by and forms a question he can see on his lips, Goldberg punches him on the nose. Or threatens to. It doesn't hurt any the less.

All I know is he's a former vaudeville comic and acrobat. He did a solo act telling jokes, with the help of a blind assistant, before he went sad. That's all he's ever tapped to me about himself. When I forgot myself and asked what happened after that, he punched me in the nose.

Only once, when he was half drunk and giving me my pail of water, I sneaked in a fast one which he answered before he knew it.

"Where did you get me, master? Did you buy me from somebody else?"

I FOUND YOU IN A CABBAGE PATCH.

Once he tapped my skull: "In the beginning was the word."

"Which word was that?"

Bong on the nose.

NO QUESTIONS.

"Watch out for the wound on my head or wherever it is."

"Shut your mouth or your teeth will fall out."

Goldberg should read that story I once heard on his transistor radio, I thought to myself. It's about a poor cabdriver driving his sled in the Russian snow. His son, a fine boy, caught pneumonia and died, and the poor cabby is unable to find anybody to talk to so as to relieve his grief a little. Nobody wants to listen to his troubles.

The customers insult him if he opens his mouth to talk. So finally he tells the story to his bony nag in the stable. And the horse, munching oats, listens patiently as the weeping old man tells him about his boy he has just buried.

Something like this could happen to you, Goldberg. Or something similar since you have no son. Maybe a nephew?

"Will you ever free me out of here, master?"

I'LL FLAY YOU ALIVE, YOU BASTARD HORSE.

We have this act we do together. Goldberg calls it, "Ask Me Another," an ironic title where I am concerned.

In the sideshow days people used to stand among the bearded ladies, fat men, Joey the snake boy, and other freaks, laughing in astonishment and disbelief at Abramowitz talking. He remembers one man staring into his mouth to see who was hiding there. Homunculus? Others suggested it was a ventriloquist's act even though the horse told them Goldberg was a deaf-mute. But in the main tent the act got thunderous storms of applause. Reporters pleaded for permission to interview Abramowitz, and he had plans to tell all; but Goldberg wouldn't have it. "His head will swell up too big," he had the talking horse say to them. "He will never wear the same size straw hat he wore last summer."

For the performance the owner dresses up in a balloony red-and-white polka-dot clown's suit with a pointed clown's hat and has borrowed the ringmaster's snaky whip, an item Abramowitz is skittish about though Goldberg says it's nothing to worry over, little more than decoration in a circus act. No animal act is without one. People like to hear the snap. He also ties something like an upside-down feather duster on Abramowitz's head that makes him look like a wilted unicorn. The little circus bands ends its brassy "Overture to William Tell"; there's a flourish of trumpets, and Goldberg cracks the whip as Abramowitz, with his loose-feathered, upside-down duster, trots once around the spotlit ring and then stops at attention, facing clown-Goldberg, his left foreleg pawing the sawdust-covered earth. Then they begin the act; Goldberg's ruddy face, as he opens his painted mouth to express himself, flushes dark red, and his melancholy eyes under black brows protrude as he painfully squeezes out the abominable sounds, his only eloquence.

"Geee gooo gaaa gaaw?"

Abramowitz's beautifully timed response is:

A. "To get to the other side."

There's a gasp from the spectators, a murmur, perhaps of puzzlement, and a moment of intense expectant silence. Then at a roll of the drums Goldberg snaps the long whip and Abramowitz translates the owner's idiocy into something that makes sense and somehow fulfills expectations; though in truth it's no more than a question following a response already given.

Q. "Why does a chicken cross the road?"

Then they laugh. And do they laugh! They pound each other on the head in helpless laughter. You'd think this trite riddle, this sad excuse for a joke were the first they've heard in their lives. And they're laughing at the translated question, of course, not the answer, which is the way Goldberg has set it up. That's his nature for you. It's the only way he works.

Abramowitz used to sink into the dumps after that, knowing what really amuses everybody is not the old-fashioned tired little riddle, but the fact it's put to them by a talking horse. That's what splits the gut.

"It's a stupid little question."

"There are no better," Goldberg said.

"You could try letting me ask one or two of my own."

YOU KNOW WHAT A GELDING IS?

I gave him no reply. Two can play at the game.

After the first applause both performers take a bow. Abramowitz trots around the ring, his head with panache held high, and when Goldberg again cracks the snaky whip, he moves nervously to the center of the ring and they go through the routine of the other infantile answers and questions in the same silly ass-backwards order. After each question Abramowitz runs around the ring as the spectators cheer.

A. "To hold up his pants."

Q. "Why does a fireman wear red suspenders?"

A. "Columbus."

Q. "What was the first bus to cross the Atlantic?"

A. "A newspaper."

Q. "What black and white and red all over?"

We did a dozen like that, and when we finished up, Goldberg cracked the foolish whip, I galloped twice more around the ring, then we took our last bows.

Goldberg pats my steaming flank and in the ocean-roar of everyone in the circus tent applauding and shouting bravo, we leave the ring, running down the ramp to our quarters, Goldberg's personal wagon van and my attached stall; after that we're private parties till tomorrow's show. Lots of customers used to come night after night, even following us to the next town to watch the performance, and they still laughed at the riddles though they had memorized them by now. That's how the season goes, and nothing much has changed one way or the other except that recently Goldberg, because the manager was complaining, added a couple of silly elephant riddles to modernize the act.

A. "From playing marbles."

Q. "Why do elephants have wrinkled knees?"

A. "To pack their dirty laundry in."

Q. "Why do elephants have long trunks?"

Neither Goldberg nor I like the new jokes, but they're the latest style. I keep in my mind that we could do the act without jokes. All you need is a talking horse.

One day Abramowitz thought he would make up a riddle of his own—it's not that hard to do. So that night after they had finished the routine, he slipped in his new joke.

A. "To say hello to his friend the chicken."

Q. "Why does a yellow duck cross the road?"

After a minute of confused silence everybody cracked up; they beat themselves silly with their fists—broken straw hats flew all over the place; but Goldberg, in unbelieving astonishment, glowered at the horse. His ruddy face turned almost black. When he cracked the whip it sounded like a river of ice breaking up. Realizing in fright that he had gone too far, Abramowitz, baring his big teeth, reared up on his hind legs and took several steps forward against the wall. But the spectators, thinking this was an extra flourish at the end of the act, applauded wildly. Goldberg's anger eased, and lowering his whip he pretended to laugh. He beamed at Abramowitz as if he were his only child and could do no wrong, though Abramowitz knew the owner was furious.

"Don't forget WHO'S WHO, you crazy horse," Goldberg, with his back to the audience, quickly tapped out on Abramowitz's nose.

He had him gallop once more around the ring,

mounted him in an acrobatic leap from the ground onto his bare back, and drove him madly to the exit.

Afterwards he Morse-coded with his hard knuckle on the horse's bony head that if he pulled anything like that again he would personally deliver him to the glue factory.

"Where they will melt you down to size. What's left over goes into dog food cans."

"It was only a joke, master," Abramowitz explained.

"To say the answer was OK, but not to ask the question all by yourself."

Out of stored-up bitterness the talking horse replied, "I did it on account of it made me feel free."

At that Goldberg whacked him hard across the neck with his murderous cane. Abramowitz, choking, staggered, but did not bleed.

"Don't, master," he gasped, "no on my old wound."

Goldberg went into slow motion, still waving the cane.

"Try it again, you tub of guts, and I'll be wearing a horsehide coat with a fur collar, gool, goon, geek, gonk." Spit collected in the corners of his mouth.

Understood.

Sometimes I think of myself as an idea, yet here I am in this filthy stall, standing with my hoofs sunk in my yellow balls of dreck. I feel old, disgusted with myself, smelling the odor of my bad breath as my teeth in the feed bag grind the hard oats into a foaming lump, while Goldberg smokes a cigar as he watches television. He feeds me well enough, if oats is your dish, but hasn't had my stall cleaned for a week. It's easy to take revenge on a horse if that's the type you are.

So the act goes on every matinee and night, keeping Goldberg in good spirits and thousands in stitches, but Abramowitz had dreams of being out in the open. They were strange dreams, if dreams; he isn't sure what they are, or come from—thoughts of freedom, or maybe self-mockery? Whoever heard of a talking horse's dreams? This occurs to him now and then. Goldberg hasn't said he knows what's going on, but Abramowitz suspects he knows more than he seems to, because when the horse, lying in his dung and soiled straw, awakens from a dangerous reverie, he hears the owner muttering in his sleep in deaf-mute talk.

Abramowitz dreams, or does something of the sort, of other lives he might live, let's say of a horse that can't talk, couldn't conceive the idea, is perfectly content to be just a horse without problems of speech. He sees himself, for instance, pulling a light wagonload of ripe apples along a rural road. There are leafy beech trees on both sides and beyond them broad green fields full of wild flowers. If he were that kind of horse, maybe he might retire to graze in such fields. More adventurously, he sees himself a racehorse in goggles, thundering along the last stretch of muddy track, slicing through a wedge of other galloping horses to win by a nose at the finish; and the jockey is definitely not Goldberg. There is no jockey; he fell off.

Or if not a racehorse, if he has to be practical about it, Abramowitz continues on as a talking horse but not in circus work anymore; and every night on the stage he recites poetry. The theater is packed and people cry out oooh and aaah, what beautiful things that horse is saying.

Sometimes he thinks of himself as altogether a free man, someone of indeterminate appearance and characteristics, who, if he has the right education, is maybe a doctor or lawyer helping poor people who need help. Not a bad idea for a useful life.

But even as I am dreaming, or whatever it is I'm doing, I hear Goldberg talking in my sleep:

As for number one, you are first and last a talking

horse, not an ordinary one who can't talk; and I have got nothing against you that you can talk, Abramowitz, but on account of what you say when you break the rules.

As for a racehorse, if you could take a good look at the brokendown type you are—overweight, with heavy sagging belly and a thick uneven dark brown coat that won't shine up no matter how much I comb or brush you, and four hairy thick bent legs, plus a pair of slight cross-eyes, you would give up this foolish idea you can be a racehorse before you do something ridiculous.

As for reciting poetry, who wants to hear a horse recite poetry? That's for the birds.

As for the third and last dream, or whatever it is that's bothering you, that you can be a doctor or lawyer, you better forget it, it's not that kind of world. A horse is a horse even if he's a talking horse; don't mix yourself up with human beings, if you know what I mean. If you're a talking horse, that's your fate. I warn you, don't be a wise guy, Abramowitz. Don't try to know everything, you might go mad. Nobody can know everything; it's not that kind of a world. Follow the rules of the game. Don't rock the boat. Don't try to make a monkey out of me; I know more than you. We got to be who we are, although this is hard for you as well as me. But that's the logic of the world. It goes by certain laws even though that's a hard proposition for some to understand. The law is the law, you can't change the order. This is the way things are put together. We are mutually related, Abramowitz, and that's all there is to it. If it makes you feel any better, I will admit to you I can't live without you and I won't let you live without me. I have my living to make and you are my talking horse I use in my act to make my living, plus so I can take care of your needs. The true freedom, like I have always told you, though you never believe me, is to understand that and live with it so you don't waste your energy resisting the rules. All you are is a horse who talks, and believe me, there are very few horses that can do that; so if you are smart, Abramowitz, it should make you happy instead of always and continually dissatisfied. Don't break up the act if you know what's good for you.

As for those yellow balls of your dreck, if you will behave yourself like a gentleman and watch out what you say, tomorrow the shovelers will come, and after, I will hose you over personally with warm water. Believe me, there's nothing like cleanliness.

Thus he mocks me in my sleep, if that's what it is. I have my doubts that I sleep much nowadays.

In short hops between towns and small cities the circus moves in wagon vans. The other horses pull them, but Goldberg won't let me, which wakes up disturbing ideas in my head. For longer hauls, from one big city to another, we ride in red-and-white circus trains. I have a stall in a freight car with some nontalking horses with braided manes and sculptured tails, from the bareback riders' act. None of us are much interested in each other. If they think at all they think a talking horse is a show-off. All they do is eat, drink, piss, and crap all day. Not a single word goes back or forth among them.

The long train rides generally give us a day off without a show, and Goldberg gets depressed and surly when we're not working the matinee or evening performance. Early in the morning of a long train-ride day he starts loving his bottle and Morse-coding me nasty remarks and threats.

"Abramowitz, you think too much, why do you bother? In the first place, your thoughts come out of you and you don't know that much, so your thoughts don't either. In other words, don't get ambitious. For instance, what are you thinking about now, tell me?"

"Answers and questions, master—some new ones to modernize the act."

"Feh, we don't need any new ones, the act is already too long."

He should know the questions I am really asking myself, though better not.

Once you start asking questions one leads to the next and in the end it's endless. And what if it turns out I'm always asking myself the same question in different words? I keep on asking myself why I can't ask this coarse lout a simple question about anything. By now I have it figured out that Goldberg is afraid of questions because a question could show he's afraid people will find out who he is. Somebody who all he does is repeat his fate, if you know what I mean. It's thinking about his that made me better understand my own. Anyway, Goldberg has some kind of past he is afraid to tell me about, though sometimes he hints. And when I mention my own past he says forget it, think of the future. What future? On the other hand, what does he think he can hide from Abramowitz, a student by nature, who spends most of his time asking himself questions Goldberg won't permit him to ask, putting one and one together, and finally making up his mind—miraculous thought—that he knows more than a horse should, even a talking horse, so therefore, given all the built-up evidence, he is positively not a horse. Not in origin, anyway.

So I came once more to the conclusion that I am a man in a horse and not just a horse that happens to be able to talk. I had figured this out in my mind before; then I said, no it can't be. I feel more like a horse bodywise; on the other hand, I talk, I think, I wish to ask questions. A. Not a horse but a man. Q. Who else does the same? So I am what I am, which is a *man* in a horse, not a *talking* horse. Something tells me there is no such thing, even though Goldberg, pointing his finger at me, says the opposite. He lives on his lies, it's his nature.

Abramowitz's four legs wobbled with emotion at the thought.

After a long day of traveling, when they were in their new quarters that night, finding the rear door to his stall unlocked—Goldberg grew careless when depressed—acting on belief as well as impulse, Abramowitz cautiously backed out. Avoiding the front of Goldberg's wagon van he trotted across the fairgrounds on which the circus was situated. Two of the circus hands who saw him trot by, perhaps because Abramowitz greeted them, "Hello, boys, marvelous evening," did not attempt to stop him. Outside the grounds, though exhilarated to be in the open, Abramowitz began to wonder if he were doing a foolish thing. He had hoped to find a wooded spot to hide in for the time being, surrounded by fields in which he could peacefully graze; but this was the industrial edge of the city, and though he clop-clopped from street to street, there were no woods nearby, not even a small park.

Where can somebody who looks like a horse go by himself?

Abramowitz tried to hide in an old riding-school stable and was driven out by an irate woman. In the end they caught up with him on a station platform where he had been waiting for a train. Quite foolishly, he knew. The conductor wouldn't let him get on though Abramowitz had explained his predicament. The stationmaster then ran out and pointed a pistol at his head. He held the horse there, deaf to his blandishments, until Goldberg arrived with his bamboo cane. The owner threatened to whip Abramowitz black and blue, and his description of the effects was so painfully vivid that Abramowitz felt as though he had been slashed into a bloody pulp. A half hour later he found himself back in his locked stall, his throbbing head encrusted with dried horse blood. Goldberg ranted in deaf-mute talk, but Abramowitz, who with lowered head pretended contrition, felt none. To escape from Goldberg he knew he must first get out of the horse he was in.

But to exit a horse as a man takes some doing. Abramowitz planned to proceed slowly and appeal to public opinion. It might take months to do what he must. Protest. Sabotage if necessary. Revolt! One night after they had taken their bows and the applause was subsiding, Abramowitz, raising his head as though to whinny his appreciation of the plaudits, suddenly cried out to all assembled in the circus tent, "Help! Get me out of here, somebody! I am a prisoner in this horse! Free a fellow man!"

After a silence that rose up like a dense forest, Goldberg, who was standing to the side, unaware of Abramowitz's passionate cry—he picked up the news later from the ringmaster—saw at once from everybody's surprised and startled expression, not to mention Abramowitz's undisguised look of triumph, that something had gone seriously wrong. The owner at once began to laugh heartily, as though whatever it was that was going on was more of the same, part of the act, a bit of personal encore by the horse. The spectators laughed too, and again warmly applauded.

"It won't do you any good," the owner Morse-coded Abramowitz afterwards. "Because nobody is going to believe you."

"Then please let me out of here on your own account, master. Have some mercy."

"On that matter," Goldberg rapped out sternly, "I

am already on record. Our lives and livings are mutually dependent, one on the other. You got nothing substantial to complain about, Abramowitz. I'm taking care on you better than you can take care on yourself."

"Maybe that's so, Mr. Goldberg, but what good is it if in my heart I am a man and not a horse, not even a talking one?"

Goldberg's ruddy face blanched as he Morse-coded the usual NO QUESTIONS.

"I'm not asking, I'm telling you something very serious."

"Watch out for hubris, Abramowitz."

That night the owner went out on the town, came back dreadfully drunk, as though he had been standing with his mouth open where it had rained brandy; and he threatened Abramowitz with the trident spear he kept in his trunk when they traveled. This is a new torment.

Anyway, the act goes on but definitely altered, not as before. Abramowitz, despite numerous warnings and various other painful threats, daily disturbs the routine. After Goldberg makes his idiot noises, his geee, gooo, gaaa, gaaw, Abramowitz purposely mixes up the responses to the usual ridiculous riddles.

A. "To get to the other side."

Q. "Why does a fireman wear red suspenders?"

A. "From playing marbles."

Q. "Why do elephants have long trunks?"

And he adds dangerous A.'s and Q.'s without permission despite the inevitability of punishment.

A. "A talking horse."

Q. "What has four legs and wishes to be free?"

At that nobody laughed.

He also mocked Goldberg when the owner wasn't carefully reading his lips; called him "deaf-mute," "stupid ears," "lock mouth"; and whenever possible addressed the public, requesting, urging, begging their assistance.

"Gevalt! Get me out of here! I am one of you! This is slavery! I wish to be free!"

Now and then when Goldberg's back was turned, or he was too lethargic with melancholy to be much attentive, Abramowitz clowned around and in other ways ridiculed the owner. He hee-hawed at his appearance, brayed at his "talk," stupidity, tyranny. Sometimes he made up little songs of freedom as he danced on his hind legs, exposing his private parts. And sometimes Goldberg, to mock the mocker, danced with him—a clown with a glum painted smile waltzing with a horse. Those who had seen the act last season were astonished, stunned by the change. They seemed concerned, uneasy.

"Help! Help, somebody help me!" Abramowitz pleaded, but nobody moved.

Sensing the tension in and around the ring the audience sometimes booed the performers, causing Goldberg, in his red-and-white polka-dot suit and white clown's cap, great embarrassment, though on the whole he kept his cool during the act and never used the ringmaster's whip. In fact he smiled as he was being insulted, whether he "listened" or not. There was a sly fixed smile on his face, and his lips twitched. And though his fleshy ears flamed like torches at the gibes and mockeries he endured, Goldberg laughed to the point of tears at Abramowitz's sallies and shenanigans; many in the big tent laughed along with him. Abramowitz was furious.

Afterwards Goldberg, once he had stepped out of his clown suit, threatened him to the point of collapse, or flayed him viciously with his cane; and the next day fed him pep pills, and painted his hide black before the performance so that people wouldn't see the wounds.

"You bastard horse, you'll lose us our living."

"I wish to be free."

"To be free you got to know when you are free. Considering your type, Abramowitz, you'll be free in the glue factory."

One night when Goldberg, after a day of profound depression, was listless and logy in the ring, could not get so much as a limp snap out of his whip, Abramowitz, thinking that where the future was concerned glue factory or his present condition of life made little difference, determined to escape either fate; he gave a solo performance for freedom, the best of his career. Though desperate, he entertained, made up hilarious riddles, recited poems he had heard on Goldberg's transistor radio which sometimes stayed on all night after he had fallen asleep; he also told stories and ended the evening with a moving speech.

He told sad stories of the lot of horses, one, for instance, beaten to death by his cruel owner, his brains battered with a log because he was too weakened by hunger to pull a heavy wagonload of wood. Another concerned a racehorse of fantastic speed, a sure winner in the Kentucky Derby, had he not, in his very first race, been doped by his owner who had placed a fortune in bets on the next best horse. One was about a flying horse shot down by a hunter who could not believe his eyes. And then Abramowitz told a story of a youth of great promise, who, out for a stroll one sunny spring day, came upon a goddess bathing in a stream. He gazed at her bare beauty in amazement and longing; seeing him staring at her she let out a piercing scream. The youth took off at a fast gallop, realizing, before he had got very far, from the noise of his snorting and the sound of pounding hoofs as he ran, that he was no longer a youth of great promise but a horse running.

Abramowitz then cried out to the faces that surrounded him, "I am also a man in a horse. Is there a doctor in the house who can help me out?"

Dead silence.

"If not a doctor, maybe a magician?"

No response except nervous laughter.

He then delivered an impassioned short speech on freedom for all. Abramowitz talked his brains blue, ending once more with a personal appeal. "Help me to recover my original form. It's not what I am but what I wish to be. I wish to be what I really am, which is a man."

At the end of the act many people in the tent were wet-eyed and the band played "The Star-Spangled Banner."

Goldberg, who had been asleep in a sawdust pile for a good part of Abramowitz's solo act, roused himself in time to join the horse in a bow. Afterwards, on the enthusiastic advice of the circus manager, he changed the name of the act from "Ask Me Another" to "Goldberg's Varieties." And wept, himself, for unknown reasons.

Back in his stall after the failure of his most passionate, most inspired pleas for assistance, Abramowitz butted his head in frustration against the stall gate until his nostrils bled in his feed bag. He thought he might drown in his blood and didn't much care. Goldberg found him lying on the floor of the stall, half in a faint, and revived him with aromatic spirits of ammonia. He bandaged his nose and spoke to him in a fatherly fashion.

"That's how the mop flops," he Morse-coded with his fingertip, "but things could be worse. Take my advice and settle for a talking horse, it's got distinction."

"Make me either into a man or make me either into a

horse," Abramowitz moaned. "It's your power, Goldberg."

"You got the wrong party, my friend."

"Why do you always say lies?"

"Why do you always ask questions you can't ask?"

"I ask because I am. I wish to be free."

"So who's free, tell me?" Goldberg asked.

"If so," said Abramowitz, "then what's to be done?"

DON'T ASK. I WARNED YOU.

He threatened to punch his nose; it bled again.

Abramowitz later that day began a hunger strike which he carried on for the better part of a week; but Goldberg threatened force-feeding with thick tubes in both nostrils, and that ended that. Abramowitz almost choked to death at the thought of it. The act went on as before, and the owner changed its name back to "Ask Me Another." When the season was over the circus headed south. Abramowitz trotted along in a cloud of dust with the other horses.

Anyway, I have my thoughts.

One fine autumn day, Goldberg washed his feet in the kitchen sink and hung his smelly white socks to dry on the gate of Abramowitz's stall before sitting down to watch astronomy on educational television. To see better he had placed a lit candle on top of the TV set. But he had carelessly left the stall gate open and Abramowitz, surprised to discover he had not given up, hopped up three steps and trotted through the messy kitchen into the living room, his eyes flaring. Confronting Goldberg staring in awe at the universe on the screen, he reared with a bray of rage to bring his hoofs down on the owner's head. Goldberg rose to protect himself. Hopping up on the chair he managed with a grunt to grab Abramowitz by both his big ears as though to lift him by them, and the horse's head and neck, up to an old wound, came off in his hands. Amid the stench of blood and bowel a man's pale head popped out of the hole in the horse. He was in his early forties, with fogged pince-nez, intense dark eyes, and a black moustache. Pulling his arms free, he grabbed Goldberg around his thick neck with both bare arms, holding on for dear life. As they tugged and struggled, Abramowitz, straining to the point of madness, slowly pulled himself out of the horse up to his navel. At that moment Goldberg broke his grip and, though the astronomy lesson was still going on, disappeared. Abramowitz made a few discreet inquiries, later, but no one could say where.

Departing the circus grounds, he cantered across a grassy soft field into a dark wood, a free centaur.

The Jewels of the Cabots

John Cheever

JOHN CHEEVER lives in Ossining, New York. Among his books are *The Wapshot Chronicle, The Wapshot Scandal, Bullet Park, World of Apples, Falconer,* and *The Stories of John Cheever.*

Funeral services for the murdered man were held in the Unitarian church in the little village of St. Botolphs. The architecture of the church was Bulfinch with columns and one of those ethereal spires that must have dominated the landscape a century ago. The service was a random collection of Biblical quotations closing with a verse. "Amos Cabot, rest in peace/Now your mortal trials have ceased. . . ." The church was full. Mr. Cabot had been an outstanding member of the community. He had once run for governor. For a month or so, during his campaign, one saw his picture on barns, walls, buildings and telephone poles. I don't suppose the sense of walking through a shifting mirror—he found himself at every turn—unsettled him as it would have unsettled me. Once, for example, when I was in an elevator in Paris, I noticed a woman carrying a book of mine. There was a photograph on the jacket and one image of me looked over her arm at another. I wanted the picture, wanted, I suppose, to destroy it. That she should walk away with my face under her arm seemed to threaten my self-esteem. She left the elevator at the fourth floor and the parting of these two images was confusing. I wanted to follow her, but how could I explain in French—or in any other language—what I felt? Amos Cabot was not at all like this. He seemed to enjoy seeing himself and when he lost the election and his face vanished (except for a few barns in the back country, where it peeled for a month or so), he seemed not perturbed.

There are, of course, the wrong Lowells, the wrong Hallowells, the wrong Eliots, Cheevers, Codmans and Englishes, but today we will deal with the wrong Cabots. Amos came from the South Shore and may never have heard of the North Shore branch of the family. His father had been an auctioneer, which meant in those days an entertainer, horse trader and sometime crook. Amos owned real estate, the hardware store, the public utilities and was a director of the bank. He had an office in the Cartwright Block, opposite the green. His wife came from Connecticut, which was, for us at that time, a distant wilderness on whose eastern borders stood the city of New York. New York was populated by harried, nervous, avaricious foreigners who lacked the character to bathe in cold water at six in the morning and to live, with composure, lives of grueling boredom. Mrs. Cabot, when I knew her, was probably in her early 40s. She was a short woman with the bright-red face of an alcoholic, although she was a vigorous temperance worker. Her hair was as white as snow. Her back and her front were prominent and there was a memorable curve to her spine that could have been caused by a cruel corset or the beginning of lordosis. No one quite knew why Mr. Cabot had married this eccentric from faraway Connecticut—it was, after all, no one's business—but she did own most of the frame tenements on the East Bank of the river, where the workers in the table-silver factory lived. Her tenements were profitable, but it would have been an unwarranted simplification to conclude that he had married for real estate. She collected the rents herself. I expect that she did her own housework and she dressed simply, but she wore on her right hand seven large diamond rings. She had evidently read somewhere that diamonds were a sound investment and the blazing stones were about as glamorous as a passbook. There were round diamonds, square diamonds, rectangular diamonds and some of those diamonds that are set in prongs. On Thursday afternoon, she would wash her diamonds in some jeweler's solution and hang them out to dry in the clothesyard. She never explained this, but the incidence of eccentricity in the village ran so high that her conduct was not thought unusual.

Mrs. Cabot spoke once or twice a year at the St. Botolphs Academy, where many of us went to school. She had three subjects: "My Trip to Alaska" (slides), "The Evils of Drink" and "The Evils of Tobacco." Drink was for her so unthinkable a vice that she could not attack it with much vehemence, but the thought of tobacco made her choleric. Could one imagine Christ on the cross, smoking a cigarette? she would ask us. Could one imagine the Virgin Mary *smoking?* A drop of nicotine fed to a pig by trained laboratory technicians had killed the beast. Etc. She made smoking irresistible and if I die of lung cancer, I shall blame Mrs. Cabot.

These performances took place in what we called the Great Study Hall. This was a large room on the second floor that could hold us all. The academy had been built in the 1850s and had the lofty, spacious and beautiful windows of that period in American architecture. In the spring and in the autumn, the building seemed gracefully suspended in its grounds, but in the winter, a glacial cold fell off the large window lights. In the Great Study Hall, we were allowed to wear coats, hats and gloves. This situation was heightened by the fact that my great-aunt Anna had bought in Athens a large collection of plaster casts, so that we shivered and memorized the donative verbs in the company of at least a dozen buck-naked gods and goddesses. So it was to Hermes and Venus as well as to us that Mrs. Cabot railed against the poisons of tobacco. She was a woman of vehement and ugly prejudice and I suppose she would have been happy to include the blacks and the Jews, but there was only one black and one Jewish family in the village and they were exemplary. The possibility of intolerance in the village did not occur to me until much later, when my mother came to our house in Westchester for Thanksgiving.

This was some years ago, when the New England highways had not been completed and the trip from New York or Westchester took over four hours. I left quite early in the morning and drove first to Haverhill, where I stopped at Miss Peacock's School and picked up my niece. I then went on to St. Botolphs, where I found Mother sitting in the hallway in an acolyte's chair. The chair had a steepled back, topped with a wooden fleur-de-lis. From what rain-damp church had this object been stolen? She wore a coat and her bag was at her feet.

"I'm ready," she said. She must have been ready for

a week. She seemed terribly lonely. "Would you like a drink?" she asked. I knew enough not to take this bait. Had I said yes, she would have gone into the pantry and returned, smiling sadly, to say: "Your brother has drunk all the whiskey." So we started back for Westchester. It was a cold, overcast day and I found the drive tiring, although I think fatigue had nothing to do with what followed. I left my niece at my brother's house in Connecticut and drove on to my place. It was after dark when the trip ended. My wife had made all the preparations that were customary for my mother's arrival. There was an open fire, a vase of roses on the piano and tea with anchovy-paste sandwiches. "How lovely to have flowers," said mother. "I so love flowers. I can't live without them. Should I suffer some financial reverses and have to choose between flowers and groceries, I believe I would choose flowers. . . ."

I do not want to give the impression of an elegant old lady, because there were lapses in her performance. I bring up, with powerful unwillingness, a fact that was told to me by her sister after Mother's death. It seems that at one time, she applied for a position with the Boston police force. She had plenty of money at the time and I have no idea why she did this. I suppose that she wanted to be a policewoman. I don't know what branch of the force she planned to join, but I've always imagined her in a dark-blue uniform with a ring of keys at her waist and a billy club in her right hand. My grandmother dissuaded her from this course, but the image of a policewoman was some part of the figure she cut, sipping tea by our fire. She meant this evening to be what she called aristocratic. In this connection, she often said: "There must be at least a drop of plebeian blood in the family. How else can one account for your taste in torn and shabby clothing? You've always had plenty of clothes, but you've always chosen rags."

I mixed a drink and said how much I had enjoyed seeing my niece.

"Miss Peacock's has changed," Mother said sadly.

"I didn't know," I said. "What do you mean?"

"They've let down the bars."

"I don't understand."

"They're letting in Jews," she said. She fired out the last word.

"Can we change the subject?" I asked

"I don't see why," she said. "You brought it up."

"My wife is Jewish, Mother," I said. My wife was in the kitchen.

"That is not possible," my mother said. "Her father is Italian."

"Her father," I said, "is a Polish Jew."

"Well," Mother said, "I come from old Massachusetts stock and I'm not ashamed of it, although I don't like being called a Yankee."

"There's a difference."

"Your father said that the only good Jew was a dead Jew, although I did think Justice Brandeis charming."

"I think it's going to rain," I said. It was one of our staple conversational switch-offs used to express anger, hunger, love and the fear of death.

My wife joined us and Mother picked up the routine. "It's nearly cold enough for snow," she said. "When you were a boy, you used to pray for snow or ice. It depended upon whether you wanted to skate or ski. You were very particular. You would kneel by your bed and loudly ask God to manipulate the elements. You never prayed for anything else. I never once heard you ask for a blessing on your parents. In the summer you didn't pray at all."

The Cabots had two daughters—Geneva and Molly. Geneva was the older and thought to be the more beautiful. Molly was my girl for a year or so. She was a lovely young woman with a sleepy look that was quickly dispelled by a brilliant smile. Her hair was pale-brown and held the light. When she was tired or excited, sweat formed on her upper lip. In the evenings, I would walk to their house and sit with her in the parlor under the most intense surveillance. Mrs. Cabot, of course, regarded sex with utter panic. She watched us from the dining room. From upstairs there were loud and regular thumping sounds. This was Amos Cabot's rowing machine. We were sometimes allowed to take walks together if we kept to the main streets and when I was old enough to drive, I took her to the dances at the club. I was intensely—morbidly—jealous and when she seemed to be enjoying herself with someone else, I would stand in the corner, thinking of suicide. I remember driving her back one night to the house on Shore Road.

At the turn of the century, someone decided that St. Botolphs might have a future as a resort and five mansions complete with follies were built at the end of Shore Road. The Cabots lived in one of these. All the mansions had towers. These were round with conical roofs, rising a story or so above the rest of the frame buildings. The towers were strikingly unmilitary and so I suppose they were meant to express romance. What did they contain? Dens, I guess, maids' rooms, broken furniture, trunks, and they must have been the favorite of hornets. I parked my car in front of the Cabots' and turned off the lights. The house above us was dark.

It was long ago, so long ago that the foliage of elm trees was part of the summer night. (It was so long ago that when you wanted to make a left turn, you cranked down the car window and *pointed* in that direction. Otherwise, you were not allowed to point. Don't point, you were told. I can't imagine why, unless the gesture was thought to be erotic.) The dances—the assemblies—were formal and I would be wearing a tuxedo handed down from my father to my brother and from my brother to me, like some escutcheon or sumptuary torch. I took Molly in my arms. She was completely responsive. I am not a tall man (I am sometimes inclined to stoop), but the conviction that I am loved and loving affects me like a military bracing. Up goes my head. My back is straight. I am six foot, seven, and sustained by some clamorous emotional uproar. Sometimes my ears ring. It can happen anywhere—in a Keisang house in Seoul, for example—but it happened that night in front of the Cabots' house on Shore Road. Molly said then that she had to go. Her mother would be watching from a window. She asked me not to come up to the house. I mustn't have heard. I went with her up the walk and the stairs to the porch, where she tried the door and found it locked. She asked me again to go, but I couldn't abandon her there, could I? Then a light went on and the door was opened by a dwarf. He was exhaustively misshapen. The head was hydrocephalic, the features were swollen, the legs were thick and cruelly bowed. I thought of the circus. The lovely young woman began to cry. She stepped into the house and closed the door and I was left with the summer night, the elms, the taste of an east wind. After this, she avoided me for a week or so and I was told the facts by Maggie, our old cook.

But other facts first. It was in the summer and in the summer, most of us went to a camp on the Cape run by the headmaster of the St. Botolphs Academy. The months were so feckless, so blue, that I can't remember them at all. I slept next to a boy named DeVarennes, whom I had known all my life. We were together most of the time. We played marbles together, slept together, played together on the same backfield and once together took a ten-day canoe trip during which we nearly drowned together. My brother claimed that we had begun to look alike. It was the most gratifying and unself-conscious relationship I had known. (He still calls me once or twice a year from San Francisco, where he lives unhappily with his wife and three unmarried daughters. He sounds drunk. "We were happy, weren't we?" he asks.) One day another boy, a stranger named Wallace, asked if I wanted to swim across the lake. I might claim that I knew nothing about Wallace, and I knew very little, but I did know or sense that he was lonely. It was as conspicuous, more conspicuous than any of his features. He did what was expected of him. He played ball, made his bed, took sailing lessons and got his lifesaving certificate, but this seemed more like a careful imposture than any sort of participation. He was miserable, he was lonely and sooner or later, rain or shine, he would say so and, in the act of confession, make an impossible claim on one's loyalty. One knew all this, but one pretended not to. We got permission from the swimming instructor and swam across the lake. We used a clumsy side stroke that still seems to me more serviceable than the overhand that is obligatory these days in those swimming pools where I spend most of my time. The side stroke is lower class. I've seen it once in a swimming pool and when I asked who the swimmer was, I was told he was the butler. When the ship sinks, when the plane ditches, I will try to reach the life raft with an overhand and drown stylishly, whereas if I had used a lowerclass side stroke, I would live forever.

We swan the lake, resting in the sun—no confidences —and swam home. When I went up to our cabin, DeVarennes took me aside. "Don't ever let me see you with Wallace again," he said. I asked why. He told me. "Wallace is Amos Cabot's bastard. His mother is a whore. They live in one of the tenements across the river."

The next day was hot and brilliant and Wallace asked if I wanted to swim the lake again. I said sure, sure, and we did. When we went back to camp, DeVarennes wouldn't speak to me. That night a northeaster blew up and it rained for three days. DeVarennes seems to have forgiven me and I don't recall having crossed the lake with Wallace again. As for the dwarf, Maggie told me he was a son of Mrs. Cabot's from an earlier marriage. He worked at the table-silver factory, but he went to work early in the morning and didn't return until after dark. His existence was meant to be kept a secret. This was unusual but not—at the time of which I'm writing—unprecedented. The Trumbulls kept Mrs. Trumbull's crazy sister hidden in the attic and Uncle Peepee Marshmallow—an exhibitionist—was often hidden for months.

It was a winter afternoon, an early winter afternoon. Mrs. Cabot washed her diamonds and hung them out to dry. She then went upstairs to take a nap. She claimed that she had never taken a nap in her life and the sounder she slept, the more vehement were her claims that she didn't sleep. This was not so much an eccentricity on her part as it was a crabwise way of presenting the facts that was prevalent in that part of the world. She woke at four and went down to gather her stones. They were gone. She called Geneva, but there was no answer. She got a rake and scored the stubble under the clothesline. There was nothing. She called the police.

As I say, it was a winter afternoon and the winters there were very cold. We counted for heat—sometimes for survival—on wood fires and large coal-burning furnaces that sometimes got out of hand. A winter night was a threatening fact and this may have partly accounted for the sentiment with which we watched—in late November and December—the light burn out in the west. (My father's journals, for example, were full of descriptions of winter twilights, not because he was at all crepuscular but because the coming of the night might mean danger and pain.) Geneva had packed a bag, gathered the diamonds and taken the last train out of town—the 4:37. How thrilling it must have been. The diamonds were meant to be stolen. They were a flagrant snare and she did what she was meant to do. She took the train to New York that night and sailed three days later for Alexandria on a Cunarder—the S.S. Serapis. She took a boat from Alexandria to Luxor, where, in the space of two months, she joined the Moslem faith and married the khedive.

I read about the theft the next day in the evening paper. I delivered papers. I had begun my route on foot, moved on to a bicycle and was assigned, when I was 16, to an old Ford truck. I was a truck driver! I hung around the linotype room until the papers were printed and then drove around to the four neighboring villages, tossing out bundles at the doors of the candy and stationery stores. During the world series, a second edition with box scores was brought out and after dark, I would make the trip again to Travertine and the other places along the shore.

The roads were dark, there was very little traffic and leaf burning had not been forbidden, so that the air was tannic, melancholy and exciting. One can attach a mysterious and inordinate amount of importance to some simple journey and this second trip with the box scores made me very happy. I dreaded the end of the world series as one dreads the end of any pleasure and had I been younger, I would have prayed. "CABOT JEWELS STOLEN" was the headline and the incident was never again mentioned in the paper. It was not mentioned at all in our house, but this was not unusual. When Mr. Abbott hanged himself from the pear tree next door, this was never mentioned.

Molly and I took a walk on the beach at Travertine that Sunday afternoon. I was troubled, but Molly's troubles were much graver. It did not disturb her that Geneva had stolen the diamonds. She only wanted to know what had become of her sister and she was not to find out for another six weeks. However, something had happened at the house two nights before. There had been a scene between her parents and her father had left. She described this to me. We were walking barefoot. She was crying. I would like to have forgotten the scene as soon as she finished her description.

Children drown, beautiful women are mangled in automobile accidents, cruise ships founder and men die lingering deaths in mines and submarines, but you will find none of this in my accounts. In the last chapter, the ship comes home to port, the children are saved, the miners will be rescued. Is this an infirmity of the genteel or a conviction that there are discernible moral truths? Mr. X. defecated in his wife's top drawer. This is a fact, but I claim that it is not a truth. In describing St. Botolphs, I would sooner stay on the West Bank of the river, where the houses were white and where the church bells rang, but over the bridge there was the table-silver factory, the tenements (owned by Mrs. Cabot) and the Commercial Hotel. At low tide, one could smell the sea gas from the inlets at Travertine. The headlines in the afternoon paper dealt with a trunk murder. The women on the streets were ugly. Even the dummies in the one store window seemed stooped, depressed and dressed in clothing that neither fitted nor became them. Even the bride in her splendor seemed to have gotten some bad news. The politics were neofascist, the factory was non-union, the food was unpalatable and the night wind was bitter. This was a provincial and a traditional world enjoying few of the rewards of smallness and traditionalism, and when I speak of the blessedness of all small places, I speak of the West Bank. On the East Bank was the Commercial Hotel, the demesne of Doris, a male prostitute who worked as a supervisor in the factory during the day and hustled the bar at night, exploiting the extraordinary moral lassitude of the place. Everybody knew Doris and many of the customers had used him at one time or another. There was no scandal and no delight involved. Doris would charge a traveling salesman whatever he could get, but he did it with the regulars for nothing. This seemed less like tolerance than like hapless indifference, the absence of vision, moral stamina, the splendid ambitiousness of romantic love. On fight night, Doris drifts down the bar. Buy him a drink and he'll put his hand on your arm, your shoulder, your waist, and move a fraction of an inch in his direction and he'll reach for the cake. The steam fitter buys him a drink, the high school dropout, the watch repairman. (Once a stranger shouted to the bartender: "Tell that son of a bitch to take his tongue out of my ear"—but he was a stranger.) This is not a transient world, these are not drifters; more than half of these men will never live in any other place, and yet this seems to be the essence of spiritual nomadism. The telephone rings and the bartender beckons to Doris. There's a customer in room eight. Why would I sooner be on the West Bank, where my parents are playing bridge with Mr. and Mrs. Eliot Pinkham in the golden light of a great gas chandelier?

I'll blame it on the roast, the roast, the Sunday roast bought from a butcher who wore a straw boater with a pheasant wing in the hatband. I suppose the roast entered our house, wrapped in bloody paper, on Thursday or Friday, traveling on the back of a bicycle. It would be a gross exaggeration to say that the meat had the detonative force of a land mine that could savage your eyes and your genitals, but its powers were disproportionate. We sat down to dinner after church. (My brother was living in Omaha at that time, so we were only three.) My father would hone the carving knife and make a cut in the meat. My father was very adroit with an ax and a crosscut saw and could bring down a large tree with dispatch, but the Sunday roast was something else. After he had made the first cut, my mother would sigh. This was an extraordinary performance, so loud, so profound that it seemed as if her life were in danger. It seemed as if her very soul might come unhinged and drift out of her open mouth. "Will you never learn, Leander, that lamb must be carved against the grain?" she would ask. Once the battle of the roast had begun, the exchanges were so swift, predictable and tedious that there would be no point in reporting them.

After five or six wounding remarks, my father would wave the carving knife in the air and shout: "Will you kindly mind your own business, will you kindly shut up?"

She would sigh once more and put her hand to her heart. Surely this was her last breath. Then, studying the air above the table, she would say: "Feel that refreshing breeze?

There was, of course, seldom a breeze. It could be airless, mid-winter, rainy, anything. The remark was one for all seasons. Was it a commendable metaphor for hope, for the serenity of love (which I think she had never experienced)? Was it nostalgia for some summer evening when, loving and understanding, we sat contentedly on the lawn above the river? Was it no better or no worse than the sort of smile thrown at the evening star by a man who is in utter despair? Was it a prophecy of that generation to come who would be so drilled in evasiveness that they would be denied forever the splendors of a passionate confrontation?

The scene changes to Rome. It is spring, when the canny swallows flock into the city to avoid the wing shots in Ostia. The noise the birds make seems like light as the light of day loses its brilliance. Then one hears, across the courtyard, the voice of an American woman. She is screaming. "You're a goddamned, fucked-up no-good insane piece of shit. You can't make a nickel, you don't have a friend in the world and in bed you stink. . . ." There is no reply and one wonders if she is railing at the dark. Then you hear a man cough. That's all you will hear from him. "Oh, I know I've lived with you for eight years, but if you ever thought I liked it, any of it, it's only because you're such a chump you wouldn't know the real thing if you had it. When I really come, the pictures *fall* off the walls. With you it's always an act. . . ." The high-low bells that ring in Rome at that time of day have begun to chime. I smile at this sound, although it has no bearing on my life, my faith, no true harmony, nothing like the revelations in the voice across the court. Why would I sooner describe church bells and flocks of swallows? Is this puerile, a sort of greeting-card mentality, a whimsical and effeminate refusal to look at facts? On and on she goes, but I will follow her no longer. She attacks his hair, his brain and his spirit, while I observe that a light rain has begun to fall and that the effect of this is to louden the noise of traffic on the *corso*. Now she is hysterical—her voice is breaking—and I think that at the height of her malediction, perhaps, she will begin to cry and ask his forgiveness. She will not, of course. She will go after him with a carving knife and he will end up in the emergency ward of the *polyclinico,* claiming to have wounded himself; but as I go out for dinner, smiling at beggars, fountains, children and the first stars of evening, I assure myself that everything will work out for the best. Feel that refreshing breeze!

My recollections of the Cabots are only a footnote to my principal work and I go to work early these winter mornings. It is still dark. Here and there, standing on street corners, waiting for buses, are women dressed in white. They wear white shoes and white stockings and white uniforms can be seen below their winter coats. Are they nurses, beauty-parlor operators, dentists' helpers? I'll never know. They usually carry a brown paper bag, holding, I guess, a ham on rye and a Thermos of buttermilk. Traffic is light at this time of day. A laundry truck delivers uniforms to the Fried Chicken Shack and in Asburn Place there is a milk truck—the last of that generation. It will be half an hour before the yellow school buses start their rounds.

I work in an apartment house called the Prestwick. It is seven stories high and dates, I guess, from the late Twenties. It is of a Tudor persuasion. The bricks are irregular, there is a parapet on the roof and the sign, advertising vacancies, is literally a shingle that hangs from iron chains and creaks romantically in the wind. On the right of the door, there is a list of perhaps 25 doctors' names, but these are not gentle healers with stethoscopes and rubber hammers, these are psychiatrists and this is the country of the plastic chair and the full ashtray. I don't know why they should have chosen this place, but they outnumber the other tenants. Now and then you see, waiting for the elevator, a woman with a grocery wagon and a child, but you mostly see the sometimes harried faces of men and women with trouble. They sometimes smile; they sometimes talk to themselves. Business seems slow these days and the doctor whose office is next to mine often stands in the hallway, staring out the window. What does a psychiatrist think? Does he wonder what has become of those patients who gave up, who refused group therapy, who disregarded his warnings and admonitions? He will know their secrets. I tried to murder my husband. I tried to murder my wife. Three years ago, I took an overdose of sleeping pills. The year before that, I cut my wrists. My mother wanted me to be a girl. My mother wanted me to be a boy. My mother wanted me to be a homosexual. Where had they gone, what were they doing? Were they still married, quarreling at the dinner table, decorating the Christmas tree? Had they divorced, remarried, jumped off bridges, taken Seconal, struck some kind of truce, turned homosexual or moved to a farm in Vermont where they planned to raise strawberries and lead a simple life? The doctor sometimes stands by the window for an hour.

My real work these days is to write an edition of *The New York Times* that will bring gladness to the hearts of men. How better could I occupy myself? The *Times* is a critical if rusty link in my ties to reality, but in these last years, its tidings have been monotonous. The prophets of doom are out of work. All one can do is to pick up the pieces. The lead story is this: "PRESIDENT'S HEART TRANSPLANT DEEMED SUCCESSFUL." There is this box on the lower left: "COST OF J. EDGAR HOOVER MEMORIAL CHALLENGED. The subcommittee on memorials threatened today to halve the $7,000,000 appropriated to commemorate the late J. Edgar Hoover with a Temple of Justice. . . ." Column three: "CONTROVERSIAL LEGISLATION REPEALED BY SENATE. The recently enacted bill, making it a felony to have wicked thoughts about the Administration, was repealed this afternoon by a stand-up vote of 43 to 7." On and on it goes. There are robust and heartening editorials, thrilling sports news and the weather, of course, is always sunny and warm, unless we need rain. Then we have rain. The air-pollutant gradient is zero and even in Tokyo, fewer and fewer people are wearing surgical masks. All highways, throughways, freeways and expressways will be closed for the holiday weekend. Joy to the world!

But to get back to the Cabots. The scene that I would like to overlook or forget took place the night after Geneva had stolen the diamonds. It involves plumbing. Most of the houses in the village had relatively little plumbing. There was usually a water closet in the basement for the cook and the ashman and a single bathroom on the second floor for the rest of the household. Some of these rooms were quite large and the Endicotts had a fireplace in their bathroom. Somewhere along the line, Mrs. Cabot decided that the bathroom was her demesne. She had a locksmith come and secure the door. Mr. Cabot was allowed to take his sponge bath every morning, but after this, the bathroom door was locked and Mrs. Cabot kept the key in her pocket. Mr. Cabot was obliged to use a chamber pot, but since he came from the South Shore, I don't suppose this was much of a hardship. It may even have been nostalgic. He was using the chamber pot late that night when Mrs. Cabot went to the door of his room. (They slept in separate rooms.) "Will you close the door?" she screamed. "Will you close the door? Do I have to listen to that horrible noise for the rest of my life?" They would both be in nightgowns, her snow-white hair in braids. She picked up the chamber pot and threw its contents at him. He kicked down the door of the locked bathroom, washed, dressed, packed a bag and walked over the bridge to Mrs. Wallace's place on the East Bank.

He stayed there for three days and then returned. He

was worried about Molly and in such a small place, there were appearances to be considered—Mrs. Wallace's as well as his own. He divided his time between the East and the West banks of the river until a week or so later, when he was taken ill. He felt languid. He stayed in bed until noon. When he dressed and went to his office, he returned after an hour or so. The doctor examined him and found nothing wrong.

One evening Mrs. Wallace saw Mrs. Cabot coming out of the drugstore on the East Bank. She watched her rival cross the bridge and then went into the drugstore and asked the clerk if Mrs. Cabot was a regular customer. "I've been wondering about that myself," the clerk said. "Of course, she comes over here to collect her rents, but I always thought she used the other drugstore. She comes in here to buy ant poison—arsenic, that is. She says they have these terrible ants in the house on Shore Road and arsenic is the only way of getting rid of them. From the way she buys arsenic, the ants must be terrible." Mrs. Wallace might have warned Mr. Cabot, but she never saw him again.

She went after the funeral to Judge Simmons and said that she wanted to charge Mrs. Cabot with murder. The drug clerk would have a record of her purchase of arsenic that would be incriminating. "He may have it," the judge said, "but he won't give it to you. What you are asking for is an exhumation of the body and a long trial in Barnstable and you have neither the money nor the reputation to support this. You were his friend, I know, for sixteen years. He was a splendid man and why don't you console yourself with the thought of how many years it was that you knew them? And another thing. He's left you and Wallace a substantial legacy. If Mrs. Cabot were provoked to contest the will, you could lose this."

I went out to Luxor to see Geneva. I flew to London in a 747. There were only three passengers; but, as I say, the prophets of doom are out of work. I went from Cairo up the Nile in a low-flying two-motor prop. The sameness of wind erosion and water erosion makes the Sahara there seem to have been gutted by floods, rivers, courses, streams and brooks, the thrust of a natural search. The scorings are watery and arboreal and as a false stream bed spreads out, it takes the shape of a tree, striving for light. It was freezing in Cairo when we left before dawn. Luxor, where Geneva met me at the airport, was hot.

I was very happy to see her, so happy I was unobservant, but I did notice that she had gotten fat. I don't mean that she was heavy; I mean that she weighed about 300 pounds. She was a fat woman. Her hair, once a coarse yellow, was now golden, but her Massachusetts accent was as strong as ever. It sounded like music to me on the upper Nile. Her husband—now a colonel—was a slender, middle-aged man, a relative of the last king. He owned a restaurant at the edge of the city and they lived in a pleasant apartment over the dining room. The colonel was humorous, intelligent—a rake, I guess—and a heavy drinker. When we went to the temple at Karnak, our dragoman carried ice, tonic and gin. I spent a week with them, mostly in temples and graves. We spent the evenings in his bar. War was threatening—the air was full of Russian planes—and the only other tourist was an Englishman who sat at the bar, reading his passport. On the last day, I swam in the Nile—overhand—and they drove me to the airport, where I kissed Geneva—and the Cabots—goodbye.

Brownstone

Renata Adler

RENATA ADLER was born in Milan, Italy, and grew up in Danbury, Connecticut. She was graduated from Bryn Mawr College, and received an M.A. from Harvard. Since 1963 she has been a staff writer-reporter for *The New Yorker.* From January 1968 to March 1969 she was film critic of the *New York Times.* She has published two collections of nonfiction pieces, *Toward a Radical Middle* and *A Year in the Dark,* and a novel, *Speedboat.*

The camel, I had noticed, was passing, with great difficulty, through the eye of the needle. The Apollo flight, the four-minute mile, Venus in Scorpio, human records on land and at sea—these had been events of enormous importance. But the camel, practicing in near obscurity for almost two thousand years, was passing through. First the velvety nose, then the rest. Not many were aware. But if the lead camel and then perhaps the entire caravan could make it, the thread, the living thread of camels, would exist, could not be lost. No one could lose the thread. The prospects of the rich would be enhanced. "Ortega tells us that the business of philosophy," the professor was telling his class of indifferent freshmen, "is to crack open metaphors which are dead."

"I shouldn't have come," the Englishman said, waving his drink and breathing so heavily at me that I could feel my bangs shift. "I have a terrible cold."

"He would probably have married her," a voice across the room said, "with the exception that he died."

"Well, I am a personality that prefers not to be annoyed."

"We should all prepare ourselves for this eventuality."

A six-year-old was passing the hors d'oeuvres. The baby, not quite steady on his feet, was hurtling about the room.

"He's following me," the six-year-old said, in despair.

"Then lock yourself in the bathroom, dear," Inez replied.

"He always waits outside the door."

"He loves you, dear."

"Well, I don't like it."

"How I envy you," the minister's wife was saying to a courteous, bearded boy, "reading 'Magic Mountain' for the first time."

The homosexual across the hall from me always takes Valium and walks his beagle. I borrow Valium from him from time to time, and when he takes a holiday the dog is left with me. On our floor of this brownstone, we are friends. Our landlord, Roger Somerset, was murdered last July. He was a kind and absentminded man, and on the night when he was stabbed there was a sort of requiem for him in the heating system. There is a lot of music in this building anyway. The newlyweds on the third floor play Bartók on their stereo. The couple on the second floor play clarinet quintets; their kids play rock. The girl on the fourth floor, who has been pining for two months, plays Judy Collins' "Maid of Constant Sorrow" all day long. We have a kind of orchestra in here. The ground floor is a shop. The owner of the shop speaks of our landlord's murder still. Shaking his head, he says that he suspects "foul play." We all agree with him. We changed our locks. But "foul play" seems a weird expression for the case.

It is all weird. I am not always well. One block away (I often think of this), there was ten months ago an immense crash. Water mains broke. There were small rivers in the streets. In a great skyscraper that was being built, something had failed. The newspapers reported the next day that by some miracle only two people had been "slightly injured" by ten tons of falling steel. The steel fell from the eighteenth floor. The question that preoccupies me now is how, under the circumstances, slight injuries could occur. Perhaps the two people were grazed in passing by. Perhaps some fragments of the sidewalk ricocheted. I knew a deliverer of flowers who, at Sixty-ninth and Lexington, was hit by a flying suicide. Situations simply do not yield to the most likely structures of the mind. A "self-addressed envelope," if you are inclined to brood, raises deep questions of identity. Such an envelope, immutably itself, is always precisely where it belongs. "Self-pity" is just sadness, I think, in the pejorative. But "joking with nurses" fascinates me in the press. Whenever someone has been quite struck down, lost faculties, members of his family, he is said to have "joked with his nurses" quite a lot. What a mine of humor every nurse's life must be.

The St. Bernard at the pound on Ninety-second Street was named Bonnie and would have cost five dollars. The attendant held her tightly on a leash of rope. "Hello, Bonnie," I said. Bonnie growled.

"I wouldn't talk to her if I was you," the attendant said.

I leaned forward to pat her ear. Bonnie snarled. "I wouldn't touch her if I was you," the attendant said. I held out my hand under Bonnie's jowls. She strained against the leash, and choked and coughed. "Now cut that out, Bonnie," the attendant said.

"Could I just take her for a walk around the block," I said, "before I decide?" "Are you out of your mind?" the attendant said. Aldo patted Bonnie, and we left.

I have a job, of course. I have had several jobs. I've had our paper's gossip column since last month. It is egalitarian. I look for people who are quite obscure, and report who is breaking up with whom and where they go and what they wear.

The person who invented this new form for us is on antidepressants now. He lives in Illinois. He says there are people in southern Illinois who have not yet been covered by the press. I often write about families in Queens. Last week, I went to a dinner party on Park Avenue. After 1 A.M., something called the Alive or Dead Game was being played. Someone would mention an old character from Tammany or Hollywood. "Dead," "Dead," "Dead," everyone would guess. "No, no. Alive. I saw him walking down the street just yesterday," or "Yes. Dead. I read a little obituary notice about him last year." One of the little truths people can subtly enrage or reassure each other with is who—when you have looked away a month, a year—is still around.

> DEAR TENANT:
>
> We have reason to believe that there are imposters posing as Con Ed repairmen and inspectors circulating in this area.
>
> Do not permit any Con Ed man to enter your premises or the building, if possible.
>
> THE PRECINCT

My cousin, who was born on February 29th, became a veterinarian. Some years ago, when he was twenty-eight (seven, by our childhood birthday count), he was drafted, and sent to Malaysia. He spent most of his military service there, assigned to the zoo. He operated on one tiger, which, in the course of abdominal surgery, began to wake up and wag its tail. The anesthetist grabbed the tail, and injected more sodium pentothal. That tiger survived. But two flamingos, sent by the city of Miami to Kuala Lumpur as a token of good will, could not bear the trip or the climate and, in spite of my cousin's efforts, died. There was also a cobra—the largest anyone in Kuala Lumpur could remember having seen. An old man had brought it, in an immense sack, from somewhere in the countryside. The zoo director called my cousin at once, around dinnertime, to say that an unprecedented cobra had arrived. Something quite drastic, however, seemed wrong with its neck. My cousin, whom I have always admired—for his leap-year birthday, for his pilot's license, for his presence of mind—said that he would certainly examine the cobra in the morning but that the best thing for it after its long journey must be a good night's rest. By morning, the cobra was dead.

My cousin is well. The problem is this. Hardly anyone about whom I deeply care at all resembles anyone else I have ever met, or heard of, or read about in the literature. I know an Israeli general who, in 1967, retook the Mitla Pass but who, since his mandatory retirement from military service at fifty-five, has been trying to repopulate the Ark. He asked me, over breakfast at the Drake, whether I knew any owners of oryxes. Most of the vegetarian species he has collected have already multiplied enough, since he has found and cared for them, to be permitted to run wild. The carnivorous animals, though, must still be kept behind barbed wire—to keep them from stalking the rarer vegetarians. I know a group that studies Proust one Sunday afternoon a month, and an analyst, with that Exeter laugh (embittered mooing noises, and mirthless heaving of the shoulder blades), who has the most remarkable terrorist connections in the Middle East.

The New York Chinese cabdriver lingered at every corner and at every traffic light, to read his paper. I wondered what the news was. I looked over his shoulder. The illustrations and the type were clear enough: newspaper print, pornographic fiction. I leaned back in my seat. A taxi-driver who happened to be Oriental with a sadomasochistic cast of mind was not my business. I lit a cigarette, looked at my bracelet. I caught the driver's eyes a moment in the rearview mirror. He picked up his paper. "I don't think you ought to read," I said, "while you are driving." Traffic was slow. I saw his mirrored eyes again. He stopped his reading. When we reached my address, I did not tip him. Racism and prudishness, I thought, and reading over people's shoulders.

But there are moments in this place when everything becomes a show of force. He can read what he likes at home. Tipping is still my option. Another newspaper event, in our brownstone. It was a holiday. The superintendent normally hauls the garbage down and sends the paper up, by dumbwaiter, each morning. On holidays, the garbage stays upstairs, the paper on the sidewalk. At 8 A.M., I went downstairs. A ragged man was lying across the little space that separates the inner door, which locks, from the outer door, which doesn't. I am not a news addict. I could have stepped over the sleeping man, picked up my *Times*, and gone upstairs to read it. Instead, I knocked absurdly from inside the door, and said, "Wake up. You'll have to leave now." He got up, lifted the flattened cardboard he had been sleeping on, and walked away, mumbling and reeking. It would have been kinder, certainly, to let the driver read, the wino sleep. One simply cannot bear down so hard on all these choices.

What is the point. That is what must be borne in mind. Sometimes the point is really who wants what. Sometimes the point is what is right or kind. Sometimes the point is a momentum, a fact, a quality, a voice, an intimation, a thing said or unsaid. Sometimes it's who's at fault, or what will happen if you do not move at once. The point changes and goes out. You cannot be forever watching for the point, or you lose the simplest thing: being a major character in your own life. But if you are, for any length of time, custodian of the point—in art, in court, in politics, in lives, in rooms—it turns out there are rear-guard actions everywhere. Now and then, a small foray is worthwhile. Just so that being constantly, complacently, thoroughly wrong does not become the safest position of them all. The point has never quite been entrusted to me.

The conversation of "The Magic Mountain" and the unrequited love of six-year-olds occurred on Saturday, at brunch. "Bring someone new," Inez had said. "Not queer. Not married, maybe separated. John and I are breaking up." The invitation was not of a kind that I had heard before. Aldo, who lives with me between the times when he prefers to be alone, refused to come. He despises brunch. He detests Inez. I went, instead, with a lawyer who has been a distant, steady friend but who, ten years ago, when we first came to New York, had once put three condoms on the night table beside the phone. We both had strange ideas then about New York. Aldo is a gentle, orderly, soft-spoken man, slow to conclude. I try to be tidy when he is here, but I have often made his cigarettes, and once his manuscript, into the bed. Our paper's publisher is an intellectual from Baltimore. He has read Wittgenstein; he's always making unimpeachable remarks. Our music critic throws a tantrum every day, in print. Our book reviewer is looking for another job. He found that the packages in which all books are mailed could not, simply could not, be opened without doing considerable damage—through staples, tape, wire, fluttering gray stuff, recalcitrance—to the reviewer's hands. He felt it was a symptom of some kind—one of those cases where incompetence at every stage, across the board, acquired a certain independent force. Nothing to do with books, he thought, worked out at all. We also do the news. For horoscopes, there are the ladies' magazines. We just cannot compete.

My late landlord was from Scarsdale. The Maid of Constant Sorrow is from Texas. Aldo is from St. Louis. Inez's versions vary about where she's from. I grew up in a New England mill town, where, in the early thirties, all the insured factories burned down. It has been difficult to get fire insurance in that region ever since.

The owner of a hardware store, whose property adjoined an insured factory at the time, lost everything. Afterward, he walked all day along the railroad track, waiting for a train to run him down. Railroad service has never been very good up there. No trains came. His children own the town these days, for what it's worth. The two cobbled streets where black people always lived have been torn up and turned into a public park since a flood that occurred some years ago. Unprecedented rains came. Retailers had to destroy their sodden products, for fear of contamination. And the black section was torn up and seeded over in the town's rezoning project. No one knows where the blacks live now. But there are Negroes in the stores and schools, and on the football team. It is assumed that the park integrated the town. Those black families must be living somewhere. It is a mystery.

The host, for some reason, was taking Instamatic pictures of his guests. It was not clear whether he was doing this in order to be able to show, at some future time, that there had been this gathering in his house. Or whether he thought of pictures in some voodoo sense. Or whether he found it difficult to talk. Or whether he was bored. Two underground celebrities—one of whom had become a sensation by never generating or exhibiting a flicker of interest in anything, the other of whom was known mainly for hanging around the first—were taking pictures, too. I was there with a movie star I've known for years. He had already been received in an enormous embrace by an Eastern European poet, whose hair was cut too short but who was neither as awkwardly spontaneous nor as drunk as he cared to seem. The party was in honor of the poet, who celebrated the occasion by insulting everyone and being fawned upon, by distinguished and undistinguished writers alike. "This group looks as though someone had torn up a few guest lists and floated the pieces on the air," somebody said.

Paul: "Two diamonds."

Inez: "Two hearts."

Mary: "Three clubs."

John: "Four kings."

Inez: "Darling, you know you can't just bid four kings."

John: "I don't see why. I might have been bluffing."

Inez: "No, darling. That's poker. This is bridge. And even in poker you can't just bid four kings."

John: "No. Well, I guess we'd better deal another hand."

The friend of the underground sensation walked up to the actor and me and said hello. Then, in a verbal seizure of some sort, he began muttering obscenities. The actor said a few calming things that didn't work. He finally put his finger on the mutterer's lips. The mutterer bit that finger extremely hard, and walked away. The actor wrapped his finger in a paper napkin, and got himself another drink. We stayed till twelve.

I went to a women's college. We had distinguished faculty in everything, digs at Nuoro and Mycenae. We had a quality of obsession in our studies. For professors who had quarrelled with their wives at breakfast, those years of bright-eyed young women, never getting any older, must have been a trial. The head of the history department once sneezed into his best student's honors thesis. He slammed it shut. It was ultimately published. When I was there, a girl called Cindy Melchior was immensely fat. She wore silk trousers and gilt mules. One day, in the overheated classroom, she laid aside her knitting and lumbered to the window, which she opened. Then she lumbered back. "Do you think," the professor asked, "you are so graceful?" He somehow meant it kindly. Cindy wept. That year, Cindy's brother Melvin phoned me. "I would have called you sooner," he said, "but I had the most terrible eczema." All the service staff on campus in those days were black. Many of them were followers of Father Divine. They took new names in the church. I remember the year when a maid called Serious Heartbreak married a janitor called Universal Dictionary. At a meeting of the faculty last fall, the college president, who is new and male, spoke of raising money. A female professor of Greek was knitting—and working on Linear B, with an abacus before her. In our time, there was a vogue for madrigals. Some of us listened, constantly, to a single record. There was a phrase we could not decipher. A professor of symbolic logic, a French Canadian, had sounds that matched but a meaning that seemed unlikely: Sheep are no angels; come upstairs. A counter-tenor explained it, after a local concert: She'd for no angel's comfort stay. Not so likely, either.

The Maid of Constant Sorrow said our landlord's murder marked a turning point in her analysis. "I don't feel guilty. I feel hated," she said. It is true, for a time, we all wanted to feel somehow a part—if only because violence offset the boredom of our lives. My grandfather said that some people have such extreme insomnia that they look at their watches every hour after midnight, to see how sorry they ought to be feeling for themselves. Aldo says he does not care what my grandfather said. My grandmother refused to concede that any member of the family died of natural causes. An uncle's cancer in middle age occurred because all the suitcases fell off the luggage rack onto him when he was in his teens, and so forth. Death was an acquired characteristic. My grandmother, too, used to put other people's ailments into the diminutive: strokelets were what her friends had. Aldo said he was bored to tearsies by my grandmother's diminutives.

When I worked, for a time, in the infirmary of a branch of an upstate university, it was becoming more difficult with each passing semester, except in the most severe cases, to determine which students had mental or medical problems. At the clinic, young men with straggly beards and stained bluejeans wept alongside girls in jeans and frayed sweaters—all being fitted with contact lenses, over which they then wore granny glasses. There was no demand for prescription granny glasses at all. For the severely depressed, the paranoids, and the hallucinators, our young psychiatrists prescribed "mood elevators," pills that were neither uppers nor downers but which affected the bloodstream in such a way that within three to five weeks many sad outpatients became very cheerful, and several saints and historical figures became again Midwestern graduate students under tolerable stress. On one, not unusual, morning, the clinic had a call from an instructor in political science. "I am in the dean's office," he said. "My health is quite perfect. They want me to have a checkup."

"Oh?" said the doctor on duty. "Perhaps you could come in on Friday."

"The problem is," the voice on the phone said, "I have always thought myself, and been thought by others, a Negro. Now, through research, I have found that my family on both sides have always been white."

"Oh," the doctor on duty said. "Perhaps you could just take a cab and come over."

Within twenty minutes, the political-science instructor appeared at the clinic. He was black. The doctor said nothing, and began a physical examination.

By the time his blood pressure was taken, the patient confided that his white ancestors were, in fact, royal. The mood elevators restored him. He and the doctor became close friends besides. A few months later, the instructor took a job with the government in Washington. Two weeks after that, he was calling the clinic again. "I have found new documentation," he said. "All eight of my great-grandparents were pure-blooded Germans—seven from Prussia, one from Alsace. I thought I should tell you, dear friend." The doctor suggested he come for the weekend. By Sunday afternoon, a higher dose of the pill had had its effect. The problem has not since recurred.

"All babies are natural swimmers," John said, lowering his two-year-old son gently over the side of the rowboat, and smiling. The child thrashed and sank. Aldo dived in and grabbed him. The baby came up coughing, not crying, and looked with pure fear at his father. John looked with dismay at his son. "He would have come up in a minute," John said to Aldo, who was dripping and rowing. "You have to give nature a chance."

"Reservations are still busy. Thank you for your patience," the voice of the airline kept saying. It was a recording. After it had said the same thing thirty-two times, I hung up. Scattered through the two cars of the Brewster-New York train last week were adults with what seemed to be a clandestine understanding of some sort. They did not look at each other. They stared out the windows, or read. "Um," sang a lady at our fourth stop on the way to Grand Central. She appeared to be reading the paper. She kept singing her "Um," as one who is getting the pitch. A young man had already been whistling "Frère Jacques" for three stops. When the

"Um" lady found her pitch and began to sing the national anthem, he looked at her with rage. The conductor passed through, punching tickets in his usual fashion, not in the aisle but directly over people's laps. Every single passenger was obliged to flick the tiny punched part of the ticket from his lap onto the floor. Conductors have this process as their own little show of force. The whistler and the singer were in a dead heat when we reached the city. The people with the clandestine understanding turned out to be inmates from an upstate asylum, now on leave with their families, who met them in New York.

I don't think much of writers in whom nothing is at risk. It is possible, though, to be too literal-minded about this question.

"$3000 for First Person Articles," for example:

> An article for this series must be a true, hitherto unpublished narrative of an unusual personal experience. It may be dramatic, inspirational, or humorous, but it must have, in the opinion of the editors, a quality of narrative and interest comparable to "How I Lost My Eye" (June '72) and "Attacked by a Killer Shark" (April '72). Contributions must be typewritten, preferably *double-spaced* . . .

I particularly like where the stress, the italics, goes.

In Corfu, I once met a polo-playing Argentine Existential psychiatrist who had lived for months in a London commune. He said that on days when the ordinary neurotics in the commune were getting on each other's nerves the few psychopaths and schizophrenics in their midst retired to their rooms and went their version of berserk, alone. On days when the neurotics got along, the psychopaths calmed down, tried to make contact, cooked meals. It was, he said, as though the sun came out for them. I hope that's true. Although altogether too much of life is mood. I receive communications almost every day from an institution called the Center for Short-Lived Phenomena. They have reporting sources all over the world, and an extensive correspondence. Under the title "Type of Event: Biological," I have received postcards about the progress of the Dormouse Invasion of Formentera ("Apart from population density, the dormouse of Formentera had a peak of reproduction in 1970. All females checked were pregnant, and perhaps this fact could have been the source of the idea of an 'invasion' "), and the Northwest Atlantic Puffin Decline. I have followed the Tanzanian Army Worm Outbreak; the San Fernando Earthquake; the Green Pond Fish Kill ("80% of the numbers involved," the Center's postcard reports, "were mummichogs"); the Samar Spontaneous Soil Burn; the Hawaiian Monk Seal Disappearance; and, also, the Naini Tal Sudden Sky Brightening.

Those are accounts of things that do not last long, but if you become famous for a single thing in this country, and just endure, it is certain you will recur enlarged. Of the eighteen men who were indicted for conspiracy to murder Schwerner, Goodman, and Chaney, seven were convicted by a Mississippi jury—a surprising thing. But then a year later, a man was wounded and a woman killed in a shootout while trying to bomb the house of some Mississippi Jews. It turned out that the informer, the man who had helped the bombers, and led the F.B.I. to them, was one of the convicted seven—the one, in fact, who was alleged to have killed two of the three boys who were found in that Mississippi dam. And what's more, and what's more, the convicted conspirator, alleged double killer, was paid thirty-six thousand dollars by the F.B.I. for bringing the bombers in. Yet the wave of anti-Semitic bombings in Mississippi stopped after the shootout. I don't know what it means. I am in this brownstone.

Last year, Aldo moved out and went to Los Angeles on a story. I called him to ask whether I could come. He said, "Are you going to stay this time?" I said I wasn't sure. I flew out quite early in the morning. On the plane, there was the most banal, unendurable pickup, lasting the whole flight. A young man and a young woman—he was Italian, I think; she was German—had just met, and settled on French as their only common language. They asked each other where they were from, and where they were going. They posed each other riddles. He took out a pencil and paper and sketched her portrait. She giggled. He asked her whether she had ever considered a career as a model. She said she had considered it but she feared that all men in the field were after the same thing. He agreed. He began to tell slightly off-color stories. She laughed and reproached him. It was like that. I wondered whether these things were always, to captive eavesdroppers, so dreary.

When I arrived at Aldo's door, he met me with a smile that seemed surprised, a little sheepish. We talked awhile. Sometimes he took, sometimes I held, my suitcase. I tried, I thought, a joke. I asked whether there was already a girl there. He said there was. He met me in an hour at the corner drugstore for a cup of coffee. We talked. We returned to the apartment. We had Scotch. That afternoon, quite late, I flew home. I called him from time to time. He had his telephone removed a few days later. Now, for a while, he's here again. He's doing a political essay. It begins, "Some things cannot be said too often, and some can." That's all he's got so far.

We had people in for drinks one night last week. The cork in the wine bottle broke. Somebody pounded it into the bottle with a chisel and a hammer. We went to a bar. I have never understood the feeling men seem to have for bars they frequent. A fine musician who was with us played Mozart, Chopin, and Beethoven on the piano. It seemed a great, impromptu occasion. Then he said, we thought, "I am now going to play some Yatz." From what he played, it turned out he meant jazz. He played it badly.

We had driven in from another weekend in the country while it was still daylight. Lots of cars had their headlights on. We weren't sure whether it was for or against peace, or just for highway safety. Milly, a secretary in a brokerage office, was married in our ground-floor shop that evening. She cried hysterically. Her mother and several people from her home town and John, whose girl she had been before he married Inez, thought it was from sentiment or shyness, or some conventional reason. Milly explained it to Aldo later. She and her husband had really married two years before—the week they met, in fact—in a chapel in Las Vegas. They hadn't wanted to tell their parents, or anybody, until he finished law school. They had torn up their Las Vegas license. She had been crying out of some legal fear of being married twice, it turned out. Their best man, a Puerto Rican doctor, said his aunt had been mugged in a cemetery in San Juan by a man on horseback. She thought it was her husband, returned from the dead. She had required sedation. We laughed. My friend across the hall, who owns the beagle, looked very sad all evening. He said, abruptly, that he was cracking up, and no one would believe him. There were sirens in the street. Inez said she knew exactly what he meant: she was cracking up also. Her escort, an Italian jeweller, said, "I too. I too have it. The most terrible anguishes, anguishes all in the night."

Inez said she knew the most wonderful man for the problem. "He may strike you at first as a phony," she said, "but then, when you're with him, you find yourself naturally screaming. It's such a relief. And he teaches you how you can practice at home." Milly said she was not much of a screamer—had never, in fact, screamed in her life. "High time you did, then," Inez said. Our sportswriter said he had recently met a girl whose problem was stealing all the suède garments of house guests, and another, in her thirties, who cried all the time because she had not been accepted at Smith. We heard many more sirens in the streets. We all went home.

At 4 A.M., the phone rang about fifty times. I did not answer it. Aldo suggested that we remove it. I took three Valium. The whole night was sirens, then silence. The phone rang again. It is still ringing. The paper goes to press tomorrow. It is possible that I know who killed our landlord. So many things point in one direction. But too strong a case, I find, is often lost. It incurs doubts, suspicions. Perhaps I do not know. Perhaps it doesn't matter. I think it does, though. When I wonder what it is that we are doing—in this brownstone, on this block, with this paper—the truth is probably that we are fighting for our lives.

Alternatives

Alice Adams

ALICE ADAMS grew up in Chapel Hill, North Carolina, and graduated from Radcliffe; since then she has lived mostly in San Francisco. Her fourth novel, *Rich Rewards,* was published by Knopf in the fall of 1980; a collection of stories, *Beautiful Girl,* was published in 1978.

It is the summer of 1935, and there are two people sitting at the end of a porch. The house is in Maine, at the edge of a high bluff that overlooks a large and for the moment peaceful lake. Tom Todd and Barbara Rutherford. They have recently met (she and her husband are houseguests of the Todds). They laugh a lot, they are excited about each other, and they have no idea what to do with what they feel. She is a very blond, bright-eyed girl in her twenties, wearing very short white shorts, swinging long thin legs below the high hammock on which she is perched, looking down at Tom. He is a fair, slender man with sad lines beside his mouth, but (not now!) now he is laughing with Babs. Some ten years older than she, he is a professor, writing a book on Shelley (Oh wild West Wind!) but the Depression has had unhappy effects on his university (Hilton, in the Middle South): 10 percent salary cuts, cancellation of sabbaticals. He is unable to finish his book (no promotion); they rely more and more on his wife's small income from her bookstore. And he himself has been depressed—but not now. What a girl, this Babs!

The house itself is old, with weathered shingles that once were green, and its shape is peculiar; it used to be the central lodge for a camp for underprivileged girls that Jessica Todd owned and ran before her marriage to Tom. The large, high living room is still full of souvenirs from that era: group pictures of girls in bloomers and middies, who danced or rather posed in discreet Greek tunics, and wore headbands; and over the fireplace, just below a moldering deer's head, there is a mouse-nibbled triangular felt banner, once dark green, that announced the name of the camp: Wabuwana. Why does Jessica keep all those things around, as though those were her happiest days? No one ever asked. Since there were no bedrooms Tom and Jessica sleep in a curtained-off alcove, with not much privacy; two very small rooms that once were storage closets are bedrooms for their children, Avery and Devlin. Babs and her husband, Wilfred Rutherford, have been put in a tent down the path, on one of a row of gray plank tent floors where all the camper girls used to sleep. Babs said, "How absolutely divine—I've never slept in a tent." "You haven't?" Jessica asked. "I think I sleep best in tents."

A narrow screened-in porch runs the length of the

house, and there is a long table out there—too long for just the four Todds, better (less lonely) with even two guests. The porch widens at its end, making a sort of round room, where Tom and Babs now are, not looking at the view.

Around the house there are clumps of hemlocks, tall Norway pines, white pines, and birches that bend out from the high bank. Across the smooth bright lake are the White Mountains, the Presidential Range—sharp blue Mount Adams and farther back, in the exceptionally clear days of early fall, such as this day is, you can see Mount Washington silhouetted. Lesser, gentler slopes take up the foreground: Mount Pleasant, Douglas Hill.

Beside Babs in the hammock lies a ukelele—hers, which Tom wants her to play.

"Oh, but I'm no good at *all*," she protests. "Wilfred can't stand it when I play!"

"I'll be able to stand it, I can promise you that, my dear."

Her accent is very Bostonian, his Southern; both tendencies seem to intensify as they talk together.

She picks up the instrument, plucks the four strings as she sings, "My dog has fleas."

"So does Louise," he sings mockingly, an echo. Tom is fond of simple ridiculous jokes but he feels it necessary always to deliver them as though someone else were talking. In fact, he says almost everything indirectly.

They both laugh, looking at each other.

They are still laughing when Jessica comes out from the living room where she has been reading (every summer she rereads Jane Austen) and walks down the length of the porch to where they are, and says, "Oh, a ukelele, how nice, Barbara. Some of our girls used to play."

Chivalrous Tom gets up to offer his chair—"Here you are, old dear." She did not want to sit so close to the hammock but does anyway, a small shapeless woman on the edge of her chair.

Jessica is only a few years older than Tom but she looks considerably more so, with graying hair and sad brown eyes, a tightly compressed mouth. She has strong and definite Anglo-Saxon notions about good behavior (they all do, this helpless group of American Protestants, Tom and Jessica, Barbara and Wilfred) which they try and almost succeed in passing on to their children. Jessica wears no makeup and is dressed in what she calls "camp clothes," meaning things that are old and shabby (what she thinks she deserves). "Won't you play something for us?" she asks Babs.

"Perhaps you will succeed in persuasion where I have failed," says Tom. As he sees it, his chief duty toward his wife is to be unfailingly polite, and he always is, although sometimes it comes across a little heavily.

Of course Jessica feels the currents between Babs and Tom but she accepts what she senses with melancholy resignation. There is a woman at home whom Tom likes too, small, blond Irene McGinnis, and Irene is crazy about Tom—that's clear—but nothing happens. Sometimes they kiss; Jessica has noticed that Verlie, the maid, always hides Tom's handkerchiefs. Verlie also likes Tom. Nothing more will happen with Babs. (But she is wrong.) It is only mildly depressing for Jessica, a further reminder that she is an aging, not physically attractive woman, and that her excellent mind is not compelling to Tom. But she is used to all that. She sighs, and says, "I think there's going to be a very beautiful sunset," and she looks across the lake to the mountains. "There's Mount Washington," she says.

Then the porch door bangs open and Wilfred walks

toward them, a heavy, dark young man with sleeves rolled up over big hairy arms; he has been washing and polishing his new Ford. He is a distant cousin of Jessica's. "Babs, you're not going to play that thing, are you?"

"No, darling, I absolutely promise."

"Well," Tom says, "surely it's time for a drink?"

"It surely is," says Babs, giggling, mocking him.

He gestures as though to slap at the calf of her long leg, but of course he does not; his hand stops some inches away.

Down a wide pine-needled path, some distance from the lodge, there is a decaying birchbark canoe, inside which white Indian pipes grow. They were planted years back by the camper girls. Around the canoe stands a grove of pines with knotted roots, risen up from the ground, in which chipmunks live. Feeding the chipmunks is what Jessica and Tom's children do when they aren't swimming or playing on the beach. Skinny, dark Avery and smaller, fairer Devlin—in their skimpy shorts they sit cross-legged on the pine needles, making clucking noises to bring out the chipmunks.

A small chipmunk comes out, bright-eyed, switching his tail back and forth, looking at the children, but then he scurries off.

Devlin asks, "Do you like Babs?" He underlines the name, meaning that he thinks it's silly.

"She's OK." Avery's voice is tight; she is confused by Babs. She doesn't know whether to think, as her mother probably does, that Babs's white shorts are too short, that she is too dressed up in her pink silk shirt for camp, or to be pleased at the novel sort of attention she gets from Babs, who said last night at dinner, "You know, Avery, when you're a little older you should have an evening dress this color," and pointed to the flame-gold gladioli on the table, in a gray stone crock.

"Her shorts are too short," says Devlin.

"What do you know about clothes? They're supposed to be short—*shorts.*" Saying this, for a moment Avery feels that she *is* Babs, who wears lipstick and anything she wants to, whom everyone looks at.

"Mother doesn't wear shorts, ever."

"So what? You think she's well dressed?"

Devlin is appalled; he has no idea what to make of what she has said. "I'll tell!" He is desperate. "I'll tell her what you said."

"Just try, you silly little sissy. Come on, I'll race you to the lodge."

Both children scramble up, Avery first, of course, and run across the slippery pines, their skinny brown legs flashing between the trees, and arrive at the house together and slam open the screen door and tear down the length of the porch to the cluster of grown-ups.

"Mother, do you know what Avery said?"

"No, darling, but please don't tell me unless it was something very amusing." This is out of character for Jessica, and Devlin stares at his mother, who strokes his light hair, and says, "Now, let's all be quiet. Barbara is going to play a song."

Babs picks up her ukelele and looks down at it as she begins her song, which turns out to be a long ballad about a lonely cowboy and a pretty city girl. She has an attractive, controlled alto voice. She becomes more and more sure of herself as she goes along, and sometimes looks up and smiles around at the group—at Tom—as she sings.

Tom has an exceptional ear, as well as a memory for words; somewhere, sometime, he has heard that ballad before, so that by the time she reaches the end he is singing with her, and they reach the last line together, looking into each other's eyes with a great stagy show of exaggeration; they sing together, "And they loved forever more."

But they are not, that night, lying hotly together on the cold beach, furiously kissing, wildly touching everywhere. That happens only in Tom's mind, as he lies next to Jessica and hears her soft sad snores. In her cot, in the tent, Babs sleeps very soundly, as she always does, and she dreams of the first boy she ever kissed, whose name was not Tom.

In the late forties, almost the same group gathers for dinner around a large white restaurant table, the Buon Gusto, in San Francisco. There are Tom and Jessica, and Babs, but she is without Wilfred, whom she has just divorced in Reno. Devlin is there, Devlin grown plump and sleek, smug with his new job of supervising window display at the City of Paris. Avery is there, with her second husband, fat, intellectual Stanley. (Her first marriage, to Paul Blue, the black trumpet player, was annulled; Paul was already married, and his first wife had lied about the divorce.)

Tom and Barbara have spent the afternoon in bed together, in her hotel room—that old love finally consummated. They are both violently aware of the afternoon behind them; they are partly still there, together in the tangled sea-smelling sheets. Barbara presses her legs close. Tom wonders if there is any smell of her on him that anyone could notice.

No one notices anything; they all have problems of their own.

In the more than ten years since they were all in Maine Jessica has sunk further into her own painful and very private despair. She is not fatter, but her body has lost all definition, and her clothes are deliberately middle-aged, as though she were eager to be done with being a sexual woman. Her melancholy eyes are large, darkly shadowed; below them her cheeks sag, and the corners of her mouth have a small sad downward turn. Tom is always carrying on—the phrase she uses to herself—with someone or other; she has little energy left with which to care. But sometimes, still, a lively rebellious voice within her cries out that it is all cruelly unfair; she has done everything that she was taught a wife is expected to do; she has kept house and cared for children and listened to Tom, laughed at his jokes and never said no when he felt like making love—done all those things, been a faithful and quiet wife when often she didn't want to at all, and there he is, unable to keep his eyes off Babs, laughing at all *her* jokes.

Tom has promised Barbara that he will leave Jessica; this winter they will get a divorce, and he will apply for a teaching job at Stanford or U.C., and he and Babs will live in San Francisco; they are both in love with the city.

Avery has recently begun psychoanalysis with a very orthodox Freudian; he says nothing, and she becomes more and more hysterical—she is lost! And now this untimely visit from her parents; agonized, she questions them about events of her early childhood, as though to get her bearings. "Was I nine or ten when I had whooping cough?"

"What?" says Jessica, who had daringly been embarked on an alternate version of her own life, in which she did not marry Tom but instead went on to graduate school herself, and took a doctorate in Classics. (But who would have hired a woman professor in the twenties?) "Tom, I'd love another drink," she says. "Barbara? you too?" Late in her life Jessica has discovered the numbing effects of drink—you can sleep!

"Oh, yes, divine."

Sipping what is still his first vermouth, Devlin repeats to himself that most women are disgusting. He excepts his mother. He is sitting next to Babs, and he cannot stand her perfume, which is Joy.

Looking at Jessica, whom, curiously, she has always liked, Barbara feels a chill in her heart. Are they doing the right thing, she and Tom? He says they are; he says Jessica has her bookstore and her student poet friends ("Fairies, most of them, from the look of them," Tom says), and that living with him does not make her happy at all; he has never made her happy. Is he only talking to himself, rationalizing? Barbara doesn't know.

All these people, so many of them Southern, make Avery's husband, Stanley, feel quite lost; in fact, he finds it hard to understand anything they say. Tom is especially opaque: the heavy Southern accent and heavier irony combine to create confusion, which is perhaps what Tom intends. Stanley thinks Tom is a little crazy, and feels great sympathy for Jessica, whom he admires. And he thinks: poor Avery, growing up in all that—no wonder Devlin's queer and Avery has to go to a shrink. Stanley feels an awful guilt toward Avery, for not supplying all that Tom and Jessica failed to give her, and for his persistent "premature ejaculations"—and putting the phrase in quotes is not much help.

"I remember your whooping cough very well indeed," says Tom, pulling in his chin so that the back of his head jerks up; it is a characteristic gesture, an odd combination of self-mockery and self-congratulation. "It was the same summer you pushed Harry McGinnis into the swimming pool." He turns to Stanley, who is as incomprehensible to him as he is to Stanley, but he tries. "Odd gesture, that. Her mother and I thought she had a sort of 'crush' on young Harry, and then she went and pushed him into the pool." He chuckles. "Don't try to tell me that ladies aren't creatures of whim, even twelve-year-old girls."

"I was nine," says Avery, and does not add: you had

a crush on Harry's mother, you were crazy about Irene that summer.

Jessica thinks the same thing, and she and Avery are both looking at Tom, so that he feels the thought.

"I remember teasing Irene about the bathing suit she wore that day," he says recklessly, staring about with his clear blue eyes at the unfamiliar room.

"What was it like?" asks Barbara, very interested.

"Oh, some sort of ruffled thing. You know how those Southern gals are," he says, clearly not meaning either his wife or his daughter.

"I must have thought the whooping cough was a sort of punishment," Avery says. "For having a crush on Harry, as you put it."

"Yes, probably," Jessica agrees, being herself familiar with many varieties of guilt. "You were awful sick—it was terrible. There was nothing we could do."

"When was the first summer you came to Maine?" Devlin asks Babs, coldly curious, nearly rude. It is clear that he wishes she never had.

"1935. In September. In fact September ninth," she says, and then blushes for the accuracy of her recall, and looks at Tom.

"Verlie took care of me," says Avery, still involved with her whooping cough.

Jessica sighs deeply. "Yes, I suppose she did."

Almost ten years later, in the middle fifties, Tom and Barbara are married. In the chapel of the little church, the Swedenborgian, in San Francisco, both their faces stream with tears as the minister says those words.

In her forties, Barbara is a striking woman still, with her small disdainful nose, her sleekly knotted pale hair, and her beautiful way of walking, holding herself forward like a present. She has aged softly, as very fine-skinned very blond women sometimes do. And

Tom is handsome still; they make a handsome couple (they always have).

Avery is there; she reflects that she is now older than Barbara was in 1935, that summer in Maine. She is almost thirty, divorced from Stanley, and disturbingly in love with two men at once. Has Barbara never loved anyone but Tom? (Has she?) Avery sees their tears as highly romantic.

She herself is a nervy, attractive girl with emphatic dark eyebrows, large dark eyes, and a friendly soft mouth, heavy breasts on an otherwise slender body. She wishes she had not worn her black silk suit, despite its chic; two friends have assured her that no one thought about wearing black to weddings anymore, but now it seems a thing not to have done. "I wore black to my father's wedding"—thank God she is not still seeing Dr. Gunderscheim, and will use that sentence only as a joke. Mainly, Avery is wondering which of the two men to marry, Charles or Christopher. (The slight similarity of the names seems ominous—what does it mean?) This wondering is a heavy obsessive worry to her; it drags at her mind, pulling it down. Now for the first time, in the small dim chapel, candlelit, it wildly occurs to her that perhaps she should marry neither of them, perhaps she should not marry at all, and she stares about the chapel, terrified.

"I pronounce you man and wife," says the minister, who is kindly, thin, white-haired. He is very old; in fact he quietly dies the following year.

And then, almost as though nothing had happened, they have all left the chapel: Tom and Barbara, Avery and Devlin, who was Tom's best man. ("I gave my father away," is another of Avery's new postwedding jokes.) But something has happened: Tom and Barbara are married. They don't believe it either. He gives her a deep and prolonged kiss (why does it look so awkward?) which embarrasses Devlin, so that he stares up and down the pretty, tree-lined street. He is thinking of Jessica, who is dead.

And he passionately wishes that she had not died, savagely blames Tom and Barbara for that death. Trivial, entirely selfish people—so he sees them; he compares the frivolity of their connection with Jessica's heavy suffering. Since Jessica's death Devlin has been in a sort of voluntary retreat. He left his window-display job and most of his friends; he stays at home on the wrong side of Telegraph Hill, without a view. He reads a lot and listens to music and does an occasional watercolor. He rarely sees Avery, and disapproves of what he understands to be her life. ("You don't think it's dykey, the way you sleep around?" was the terrible sentence he spoke to her, on the eve of Jessica's funeral, and it has never been retracted.) Sometimes in his fantasies it is ten years back, and Tom and Jessica get a divorce and she comes out to live in San Francisco. He finds her a pretty apartment on Telegraph Hill and her hair grows beautifully white and she wears nice tweeds and entertains at tea. And Tom and Barbara move to hell—Los Angeles or Mexico or somewhere. Most people who know him assume Devlin to be homosexual; asexual is actually the more accurate description.

They stand there, that quite striking group, all blinking in a brilliant October sun that instantly dries all tears; for several moments they are all transfixed there, unable to walk, all together, to their separate cars, to continue to the friend's house where there is to be the wedding reception. (Why this hesitation? do none of them believe in the wedding? what is a marriage?)

Five years later, in the early sixties, Avery drives up to Maine from Hilton, for various reasons which do not include a strong desire to see Tom and Barbara. She has been married to Christopher for four years, and she came out from San Francisco to Hilton to see how it was away from him. Away from him she fell wildly in love with a man in Hilton named Jason Valentine, and now (for various reasons) she has decided that she needs some time away from Jason.

She drives smoothly, quietly, along the pine-needled road in her Corvair to find no one there. No car.

But the screen door is unlatched, and she goes in, stepping up from the old stone step onto the long narrow porch, from which the long table has been removed, replaced with a new one that is small and round. (But where did they put the old one?) And there are some bright yellow canvas chairs, new and somehow shocking against the weathered shingled wall.

Inside the house are more violent changes, more bright new fabrics: curtains, bandanna-red, and a bandanna bedspread on the conspicuous wide bed. Beside the fireplace is a white wicker sofa (new) with chintz cushions—more red. So much red and so much newness make Avery dizzy; almost angrily she wonders where the old things are, the decaying banners and sepia photographs of girls in Greek costumes. She goes into the kitchen and it is all painted yellow, into what was the large closet where she used to sleep—but a wall has been knocked out between her room and Devlin's; it is all one room now, a new room, entirely strange, with a new iron bed, a crocheted bedspread, which is white. Is that where they will expect her to sleep? She wishes there were a phone. Tomorrow she will have to drive into town to call Jason at his studio.

Needing a drink, Avery goes back into the kitchen, and finds a bottle of an unfamiliar brand of bourbon. She gets ice from the refrigerator (terrifyingly new—so white!), water from the tap—thank God, the same old sink. With her clutched drink she walks quickly through the living room to the porch, down to the end. She looks out across the lake with sentimentally teared eyes, noting that it is clear but not quite clear enough to see Mount Washington.

Being in love with Jason, who is a nonpracticing architect (he would rather paint), who worries about his work (his nonwork), who loves her but is elusive (she has no idea when they will see each other again), has tightened all Avery's nerves: she is taut, cries easily, and is all concentrated on being in love with Jason.

A car drives up, a Mustang—Barbara is faithful to Fords. And there they are saying, "Avery, but we didn't ex*pect* you, we went into *Port*land, for *lob*sters. Oh, dear, how awful, we only bought *two!*" Embracing, laughing. Tears (why?) in everyone's eyes.

They settle down, after packages are put away, Avery's bags in the new guest room, and they watch the sunset: a disappointing pale pastel. And they drink a lot.

Barbara is nervous, both because of this shift in schedule and because of Avery, whom she regards as an intellectual, like Tom. She is always afraid of what Avery will say—a not-unfounded fear. Also, she is upset about the prospect of two lobsters for three people.

What he considers her untimely arrival permits Tom's usual ambivalence about Avery to yield to a single emotion: extreme irritation. How inconsiderate she is—always has been! Besides, he was looking forward to his lobster.

Avery chooses this unpropitious moment to announce that she is leaving Christopher. "We've been making each other miserable," she says. "We have been, for a long time." She trails off.

Tom brightens. "Well, old dear, I always think incompatibility is a good reason not to live together."

He has no notion of his own prurience in regard to his daughter.

She does. She says, "Oh, Christ."

Barbara goes into the kitchen to divide up the lobster; a skilled hostess, she does quite well, and she makes a good mayonnaise, as she listens to the jagged sounds of the quarrel on the porch. Avery and Tom. She sighs.

Now darkness surrounds the house, and silence, except for a faint soft lapping of small waves on the shore, and tiny noises from the woods: small animals shifting weight on the leaves, a bird moving on a branch.

"Although I have what I suppose is an old-fashioned prejudice against divorce," Tom unfortunately says.

"Christ, is that why you stayed married to mother and made her as miserable as you could? Christ, I have a prejudice against misery!" Avery feels her voice (and herself) getting out of control.

Barbara announces dinner, and they go to the pretty new table, where places are set, candles lit. Barbara distributes the lobster, giving Tom the major share, but he scowls down at his plate.

As Avery does at hers—in Hilton, with Jason, she was generally too overstimulated, too "in love" to eat; now she is exhausted and very hungry. She turns to Barbara, as though for help. "Don't you ever wish you'd got married before you did? What a waste those years were. That time in San Francisco, why not then?"

Startled, Barbara has no idea what to answer. She has never allowed herself to think in these terms, imaginatively to revise her life. "I feel lucky we've had these years we have had," she says—which, for her, is the truth. She loves Tom; she feels that she is lucky to be his wife.

"But those last years were horrible for mother," Avery says. "You might have spared her that time."

"I think I might be in a better position than you to be

the judge of that." Enraged, Tom takes a characteristic stance: his chin thrust out, he is everyone's superior—he is especially superior to women and children, particularly his own.

"Oh, yeah?" In her childhood, this was considered the rudest remark one could make; then Avery would never have said it to Tom. "You think she just plain died of a heart attack, don't you? Well, her room was full of empty sherry bottles. All over. Everywhere those drab brown empty bottles, smelling sweet. Julia told me, when she cleaned it out."

This information (which is new) is so shocking (and so absolutely credible) to Tom that he must dismiss it at once. His desperate and hopeless guilts toward Jessica have forced him to take a sanctimonious tone in speaking of her. He must dismiss this charge at once. "As a matter of face, Julia is quite unreliable, as Verlie was," he says.

Avery explodes. "Julia is unreliable! Verlie was! Christ—why? because they're black? because they're women?"

Barbara has begun to cry. "You've got to stop this," she says. "Why quarrel about the past? It's over—"

Tom and Avery stare at each other, in terrible pain; they would like to weep, to embrace, but they are unable to do either.

Tom draws himself up stiffly—stiffly he turns to Barbara. "You're quite right, old dear," he says.

Several things attack Avery's mind at once: one, that she would like to say, goddam you both, or something obscene, and take off down the turnpike, back to Boston; two, she is too drunk for the turnpike; and three, she has just noticed that Tom speaks to Barbara exactly as though she were Jessica, as though neither of them were people but something generic named Wife.

And so the moment goes, the awful emotions subside, and they all retreat to trivia. Although Avery's hands still shake, she comments on the mayonnaise (she is not excruciatingly Southern Jessica's daughter for nothing), which Barbara gratefully takes up.

"I'm never sure it will come out right," she says. "I've had the most embarrassing failures, but of course tonight, just for family—" She is unable to finish the sentence, or to remember what she meant.

Later, during the next few years before Tom's death, Avery looks back and thinks that yes, she should have left then, drunk or not. She could have found a motel. That would have been a strong gesture, a refusal to put up with any more of what she saw as Tom's male imperialism, his vast selfishness. (But poor Avery was constantly plagued with alternatives; she constantly rewrote her life into new versions in which she did not marry Stanley. Or Christopher. Sometimes she thought she should have stayed with Paul Blue; in that version, of course, he was not married.) After Tom died she thought that perhaps it was just as well she hadn't left, but she was never quite sure.

Against everyone's advice, early in the summer after Tom died, Barbara drove alone to Maine. Even Devlin had called to dissuade her (in fact ever since Tom's funeral, to which Avery did not even come—Tom had died while she was in Mount Zion Hospital being treated for depression—a new and warm connection had been established between Barbara and Devlin; they wrote back and forth; she phoned him for various pieces of advice—she had begun to rely on him as she was used to relying on Tom).

Devlin said, "Darling Barbara, do you see it as an exercise in masochism? I wouldn't have thought it of you."

"Angel, you don't understand. I love that house. I've been extremely happy there."

"Barbara, let me be blunt: don't you think you'll be fantastically lonely?"

"No, I don't."

And so, after visits with friends and relatives in Boston, Barbara drives on to Maine in her newest Ford, and arrives in a twilight of early July. She parks near the house, gets out, pausing only briefly to observe the weather, which is clear, and to smile at the warm familiar smell of pines. Then she walks briskly over to the porch and opens the padlock on the screen door.

Her first reaction, stepping up onto the porch, could be considered odd: she decides that those yellow chairs are wrong for the porch. This pleases her: changing them for something else will give her something to do. She enters the living room, sniffs at the musty, airless space, and goes into the kitchen, where last summer she hid a bottle of bourbon in the flour bin. (Sometimes stray hunters or fishermen break into the house and take things.) No one has taken it, and she makes herself a good stiff drink, and goes to the rounded end of the porch, to sit and rest.

And much more clearly than she can remember anything that happened last month, last winter or fall, she sees that scene of over thirty years ago, sees Tom (how young he was, how handsome), as he urged her to play her ukelele (play what? did he name a song?), and she sees Jessica come out to where they are (making some reference to the girls who used to come to camp—poor Jessica), and Wilfred, as always angrily serious, puffing although not yet fat, and then wild, skinny Avery (why did she and Jason Valentine not marry?) and frightened Devlin, holding his mother's arm. She sees all those people, and herself among them, and for an instant she has a sense that she *is* all of them—that she is Jessica as well as Barbara, is Wilfred, Avery, Devlin, and Tom.

But this is an unfamiliar mood, or sense, for her, and she shakes it off, literally shaking her head and lifting her chin. She remembers then that she put the old chairs and the table in the shed next to the kitchen.

Three days later Barbara has restored the lodge to what (to herself) she calls its "old look." The old chairs and old long table are back. She has even put up some of Jessica's old pictures in the living room.

She has no idea why she made such an effort, except that she firmly believes (always has) in the efficacy of physical work; she was driven by a strong, controlling instinct, and she also believes in her instincts. She even laughs to herself at what could seem a whim, and in writing a note to Devlin she says, "You'd have thought I was restoring Williamsburg, and you should see my blisters!"

And so at the end of her day she is seated there at the end of the porch, and everything but herself looks just as it did when she first saw it. She drinks the two stiff highballs that she allows herself before dinner, and she remembers all the best times with Tom, San Francisco hotels and Paris honeymoon, the big parties in Hilton, and she sheds a few tears, but she does not try to change anything that happened. She does not imagine an altered, better life that she might have had.

The Faithful

James Alan McPherson

JAMES ALAN MCPHERSON was born in Savannah, Georgia, in 1943. He attended college in Georgia, graduate school in Cambridge and in Iowa City. Since 1969 he has been a contributing editor for *The Atlantic*.

There is John Butler, a barber, looking out his shop window on a slow Monday morning. Impeccable, as usual, in his starched white jacket, he stands and surveys the procession of colors blending into the avenue, a living advertisement of his profession. The colors are blurred; the window needs a cleaning; the red lettering has been allowed to fade, almost to a mere outline. Some of the passing faces he cannot recognize. But some recognize him behind the window and wave as they hurry past. Others, wanting to avoid all contact with the shop, pretend that he is not there. They ease out of view without acknowledging his nodding head. Still, he stands in his usual place between the edge of the window and the door; and when a familiar face moves by the window without glancing toward the shop, he shares the embarrassment and turns his own eyes away. In his mind he forgives the workers; but the shiftless, the workless, the timeless strollers up and down the avenue he does not spare.

"They still tryin' to starve us out," he says, turning to the members of his shop. Today it consists of Ray Powell, the second barber; Mickey Norris, who has again played hooky from school in order to earn a few dollars shining shoes; and two loafers, who have come in for a game of checkers and a chance to enjoy it. All wince to hear him start again.

"Maybe I'll go on down the block a minute," Mickey says, moving toward the door.

"Maybe you better go on to school," Butler tells him. "There ain't go'n be no work in here today."

Mickey, a sly boy, does not stray far from the green metal chair.

Butler gives him a severe look. "Not tomorrow either," he adds.

Mickey slinks back to the chair and sits, his hands going into his pockets for coins to toss.

Ray, a fat brown man who likes to give the impression of habitual efficiency, runs the edge of a hand towel between the teeth of his own black comb and puckers his lips in an exaggeration of effort. "It's just the first of the week, Reverend," he says. "Things are bound to pick up."

One of the loafers, Norm Tyson from the Projects, knows better: he allows his opponent an advantage on the board and, before the man can incorporate it, says: "Looks like it's yours."

And then the two of them leave.

Just after noon, when Ray has gone across the street for lunch and Mickey has wandered off until evening, a young man looks in the door. A massive black tiara of hair encircles his head; his matching light green shirt and bell-bottom trousers advertise his wealth. Butler flashes his most hospitable smile and rises from his chair.

"How much for a quick one?" the young man asks from the door.

"For all that, two-fifty, maybe three dollars," Butler says.

The young man snorts and throws back his arms in playful amazement. "Just for a *trim?* You wouldn't wanna mess up my vibrations, would you?"

Butler loosens the smile and lowers his voice. "No," he says. "Better go somewhere else. I got me some heavy hands."

The young man laughs. "A heavy hand make a rusty register in your business, don't it?" And backs out the door before the barber can form an answer.

At the end of the day some regulars do come in; but they are losing more hairs than Butler clips. Still, they lower their heads, more from respect than necessity, and allow him limited operations around the edges. These balding faithfuls—John Gilmore or Dick Kendricks or Willie Russell—the backbone of his Sunday congregation, fold their hands beneath the white sheet square and abide, in their turn, his wandering frustrations. "These whites have bull-shitted our young men," he says. "Now, me, I'm as proud as the next man. But our boys didn't stop gettin' haircuts until these white boys started that mess. That's a fact. Wasn't no more than a couple years ago, they'd be lined up against that wall on a Saturday night laughin' at the white boys. But soon as they see these white kids runnin' round wild, all at once they hair ain't long enough no more."

John Gilmore keeps his head lowered, his lips tight, his eyes watching his hands work beneath the sheet.

Ray, sitting in his own chair, looks up from the paper he has been reading and says: "Hey, I see where they arrested a big shot for tax evasion. First of the year they bound to hamstring *one* for example." But no one picks it up. Ray rattles and folds the paper, and eases back into his reading.

"They know what they doin'," Butler continues. "Why, they tell me Miss Dawson's boy can't git into the university on that new free program because those folk up there think he's a Tom. As *smart* as that boy is, he can't git in. But you see old Buggsy Brooks goin' up there. They *took him out of jail,*" he says, bending close to Gilmore's ear for emphasis. "You ought to see him struttin' around, hair on his head big as a basketball. Never read a book through in his life."

But no one, not even Gilmore who knows the true state of affairs, can muster the hardness of heart to take him on.

Once, there had been violent betting and spit-infested verbal battles and crowded-round checker games and hot clothes and numbers passing through; once, Butler would hum radio spirituals as he went about his work, or else trade righteous homilies with Ray, busy in the other chair. The men who remember those days—Gilmore, Kendricks, and the others—would like to have them back; but there is an unspoken fear of being too possessive about the past and a determination not to allow the present to slip out of focus. They recognize another world outside the shop door, and find it much easier to pay up and walk away when Butler is done with his work.

"If it wasn't for you belonging to his church," John Gilmore tells his wife after each visit, "I wouldn't go in there."

"Now don't you be no trouble to him," Marie Gilmore reminds her husband. "He ain't got much longer to go."

On Sundays Butler now converts his sermons. The themes still resemble something familiar to his congregation, but lately the images have been doing different work. The relative few who still come into the church to hear it are growing bored. Some have already visited Reverend Tarwell and his more magical thumpings over on 138th. They like what they hear. There is talk that Tarwell plans to have himself crucified next month at Easter Sunrise Service and preach the entire sermon from the cross. Such resurrected remnants of the South appeal to them; the oldest have ever been homesick. Besides, Butler seems to have an obsession with a single theme:

"I was walkin' down here this morning', brothers and sisters," he begins, his rising voice mellowing into a comfortable chant, "thinkin' about the rift there is these days between father and son; thinkin' about the breach there is between son and son and daughter and daughter. I'm thinkin' this mornin' about old bloody Cain and his guiltless brother; about old man Abraham castin' his son out into the wilderness; about that old rascal, Saul, lettin' his *wine* turn him against young David. I see little Joseph tossed in the dark pit, strip naked of his garment by his brothers. And hungry Esau, just a-droolin' at the mouth, sellin' his birthright for a mess of *pottage*. There's old slick Jacob now, a-crawlin' in to blind Isaac's bedside underneath the *fleece* of a wild and wooly animal; and Esau standin' outside the door, just a-weepin' away. Next to him is old rebellious Absalom, up in an *oak* tree, swingin' by his hair with Joab ridin' *down* on him. Just look at that boy cuss. I want to cut him down, Church, but I ain't got the strength. My arm is raised up to him, but my *razor's* kind of rusty. So can I git an *a-men* over here . . .?"

Some of the people on his left say a weak "a-men."

"Can I hear an *a-men* over there . . .?"

Some few on the right say "a-men."

"My razor growin' *sharper* by the second . . ."

"You better lay off that stuff," Ella, his wife, tells him at Sunday dinner. "The church done got tired of that one record you keep playin'." They have not been invited out for Sunday dinner in over five months.

"They ain't got no cause to complain," Butler tells her. "I give them a good service. Besides, most of them don't even listen to nothin' but the names."

"Just the same, you better lay off it for a while. It ain't their fault you goin' out of business."

Butler looks over at her. She is chewing with a deliberation calculated to enrage him into an argument. "Whose fault you reckon it is?" he demands.

She continues chewing, looking wise.

Butler looks at his own food. "All right," he says. "It's *my* fault."

"It ain't that you *have* to do Afros. Ray could do that and you could do your own customers. There ain't nothin' wrong with dividin' up the work thataway."

"Ray ain't go'n do fancy cuts in *my* place. First thing you know, these young fellows come hangin' round there and drive the old customers away."

She chews for a while, sips her coffee, and watches him. She takes her time in swallowing, smacks her lips, and then says: "Then you won't have a place for much longer."

He scrapes at his own plate, trying to avoid her eyes.

"And the way *you* goin'," she adds, "you won't be preachin' much longer either."

This thought he takes to bed with him while she lingers in the kitchen and sips, with irritating emphasis, another cup of coffee.

On another slow Monday morning, Ray, shaping his own moustache at the mirror, says: "You know, Reverend, I been thinking. Maybe we ought to go into processes. Nobody can say *now* that's imitating the white man. And there's guys on the block still wearing them."

Butler turns from the window, his face twitching. Images of winos and hustlers flash through his mind. "That's what you been thinkin', huh?" he says to Ray.

"Yeah, Reverend," Ray says, laughing to himself in the mirror. "Since the white folks always imitating us, maybe we could even process some of them."

"I don't process," Butler answers.

"It's work," Ray says, dropping the laugh and looking serious.

"It's devil's work," Butler says.

"Right now, I'd say we ain't got much of a choice."

Butler stands behind him. They exchange looks in the mirror. Ray works the scissors in his right hand, shaking off the hairs. Then he begins to clip his moustache again, drawing in his chin. Butler watches. After a while he says: "Ray, I know you think I'm a fool. I can't help that. But when you get to be my age change is just hard. You can shape a boy's life by what you do to his hair," he says, looking over at Mickey tossing coins against the wall. "Now everybody can't do that, but I'm proud to say I done it more than once in my lifetime. And I want to do it some more. But scrapin' a few loose hairs off every Tom, Dick, and Harry that come in here, just to get the money, why anybody can do that. You understand what I'm sayin'?"

Ray lowers the scissors but does not answer.

"You, Mickey? You understand?"

Mickey thinks it over, tossing another coin to the wall. After a while he says, "Naw, suh," and nods his head.

Butler walks back to the window. "That's what I figured," he finally says, looking out.

A little after one o'clock John Gilmore comes in for a quick shave during his lunch hour. Lying almost parallel in the chair, his rust-brown lips and eyelids showing through the lather, he makes careful conversation while Butler exercises the repressed magic in his hands. "Times being what they is in religion and all," he says, "I been wonderin' what you been plannin' to do."

"About what?" Butler says, not pausing in his work.

"Well," Gilmore begins, "Marie say Second Calvary ain't drawin' no stronger membership. In fact, a lot of folks thinkin' about plain quittin'."

"That's their business," he answers, holding back Gilmore's ear. "They git what they pay for."

Gilmore waits until his ear is allowed to fall back into place. Then he says: "I hear Reverend Tarwell thinkin' 'bout *you* for assistant pastor of his place. Times bein' good for the colored like they is, he thinkin' 'bout goin' into politics in a few years. When he step down, there sure go'n be a crowd over at his place for somebody."

Butler paused to wipe the razor. "Ain't most of his people from South Carolina?" he asks.

"Some."

"Well, most of mine from Alabama. There's two different styles."

Gilmore licks some lather off his lip with a delicate flicker of his tongue. He moistens both lips in the process. "That don't make a difference no more," he says. "People thinkin' 'bout *unity* these days. All of us in the same boat no matter where we from."

"Guess so," Butler says lightly. But after cleaning his razor again he says: "Where you from?"

"Alabama."

"Then why you worryin' about Tarwell's church? Why don't he bring his people over to *mine*?"

Gilmore tightens his lips.

"He's the one plannin' to leave the community, not me."

"I'll tell him that," Gilmore says, closing his eyes tight and easing into a resolved silence.

Late on Thursday afternoon, Ray, his eyes averted, says he has to go. "It was a good shop, Reverend," he says, "but I got me a family to support."

"Where you goin' to?" Butler asks.

"This new parlor over on 145th."

"Its all set up, huh?"

Ray says, "Yeah."

"Well," Butler says, forcing a smile, "maybe my luck will change some now with you gone."

Ray looks sad. His fat jaws break out in sweat. He wipes it away, turning up the edge of his moustache. Lately he has taken to wearing his hair long about his ears: a steady warning, but of unsuspected proportions. "It ain't nothing to do with *luck,* Reverend," he sighs. "God-*damn!* Everybody done switched over but *us*. Even the *barber schools* don't teach them old down-home cuts no more. You just *plain stubborn!*" Now he pauses, checking a great part of what has been building up in him. "Look, you want to get in on the money? It's easy as pie. There ain't no work involve in it. All you have to do is trim. *Trim!*" He sighs, smoothing down his ruffed moustache while stroking his face again. "You getting to be an old man, Reverend. You should be looking ahead. That's what I'm doing. That's *all* I'm doing."

"I'll take over your regulars."

"What regulars?" Ray says. "There ain't no regulars to divide. I cut your hair, you cut mine. Sometime Willie Russell or Jack Gilmore come in here out of guilt and let you burn their ears. What's gonna happen when they get tired? Who you go'n cut them, your*self?*"

"You can take your stuff with you," Butler tells him, oblivious of Ray's exasperation. "But mind you don't take the goodwill over there to 145th."

Ray, locking his mouth against more hot words, sprawls into his own chair, penitent and brooding. Mickey, smoking a cigarette and listening in the john, blows a stream of smoke into the air and thinks his own thoughts.

"Now old Isaac," he tells his people on another Sunday morning, "he's a-layin' down to die. He done followed out God's directions and now ain't worried about but one thing: makin' his dyin' bed comfortable. He done married to Rebekah, accordin' to his *father's* will; he done planted, in his old age, the *seed* of a great nation in her wombs. But now he's tired, Church, his eyesight is a-failin' and he's hungry for *red meat*. He's just about ready to lay his blessin' on anybody, just as long as he can get a taste of venison steak. But God, Glory Glory, is a-workin' against him, as he always works against the *unwise*. He can't run the risk of that blessin' fallin' on Esau, who is all covered with hair. So he has to make Rebekah his instrument, one more time, to see that his work gits done. I want you to picture old Isaac now, just layin' in his darkness pantin' for meat. And Jacob, God's beloved, sneakin' in to blind Isaac's bedside, a goatskin on his head, a service tray in his hand. But look here, Church: yonder, over there, runnin' up from the woods with his hair holdin' him down, here come old Esau just a-hustlin' home. It's gonna be a close one, Church; both these boys is *movin' fast*. Now who go'n put money down on Esau? I say who go'n *bet* on Jacob? Both these boys is hustlin' on in. Who go'n lay somethin' on Esau this mornin' now . . .?"

No one responds.

". . . Well, then, who go'n *bet* on Jacob . . . ?"

Most of them are confused. But some of the oldest, and most faithful, lay uninspired "a-mens" on Jacob.

". . . The race is gettin' closer by the minute . . ."

Marie Gilmore, dressed in her best white usher's uniform, gets up and leaves the room.

There is John Butler, the barber, on another Monday morning; again loitering by the window, again considering the rhythm of the street. He has not housed a complete checker game for almost a month.

"How do you do one of these Afros?" he asks Mickey, turning from the window.

"Nothin' to it, Rev," says Mickey, a careful boy who bears the jokings of his buddies concerning his own close-cut hair in order to keep some steady work. "Nothin' to it," he repeats, anticipation in his wise eyes. "You just let it grow, put some stuff on it, and keep it even all the time."

"What kind of stuff? Sound like a process to me."

"Naw, Rev," Mickey says.

"What is this *stuff?*"

"It's just to keep dandruff out."

"You think I could do one?"

"Hell, Rev, *any*body can do it."

Butler thinks a bit. "Mickey, what does it do for these kids?"

Mickey looks up at him, his face suggesting the fire of deeply held knowledge. "What *don't* it do for you?" is his answer.

Butler considers this.

Just before closing time that same day John Gilmore comes in. He does not need a shave or even a trim. Nor does he offer much conversation. Butler waits. Finally Gilmore musters sufficient courage.

"Marie says she ain't comin' back to Second Calvary no more."

"Gone over to Tarwell, I bet."

Gilmore nods. His large hands dangle between his legs as he sits on the green metal chair across from Butler.

"She was a fine usher," Butler says. "Now Tarwell done beat me out of somethin' fine."

"You beat *yourself*," Gilmore says. "She didn't no more want to go over there than I want to stop comin' in here."

Butler looks into him. Gilmore looks down at his hands.

"So that's how it is?"

Gilmore nods again.

"And you call yourself a *Alabama* boy."

"That's been over a long time ago. Things change."

"I suppose you fixin' to grow yourself an Afro too, with that bald spot on your head."

Gilmore grows irritated. He gets up and moves toward the door. "I ain't fixin' to do *nothin'*," he says. "But if I was you I'd be fixin' to close up shop for a while so's I could reread my Bible for a spell."

"I know the Good Book," Butler says. "Thank you kindly."

Gilmore turns at the door, his long right hand holding

it open. "Or maybe give up the Good Book and go back down home where you can cut the kind of hair you want."

"Maybe *all* of us ought to go back," Butler calls after him. But John Gilmore has already closed the door.

Through the ebb of the afternoon he slumps in his chair, taking inventory of his situation. He is not a poor man: the title to the shop is clear; the upper floor of his duplex is rented out to a shoolteacher; and there is, besides, a little money in the bank. But there is Mickey to consider if he should close up shop; his salary comes to three-fifty a week, regardless. He would not like to see Mickey leave too. He would not like to see Mickey over on 145th, picking up ideas which have always been alien to his shop. He thinks some more about Mickey. Then he thinks about the South. Closing time comes, and goes. Mickey, passing down the street, sees him there and comes in. Butler sends him for coffee and then leans back again and closes his eyes. He thinks about going home, but again he thinks about the South. His feet braced against the footrest, the chair swinging round on its own, he recalls the red dirt roads of Alabama.

"Gimme a 'fro."

Having lost all sense of direction, he has to raise himself before the sound can be connected.

"Gimme a 'fro, please?"

A boy is standing next to his chair. He is Tommy Gilmore, youngest son of his former customer. Butler once baptized him during the heat of a summer revival. Tommy's hair is gray-black and tightly curled, his mouth is open, his dungarees faded and torn at the knee; a dollar bill is held up to Butler in the edge of his fist.

"What you want?"

"A haircut."

"It's after closing time," Butler tells him. Then he sees the dollar. "And anyway, it's gonna cost you one-fifty. You got that much?"

The boy hands up the dollar.

"That ain't enough," Butler says, handing it back. "What else you got in your pocket? How much Marie give you?"

"Ain't got no more," the boy mumbles.

Greed lifts its thumb, but charity quickly waves it away. "You sure that's all you got?"

"Yes, sir."

Butler moves over to the hot-water heater and takes the board from behind it. He lays it across the armrests of his chair, takes a fresh cloth from the drawer and gives it a decisive snap. "Sit down, Mister," he tells the boy. "I'm gonna give you the nicest schoolboy you ever seen."

Tommy does not move. His fist tightens around the dollar. Part of it disappears into the vise. His eyes narrow cynically. "A schoolboy ain't no 'fro," he states.

"Git up on the board, son."

"You go'n *gimme* one?"

"I'm a barber, ain't I?"

The boy mounts.

Butler secures him, and then ties the cloth.

Mickey comes in with the coffee, surveys the room, and then sets the steaming cup on the counter below the mirror.

Butler fastens the safety pin in the knot behind the boy's neck. "Now look here, Mickey, and you'll learn something," he says as Mickey stands back to inspect the boy in the chair.

Mickey's eyes flicker over the scene, the curiosity in him slowly changing to doubt. "How you go'n do it,

Rev? You ain't got no *comb,* you ain't got no *stuff,* and it ain't even *long* enough yet."

The boy begins to wiggle in the chair. The board shifts under him. "It is *too* long enough," he says.

"Naw, it ain't," says Mickey, malice in his eyes, his eyes on the younger boy's face, his head solemnly swaggering. "You got to go four, five months before you get enough. And you ain't got but one or two yet."

"Shut your trap, Mickey," Butler orders. He straightens the board with one hand and places the other on the struggling boy's shoulder. "I'm goin' to work on it now," he says, pressing down.

"But it ain't go'n do no *good!*"

"Shut up or go on home!" Butler says.

Mickey struts over to his own green chair at the end of the row, his face beaming the aloofness of a protected bettor on a fixed poker game. He sits, watching with animal intensity. The boy sees him and begins to squirm again.

"Quiet down, now," the barber says, this time pressing down on the boy's head. "I know what I'm doin'."

The boy obeys, whimpering some. Butler begins to use his shears. The hair is hard and thick, tightly curled and matted; but, deep inside it, near the scalp, he sees red dust rising. He is furious in his work, a starved man: turning and clipping and holding and brushing and shaping and holding and looking and seeing, beyond it all, the red dust rising. In ten minutes it is done. He stands back for a final look, then opens the pin, undoes the knot. Again he shapes the white sheet-square; again he brushes. The boy steps down, still whimpering softly. The board goes back behind the hot-water tank. And Butler lifts him up to the long mirror. The last whiffs of steam curl out from the cooling coffee. Mickey tightens his mouth and reaches into his pocket for a coin to toss against the wall. The boy looks into the mirror.

There is the barber: under the single bulb which sends light out through the windows of his shop. Gesturing, mouthing, making swift movements with his hands in the face of the shouting John Gilmore, who stands between him and the window. The boy is clinging to the man, crying softly. There is Mickey, still in his green chair against the wall, his own eyes, his own mind deciding.

"If you didn't call yourself a minister of God, I'd *kick your ass!*" the tight-fisted John Gilmore is saying. His bottom lip is pushed far out from his face.

"Didn't you ever have a schoolboy when you was his age? Just answer me that."

"I went to a different school. But my son ain't no *plantation* Negro."

"He didn't have nothin' but a dollar anyhow."

"Then you should of send him somewheres else!"

Tommy's mouth is open. He is crying without sound

"*Look* at him! You can't *tell* me he don't look better now."

"We go'n close you down, old man. You hear what I'm sayin'? We go'n close this joint down and your church *too!*"

"You go'n close us *all* down."

"We go'n run all you Toms from the community . . ."

Mickey slides his hand into his pocket, rattling the coins.

On still another Sunday morning he stands, tired now, old, facing the last few strays of a scattered flock. It is almost Easter. Word is going around that Tarwell has already nailed the cross together in the basement of his church. Some say they have seen it. Others, some of those who are sitting here, are still reserving judgment. Marie Gilmore is back; but she has not come for the sermon. She sits at the back of the room in a purple dress, her eyes cast down. Butler, looking fierce and defensive, stares at the six or so faces peering up at him. Some look sheepish; some impatient; some look numb as always, waiting to be moved. He stands before them, his two hands gripping the edges of the pulpit. They wait. Several plump ladies fan themselves, waiting. One, Betty Jessup, sitting on the front pew, leans forward and whispers: "You fixin' to preach, or what?"

He does not answer.

Now the people begin to murmur among themselves: "What's wrong with him?" "When's he gonna start?"

"We are a stiff-necked people," he begins, his voice unusually steady, the music gone. "Our heads turn thisaway and thataway, but only in one direction at a time." He pauses. "We'll be judged for it."

"Who go'n judge us?" Marie Gilmore suddenly fires from the back of the room. They all turn, their mouths hanging loose. Marie Gilmore rises. "Who's to say what's to be judged and what ain't?" she says through trembling lips. "Who's left to say for certain he knows the rules or can show us where they written down?" she says.

The people are amazed. Several of them wave their hands and nod their heads to quiet her. Marie Gilmore does not notice. Her eyes are fixed on Butler.

He stands behind the pulpit and does not say anything.

At Sunday dinner Ella says: "Well, what you go'n do *now?*"

"Send that truant officer after Mickey," he says quietly.

"What else?"

He shifts his eyes about the room, looking for something.

Ella sighs and strikes her chest. "Lord, why I had to marry a man with a *hard head?*"

Butler looks her in the face. "Because you couldn't do no better," he tells her.

Usurpation
(Other People's Stories)

Cynthia Ozick

CYNTHIA OZICK is the author of *Trust,* a novel (New American Library); *The Pagan Rabbi and Other Stories* (Knopf), nominated for a 1972 National Book Award; *Bloodshed and Three Novellas;* and *Levitation: Five Fictions.* She has also published essays, poetry, criticism, reviews, and translations in numerous periodicals and anthologies, and has been the recipient of several prizes, including the Award for Literature of the American Academy of Arts and Letters. Her home is in New Rochelle, New York.

Occasionally a writer will encounter a story that is his, yet is not his. I mean, by the way, a writer of *stories,* not one of these intelligences that analyze society and culture, but the sort of ignorant and acquisitive being who moons after magical tales. Such a creature knows very little: how to tie a shoelace, when to go to the store for bread, and the exact stab of a story that belongs to him, and to him only. But sometimes it happens that somebody else has written the story first. It is like being robbed of clothes you do not yet own. There you sit, in the rapt hall, seeing the usurper on the stage caressing the manuscript that, in its deepest turning, was meant to be yours. He is a transvestite, he is wearing your own hat and underwear. It seems unjust. There is no way to prevent him.

You may wonder that I speak of a hall rather than a book. The story I refer to has not yet been published in a book, and the fact is I heard it read aloud. It was read by the author himself. I had a seat in the back of the hall, with a much younger person pressing the chair-arms on either side of me, but by the third paragraph I was blind and saw nothing. By the fifth paragraph I recognized my story—knew it to be mine, that is, with the same indispensable familiarity I have for this round-flanked left-side molar my tongue admires. I think of it, in all that waste and rubble amid gold dental crowns, as my pearl.

The story was about a crown—a mythical one, made of silver. I do not remember its title. Perhaps it was simply called "The Magic Crown." In any event, you will soon read it in its famous author's new collection. He is, you may be sure, very famous, so famous that it was startling to see he was a real man. He wore a conventional suit and tie, a conventional haircut and conventional eyeglasses. His whitening mustache made him look conventionally distinguished. He was not at all as I had expected him to be—small and astonished, like his heroes.

This time the hero was a teacher. In the story he was always called "the teacher," as if how one lives is what one is.

> The teacher's father is in the hospital, a terminal case. There is no hope. In an advertisement the teacher reads about a wonder-curer, a rabbi who can work miracles. Though a rational fellow and a devout skeptic, in desperation he visits the rabbi and learns that a cure can be effected by the construction of a magical silver crown, which costs nearly five hundred dollars. After it is made the rabbi will give it a special blessing and the sick man will recover. The teacher pays and in a vision sees a glowing replica of the marvelous crown. But afterward he realizes that he has been mesmerized.
>
> Furiously he returns to the rabbi's worn-out flat to demand his money. Now the rabbi is dressed like a rich dandy. "I telephoned the hospital and my father is still sick." The rabbi chides him—he must give the crown time to work. The teacher insists that the crown he paid for be produced. "It cannot be seen," says the rabbi, "it must be believed in, or the blessing will not work."
>
> The teacher and the rabbi argue bitterly. The rabbi calls for faith, the teacher for his stolen money. In the heart of the struggle the teacher confesses with a terrible cry that he has really always hated his father anyway. The next day the father dies.

With a single half-archaic word the famous writer pressed out the last of the sick man's breath: he "expired."

Forgive me for boring you with plot-summary. I know there is nothing more tedious, and despise it myself. A rabbi whose face I have not made you see, a teacher whose voice remains a shadowy moan: how can I burn the inside of your eyes with these? But it is not my story, and therefore not my responsibility. I did not invent any of it.

From the platform the famous writer explained that the story was a gift, he too had not invented it. He took it from an account in a newspaper—which one he would not tell: he sweated over fear of libel. Cheats and fakes always hunt themselves up in stories, sniffing out twists, insults, distortions, transfigurations, all the drek of the imagination. Whatever's made up they grab, thick as lawyers against the silky figurative. Still, he swore it really happened, just like that—a crook with his crooked wife, calling himself rabbi, preying on gullible people, among them educated men, graduate students even; finally they arrested the fraud and put him in jail.

Instantly, the famous writer said, at the smell of the word "jail," he knew the story to be his.

This news came to me with a pang. The silver crown given away free, and where was I?—I who am pocked with newspaper-sickness, and hunch night after night (it pleases me to read the morning papers after midnight) catatonically fixed on shipping lists, death columns, lost wallets, maimings, muggings, explosions, hijackings, bombs, while the unwashed dishes sough thinly all around.

It has never occurred to me to write about a teacher; and as for rabbis, I can make up my own craftily enough. You may ask, then, what precisely in this story attracted me. And not simply attracted: seized me by the lung and declared itself my offspring—a changeling in search of its natural mother. Do not mistake me: had I only had access to a newspaper that crucial night (the *Post*, the *News*, the *Manchester Guardian, St. Louis Post-Dispatch, Boston Herald-Traveler*, ah, which, which? and where was I? in a bar? never; buying birth control pills in the drug store? I am a believer in fertility; reading, God forbid, a *book?*), my own story would have been less logically decisive. Perhaps the sick father would have recovered. Perhaps the teacher would not have confessed to hating his father. I might have caused the silver crown to astonish even the rabbi himself. Who knows what I might have sucked out of those swindlers! The point is I would have fingered out the magical parts.

Magic—I admit it—is what I lust after. And not ordinary magic, which is what one expects of pagan peoples; their religions declare it. After all, half the world asserts that once upon a time God became a man, and moreover that whenever a priest in sacral ceremony wills it, that same God-man can climb into a little flat piece of unleavened bread. For most people nowadays it is only the *idea* of a piece of bread turning into God—but is that any better? As for me, I am drawn not to the symbol, but to the absolute magic act. I am drawn to what is forbidden.

Forbidden. The terrible Hebrew word for it freezes the tongue—*asur*: Jewish magic. Trembling, we have heard in Deuteronomy the No that applies to any slightest sniff of occult disclosure: how mighty is Moses, peering down the centuries into the endlessness of this allure! Astrologists, wizards and witches: *asur*. The Jews have no magic. For us bread may not tumble into body. Wine is wine, death is death.

And yet with what prowess we have crept down the centuries after amulets, and hidden countings of letters, and the silver crown that heals: so it is after all nothing to marvel at that my own, my beloved, subject should be the preternatural—everything anti-Moses, all things blazing with their own wonder. I long to be one of the ordinary peoples, to give up our agnostic God whom even the word "faith" insults, who cannot be imagined in any form, whom the very hope of imagining offends, who is without body and cannot enter body . . . oh, why can we not have a magic God like other peoples?

Some day I will take courage and throw over being a Jew, and then I will make a little god, a silver godlet, in the shape of a crown, which will stop death, resurrect fathers and uncles; out of its royal points gardens will burst. —That story! Mine! Stolen! I considered: was it possible to leap up on the stage with a living match and burn the manuscript on the spot, freeing the crown out of the finished tale, restoring it once more to a public account in the *Times?* But no. Fire, even the little humble wobble of a match, is too powerful a magic in such a place, among such gleaming herds. A conflagration of souls out of lust for a story! I feared so terrible a spell. All the same, he would own a carbon copy, or a photographic copy: such a man is meticulous about the storage-matter of his brain. A typewriter is a volcano. Who can stop print?

If I owned a silver godlet right now I would say: Almighty small Crown, annihilate that story; return, return the stuff of it to me.

A peculiar incident. Just as the famous writer came to the last word—"expired"—I saw the face of a goat. It was thin, white, blurry-eyed; a scraggly fur beard hung from its chin. Attached to the beard was a transparent voice, a voice like a whiteness—but I ought to explain how I came just then to be exposed to it. I was leaning against the wall of that place. The fading hiss of "expired" had all at once fevered me; I jumped from my seat between the two young people. Their perspiration had dampened the chair-arms, and the chill of their sweat, combined with the hotness of my greed for this magic story which could not be mine, turned my flesh to a sort of vapor. I rose like a heated gas, feeling insubstantial, and went to press my head against the cold side wall along the aisle. My brain was all gas, it shuddered with envy. Expired! How I wished to write a story containing that unholy sound! How I wished it was I who had come upon the silver crown . . . I must have looked like an usher, or in some fashion a factotum of the theater, with my skull drilled into the wall that way.

In any case I was taken for an official: as someone in authority who lolls on the job.

The goat-face blew a breath deep into my throat.

"I have stories. I want to give him stories."

"*What* do you want?"

"Him. Arrange it, can't you? In the intermission, what d'you say?"

I pulled away; the goat hopped after me.

"How? When?" said the goat. "Where?" His little beard had a tremor. "If he isn't available here and now, tell me his mailing address. I need criticism, advice, I need help—"

We become what we are thought to be; I became a factotum.

I said pompously, "You should be ashamed to pursue the famous. Does he know you?"

"Not exactly. I'm a cousin—"

"*His* cousin?"

"No. That rabbi's wife. She's an old lady, my mother's uncle was her father. We live in the same neighborhood."

"What rabbi?"

"The one in the papers. The one he swiped the story from."

"That doesn't oblige him to read you. You expect too much," I said. "The public has no right to a writer's private mind. Help from high places doesn't come like manna. His time is precious, he has better things to do." All this, by the way, was quotation. A famous writer—not this one—to whom I myself sent a story had once stung me with these words; so I knew how to use them.

"Did he say you could speak for him?" sneered the

goat. "Fame doesn't cow me. Even the famous bleed."

"Only when pricked by the likes of you," I retorted. "Have you been published?"

"I'm still young."

"Poets before you died first and published afterward. Keats was twenty-six, Shelley twenty-nine, Rimbaud—"

"I'm like these, I'll live forever."

"Arrogant!"

"Let the famous call me that, not you."

"At least I'm published," I protested; so my disguise fell. He saw I was nothing so important as an usher, only another unknown writer in the audience.

"Do *you* know him?" he asked.

"He spoke to me once at a cocktail party."

"Would he remember your name?"

"Certainly," I lied. The goat had speared my dignity.

"Then take only one story."

"Leave the poor man alone."

"*You* take it. Read it. If you like it—look, only if you like it!—give it to him for me."

"He won't help you."

"Why do you think everyone is like you?" he accused—but he seemed all at once submerged, as if I had hurt him. He shook out a vast envelope, pulled out his manuscript, and spitefully began erasing something. Opaque little tears clustered on his eyelashes. Either he was weeping or he was afflicted with pus. "Why do you think I don't deserve some attention?"

"Not of the great."

"Then let me at least have yours," he said.

The real usher just then came like a broom. Back! Back! Quiet! Don't disturb the reading! Before I knew it I had been swept into my seat. The goat was gone, and I was clutching the manuscript.

The fool had erased his name.

That night I read the thing. You will ask why. The newspaper was thin, the manuscript fat. It smelled of stable: a sort of fecal stink. But I soon discovered it was only the glue he had used to piece together parts of corrected pages. An amateur job.

If you are looking for magic now, do not. This was no work to marvel at. The prose was not bad, but not good either. There are young men who write as if the language were an endless bolt of yard goods—you snip off as much as you need for the length of fiction you require: one turn of the loom after another, everything of the same smoothness, the texture catches you up nowhere.

I have said "fiction." It was not clear to me whether this was fiction or not. The title suggested it was: "A Story of Youth and Homage." But the narrative was purposefully inconclusive. Moreover, the episodes could be interpreted on several "levels." Plainly it was not just a story, but meant something much more, and even that "much more" itself meant much more. This alone soured me; such techniques are learned in those hollowed-out tombstones called Classes in Writing. In my notion of these things, if you want to tell a story you tell it. I am against all these masks and tricks of metaphor and fable. That is why I am attracted to magical tales: they mean what they say; in them miracles are not symbols, they are conditional probabilities.

The goat's story was realistic enough, though self-conscious. In perfectly ordinary, mainly trite, English it pretended to be incoherent. That, as you know, is the fashion.

I see you are about to put these pages down, in fear of another plot-summary. I beg you to wait. Trust me a little. I will get through it as painlessly as possible—I promise to abbreviate everything. Or, if I turn out to be long-winded, at least to be interesting. Besides, you can see what risks I am taking. I am unfamiliar with the laws governing plagiarism, and here I am, brazenly giving away stories that are not rightfully mine. Perhaps one day the goat's story will be published and acclaimed. Or perhaps not: in either case he will recognize his plot as I am about to tell it to you, and what furies will beat in him! What if, by the time *this* story is published, at this very moment while you are reading it, I am on my back in some filthy municipal dungeon? Surely so deep a sacrifice should engage your forgiveness.

Then let us proceed to the goat's plot:

> An American student at a yeshiva in Jerusalem is unable to concentrate. He is haunted by worldly desires; in reality he has come to Jerusalem not for Torah but out of ambition. Though young and unpublished, he already fancies himself to be a writer worthy of attention. Then why not the attention of the very greatest?
>
> It happens that there lives in Jerusalem a writer who one day will win the most immense literary prize on the planet. At the time of the story he is already an old man heavy with fame, though of a rather parochial nature; he has not yet been to Stockholm—it is perhaps two years before the Nobel Prize turns him into a mythical figure. ["Turns him into a mythical figure" is an excellent example of the goat's prose, by the way.] But the student is prescient, and fame is fame. He composes a postcard:
>
> > There are only two religious
> > writers in the world. You are
> > one and I am the other. I will
> > come to visit you.
>
> It is true that the old man is religious. He wears a skullcap, he threads his tales with strands of the holy phrases. And he cannot send anyone away from his door. So when the student appears, the old writer invites him in for a glass of tea, though homage fatigues him; he would rather nap.

The student confesses that his own ambitiousness has brought him to the writer's feet; he too would wish one day to be revered as the writer himself is revered.

—I wish, says the old writer, I had been like you in my youth. I never had the courage to look into the face of anyone I admired, and I admired so many! But they were all too remote; I was very shy. I wish now I had gone to see them, as you have come to see me.

—Whom did you admire most? asks the student. In reality he has no curiosity about this or anything else of the kind, but he recognizes that such a question is vital to the machinery of praise. And though he has never read a word the old man has written, he can smell all around him, even in the old man's trousers, the smell of fame.

—The Rambam, answers the old man. —Him I admired more than anyone.

—Maimonides? exclaims the student. —But how could you visit Maimonides?

—Even in my youth, the old man assents, the Rambam had already been dead for several hundred years. But even if he had not been dead, I would have been too shy to go and see him. For a shy young man it is relieving to admire someone who is dead.

—Then to become like you, the student says meditatively, it is necessary to be shy?

—Oh yes, says the old man. —It is necessary to be shy. The truest ambition is hidden in shyness. All ambitiousness is hidden. If you want to usurp my place you must not show it, or I will only hang on to it all the more tightly. You must always walk with your head down. You must be a true *ba'al ga'avah*.

—A *ba'al ga'avah?* cries the student.—But you contradict yourself! Aren't we told that the *ba'al ga' avah* is the man whom God most despises? The self-righteous self-idolator? It's written that him alone God will cause to perish. Sooner than a murderer!

It is plain that the young man is in good command of the sources; not for nothing is he a student at the yeshiva. But he is perplexed, rattled. —How can I be like you if you tell me to be a *ba'al ga'avah?* And why would you tell me to be such a thing?

—The *ba'al ga'avah,* explains the writer, is a supplanter: the man whose arrogance is godlike, whose pride is like a tower. He is the one who most subtly turns his gaze downward to the ground, never looking at what he covets. I myself was never cunning enough to be a genuine *ba'al ga'avah;* I was always too timid for it. It was never necessary for me to feign shyness, I was naturally like that. But you are not. So you must invent a way to become a genuine *ba'al ga'avah,* so audacious and yet so ingenious that you will fool God and will live.

The student is impatient. —How does God come into this? We're talking only of ambition.

—Of course. Of *serious* ambition, however. You recall: "All that is not Torah is levity." This is the truth to be found at the end of every incident, even this one. —You see, the old man continues, my place can easily be taken. A blink, and it's yours. I will not watch over it if I forget that someone is after it. But you must make me forget.

—How? asks the student, growing cold with greed.

—By never coming here again.

—It's a joke!

—And then I will forget you. I will forget to watch over my place. And then, when I least look for it to happen, you will come and steal it. You will be so quiet, so shy, so ingenious, so audacious, I will never suspect you.

—A nasty joke! You want to get rid of me! It's mockery, you forget what it is to be young. In old age everything is easier, nothing burns inside you.

But meanwhile, inside the student's lungs, and within the veins of his wrists, a cold fog shivers.

—Nothing burns? Yes; true. At the moment, for instance, I covet nothing more lusty than my little twilight nap. I always have it right now.

—They say (the student is as cold now as a frozen path, all his veins are paths of ice), they say you're going to win the Nobel Prize! For literature!

—When I nap I sleep dreamlessly. I don't dream of such things. Come, let me help you cease to covet.

—It's hard for me to keep my head down! I'm young, I want what you have, I want to be like you!

Here I will interrupt the goat's story to apologize. I would not be candid if I did not confess that I am rewriting it; I am almost making it my own, and that will never do for an act of plagiarism. I don't mean only that I have set it more or less in order, and taken out the murk. That is only by the way. But, by sticking to what one said and what the other answered, I have broken my promise; already I have begun to bore you. Boring! Oh, the goat's story was boring! Philosophic stories make excellent lullabies.

So, going on with my own version (I hate stories with ideas hidden in them), I will spring out of paraphrase and invent what the old man does.

Right after saying "Let me help you cease to covet," he gets up and, with fuzzy sleepy steps, half-limps to a table covered by a cloth that falls to the floor. He separates the parts of the cloth, and now the darkness underneath the table takes him like a tent. In he crawls, the flaps cling, his rump makes a bulge. He calls out two words in Hebrew: *ohel shalom!* and backs out, carrying with him a large black box. It looks like a lady's hat box.

"An admirer gave me this. Only not an admirer of our

own time. A predecessor. I had it from Tchernikhovsky. The poet. I presume you know his work?"

"A little," says the student. He begins to wish he had boned up before coming.

"Tchernikhovsky was already dead when he brought me this," the old man explains. "One night I was alone, sitting right there—where you are now. I was reading Tchernikhovsky's most famous poem, the one to the god Apollo. And quite suddenly there was Tchernikhovsky. He disappointed me. He was a completely traditional ghost, you could see right through him to the wall behind. This of course made it difficult to study his features. The wall behind—you can observe for yourself—held a bookcase, so where his nose appeared to be I could read only the title of a Tractate of the Mishnah. A ghost can be seen mainly in outline, unfortunately, something like an artist's charcoal sketch, only instead of the blackness of charcoal, it is the narrow brilliance of a very fine white light. But what he carried was palpable, even heavy—this box. I was not at all terror-stricken, I can't tell you why. Instead I was bemused by the kind of picture he made against the wall—'modern,' I would have called it then, but probably there are new words for that sort of thing now. It reminded me a little of a collage: one kind of material superimposed on another kind which is utterly different. One order of creation laid upon another. Metal on tissue. Wood on hide. In this case it was a three-dimensional weight superimposed on a line—the line, or luminous congeries of lines, being Tchernikhovsky's hands, ghost hands holding a real box."

The student stares at the box. He waits like a coat eager to be shrunk.

"The fact is," continues the old writer, "I have never opened it. Not that I'm not as inquisitive as the next mortal. Perhaps more so. But it wasn't necessary.

There is something about the presence of an apparition which satisfies all curiosity forever—the deeper as well as the more superficial sort. For one thing, a ghost will tell you everything, and all at once. A ghost may *look* artistic, but there is no finesse to it, nothing indirect or calculated, nothing suggesting *raffinement*. It is as if everything gossamer had gone simply into the stuff of it. The rest is all grossness. Or else Tchernikhovsky himself, even when alive and writing, had a certain clumsiness. This is what I myself believe. All that pantheism and earth-worship! That pursuit of the old gods of Canaan! He thickened his tongue with clay. All pantheists are fools. Likewise trinitarians and gnostics of every kind. How can a piece of creation be its own Creator?

"Still, his voice had rather a pretty sound. To describe it is to be obliged to ask you to recall the sound of prattle: a baby's purr, only shaped into nearly normal cognitive speech. A most pleasing combination. He told me that he was reading me closely in Eden and approved of my stories. He had, he assured me, a number of favorites, but best of all he liked a quite short tale—no more than a notebook sketch, really—about why the Messiah will not come.

"In this story the Messiah is ready to come. He enters a synagogue and prepares to appear at the very moment he hears the congregation recite the 'I believe.' He stands there and listens, waiting to make himself visible on the last syllable of the verse 'I believe in the coming of the Messiah, and even if he tarry I will await his coming every day.' He leans against the Ark and listens, listens and leans—all the time he is straining his ears. The fact is he can hear nothing: the congregation buzzes with its own talk—hats, mufflers, business, wives, appointments, rain, lessons, the past, next week . . . the prayer is obscured, all its syllables are drowned in everydayness, and the Messiah retreats; he has not heard himself summoned.

"This, Tchernikhovsky's ghost told me, was my best story. I was at once suspicious. His baby-voice hinted at ironies, I caught a tendril of sarcasm. It was clear to me that what he liked about this story was mainly its climactic stroke: that the Messiah is prevented from coming. I had written to lament the tarrying of the Messiah; Tchernikhovsky, it seemed, took satisfaction exactly in what I mourned. 'Look here,' he tinkled at me—imagine a crow linked to a delicious little gurgle, and the whole sense of it belligerent as a prizefighter and coarse as an old waiter—'now that I'm dead, a good quarter-century of deadness under my dust, I've concluded that I'm entirely willing to have you assume my eminence. For one thing, I've been to Sweden, pulled strings with some deceased but still influential Academicians, and arranged for you to get the Nobel Prize in a year or two. Which is beyond what I ever got for myself. But I'm aware this won't interest you as much as a piece of eternity right here in Jerusalem, so I'm here to tell you you can have it. You can'—he had a babyish way of repeating things—'assume my eminence.'

"You see what I mean about grossness. I admit I was equally coarse. I answered speedily and to the point. I refused.

" 'I understand you,' he said. 'You don't suppose I'm pious enough, or not pious in the right way. I don't meet your yeshiva standards. Naturally not. You know I used to be a doctor, I was attracted to biology, which is to say to dust. Not spiritual enough for you! My Zionism wasn't of the soul, it was made of real dirt. What I'm offering you is something tangible. Have some common sense and take it. It will do for you what the Nobel Prize can't. Open the box and put on whatever's inside. Wear it for one full minute and the thing will be accomplished.' "

"For God's sake, what *was* it?" shrieks the student, shriveling into his blue city-boy shirt. With a tie: and in Jerusalem! (The student is an absurdity, a crudity. But of course I've got to have him; he's left over from the goat's story, what else am I to do?)

"Inside the box," replies the old writer, "was the most literal-minded thing in the world. From a ghost I expected as much. The whole idea of a ghost is a literal-minded conception. I've used ghosts in my own stories, naturally, but they've always had a real possibility, by which I mean an ideal possibility: Elijah, the True Messiah . . ."

"For God's sake, the box!"

"The box. Take it. I give it to you."

"What's in it?"

"See for yourself."

"Tell me first. Tchernikhovsky told *you*."

"That's a fair remark. It contains a crown."

"What kind of crown?"

"Made of silver, I believe."

"*Real* silver?"

"I've never looked on it, I've explained this. I *refused* it."

"Then why give it to me?"

"Because it's meant for that. When a writer wishes to usurp the place and power of another writer, he simply puts it on. I've explained this already."

"But if I wear it I'll become like Tchernikhovsky—"

"No, no, like me. Like me. It confers the place and power of the giver. And it's what you want, true? To be like me?"

"But this isn't what you advised a moment ago. *Then* you said to become arrogant, a *ba'al ga'avah,* and to conceal it with shyness—"

(Quite so. A muddle in the plot. That was the goat's story, and it had no silver crown in it. I am still stuck with these leftovers that cause seams and cracks in my own version. I will have to mend all this somehow. Be patient. I will manage it. Pray that I don't bungle it.)

"Exactly," says the old writer. "That's the usual way. But if you aren't able to feign shyness, what is necessary is a short cut. I warned you it would demand audacity and ingenuity. What I did not dare to do, you must have the courage for. What I turned down you can raise up. I offer you the crown. You will see what a short cut it is. Wear it and immediately you become a *ba'al ga'avah.* Still, I haven't yet told you how I managed to get rid of Tchernikhovsky's ghost. Open the box, put on the crown, and I'll tell you."

The student obeys. He lifts the box onto the table. It seems light enough, then he opens it, and at the first thrust of his hand into its interior it disintegrates, flakes off into dust, is blown off at a breath, consumed by the first alien molecule of air, like something very ancient removed from the deepest clay tomb and unable to withstand the corrosive stroke of light.

But there, in the revealed belly of the vanished box, is the crown.

It appears to be made of silver, but it is heavier than any earthly silver—it is heavy, heavy, heavy, dense as a meteorite. Puffing and struggling, the student tries to raise it up to his head. He cannot. He cannot lift even a corner of it. It is weighty as a pyramid.

"It won't budge."

"It will after you pay for it."

"You didn't say anything about payment!"

"You're right. I forgot. But you don't pay in money. You pay in a promise. You have to promise that if you decide you don't want the crown you'll take it off immediately. Otherwise it's yours forever."

"I promise."

"Good. Then put it on."

And now lightly, lightly, oh so easily as if he lifted a straw hat, the student elevates the crown and sets it on his head.

"There. You are like me. Now go away."

And oh so lightly, lightly, as easily as if the crown were a cargo of helium, the student skips through Jerusalem. He runs! He runs into a bus, a joggling mob crushed together, everyone recognizes him, even the driver: he is praised, honored, young women put out their hands to touch his collar, they pluck at his pants, his fly unzips and he zips it up again, oh fame! He gets off the bus and runs to his yeshiva. Crowds on the sidewalk, clapping. So this is what it feels like! He flies into the yeshiva like a king. Formerly no one blinked at him, the born Jerusalemites scarcely spoke to him, but now! It is plain they have all read him. He hears a babble of titles, plots, characters, remote yet familiar—look, he thinks, the crown has supplied me with a ready-made bibliography. He reaches up to his head to touch it: a flash of cold. Cold, cold, it is the coldest silver on the planet, a coldness that stabs through into his brain. Frost encases his brain, inside his steaming skull he hears more titles, more plots, names of characters, scholars, wives, lovers, ghosts, children, beggars, villages, candlesticks—what a load he carries, what inventions, what a teeming and a boiling, stories, stories, stories! His own; yet not his own. The Rosh Yeshiva comes down the stairs from his study: the Rosh Yeshiva, the Head, a bony miniaturized man grown almost entirely inward and upward into a spectacular dome, a brow shaped like the front of an academy, hollowed-out temples for porticoes, a resplendent head with round dead-end eyeglasses as denying as bottle-bottoms and curl-scribbled beard and small attachments of arms and little antlike legs thin as hairs; and the Rosh Yeshiva, who has never before let fall a syllable to this obscure tourist-pupil from America, suddenly cries out the glorious blessing reserved for finding oneself in the presence of a sage: Blessed are You, O God, Imparter of wisdom to those who fear Him! And the student in his crown understands that there now cleave to his name sublime parables interpreting the divine purpose, and he despairs, he is afraid, because suppose he were obliged to write one this minute? Suppose these titles clamoring all around him are only empty pots, and he must fill them up with stories? He runs from the yeshiva, elbows out, scattering admirers and celebrants, and makes for the alley behind the kitchen—no one ever goes there, only the old cats who scavenge in the trash barrels. But behind him—crudely sepulchral footsteps, like thumps inside a bucket, he runs, he looks back, he runs, he stops—Tchernikhovsky's ghost! From the old writer's description he can identify it easily. "A mistake," chimes the ghost, a pack of bells, "it wasn't for you."

"What!" screams the student.

"Give it back."

"What!"

"The crown," pursues the baby-purr voice of Tchernikhovsky's ghost. "I never meant for that old fellow to give it away."

"He said it was all right."

"He tricked you."

"No he didn't."

"He's sly sly sly."

"He said it would make me just like him. And I am."

"No."

"Yes!"

"Then predict the future."

"In two years, the Nobel Prize for Literature!"

"For him, not for you."

"But I'm *like* him."

" 'Like' is not the same as the same. You want to be the same? Look in the window."

The student looks into the kitchen window. Inside, among cauldrons, he can see the roil of the students in their caps, spinning here and there, in the pantry, in the Passover dish closet even, past a pair of smoky vats, in search of the fled visitor who now stares and stares until his concentration alters seeing; and instead of looking behind the pane, he follows the light on its surface and beholds a reflection. An old man is also looking into the window; the student is struck by such a torn rag of a face. Strange, it cannot be Tchernikhovsky: he is all web and wraith; and anyhow a ghost has no reflection. The old man in the looking-glass window is wearing a crown. A silver crown!

"You see?" tinkles the ghost. "A trick!"

"I'm old!" howls the student.

"Feel in your pocket."

The student feels. A vial.

"See? Nitroglycerin."

"What is this, are you trying to blow me up?"

Again the small happy soaring of the infant's grunt. "I remind you that I am a physician. When you are seized by a pulling, a knocking, a burning in the chest, a throb in the elbow-crook, swallow one of these tablets. In coronary insufficiency it relaxes the artery."

"Heart failure! Will I die? Stop! I'm young!"

"With those teeth? All gums gone? That wattle? Dotard! Bag!"

The student runs; he remembers his perilous heart; he slows. The ghost thumps and chimes behind. So they walk, a procession of two, a very old man wearing a silver crown infinitely cold, in his shadow a ghost made all of lit spider-thread, giving out now and then with baby's laughter and odd coarse curses patched together from Bible phrases; together they scrape out of the alley onto the boulevard—an oblivious population there.

"My God! No one knows me. Why don't they know me here?"

"Who should know you?" says Tchernikhovsky.

"In the bus they yelled out dozens of book titles. In the streets! The Rosh Yeshiva said the blessing for seeing a sage!"

But now in the bus the passengers are indifferent; they leap for seats; they snore in cozy spots standing up, near poles; and not a word. Not a gasp, not a squeal. Not even a pull on the collar. It's all over! A crown but no king.

"It's stopped working," says the student, mournful.

"The crown? Not on your life."

"Then you're interfering with it. You're jamming it up."

"That's more like the truth."

"Why are you following me?"

"I don't like misrepresentation."

"You mean you don't like magic."

"They're the same thing."

"Go away!"

"I never do that."

"*He* got rid of you."

"Sly sly sly. He did it with a ruse. You know how? He refused the crown. He took it but he hid it away. No one ever refused it before. Usurper! Coveter! *Ba'al ga'avah!* That's what he is."

The student protests, "But he *gave* me the crown. 'Let me help you cease to covet,' that's exactly what he said, why do you call him *ba'al ga'avah?*"

"And himself? *He's* ceased to covet, is that it? That's what you think? You think he doesn't churn saliva over the Nobel Prize? Ever since I told him they were speculating about the possibility over at the Swedish Academicians' graveyard? Day and night that's all he dreams of. He loves his little naps, you know why? To sleep, perchance to dream. He imagines himself in a brand-new splendiferous bow-tie, rear end trailing tails, wearing his skullcap out of public arrogance, his old wife up there with him dressed to the hobbledorfs—in Stockholm, with the King of Sweden! That's what he sees, that's what he dreams, he can't work, he's in a fever of coveting. You think it's different when you're old?"

"I'm not old!" the student shouts. A willful splinter, he peels himself from the bus. Oh, frail, his legs are straw, the dry knees wrap close like sheaves, he feels himself pouring out, sand from a sack. Old!

Now they are in front of the writer's house. "Age makes no matter," says the ghost, "the same, the same. Ambition levels, lust is unitary. Lust you can always count on. I'm not speaking of the carnal sort. Carnality's a brevity—don't compare wind with mountains! But lust! Teetering on the edge of the coffin there's lust. After mortality there's lust, I guarantee you. In Eden there's nothing but lust." The ghost raps on the door—with all his strength, and his strength is equal to a snowflake. Silence, softness. "Bang on the thing!" he commands, self-disgusted; sometimes he forgets he is incorporeal.

The student obeys, shivering; he is so cold now his three or six teeth clatter like chinaware against a waggling plastic bridge anchored in nothing, his ribs shake in his chest, his spine vibrates without surcease. And what of his heart? Inside his pocket he clutches the vial.

The old writer opens up. His fists are in his eyes.

"We woke you, did we?" gurgles Tchernikhovsky's ghost.

"You!"

"Me," says the ghost, satisfied. "*Ba'al ga'avah!* Spiteful! You foisted the crown on a kid."

The old writer peers. "Where?"

The ghost sweeps the student forward. "I did him the service of giving him long life. Instantly. Why wait for a good thing?"

"I don't want it! Take it back!" the student cries, snatching at the crown on his head; but it stays on. "You said I could give it back if I don't want it any more!"

Again the old writer peers. "Ah. You keep your promise. So does the crown."

"What do you mean?"

"It promised you acclaim. But it generates this pest. Everything has its price."

"Get rid of it!"

"To get rid of the ghost you have to get rid of the crown."

"All right! Here it is! Take it back! It's yours!"

The ghost laughs like a baby at the sight of a teat. "Try and take it off then."

The student tries. He tears at the crown, he flings his head upward, backward, sideways, pulls and pulls. His fingertips flame with the ferocious cold.

"How did *you* get rid of it?" he shrieks.

"I never put it on," replies the old writer.

"No, no, I mean the ghost, how did you get rid of the ghost!"

"I was going to tell you that, remember? But you ran off."

"You sent me away. It was a trick, you never meant to tell."

The ghost scolds: "No disputes!" And orders, "Tell now."

The student writhes; twists his neck; pulls and pulls. The crown stays on.

"The crown loosens," the old writer begins, "when the ghost goes. Everything dissolves together—"

"But *how?*"

"You find someone to give the crown to. That's all. You simply pass it on. All you do is agree to give away its powers to someone who wants it. Consider it a test of your own generosity."

"Who'll want it? Nobody wants such a thing!" the student shrieks. "It's stuck! Get it off! Off!"

"*You* wanted it."

"Prig! Moralist! *Ba'al ga'avah!* Didn't I come to you for advice? Literary advice, and instead you gave me this! I wanted help! You gave me metal junk! Sneak!"

"Interesting," observes the ghost, "that I myself acquired the crown in exactly the same way. I received it from Ibn Gabirol. Via ouija board. I was skeptical about the method but discovered it to be legitimate. I consulted him about some of his verse-forms. To be specific, the problem of enjambment, which is more difficult in Hebrew than in some other languages. By way of reply he gave me the crown. Out of the blue it appeared on the board—naked, so to speak, and shining oddly, like a fish without scales. Of course there wasn't any ghost attached to the crown then. I'm the first, and you don't think I *like* having to materialize thirty minutes after someone's put it on? What I need is to be left in peace in Paradise, not this business of being on call the moment someone—"

"Ibn Gabirol?" the old writer breaks in, panting, all attention. Ibn Gabirol! Sublime poet, envied beyond envy, sublimeness without heir, who would not covet the crown of Ibn Gabirol?

"He said *he* got it from Isaiah. The quality of

ownership keeps declining apparently. That's why they have me on patrol. If someone unworthy acquires it—well, that's where I put on my emanations and dig in. Come on," says the ghost, all at once sounding American, "let's go." He gives the student one of his snowflake shoves. "Where you go, I go. Where I go, you go. Now that you know the ropes, let's get out of here and find somebody who deserves it. Give it to some goy for a change. 'The righteous among the Gentiles are as judges in Israel.' My own suggestion is Oxford, Mississippi, Faulkner, William."

"Faulkner's dead."

"He is? I ought to look him up. All right then. Someone not so fancy. Norman Mailer."

"A Jew," sneers the student.

"Can you beat that. Never mind, we'll find someone. Keep away from the rot of Europe—Kafka had it once. Maybe a black. An Indian. Spic maybe. We'll go to America and look."

Moistly the old writer plucks at the ghost. "Listen, this doesn't cancel the Prize? I still get it?"

"In two years you're in Stockholm."

"And me?" cries the student. "What about me? What happens to me?"

"You wear the crown until you get someone to take it from you. Blockhead! Dotard! Don't you *listen?*" says the ghost: his accent wobbles, he elides like a Calcuttan educated in Paris.

"No one wants it! I told you! Anyone who really needs it you'll say doesn't deserve it. If he's already famous he doesn't need it, and if he's unknown you'll think he degrades it. Like me. Not fair! There's no *way* to pass it on."

"You've got a point." The ghost considers this. "That makes sense. Logic."

"So get it off me!"

"However, again you forget lust. Lust overcomes logic."

"Stop! Off!"

"The King of Sweden," muses the old writer, "speaks no Hebrew. That will be a difficulty. I suppose I ought to begin to study Swedish."

"Off! Off!" yells the student. And tugs at his head, yanks at the crown, pulling, pulling, seizing it by the cold points. He throws himself down, wedges his legs against the writer's desk, tumbling after leverage; nothing works. Then methodically he kneels, lays his head on the floor, and methodically begins to beat the crown against the wooden floor. He jerks, tosses, taps, his white head in the brilliant crown is a wild flashing hammer; then he catches at his chest; his knuckles explode; then again he beats, beats, beats the crown down. But it stays stuck, no blow can knock it free. He beats. He heaves his head. Sparks spring from the crown, small lightnings leap. Oh, his chest, his ribs, his heart! The vial, where is the vial? His hands squirm toward his throat, his chest, his pocket. And his head beats the crown down against the floor. The old head halts, the head falls, the crown stays stuck, the heart is dead.

"Expired," says the ghost of Tchernikhovsky.

Well, that should be enough. No use making up any more of it. Why should I? It is not my story. It is not the goat's story. It is no one's story. It is a story nobody wrote, nobody wants, it has no existence. What does the notion of a *ba'al ga'avah* have to do with a silver crown? One belongs to morals, the other to magic. Stealing from two disparate tales I smashed their elements one into the other. Things must be brought together. In magic all divergences are linked and locked. The fact is I forced the crown onto the ambitious student in order to punish.

To punish? Yes. In life I am, though obscure, as generous and reasonable as those whom wide glory has sweetened; earlier you saw how generously and reasonably I dealt with the goat. So I am used to being taken for everyone's support, confidante, and consolation—it did not surprise me, propped there against the wall in the dark, when the goat begged me to read his story. Why should he not? My triumph is that, in my unrenown, everyone trusts me not to lie. But I always lie. Only on paper I do not lie. On paper I punish, I am malignant.

For instance: I killed off the student to punish him for arrogance. But it is really the goat I am punishing. It is an excellent thing to punish him. Did he not make his hero a student at the yeshiva, did he not make him call himself "religious"? But what is that? What is it to be "religious"? Is religion any different from magic? Whoever intends to separate them ends in proving them to be the same.

The goat was a *ba'al ga'avah!* I understood that only a *ba'al ga'avah* would dare to write about "religion."

So I punished him for it. How? By transmuting piety into magic.

Then—and I require you to accept this with the suddenness I myself experienced it: *as if by magic*—again I was drawn to look into the goat's story; and found, on the next-to-last page, an address. He had rubbed out (I have already mentioned this) his name; but here was a street and a number:

18 Herzl Street
Brooklyn, N.Y.

A street fashioned—so to speak—after the Messiah. Here I will halt you once more to ask you to take no notice of the implications of the goat's address. It is an aside worthy of the goat himself. It is he, not I, who would grab you by the sleeve here and now in order to explain exactly who Theodore Herzl was—oh, how I despise writers who will stop a story dead for the sake of showing off! Do you care whether or not Maimonides (supposing you had ever heard of that lofty saint) tells us that the messianic age will be recognizable simply by the resumption of Jewish political independence? Does it count if, by that definition, the Messiah turns out to be none other than a Viennese journalist of the last century? Doubtless Herzl was regarded by his contemporaries as a *ba'al ga'avah* for brazening out, in a modern moment, a Hebrew principality. And who is more of a *ba'al ga'avah* than the one who usurps the Messiah's own job? Take Isaiah—was not Isaiah a *ba'al ga'avah* when he declared against observance—"I hate your feasts and your new moons"—and in the voice, no less, of the Creator Himself?

But thank God I have no taste for these notions. Already you have seen how earnestly my mind is turned toward hatred of metaphysical speculation. Practical action is my whole concern, and I have nothing but contempt for significant allusions, nuances, buried effects.

Therefore you will not be astonished at what I next undertook to do. I went—ha!—to the street of the Messiah to find the goat.

It was a place where there had been conflagrations. Rubble tentatively stood: brick on brick, about to fall. One remaining configuration of wall, complete with windows but no panes. The sidewalk underfoot stirred with crumbs, as of sugar grinding: mortar reduced to sand. A desert flushed over tumbled yards. Lintels and doors burned out, foundations squared like pebbles on a beach: in this spot once there had been cellars, stoops, houses. The smell of burned wood wandered. A civilization of mounds—who had lived here? Jews. There were no buildings left. A rectangular stucco fragment—of what? synagogue maybe—squatted in a space. There was no Number 18—only bad air, light flying in the gape and gash where the fires had driven down brick, mortar, wood, mothers, fathers, children pressing library cards inside their pockets—gone, finished.

And immediately—as if by magic—the goat!

"You!" I hooted, exactly as, in the story that never was, the old writer had cried it to Tchernikhovsky's shade.

"You've read my stuff," he said, gratified. "I knew you could find me easy if you wanted to. All you had to do was want to."

"Where do you live?"

"Number 18. I knew you'd want to."

"There isn't any 18."

He pointed. "It's what's left of the shul. No plumbing, but it still has a good kitchen in the back. I'm what you call a squatter, you don't mind?"

"Why should I mind?"

"Because I stole the idea from a book. It's this story about a writer who lives in an old tenement with his typewriter and the tenement's about to be torn down—"

The famous author who had written about the magic crown had written that story too; I reflected how some filch their fiction from life, others filch their lives from fiction. What people call inspiration is only pilferage. "You're not living in a tenement," I corrected, "you're living in a synagogue."

"What used to be. It's a hole now, a sort of cave. The Ark is left though, you want to see the Ark?"

I followed him through shards. There was no front door.

"What happened to this neighborhood?" I said.

"The Jews went away."

"Who came instead?"

"Fire."

The curtain of the Ark dangled in charred shreds. I peered inside the orifice which had once closeted the Scrolls: all blackness there, and the clear sacrificial smell of things that have been burned.

"See?" he said. "The stove works. It's the old wood-burning kind. For years they didn't use it here, it just sat. And now—resurrection." Ah: the clear sacrificial smell was potatoes baking.

"Don't you have a job?"

"I write, I'm a writer. And no rent to pay anyhow."

"How do you drink?"

"You mean *what.*" He held up a full bottle of Schapiro's kosher wine. "They left a whole case intact."

"But you can't wash, you can't even use the toilet."

"I pee and do my duty in the yard. Nobody cares. This is freedom, lady."

"Dirt," I said.

"What's dirt to Peter is freedom to Paul. Did you like my story? Sit."

There was actually a chair, but it had a typewriter on it. The goat did not remove it.

"How do you take a bath?" I persisted.

"Sometimes I go to my cousin's. I told you. The rabbi's wife."

"The rabbi from this synagogue?"

"No, he's moved to Woodhaven Boulevard. That's Queens. All the Jews from here went to Queens, did you know that?"

"*What* rabbi's wife?" I blew out, exasperated.

"I *told* you. The one with the crown. The one they wrote about in the papers. The one *he* lifted the idea of that story from. A rip-off that was, my cousin ought to sue."

Then I remembered. "All stories are rip-offs," I said. "Shakespeare stole his plots. Dostoyevski dug them out of the newspaper. Everybody steals. The Decameron's stolen. Whatever looks like invention is theft."

"Great," he said, "that's what I need. Literary talk."

"What did you mean, you knew I would want to come?—Believe me, I didn't come for literary talk."

"You bet. You came because of my cousin. You came because of the crown."

I was amazed: instantly it coursed in on me that this was true. I had come because of the crown; I was in pursuit of the crown.

I said: "I don't care about the crown. I'm interested in the rabbi himself. The crown-blesser. What I care about is the psychology of the thing."

This word—"psychology"—made him cackle. "He's in jail, I thought you knew that. They got him for fraud."

"Does his wife still have any crowns around?"

"One."

"Here's your story," I said, handing it over. "Next time leave your name in. You don't have to obliterate it, rely on the world for that."

The pus on his eyelids glittered. "Alex will obliterate the world, not vice versa."

"How? By bombing it with stories? The first anonymous obliteration. The Flood without a by-line," I said. "At least everything God wrote was publishable. Alex what?"

"Goldflusser."

"You're a liar."

"Silbertsig."

"Cut it out."

"Kupferman. Bleifischer. Bettler. Kenigman."

"All that's mockery. If your name's a secret—"

"I'm lying low, hiding out, they're after me because I helped with the crowns."

I speculated, "You're the one who made them."

"No. She did that."

"Who?"

"My cousin. The rabbi's wife. She crocheted them. What he did was go buy the form—you get it from a costume loft, stainless steel. She used to make these little pointed sort of *gloves* for it, to protect it, see, and the shine would glimmer through, and then the customer would get to keep the crown-cover, as a sort of guarantee—"

"My God," I said, "what's all that about, why didn't *she* go to jail?"

"Crocheting isn't a crime."

"And you?" I said. "What did you do in all that?"

"Get customers. Fraudulent solicitation, that's a crime."

He took the typewriter off the chair and sat down. The wisp of beard wavered. "Didn't you like my story?" he accused. The pages were pressed with an urgency between his legs.

"No. It's all fake. It doesn't matter if you've been to Jerusalem. You've got the slant of the place all wrong. It doesn't matter about the yeshiva either. It doesn't matter if you really went to see some old geezer over there, you didn't get anything right. It's a terrible story."

"Where do you come off with that stuff?" he burst out. "Have *you* been to Jerusalem? Have *you* seen the inside of a yeshiva?"

"No."

"So!"

"I can tell when everything's fake," I said. "What I mean by fake is raw. When no one's ever used it before, it's something new under the sun, a whole new combination, that's bad. A real story is whatever you can predict, it has to be familiar, anyhow you have to know how it's going to come out, no exotic new material, no unexpected flights—"

He rushed out at me: "What you want is to bore people!"

"I'm a very boring writer," I admitted; out of politeness I kept from him how much his story, and even my own paraphrase of it, had already bored me. "But in *principle* I'm right. The only good part in the whole thing was explaining about the *ba'al ga'avah.* People hate to read foreign words, but at least it's ancient wisdom. Old, old stuff."

Then I told him how I had redesigned his story to include a ghost.

He opened the door of the stove and threw his manuscript in among the black-skinned potatoes.

"Why did you do that?"

"To show you I'm no *ba'al ga'avah.* I'm humble enough to burn up what somebody doesn't like."

I said suspiciously, "You've got other copies."

"Sure. Other potatoes too."

"Look," I said, riding malice, "it took me two hours to find this place, I have to go to the yard."

"You want to take a leak? Come over to my cousin's. It's not far. My cousin's lived in this neighborhood sixty years."

Furiously I went after him. He was a crook leading me to the house of crooks. We walked through barrenness and canker, a ruined city, store-windows painted black, one or two curtained by gypsies, some boarded, barred, barbed, old newspapers rolling in the gutter, the sidewalks speckled with viscous blotch. Overhead a smell like kerosene, the breath of tenements. The cousin's toilet stank as if no one had flushed it in half a century; it had one of those tanks high up, attached to the ceiling, a perpetual drip running down the pull chain. The sink was in the kitchen. There was no soap; I washed my hands with Ajax powder while the goat explained me to his cousin.

"She's interested in the crown," he said.

"Out of business," said the cousin.

"Maybe for her."

"Not doing business, that's all. For nobody whatsoever."

"I'm not interested in buying one," I said, "just in finding out."

"Crowns is against the law."

"For healing," the goat argued, "not for showing. She knows the man who wrote that story. You remember about that guy, I told you, this famous writer who took—"

"Who took! Too much fame," said the cousin, "is why Saul sits in jail. Before newspapers and stories we were left in peace, we helped people peacefully." She condemned me with an oil-surfaced eye, the colorless slick of the ripening cataract. "My husband, a holy man, him they put in jail. Him! A whole year, twelve months! A man like that! Brains, a saint—"

"But he fooled people," I said.

"In helping is no fooling. Out, lady. You had to pee, you peed. You needed a public facility, very good, now out. I don't look for extra customers for my toilet bowl."

"Goodbye," I said to the goat.

"You think there's hope for me?"

"Quit writing about ideas. Stay out of the yeshiva, watch out for religion. Don't make up stories about famous writers."

"Listen," he said—his nose was speckled with pustules of lust, his nostrils gaped—"you didn't like that one, I'll give you another. I've got plenty more, I've got a crateful."

"What are you talking," said the cousin.

"She knows writers," he said, "in person. She knows how to get things published."

I protested, "I can hardly get published myself—"

"You published something?" said the cousin.

"A few things, not much."

"Alex, bring Saul's box."

"That's not the kind of stuff," the goat said.

"Definitely. About expression I'm not so concerned like you. What isn't so regular, anyone with a desire and a pencil can fix it."

The goat remonstrated, "What Saul has is something else, it's not *writing*—"

"With connections," said the cousin, "nothing is something else, everything is writing. Lady, in one box I got my husband's entire holy life work. The entire theory of healing and making the dead ones come back for a personal appearance. We sent maybe to twenty printing houses, nothing doing. You got connections, I'll show you something."

"Print," I reminded her, "is what you said got the rabbi in trouble."

"Newspapers. Lies. False fame. Everything with a twist. You call him rabbi, who made from him a rabbi? The entire world says rabbi, so let it be rabbi. There he sits in jail, a holy man what did nothing his whole life to harm. Whatever a person asked for, this was what he gave. Whatever you wanted to call him, this was what he became. Alex! Take out Saul's box, it's in the bottom of the dresser with the crown."

"The crown?" I said.

"The crown is nothing. What's something is Saul's brain. Alex!"

The goat shut his nostrils. He gave a snicker and disappeared. Through the kitchen doorway I glimpsed a sagging bed and heard a drawer grind open.

He came back lugging a carton with a picture of tomato cans on it. On top of it lay the crown. It was gloved in a green pattern of peephole diamonds.

"Here," said the cousin, "is Saul's ideas. Listen, that famous writer what went to steal from the papers—a fool. If he could steal what's in Saul's brain what would he need a newspaper? Read!" She dipped a fist into a hiss of sheets and foamed up a sheaf of them. "You'll see, the world will rush to put in print. The judge at the trial—I said to him, look in Saul's box, you'll see the truth, no fraud. If they would read Saul's papers, not only would he not sit in jail, the judge with hair growing from his ears they would throw out!"

I looked at the goat; he was not laughing. He reached out and put the crown on my head.

It felt lighter than I imagined. It was easy to forget you were wearing it.

I read:

> Why does menkind not get what they wish for? This is an easy solution. He is used to No. Always No. So it comes he is afraid to ask.

"The power of positive thinking," I said. "A philosopher."

"No, no," the cousin intervened, "not a philosopher,

what do philosophers know to heal, to make real shadows from the dead?"

Through thinning threads of beard the goat said, "not a philosopher."

I read:

> Everything depends what you ask. Even you're not afraid to ask, plain asking is not sufficient. If you ask in a voice, there got to be an ear to listen in. The ear of Ha-shem, King of the Universe. (His Name we don't use it every minute like a shoelace.) A Jew don't go asking Ha-shem for inside information, for what reason He did this, what ideas He got on that, how come He let happen such-and-such a pogrom, why a good person loved by one and all dies with cancer, and a lousy bastard he's rotton to his partner and cheats and plays the numbers, this fellow lives to 120. With questions like this don't expect no replies, Ha-shem don't waste breath on trash from fleas. Ha-shem says, My secrets are My secrets, I command you what you got to do, the rest you leave to Me. This is no news that He don't reveal His deepest business. From that territory you get what you deserve, silence.

"What are you up to?" said the goat.

"Silence."

"Ssh!" said the cousin. "Alex, so let her read in peace!"

> For us, not one word. He shuts up, His mouth is locked. So how come G–d conversed in history with Adam, with Abraham, with Moses? All right, you can argue that Moses and Abraham was worth it to G–d to listen to, what they said Ha-shem wanted to hear. After all they fed Him back His own ideas. An examination, and already they knew the answers. Smart guys, in the whole history of menkind no one else like these couple of guys. But with

> Adam, new and naked with no clothes on, just when the whole world was born, was Adam different from me and you? What did Adam know? Even right from wrong he didn't know yet. And still G–d thought, to Adam it's worthwhile to say a few words, I'm not wasting my breath. So what was so particular about Adam that he got Ha-shem's attention, and as regards me and you He don't blink an eye? Adam is better than me and you? We don't go around like a nudist colony, between good and lousy we already know what's what, with or without apples. To me and you G–d should also talk!

"You're following?" the cousin urged. "You see what's in Saul's brain? A whole box full like this, and sits in jail!"

> But when it comes wishes, when it comes dreams, who says No? Who says Ha-shem stops talking? Wishes, dreams, imaginations—like fishes in the head. Ha-shem put in Joseph's head two good dreams, were they lies? The truth and nothing but the truth! Q.E.D. To Adam Ha-shem spoke one way, and when He finishes with Moses he talks another way. In a dream, in a wish. That *apikoros* Sigmund Freud, he also figured this out. Whomever says Sigmund Freud stinks from sex, they're mistaken. A wish is the voice, a dream is the voice, an imagination is the voice, all is the voice of Ha-shem the Creator. Naturally a voice is a biological thing, who says No? Whatsoever happens inside the human is a biological thing.

"What are you up to?" the goat asked again.

"Biology."

"Don't laugh. A man walked in here shaking all over, walked out O.K., I saw it myself."

The cousin said mournfully, "A healer."

"I wrote a terrific story about that guy, I figured what had was cystic fibrosis, I can show you—"

"There isn't any market for medical stories," I said.

"This was a miracle story."

"There are no miracles."

"That's right!" said the cousin. She dug down again into the box. "One time only, instead of plain writing down, Saul made up a story on this subject exactly. On a yellow piece paper. Aha, here. Alex, read aloud."

The goat read:

> One night in the middle of dim stars Ha-shem said, No more miracles! An end with miracles, I already did enough, from now on nothing.
>
> So a king makes an altar and bows down. "O Ha-shem, King of the Universe, I got a bad war on my hands and I'm taking a beating. Make a miracle and save the whole country." Nothing doing, no miracle.
>
> Good, says Ha-shem, this is how it's going to be from now on.
>
> So along comes the Germans, in the camp they got a father and a little son maybe twelve years old. And the son is on the list to be gassed tomorrow. So the father runs around to find a German to bribe, G–d knows what he's got to bribe him with, maybe his wife's diamond ring that he hid somewhere and they didn't take it away yet. And he fixes up the whole thing, tomorrow he'll bring the diamond to the German and they'll take the boy off the list and they won't kill him. They'll slip in some other boy instead and who will know the difference?
>
> Well, so that could be the end, but it isn't. All day after everything's fixed up, the father is thinking and thinking, and in the middle of the night he goes to an old rabbi that's in the camp also, and he tells the rabbi he's going to save his little son.
>
> And the rabbi says, "So why come to me? You made your decision already." The father says, "Yes, but they'll put another boy in his place." The rabbi says,

"Instead of Isaac, Abraham put a ram. And that was for G–d. You put another child, and for what? To feed Moloch." The father asks, "What is the law on this?" "The law is, Don't kill."

The next day the father don't bring the bribe. And his eyes don't never see his beloved little child again. Well, so that could be the end, but it isn't. Ha-shem looks at what's happening, here is a man what didn't save his own boy so he wouldn't be responsible with killing someone else. Ha-shem says to Himself, I made a miracle anyhow. I blew in one man so much power of My commandments that his own flesh and blood he lets go to Moloch, so long he shouldn't kill. That I created even one such person like this is a very great miracle, and I didn't even notice I was doing it. So now positively no more.

And after this the destruction continues, no interruptions. Not only the son is gassed, but also the father, and also the boy what they would have put in his place. And also and also and also, until millions of bones of alsos goes up in smoke. About miracles Ha-shem don't change his mind except by accident. So the question menkind has to ask their conscience is this: If the father wasn't such a good commandment-keeper that it's actually a miracle to find a man like this left in the world, what could happen instead? And if only one single miracle could slip through before G–d notices it, which one? Suppose this father didn't use up the one miracle, suppose the miracle is that G–d will stop the murderers altogether, suppose! Instead: nothing doing, the father on account of one kid eats up the one miracle that's lying around loose. For the sake of one life, the whole world is lost.

But on this subject, what's written in our holy books? What the sages got to say? The sages say different: If you save one life only, it's like the whole world is saved. So which is true? Naturally, whatever's written is what's true. What does this prove? It proves that if you talk miracle, that's when everything becomes false. Men and women! Remember! No stories from miracles! No stories and no belief!

"You see?" said the cousin. "Here you have Saul's theories exactly. Whoever says miracles, whoever says magic, tells a lie. On account of a lie a holy man sits in a cage."

"And the crown?" I asked.

She ignored this. "You'll help to publish. You'll give to the right people, you'll give to connections—"

"But why? Why do you need this?"

"What's valuable you give away, you don't keep it for yourself. Listen, is the Bible a secret? The whole world takes from it. Is Talmud a secret? Whatever's a lie should be a secret, not what's holy and true!"

I appealed to the goat. He was licking his fingertips. "I can't digest any of this—"

"You haven't had a look at Saul," he said, "that's why."

The cousin said meanly, "I saw you put on her the crown."

"She wants it."

"The crown is nothing."

"She wants it."

"Then show her Saul."

"You mean in prison?" I said.

"In the bedroom on the night table."

The goat fled. This time he returned carrying a small gilded tin frame. In it was a snapshot of another bearded man.

"Look closely."

But instead of examining the photograph, I all at once wanted to study the goat's cousin. She was one of those tiny twig-thin old women who seem to enlarge the more you get used to their voices. It was as if her whine and her whirr were a pump, and pumped her up; she was now easily as tall as I (though I am myself not very tall) and expanding curiously. She was wearing a checked nylon housedress and white socks in slippers, above which bulged purplish varicose nodules. Her eyes were terribly magnified by metal-rimmed lenses, and looked out at me with the vengefulness of a pair of greased platters. I was astonished to see that a chromium crown had buried itself among the strings of her wandering hairs: having been too often dyed ebony, they were slipping out of their follicles and onto her collarbone. She had an exaggerated widow's peak and was elsewhere a little bit bald.

The goat too wore a crown.

"I thought there was only one left," I objected.

"Look at Saul, you'll see the only one."

The man in the picture wore a silver crown. I recognized him, though the light was shut off in him and the space of his flesh was clearly filled.

"Who is this?" I said.

"Saul."

"But I've seen him!"

"That's right," the cousin said.

"Because you wanted to," said the goat.

"The ghost I put in your story," I reminded him, "this is what it looked like."

The cousin breathed. "You published that story?"

"It's not even written down."

"Whose ghost was it?" asked the goat.

"Tchernikhovsky's. The Hebrew poet. A *ba'al ga' avah*. He wrote a poem called 'Before the Statue of Apollo.' In the last line God is bound with leather thongs."

"Who binds him?"

"The Jews. With their phylacteries. I want to read more," I said.

The two of them gave me the box. The little picture

they set on the kitchen table, and they stood over me in their twinkling crowns while I splashed my hands through the false rabbi's stories. Some were already browning at the margins, in ink turned violet, some were on lined school paper, written with a ball-point pen. About a third were in Yiddish; there was even a thin notebook all in Russian; but most were pressed out in pencil in an immigrant's English on all kinds of odd loose sheets, the insides of old New Year greeting cards, the backs of cashiers' tapes from the supermarket, in one instance the ripped-out leather womb of an old wallet.

Saul's ideas were:

> sorcery, which he denied.
> levitation, which he doubted.
> magic, which he sneered at.
> miracles, which he denounced.
> healing, which he said belonged in hospitals.
> instant cures, which he said were fancies and delusions.
> the return of deceased loved ones, which he said were wishful hallucinations.
> the return of dead enemies, which ditto.
> plural gods, which he disputed.
> demons, which he derided.
> amulets, which he disparaged and repudiated.
> Satan, from which hypothesis he scathingly dissented.

He ridiculed everything. He was a rationalist.

"It's amazing," I said, "that he looks just like Tchernikhovsky."

"What does Tchernikhovsky look like?" one of the two crowned ones asked me; I was no longer sure which.

"I don't know, how should I know? Once I saw his picture in an anthology of translations, but I don't remember it. Why are there so many crowns in this room? What's the point of these crowns?"

Then I found the paper on crowns:

> You take a real piece mineral, what kings wear. You put it on, you become like a king. What you wish, you get. But what you get you shouldn't believe in unless it's real. How do you know when something's real? If it lasts. How long? This depends. If you wish for a Pyramid, it should last as long like a regular Pyramid lasts. If you wish for long life, it should last as long like your own grandfather. If you wish for a Magic Crown, it should last as long like the brain what it rests on.

I interrupted myself: "Why doesn't he wish himself out of prison? Why didn't he wish himself out of getting sentenced?"

"He lets things take their course."

Then I found the paper on things taking their course:

> From my own knowledge I knew a fellow what loved a woman, Beylinke, and she died. So he looked and looked for a twin to this Beylinke, and it's no use, such a woman don't exist. Instead he married a different type altogether, and he made her change her name to Beylinke and make love on the left side, like the real Beylinke. And if he called Beylinke! and she forgot to answer (her name was Ethel) he gave her a good knock on the back, and one day he knocked hard into the kidney and she got a growth and she died. And all he got from his forcing was a lonesome life.
>
> Everything is according to destiny, you can't change nothing. Not that anybody can know what happens before it happens, not even Ha-shem knows which dog will bite which cat next week in Persia.

"Enough," said one of the two in the crowns. "You read and you took enough. You ate enough and you drank enough from this juice. Now you got to pay."

"To pay?"

"The payment is, to say thank you what we showed you everything, you take and you publish."

"Publishing isn't the same as Paradise."

"For some of us it is," said one.

"She knows from Paradise!" scoffed the other.

They thrust the false rabbi's face into my face.

"It isn't English, it isn't even coherent, it's inconsistent, it's crazy, nothing hangs together, nobody in his right mind would—"

"Connections you got."

"No."

"That famous writer."

"A stranger."

"Then somebody else."

"There's no one. I can't make magic—"

"*Ba'al ga'avah!* You're better than Saul? Smarter? Cleverer? You got better ideas? You, a nothing, they print, and he sits in a box?"

"I looked up one of your stories. It stank, lady. The one called 'Usurpation.' Half of it's swiped, you ought to get sued. You don't know when to stop. You swipe other people's stories and you go on and on, on and on, I fell asleep over it. Boring! Long-winded!"

The mass of sheets pitched into my lap. My fingers flashed upward: there was the crown, with its crocheted cover, its blunted points. Little threads had gotten tangled in my hair. If I tugged the roots would shriek. Tchernikhovsky's paper eyes looked frightened. Crevices opened on either side of his nose and from the left nostril the gray bone of his skull poked out, a cheekbone like a pointer.

"I don't have better ideas," I said. "I'm not interested in ideas, I don't care about ideas. I hate ideas. I only care about stories."

"Then take Saul's stories!"

"Trash. Justice and mercy. He tells you how to live, what to do, the way to think. Righteousness fables, morality tales. Didactic stuff. Rabbinical trash," I said. "What I mean is *stories*. Even you," I said to the goat, "wanting to write about writers! Morality, morality! You people eat yourself up with morality and mortality!"

"What else should a person eat?"

Just then I began to feel the weight of the crown. It pressed unerringly into the secret tunnels of my brain. A pain like a grief leaped up behind my eyes, up through the temples, up, up, into the marrow of the crown. Every point of it was a spear, a nail. The crown was no different from the bone of my head. The false rabbi Tchernikhovsky tore himself from the tin prison of his frame and sped to the ceiling as if gassed. He had bluish teeth and goblin's wings made of brown leather. Except for the collar and cravat that showed in the photograph, below his beard he was naked. His testicles were leathery. His eyeballs were glass, like a doll's. He was solid as a doll; I was not so lightheaded as to mistake him for an apparition. His voice was as spindly as a harpsichord: "Choose!"

"Between what and what?"

"The Creator or the creature. God or god. The Name of Names or Apollo."

"Apollo," I said on the instant.

"Good," he tinkled, "blessings," he praised me, "flowings and flowings, streams, brooks, lakes, waters out of waters."

Stories came from me then, births and births of tellings, narratives and suspenses, turning-points and palaces, foam of the sea, mermen sewing, dragons pullulating out of quicksilver, my mouth was a box, my ears flowed, they gushed legends and tales, none of them of my own making, all of them acquired, borrowed, given, taken, inherited, stolen, plagiarized, usurped, chronicles and sagas invented at the beginning of the world by the offspring of giants copulating with the daughters of men. A king broke out of the shell of my left eye and a queen from the right one, the box of my belly lifted its scarred lid to let out frogs and swans, my womb was cleft and stories burst free of their balls of blood. Stories choked the kitchen, crept up the toilet tank, replenished the bedroom, knocked off the goat's crown, knocked off the cousin's crown, my own crown in its coat contended with the vines and tangles of my hair, the false rabbi's beard had turned into strips of leather, into whips, the whips struck at my crown, it slid to my forehead, the whips curled round my arm, the crown sliced the flesh of my forehead.

At last it fell off.

The cousin cried out her husband's name.

"Alex," I called to the goat: the name of a conqueror, Aristotle's pupil, the arrogant god-man.

In the hollow streets which the Jews had left behind there were scorched absences, apparitions, usurpers. Someone had broken the glass of the kosher butcher's abandoned window and thrown in a pig's head, with anatomical tubes still dripping from the neck.

When we enter Paradise there will be a cage for story-writers, who will be taught as follows:

All that is not Law is levity.

But we have not yet ascended. The famous writer has not. The goat has not. The false rabbi has not; he sits out his year. A vanity press is going to bring out his papers. The bill for editing, printing, and binding will be $1,847.45. The goat's cousin will pay for it from a purse in the bottom bowel of the night table.

The goat inhabits the deserted synagogue, drinking wine, littering the yard with his turds. Occasionally he attends a public reading. Many lusts live in his chin-hairs, like lice.

Only Tchernikhovsky and the shy old writer of Jerusalem have ascended. The old writer of Jerusalem is a fiction; murmuring psalms, he snacks on leviathan and polishes his Prize with the cuff of his sleeve. Tchernikhovsky eats nude at the table of the nude gods, clean-shaven now, his limbs radiant, his youth restored, his sex splendidly erect, the discs of his white ears sparkling, a convivial fellow; he eats without self-restraint from the celestial menu, and when the Sabbath comes (the Sabbath of Sabbaths, which flowers every seven centuries in the perpetual Sabbath of Eden), as usual he avoids the congregation of the faithful before the Footstool and the Throne. Then the taciturn little Canaanite idols call him, in the language of the spheres, kike.

Are You a Doctor?

Raymond Carver

RAYMOND CARVER was born in Clatskanie, Oregon, and grew up in Yakima, Washington. His stories have appeared in *Esquire, Harper's Bazaar, The Iowa Review*, and other magazines. He has published two books of stories, *Will You Please Be Quiet, Please?* which was a National Book Award nominee in fiction in 1977, and *Furious Seasons.* He has published two books of poems, *Winter Insomnia* and *At Night the Salmon Move*, and is currently a professor of English and teaching in the Creative Writing Program at Syracuse University.

FOR GORDON LISH

In slippers, pajamas, and robe, he hurried out of the study when the telephone began to ring. Since it was past ten, he assumed it was his wife. She called—late like this, after a few drinks—each night she was out of town. She was a buyer, and all this week she had been away on business.

"Hello, dear. Hello," he said again.

"Who is this?" a woman asked.

"Well, who is this? What number do you want?"

"Just a minute," the woman said. "It's 273-8063."

"That's my number," he said. "How did you get it?"

"I don't know. It was written down on a piece of paper when I got in from work," the woman said.

"Who wrote it down?"

"I don't know for sure. The baby sitter, I guess. It must be her."

"Didn't you ask her?" he said.

"No. She doesn't have a phone either, or I'd call."

"Well, I don't know how she got it," he said, "but it's my telephone number, and it's unlisted. I'd appreciate it if you'd just toss it away. Hello? Did you hear me?"

"Yes, I heard," the woman said.

"Is there anything else then?" he said. "It's late and I'm busy." He hadn't meant to be curt, but one couldn't take chances. He sat down on the chair by the telephone and said, "I didn't mean to be short. I only meant that it's late, and I'll admit I'm concerned how you happen to have my number." He pulled off his slipper and began massaging his foot, waiting.

"I don't know either," she said. "I told you I just found the number written down, no note or anything. I'll ask Annette—that's the sitter—when I see her tomorrow. I didn't mean to disturb you. I only just now found the note. I've been in the kitchen ever since I came in from work."

"It's all right," he said. "Forget it. Just throw it away or something and forget it. There's no problem, so don't worry." He moved the received from one ear to the other.

"You sound like a nice man," the woman said.

"Do I? Well, that's nice of you to say." He knew he

should hang up now, but it was good to hear a voice, even his own, in the quiet room.

"Oh, yes," she said. "I can tell."

He let go his foot.

"What's your name, if you don't mind my asking?" she said.

"My name is Arnold," he said.

"And what's your first name?" she said.

He hesitated. "Arnold is my first name."

"Oh, forgive me," she said. "Arnold is you *first* name? And your second name, Arnold? What's your second name?"

"I really must hang up," he said.

"Arnold, for goodness sake, I'm Clara Holt. Now your name is Mr. Arnold what?"

"Arnold Breit," he said, and then quickly added, "Clara Holt. That's nice. But I really think I should hang up now, Miss Holt. I'm expecting a call."

"I'm sorry, Arnold, I didn't mean to take up your time," she said.

"That's all right," he said. "It's been nice talking to you."

"You're kind to say that, Arnold."

"Will you hold the phone a minute?" he said. "I have to check on something." He went into the study for a cigar, took a minute lighting it with the desk lighter, then removed his glasses and looked at himself in the mirror over the fireplace. When he returned to the telephone he was half afraid she might be off the line.

"Hello."

"Hello, Arnold," she said.

"I thought you might have hung up."

"Oh no," she said.

"About your having my number," he said. "Nothing to worry over, I don't suppose. Just throw it away, I suppose."

"I will, Arnold," she said.

"Well, I must say good-by then."

"Yes, of course," she said. "I'll say good night now."

He heard her draw breath.

"I know I'm imposing, Arnold, but do you think we could meet somewhere we could talk? Just for a few minutes?"

"I'm afraid that's impossible," he said.

"Just for a minute, Arnold. My finding your number and everything. I feel, I feel strongly about this, Arnold."

"I'm an old man," he said.

"Oh, you're not," she said.

He let it go at that.

"Could we meet somewhere, Arnold?" Then: "You see, I haven't told you everything. There's something else."

"What do you mean?" he said. "What is this exactly? Hello?"

She had hung up.

When he was preparing for bed, his wife called, somewhat intoxicated he could tell, and they chatted for a while, but he said nothing about the other call. Later, as he was turning the covers down, the telephone rang again.

He picked up the receiver. "Hello! Arnold Breit speaking."

"Arnold, I'm sorry we got cut off. As I was saying, I think it's important we meet."

The next afternoon as he put the key into the lock, he could hear the telephone ringing. He put his brief case down and, still in his hat, coat, and gloves, hurried over to the end table and picked up the receiver.

"Arnold, I'm sorry to bother you again," the woman

said. "But you must come to my house tonight around nine or nine-thirty. Can you do that much for me, Arnold?"

His heart moved when he heard her use his name. "I couldn't do that," he said.

"Please, Arnold," she said. "It's important or I wouldn't be asking. I can't leave the house tonight, because my daughter is sick with a cold. Cheryl is sick, and now I'm afraid for the boy."

"And your husband?" He waited.

"I'm not married," she said. "You will come, won't you?"

"I can't promise," he said.

"I implore you to come," she said. Then she gave him the address and hung up.

" 'I implore you to come,' " he repeated, still holding the receiver. He slowly took off his gloves and then his coat. He felt he had to be careful. He went to wash up. When he looked in the bathroom mirror he discovered the hat. It was then that he made the decision to go to see her, and he took off his hat and glasses and began to soap his face. Then he checked his nails.

"You're sure this is the right street?" he asked the driver.

"This is the street and there's the house," the driver said.

"Keep going," he said. "Let me out at the end of the block."

He paid the driver. Lights from the upstairs windows illuminated the balconies, and he could see planters sitting on the balustrades, here and there a piece of lawn furniture. At one balcony a large man in a sweater leaned on his arms over the railing and watched him walk toward the door.

He pushed the button under *C. Holt*. The buzzer sounded, and he quickly stepped to the door and entered. He climbed the stairs slowly, stopping to rest briefly at each landing. He remembered the hotel in Luxembourg, the five flights he and his wife had climbed so many years ago. He felt a sudden pain in his side, imagined heart trouble, and imagined his legs folding under him and a loud fall to the bottom of the stairs. He took out his handkerchief and wiped his forehead, then removed his glasses and began wiping the lenses, waiting for his heart to quiet.

He looked down the hall. For an apartment house of this size, it seemed unusually quiet. He stopped at her door, removed his hat, and knocked lightly. The door opened a crack to reveal a plump little girl in pajamas.

"Are you Arnold Breit?" she said.

"Yes, I am," he said. "Is your mother home?"

"She said for you to come in. She said she went to the drugstore for some cough syrup and aspirin."

He shut the door behind him. "What is your name? Your mother told me, but I forgot."

When the girl said nothing, he tried again.

"Cheryl," she said. "C-h-e-r-y-l."

"Yes, now I remember. Well, I was close, you must admit."

She sat on a hassock across the room and looked at him.

"So you're sick, are you?" he said.

She shook her head.

"Not sick?"

"No," she said.

He looked around. The room was lighted by a brass floor lamp that had a large ashtray and a magazine rack affixed to the pole. A television set stood against the far wall. It was on with the volume down. A narrow hall next to the kitchen led to the back of the apartment. The furnace was up, the air close with a medicinal smell. A number of hairpins and rollers lay on the coffee table. A pink bathrobe hung over the back of a couch.

He looked at the child again, then raised his eyes toward the kitchen and the glass doors that gave off the kitchen onto the balcony. The doors stood slightly ajar, and a little chill went through him as he recalled the large man in the sweater.

"Mama went out for a minute," the child said, as if suddenly waking up.

He leaned forward on his toes, hat in hand, and stared at her. "I think I'd better go," he said.

A key turned in the lock, the door swung open, and a small, pale, freckled woman of about thirty entered carrying a paper sack.

"Arnold? I'm glad to see you." She glanced at him quickly, uneasily, and shook her head gently from side to side as she walked out to the kitchen with the sack. He heard a cupboard door shut. The child sat on the hassock and watched him. He leaned his weight first on one leg and then the other, then placed the hat on his head and removed it with the same gesture as the woman reappeared.

"Are you a doctor?" she asked suddenly.

"No," he said startled. "No, I am not."

"Cheryl is sick, you see. I thought I'd ask. Why didn't you take the man's coat?" she said, turning to the child. "Please forgive her. We're not used to company."

He was embarrassed. "I can't stay," he said. "I really shouldn't have come."

"Please sit down," she said. "We can't talk like this. Let me give her some medicine first. Then we can talk."

"I really must go," he said. "From the tone of your

voice, I thought there was something urgent. But I really must go." He looked down at his hands and was aware he had been gesturing feebly.

"I'll put on tea water," he heard her say, as if she hadn't been listening. "Then I'll give Cheryl her medicine, and then we can talk."

She took the child by the shoulders and steered her into the kitchen. He saw the woman pick up a spoon, open a bottle of something after scanning the label, and pour out two doses.

"Now you say good night to Mr. Breit, honey, and go to your room."

He nodded to the child and then followed the woman to the kitchen. He did not take the chair she indicated, but instead one that let him face the balcony, the bedroom hall, and the small living room. "Do you mind if I smoke a cigar?" he asked.

"I don't mind," she said. "I don't think it will bother me, Arnold. Please do."

He decided against it. He put his hands on his knees, leaned foward, and gave his face a serious expression. "This is still very much of a mystery to me," he said. "It's quite out of the ordinary, I assure you."

"I understand, Arnold," she said. "You'd probably like to hear the story of how I got your number?"

"I would indeed," he said.

They sat across from each other waiting for the water to boil. He could hear the television. He looked around the kitchen and then out toward the balcony again. The water began to bubble.

"You were going to tell me about the number," he said.

"What, Arnold? I'm sorry," she said.

He cleared his throat. "Tell me how you acquired my number," he said.

"I checked with Annette. The baby sitter—but of course you know that. Anyway, she told me the phone rang while she was here and it was somebody wanting me. They left a number to call, and it was your number she took down. That's all I know." She moved a cup around in front of her. "I'm sorry I can't tell you any more."

"Your water is boiling," he said.

She put out spoons, milk, and sugar, and poured the steaming water over tea bags.

He added sugar and stirred his tea. "You said it was urgent that I come."

"Oh that, Arnold," she said, turning away. "I don't know what made me say that. I can't imagine what I was thinking."

"Then there's nothing?" he said.

"No. I mean, yes." She shook her head. "What you said, I mean. Nothing."

"I see," he said. He went on stirring his tea. He could hear the television from down the hall.

"It's unusual," he said after a minute, almost to himself. "Quite unusual." He smiled weakly, then moved the cup to one side and touched his lips with the napkin.

"You aren't leaving?" she said.

"I must," he said. "I'm expecting a call at home."

"Not yet, Arnold."

She scraped her chair back and stood up. Her eyes were a pale green, set deep in her pale face and surrounded by what he had at first thought was dark make-up. Appalled at himself, knowing he would despise himself for it, he stood and put his arms clumsily around her waist. She let herself be kissed, fluttering and closing her eyelids briefly.

"It's late," he said, letting go, turning away unsteadily. "You've been very gracious, but I must be leaving, Mrs. Holt. Thank you. Thanks for the tea."

"You will come again, won't you, Arnold?" she said.

He shook his head.

She followed him to the door, where he held out his hand. He could still hear the television from the hall. It seemed louder, as if the volume had been turned up. He remembered the other child then, the boy. Where was he? She took his hand, raised it quickly to her lips.

"You mustn't forget me, Arnold."

"I won't," he said. "Clara. Clara Holt."

"I'm glad you came tonight," she said. "We had a good talk." She picked at something, a hair, a thread, on his suit collar. "I'm very glad you came, and I feel certain you'll come again." He looked at her carefully, but she was staring past him now as if she were trying to remember something. "Now—good night, Arnold," she said, and with that she shut the door, almost catching his overcoat.

"Strange," he said, as he started down the stairs. He took a long breath as he reached the sidewalk, paused a minute to look back at the building. But he was unable to determine which balcony was hers. The large man moved slightly against the railing and continued looking down at him. He began walking, hands deep in his coat pockets.

When he reached home, the telephone was ringing. He stood very quietly in the middle of the room holding the key between his fingers until the ringing stopped. Then, carefully, tenderly, he put a hand against his chest and felt, through the layers of clothes, his beating heart. After a time he made his way into the bedroom.

Almost immediately the telephone began to ring, and this time he answered it. "Arnold. Arnold Breit speaking," he said.

"Arnold? My, aren't we formal tonight?" his wife said, her voice strong, teasing. "I've been calling since nine. Out living it up, Arnold?"

He remained silent and considered her voice.

"Are you there, Arnold?" she said. "You don't sound like yourself."

His Son, in His Arms, in Light, Aloft

Harold Brodkey

HAROLD BRODKEY was born in Staunton, Illinois, and now lives in New York City. His stories have appeared in *The New Yorker* and *Esquire*. He is the author of *First Love and Other Stories*.

My father is chasing me.

My God, I feel it up and down my spine, the thumping on the turf, the approach of his hands, his giant hands, the huge ramming increment of his breath as he draws near: a widening effort. I feel it up and down my spine and in my mouth and belly—Daddy is so swift: who ever heard of such swiftness? Just as in stories. . . .

I can't escape him, can't fend him off, his arms, his rapidity, his will. His interest in me.

I am being lifted into the air—and even as I pant and stare blurredly, limply, mindlessly, a map appears, of the dark ground where I ran: as I hang limply and rise anyway on the fattened bar of my father's arm, I see that there's the grass, there's the path, there's a bed of flowers.

I straighten up. There are the lighted windows of our house, some distance away. My father's face, full of noises, is near: it looms: his hidden face: is that you, old money-maker? My butt is folded on the trapeze of his arm. My father is as big as an automobile.

In the oddly shrewd-hearted torpor of being carried home in the dark, a tourist, in my father's arms, I feel myself attached by my heated-by-running dampness to him: we are attached, there are binding oval stains of warmth.

In most social talk, most politeness, most literature, most religion, it is as if violence didn't exist—except as sin, something far away. This is flattering to women. It is also conducive to grace—because the heaviness of fear, the shadowy henchmen selves that fear attaches to us, that fear sees in others, is banished.

Where am I in the web of jealousy that trembles at every human movement?

What detectives we have to be.

What if I am wrong? What if I remember incorrectly? It does not matter. This is fiction—a game—of pleasures, of truth and error, as at the sensual beginning of a sensual life.

My father, Charley, as I knew him, is invisible in any photograph I have of him. The man I hugged or ran toward or ran from is not in any photograph: a photograph shows someone of whom I think: *Oh, was he like that?*

But in certain memories, *he* appears, a figure, a presence, and I think, *I know him.*

It is embarrassing to me that I am part of what is unsayable in any account of his life.

When Momma's or my sister's excesses, of mood, or of shopping, angered or sickened Daddy, you can smell him then from two feet away: he has a dry, achy little stink of a rapidly fading interest in his life with us. At these times, the women in a spasm of wit turn to me; they comb my hair, clean my face, pat my bottom or my shoulder, and send me off; they bid me to go cheer up Daddy.

Sometimes it takes no more than a tug at his newspaper: the sight of me is enough; or I climb on his lap, mimic his depression; I stand on his lap, press his head against my chest. . . . His face is immense, porous, complex with stubble, bits of talcum on it, unlikely colors, unlikely features, a bald brow with a curved square of lamplight in it. About his head there is a nimbus of sturdy wickedness, of unlikelihood. If his mood does not change, something tumbles and goes dead in me.

Perhaps it is more a nervous breakdown than heartbreak: I have failed him: his love for me is very limited: I must die now. I go somewhere and shudder and collapse—a corner of the dining room, the back stoop or deck: I lie there, empty, grief-stricken, literally unable to move—I have forgotten my limbs. If a memory of them comes to me, the memory is meaningless. . . .

Momma will then stalk in to wherever Daddy is and say to him, "Charley, you can be mad at me, I'm used to it, but just go take a look and see what you've done to the child. . . ."

My uselessness toward him sickens me. Anyone who

fails toward him might as well be struck down, abandoned, eaten.

Perhaps it is an animal state: I have-nothing-left I-have-no-place-in this-world.

Well, this is his house. Momma tells me in various ways to love him. Also, he is entrancing—he is so big, so thunderish, so smelly, and has the most extraordinary habits, reading newspapers, for instance, and wiggling his shoe: his shoe is gross: kick someone with that and they'd fall into next week.

Some memories huddle in a grainy light. What it is is a number of similar events bunching themselves, superimposing themselves, to make a false memory, a collage, a mental artifact. Within the boundaries of one such memory one plunges from year to year, is small and helpless, is a little older: one remembers it all but it is nothing that happened, that clutch of happenings, of associations, those gifts and ghosts of a meaning.

I can, if I concentrate, whiten the light—or yellow-whiten it, actually—and when the graininess goes, it is suddenly one afternoon.

I could not live without the pride and belonging-to-himness of being that man's consolation. He had the disposal of the rights to the out-of-doors—he was the other, the other-not-a-woman: he was my strength, literally, my strength if I should cry out.

Flies and swarms of the danger of being unfathered beset me when I bored my father: it was as if I were covered with flies on the animal plain where some ravening wild dog would leap up, bite and grip my muzzle, and begin to bring about my death.

I had no protection: I was subject now to the appetite of whatever inhabited the dark.

A child collapses in a sudden burst of there-is-nothing-here, and that is added onto nothingness, the nothing of being only a child concentrating on there being nothing there, no hope, no ambition: there is a despair but one without magnificence except in the face of its completeness: *I am a child and am without strength of my own.*

I have—in my grief—somehow managed to get to the back deck: I am sitting in the early evening light; I am oblivious to the light. I did and didn't hear his footsteps, the rumble, the house thunder dimly (behind and beneath me), the thunder of his-coming-to-rescue-me. . . . I did and didn't hear him call my name.

I spoke only the gaping emptiness of grief—that tongue—I understood I had no right to the speech of fathers and sons.

My father came out on the porch. I remember how stirred he was, how beside himself that I was so unhappy, that a child, a child he liked, should suffer so. He laid aside his own mood—his disgust with life, with money, with the excesses of the women—and he took on a broad-winged, malely flustering, broadwinged optimism—he was at the center of a great beating (of the heart, a man's heart, of a man's gestures, will, concern), dust clouds rising, a beating determination to persuade me that the nature of life, of *my* life, was other than I'd thought, other than whatever had defeated me—he was about to tell me there was no need to feel defeated, he was about to tell me that I was a good, or even a wonderful, child.

He kneeled—a mountain of shirtfront and trousers; a mountain that poured, clambered down, folded itself, re-formed itself: a disorderly massiveness, near to me, fabric-hung-and-draped: Sinai. He said, "Here, here, what is this—what is a child like you doing being so sad?" And: "Look at me. . . . It's all right. . . . Everything is all right. . . ." The misstatements of consolation are lies about the absolute that require faith—and no memory: the truth of consolation can be investigated if one is a proper child—that is to say, affectionate—only in a non-skeptical way.

"It's not all right!"

"It is—it is." It was and wasn't a lie: it had to do with power—and limitations: my limitations and his power: he could make it all right for me, everything, provided my everything was small enough and within his comprehension.

Sometimes he would say, "Son—" He would say it heavily—"Don't be sad—I don't want you to be sad—I don't like it when you're sad—"

I can't look into his near and, to me, factually incredible face—incredible because so large (as at the beginning of a love affair): I mean as a *face:* it is the focus of so many emotions and wonderments: he could have been a fool or was—it was possibly the face of a fool, someone self-centered, smug, an operator, semi-criminal, an intelligent psychoanalyst; it was certainly a mortal face—but what did the idea or word mean to me then—*mortal?*

There was a face; it was as large as my chest; there were eyes, inhumanly big, humid—what could they mean? How could I read them? How do you read eyes? I did not know about comparisons: how much more affectionate he was than other men, or less, how much better than common experience or how much worse in this area of being fathered my experience was with him: I cannot say even now: it is a statistical matter, after all, a matter of averages: but who at the present date can phrase the proper questions for the poll? And who will understand the hesitations, the blank looks, the odd expressions on the faces of the answerers?

The odds are he was a—median—father. He himself had usually a conviction he did pretty well: sometimes he despaired—of himself: but blamed me: my love: or something: or himself as a father: he wasn't good at managing stages between strong, clear states of feeling. Perhaps no one is.

Anyway, I knew no such terms as *median* then: I did not understand much about those part of his emotions which extended past the rather clear area where my emotions were so often amazed. I chose, in some ways, to regard him seriously: in other ways, I had no choice—he was what was given to me.

I cannot look at him, as I said: I cannot see anything: if I look at him without seeing him, my blindness insults him: I don't want to hurt him at all: I want nothing: I am lost and have surrendered and am really dead and am waiting without hope.

He knows how to rescue people. Whatever he doesn't know, one of the things he knows in the haste and jumble of his heart, among the blither of tastes in his mouth and opinions and sympathies in his mind and so on, is the making yourself into someone who will help someone who is wounded. The dispersed and unlikely parts of him come together for a while in a clucking and focused arch of abiding concern. Oh how he plows ahead; oh how he believes in rescue! He puts—he *shoves*—he works an arm behind my shoulders, another under my legs: his arms, his powers shove at me, twist, lift and jerk me until I am cradled in the air, in his arms: "You don't have to be unhappy—you haven't hurt anyone—don't be sad—you're a *nice* boy. . . ."

I can't quite hear him, I can't quite believe him. I can't be *good*—the confidence game is to believe him, is to be a good child who trusts him—we will both smile then, he and I. But if I hear him, I have to believe him still. I am set up that way. He is so big; he is the possessor of so many grandeurs. If I believe him, hope and pleasure will start up again—suddenly—the blankness in me will be relieved, broken by these—meanings—that it seems he and I share in some big, attaching way.

In his pride he does not allow me to suffer: I belong to him.

He is rising, jerkily, to his feet and holding me at the same time. I do not have to stir to save myself—I only have to believe him. He rocks me into a sad-edged relief and an achingly melancholy delight with the peculiar lurch as he stands erect of establishing his balance and rectifying the way he holds me, so he can go on holding me, holding me aloft, against his chest: I am airborne: I liked to have that man hold me—in the air: I knew it was worth a great deal, the embrace, the gift of altitude. I am not exposed on the animal plain. I am not helpless.

The heat his body gives off! It is the heat of a man sweating with regret. His heartbeat, his burning, his physical force: ah, there is a large rent in the nothingness: the mournful apparition of his regret, the proof of his loyalty wake me: I have a twin, a massive twin, mighty company: Daddy's grief is at my grief: my nothingness is echoed in him (if he is going to have to live without me): the rescue was not quite a secular thing. The evening forms itself, a classroom, a brigade of shadows, of phenomena—the tinted air slides: there are shadowy skaters everywhere: shadowy cloaked people step out from behind things which are then hidden behind their cloaks. An alteration in the air proceeds from openings in the ground, from leaks in the sunlight which is being disengaged, like a stubborn hand, or is being stroked shut like my eyelids when I refuse to sleep: the dark rubs and bubbles noiselessly—and seeps—into the landscape. In the rubbed distortion of my inner air, twilight soothes: there are two of us breathing in close proximity here (he is telling me that grownups sometimes have things on their minds, he is saying mysterious things which I don't comprehend); I don't want to look at him: it takes two of my eyes to see one of his—and then I mostly see myself in his eye: he is even more unseeable from here, this holder: my head falls against his neck: "I know what you like—you'd like to go stand on the wall—would you like to see the sunset?" Did I nod? I think I did: I nodded gravely: but perhaps he did not need an answer since he thought he knew me well.

We are moving, this elephant and I, we are lumbering, down some steps, across grassy, uneven ground—the spoiled child in his father's arms—behind our house was a little park—we moved across the grass of the little park. There are sun's rays on the dome of the moorish bandstand. The evening is moist, fugitive, momentarily sneaking, half welcomed in this hour of crime. My father's neck. The stubble. The skin where the stubble stops. Exhaustion has me: I am a creature of failure, a locus of childishness, an empty skull: I am this being-young. We overrun the world, he and I, with his legs, with our eyes, with our alliance. We move on in a ghostly torrent of our being like this.

My father has the smell and feel of wanting to be my father. Guilt and innocence stream and re-stream in him. His face, I see now in memory, held an untiring surprise: as if some grammar of deed and purpose—of comparatively easy tenderness—startled him again and again, startled him continuously for a while. He said, "I guess we'll just have to cheer you up—we'll have to show you life isn't so bad—I guess we weren't any too careful of a little boy's feelings, were we?'' I wonder if all comfort is alike.

A man's love is, after all, a fairly spectacular thing.

He said—his voice came from above me—he spoke out into the air, the twilight—''We'll make it all right—just you wait and see. . . .''

He said, ''This is what you like,'' and he placed me on the wall that ran along the edge of the park, the edge of a bluff, a wall too high for me to see over, and which I was forbidden to climb: he placed me on the stubbed stone mountains and grouting of the wall-top. He put his arm around my middle: I leaned against him: and faced outward into the salt of the danger of the height, of the view (we were at least one hundred and fifty feet, we were, therefore, hundreds of feet in the air); I was flicked at by narrow, abrasive bands of wind, evening wind, veined with sunset's sun-crispness, strongly touched with coolness.

The wind would push at my eyelids, my nose, my lips. I heard a buzzing in my ears which signaled how high, how alone we were: this view of a river valley at night and of parts of four counties was audible. I looked into the hollow in front of me, a grand hole, an immense, bellying deep sheet or vast sock. There were numinous fragments in it—birds in what sunlight was left, bits of smoke faintly lit by distant light or mist, hovering inexplicably here and there: rays of yellow light, high up, touching a few high clouds.

It had a floor on which were creeks (and the big river), a little dim, a little glary at this hour, rail lines, roads, highways, houses, silos, bridges, trees, fields, everything more than half hidden in the enlarging dark: there was the shrinking glitter of far-off noises, bearded and stippled with huge and spreading shadows of my ignorance: it was panorama as a personal privilege. The sun at the end of the large, sunset-swollen sky, was a glowing and urgent orange; around it were the spreading petals of pink and stratospheric gold: on the ground were occasional magenta flarings; oh it makes you stare and gasp; a fine, astral (not a crayon) red hole in a broad, magnificent band across the middlewestern sky: below us, for miles, shadowiness tightened as we watched (it seemed); above us, tinted clouds spread across the vast shadowing sky: there were funereal lights and sinkings everywhere. I stand on the wall and lean against Daddy, only somewhat awed and abstracted: the view does not own me as it usually does: I am partly in the hands of the jolting—amusement—the conceit—of having been resurrected by my father.

I understood that he was proffering me oblivion plus pleasure, the end of a sorrow to be henceforth remembered as Happiness. This was to be my privilege. This amazing man is going to rescue me from any anomaly or barb or sting in my existence: he is going to confer happiness on me: as a matter of fact, he has already begun.

"Just you true me—you keep right on being cheered up—look at that sunset—that's some sunset, wouldn't you say?—everything is going to be just fine and dandy—you trust me—you'll see—just you wait and see. . . ."

Did he mean to be a swindler? He wasn't clearminded—he often said, "I mean well." He did not think other people meant well.

I don't feel it would be right to adopt an Oedipal theory to explain what happened between him and me: only a sense of what he was like as a man, what certain moments were like, and what was said.

It is hard in language to get the full, irregular, heavy sound of a man.

He liked to have us "all dressed and nice when I come home from work," have us wait for him in attitudes of serene all-is-well contentment. As elegant as a Spanish prince I sat on the couch toying with an oversized model truck—what a confusion of social pretensions, technologies, class disorder there was in that. My sister would sit in a chair, knees together, hair brushed: she'd doze off if Daddy was late. Aren't we happy! Actually, we often are.

One day he came in plungingly, excited to be home and to have us as an audience rather than outsiders who didn't know their lines and who often laughed at him as part of their struggle to improve their parts in his scenes. We were waiting to have him approve of our tableau—he usually said something about what a nice family we looked like or how well we looked or what a pretty group or some such thing—and we didn't realize he was the tableau tonight. We held our positions, but we stared at him in a kind of mindless what-should-we-do-besides-sit-here-and-be-happy-and-nice? Impatiently he said, "I have a surprise for you, Charlotte—Abe Last has a heart after all." My father said something on that order: or "—a conscience after all"; and then he walked across the carpet, a man somewhat jerky with success—a man redolent of vaudeville, of grotesque and sentimental movies (he liked grotesquerie, prettiness, sentiment). As he walked, he pulled banded packs of currency out of his pockets, two or three in each hand. "There," he said, dropping one, then three in Momma's dressed-up lap. "There," he said, dropping another two: he uttered a "there" for each subsequent pack. "Oh, let me!" my sister cried and ran over to look—and then she grabbed two packs and said, "Oh, Daddy, how much *is* this?"

It was eight or ten thousand dollars, he said. Momma

said, "Charley, what if someone sees—we could be robbed—why do you take chances like this?"

Daddy harrumphed and said, "You have no sense of fun—if you ask me, you're afraid to be happy. I'll put it in the bank tomorrow—if I can find an honest banker—here, young lady, put that money down:you don't want to prove your mother right, do you?"

Then he said, "I know one person round here who knows how to enjoy himself—" and he lifted me up, held me in his arms.

He said, "We're going outside, this young man and I."

"What should I do with this money!"

"Put it under your mattress—make a salad out of it: you're always the one who worries about money," he said in a voice solid with authority and masculinity, totally pieced out with various self-satisfactions—as if he had gained a kingdom and the assurance of appearing as glorious in the histories of his time; I put my head back and smiled at the superb animal, at the rosy—and cowardly—panther leaping; and then I glanced over his shoulder and tilted my head and looked sympathetically at Momma.

My sister shouted, "I know how to enjoy myself—I'll come too! . . ."

"Yes, yes," said Daddy, who was *never* averse to enlarging spheres of happiness and areas of sentiment. He held her hand and held me on his arm.

"Let him walk," my sister said. And: "He's getting bigger—you'll make a sissy out of him, Daddy. . . ."

Daddy said, "Shut up and enjoy the light—it's as beautiful as Paris and in our own backyard."

Out of folly, or a wish to steal his attention, or greed, my sister kept on: she asked if she could get something with some of the money; he dodged her question; and she kept on; and he grew peevish, so peevish, he returned to the house and accused Momma of having never taught her daughter not to be greedy—he sprawled, impetuous, displeased, semi-frantic in a chair: "I can't enjoy myself—there is no way a man can live in this house with all of you—I swear to God this will kill me soon. . . ."

Momma said to him, "I can't believe in the things you believe in—I'm not a girl anymore: when I play the fool, it isn't convincing—you get angry with me when I try. You shouldn't get angry with her—you've spoiled her more than I have—and how do you expect her to act when you show her all that money—how do you think money affects people?"

I looked at him to see what the answer was, to see what he would answer. He said, "Charlotte, try being a rose and not a thorn."

At all times, and in all places, there is always the possibility that I will start to speak or will be looking at something and I will feel his face covering mine, as in a kiss and as a mask, turned both ways like that: and I am inside him, his presence, his thoughts, his language: *I* am languageless then for a moment, an automation of repetition, a bagged piece of an imaginary river of descent.

I can't invent everything for myself: some always has to be what I already know: some of me always has to be him.

When he picked me up, my consciousness fitted itself to that position: I remember it—clearly. He could punish me—and did—by refusing to lift me, by denying me that union with him. Of course, the union was not one-sided: I was his innocence—as long as I was not an accusation, that is. I censored him—in that when he felt himself being, consciously, a father, he held back part of his other life, of his whole self: his shadows, his impressions, his adventures would not readily fit into me—what a gross and absurd rape that would have been.

So he was *careful*—he *walked on eggs*—there was an odd courtesy of his withdrawal behind his secrets, his secret sorrows and horrors, behind the curtain of what-is-suitable-for-a-child.

Sometimes he becomes simply a set of limits, of walls, inside which there is the caroming and echoing of my astounding sensibility amplified by being his son and in his arms and aloft; and he lays his sensibility aside or models his on mine, on my joy, takes his emotional coloring from me, like a mirror or a twin: his incomprehensible life, with its strengths, ordeals, triumphs, crimes, horrors, his sadness and disgust, is enveloped and momentarily assuaged by my direct and indirect childish consolation. My gaze, my enjoying him, my willingness to be him, my joy at it, supported the baroque tower of his necessary but limited and maybe dishonest optimism.

One time he and Momma fought over money and he left: he packed a bag and went. Oh it was sad and heavy at home. I started to be upset, but then I retreated into an impenetrable stupidity: not knowing was better than being despairing. I was put to bed and I did fall asleep: I woke in the middle of the night; he had returned and was sitting on my bed—in the dark—a huge shadow in the shadows. He was stroking my forehead. When he saw my eyes open, he said in a sentimental, heavy voice, "I could never leave *you*—"

He didn't really mean it: I was an excuse: but he did mean it—the meaning and not-meaning were like the rise and fall of a wave in me, in the dark outside of me, between the two of us, between him and me (at other moments he would think of other truths, other than the one of he-couldn't-leave-me sometimes). He bent over sentimentally, painedly, not nicely, and he began to hug me; he put his head down, on my chest; my small heartbeat vanished into the near, sizable, anguished, angular, emotion-swollen one that was his. I kept advancing swiftly into wakefulness, my consciousness came rushing and widening blurredly, embracing the dark, his presence, his embrace. It's Daddy, it's Daddy—it's dark still—wakefulness rushed into the dark grave or grove of his hugely extended presence. His affection. My arms stumbled: there was no adequate embrace in me—I couldn't lift *him*—I had no adequacy yet except that of my charm or what-have-you, except things the grown-ups gave me—not things: traits, qualities. I mean my hugging his head was nothing until he said, "Ah, you love me. . . . You're all right. . . ."

Momma said: "They are as close as two peas in a pod—they are just alike—that child and Charley. That child is God to Charley. . . ."

He didn't always love me.

In the middle of the night that time, he picked me up after a while, he wrapped me in a blanket, held me close, took me downstairs in the dark; we went outside, into the night; it was dark and chilly but there was a moon—I thought he would take me to the wall but he just stood on our back deck. He grew tired of loving me; he grew abstracted and forgot me: the love that had just a moment before been so intently and tightly clasping and nestling went away, and I found myself released, into the cool night air, the floating damp, the silence, with the darkened houses around us.

I saw the silver moon, heard my father's breath, felt the itchiness of the woolen blanket on my hands, noticed its wool smell. I did this alone and I waited. Then when he didn't come back, I grew sleepy and put my head down against his neck: he was nowhere near me. Alone in his arms, I slept.

Over and over a moment seems to recur, something seems to return in its entirety, a name seems to be accurate: and we say it always happens like this. But we are wrong, of course.

I was a weird choice as someone for him to love.

So different from him in the way I was surprised by things.

I am a child with this mind. I am a child he has often rescued.

Our attachment to each other manifests itself in sudden swoops and grabs and rubs of attention, of being entertained, by each other, at the present moment.

I ask you, how is it possible it's going to last?

Sometimes when we are entertained by each other, we are bold about it, but just as frequently, it seems embarrassing, and we turn our faces aside.

His recollections of horror are more certain than mine. His suspicions are more terrible. There are darknesses in me I'm afraid of, but the ones in him don't frighten me but are like the dark in the yard, a dark a child like me might sneak into (and has)—a dark full of unseen shadowy almost-glowing presences—the fear, the danger—are desirable—difficult—with the call-to-be-brave: the childish bravura of *I must endure this* (knowing I can run away if I choose).

The child touches with his pursed, jutting, ignorant lips the large, handsome, odd, humid face of his father who can run away too. More dangerously.

He gave away a car of his that he was about to trade in on a new one: he gave it to a man in financial trouble; he did it after seeing a movie about crazy people being loving and gentle with each other and everyone else: Momma said to Daddy, "You can't do anything you want—you can't listen to your feelings—you have a family. . . ."

After seeing a movie in which a child cheered up an old man, he took me to visit an old man who probably was a distant relative, and who hated me at sight, my high coloring, the noise I might make, my father's affection for me: "Will he sit still? I can't stand noise. Charley, listen, I'm in bad shape—I think I have cancer and they won't tell me—"

"Nothing can kill a tough old bird like you, Ike. . . ."

The old man wanted all of Charley's attention—and strength—while he talked about how the small threads and thicker ropes that tied him to life were being cruelly tampered with.

Daddy patted me afterward, but oddly he was bored and disappointed in me as if I'd failed at something.

He could not seem to keep it straight about my value to him or to the world in general; he lived at the center of his own intellectual shortcomings and his moral pride: he needed it to be true, as an essential fact, that goodness—or innocence—was in him or was protected by him, and that, therefore, he was a good *man* and superior to other men, and did not deserve—certain common masculine fates—horrors—tests of his courage—certain pains. It was necessary to him to have it be true that he knew what real goodness was and had it in his life.

Perhaps that was because he didn't believe in God, and because he felt (with a certain self-love) that people, out in the world, didn't appreciate him and were needlessly difficult—"unloving": he said it often—and because it was true he was shocked and guilty and even enraged when he was "forced" into being unloving himself, or when he caught sight in himself of such a thing as cruelty, or cruel nosiness, or physical cowardice—God, how he hated being a coward—or hatred, physical hatred, even for me, if I was coy or evasive or disinterested or tired of him: it tore him apart literally—bits of madness, in varying degrees would grip him as in a Greek play: I see his mouth, his salmon-colored mouth, showing various degrees of sarcasm—sarcasm mounting into bitterness and even a ferocity without tears that always suggested to me, as a child, that he was near tears but had forgotten in his ferocity that he was about to cry.

Or he would catch sight of some evidence, momentarily inescapable—in contradictory or foolish statements of his or in unkept promises that it was clear he had never meant to keep, had never made any effort to keep—that he was a fraud; and sometimes he would laugh because he was a fraud—a good-hearted fraud, he believed—or he would be sullen or angry, a fraud caught either by the tricks of language so that in expressing affection absentmindedly he had expressed too much; or caught by greed and self-concern: he hated the evidence that he was mutable as hell: that he loved sporadically and egoistically, and often with rage and vengeance, and that madness I mentioned earlier: he couldn't stand those things: he usually forgot them; but sometimes when he was being tender, or noble, or self-sacrificing, he would sigh and be very sad—maybe because the good stuff was temporary. I don't know. Or sad that he did it only when he had the time and was in the mood. Sometimes he forgot such things and was superbly confident—or was that a bluff?

I don't know. I really can't speak for him.

I look at my hand and then at his; it is not really conceivable to me that both are hands: mine is a sort of a hand. He tells me over and over that I must not upset him—he tells me of my power over him—I don't know how to take such a fact—is it a fact? I stare at him. I gasp with the ache of life stirring in me—again: again: *again*—I ache with tentative and complete and then again tentative belief.

For a long time piety was anything at all sitting still or moving slowly and not rushing at me or away from me but letting me look at it or be near it without there being any issue of safety-about-to-be-lost.

This world is evasive.

But someone who lets you observe him is not evasive, is not hurtful, at that moment: it is like in sleep where *the other* waits—the Master of Dreams—and there are doors, doorways opening into farther rooms where there is an altered light, and which I enter to find—what? That someone is gone? That the room is empty? Or perhaps I find a vista, of rooms, of archways, and a window, and a peach tree in flower—a tree with peach-colored flowers in the solitude of night.

I am dying of grief, Daddy. I am waiting here, limp with abandonment, with exhaustion: perhaps I'd better believe in God. . . .

My father's virtues, those I dreamed about, those I saw when I was awake, those I understood and misunderstood, were, as I felt them, in dreams or wakefulness, when I was a child, like a broad highway opening into a small dusty town that was myself; and down that road came bishops and slogans, Chinese processions, hasidim in a dance, the nation's honor and glory *in its young people*, baseball players, singers who sang "with their whole hearts," automobiles and automobile grilles, and grave or comic bits of instruction. This man is attached to me and makes me light up with festal affluence and oddity; he says, "I think you love me."

He was right.

He would move his head—his giant face—and you could observe in his eyes the small town which was me in its temporary sophistication, a small town giving proof on every side of its arrogance and its prosperity and its puzzled contentment.

He also instructed me in hatred: he didn't mean to, not openly: but I saw and picked up the curious buzzing of his puckered distastes, as nastiness of dismissal that he had: a fetor of let-them-all-kill-each-other. He hated lots of people, whole races: he hated ugly women.

He conferred an odd inverted splendor on awfulness—because *he* knew about it: he went into it every day. He told me not to want that, not to want to know about that: he told me to go on being just the way I was—"a nice boy."

When he said something was unbearable, he meant it; he meant he could not bear it.

In my memories of this time of my life, it seems to be summer all the time, even when the gound is white: I suppose it seems like summer because I was never cold.

Ah: I wanted to see. . . .

My father, when he was low (in spirit) would make rounds, inside his head, checking on his consciousness, to see if it was safe from inroads by "*the unbearable*": he found an all-is-well in a quiet emptiness. . . .

In an uninvadedness, he found the weary complacency and self-importance of All is Well.

(The women liked invasions—up to a point.)

One day he came home, mysterious, exalted, hatted and suited, roseate, handsome, a little sweaty—it really was summer that day. He was exalted—as I said—but nervous toward me—anxious with promises.

And he was, oh, somewhat angry, justified, toward the world, toward me, not exactly as a threat (in case I didn't respond) but as a jumble.

He woke me from a nap, an uneasy nap, lifted me out of bed, me, a child who had not expected to see him that afternoon—I was not particularly happy that day, not particularly pleased with him, not pleased with him at all, really.

He dressed me himself. At first he kept his hat on. After a while, he took it off. When I was dressed, he said, "You're pretty sour today," and he put his hat back on.

He hustled me down the stairs; he held my wrist in his enormous palm—immediate and gigantic to me and blankly suggestive of a meaning I could do nothing about except stare at blankly from time to time in my childish life.

We went outside into the devastating heat and glare, the blathering, humming afternoon light of a midwestern summer day: a familiar furnace.

We walked along the street, past the large, silent houses, set, each one, in hard, pure light. You could not look directly at anything, the glare, the reflections were too strong.

Then he lifted me in his arms—aloft.

He was carrying me to help me because the heat was bad—and worse near the sidewalk which reflected it upward into my face—and because my legs were short and I was struggling, because he was in a hurry and because he liked carrying me, and because I was sour and blackmailed him with my unhappiness, and he was being kind with a certain—limited—mixture of exasperation-turning-into-a-degree-of-mortal-love.

Or it was another time, really early in the morning, when the air was partly asleep, partly adance, but in veils, trembling with heavy moisture. Here and there, the air broke into a string of beads of pastel colors, pink, pale green, small rainbows, really small, and very narrow. Daddy walked rapidly. I bounced in his arms. My eyesight was unfocused—it bounced too. Things were more than merely present: they pressed against me: they had the aliveness of myth, of the beginning of an adventure when nothing is explained as yet.

All at once we were at the edge of a bankless river of yellow light. To be truthful, it was like a big, wooden beam of fresh, unweathered wood: but we entered it: and then it turned into light, cooler light than in the hot humming afternoon but full of bits of heat that stuck to me and then were blown away, a semi-heat, not really friendly, yet reassuring: and very dimly sweaty; and it grew, it spread: this light turned into a knitted cap of light, fuzzy, warm, woven, itchy: it was pulled over my head, my hair, my forehead, my eyes, my nose, my mouth.

So I turned my face away from the sun—I turned it so it was pressed against my father's neck mostly—and then I knew, in a childish way, knew from the heat (of his neck, of his shirt collar), knew by childish deduction, that his face was unprotected from the luminousness all around us: and I looked; and it was so; his face, for the moment unembarrassedly, was caught in that light. In an accidental glory.

I-80 Nebraska, M.490—M.205

John Sayles

JOHN SAYLES was born in 1950 in Schenectady, New York. He is the author of the novels *Pride of the Bimbos*, *Union Dues*, and a collection of stories *The Anarchist's Convention.* He now lives in Hoboken, New Jersey.

"This is that Alabama Rebel, this is that Alabama Rebel, do I have a copy?"

"Ahh, 10-4 on that, Alabama Rebel."

"This is that Alabama Rebel westbound on 80, ah, what's your handle, buddy, and where you comin from?"

"This is that, ah, Toby Trucker, eastbound for that big O town, round about the 445 marker."

"I copy you clear, Toby Trucker. How's about that Smokey Bear situation up by that Lincoln town?"

"Ah, you'll have to hold her back a little through

there, Alabama Rebel, ah, place is crawling with Smokies like usual. Saw three of em's lights up on the overpass just after the airport there."

"And how bout that Lincoln weigh station, they got those scales open?"

"Ah, negative on that, Alabama Rebel, I went by the lights was off, probably still in business back to that North Platte town."

"They don't get you coming they get you going. How bout that you-know-who, any sign of him tonight? That Ryder P. Moses?"

"Negative on that, thank God. Guy gives me the creeps."

"Did you, ah, ever actually hear him, Toby Trucker?"

"A definite 10-4 on that one, Alabama Rebel, and I'll never forget it. Coming down from that Scottsbluff town three nights ago I copied him. First he says he's northbound, then he says he's southbound, then he's right on my tail singing 'The Wabash Cannonball.' Man blew by me outside of that Oshkosh town on 26, must of been going a hundred plus. Little two-lane blacktop and he thinks he's Parnelli Jones at the Firecracker 500."

"You see him? You see what kind of rig he had?"

"A definite shit-no negative on that. I was fighting to keep the road. The man aint human."

"Ah, maybe not, Toby Trucker, maybe not. Never copied him myself, but I talked with a dozen guys who have in the last couple weeks."

"Ahh, maybe you'll catch him tonight."

"Long as he don't catch me."

"Got a point there, Alabama Rebel. Ahhhh, I seem to be losing you here—"

"10-4. Coming up to that Lincoln town, buddy. I thank you kindly for the information and ah, I hope you stay out of trouble in that big O town and maybe we'll modulate again some night. This is that Alabama Rebel, over and out."

"This is Toby Trucker, eastbound, night now."

Westbound on 80 is a light-stream, ruby-strung big rigs rolling straight into the heart of Nebraska. Up close they are a river in breakaway flood, bouncing and pitching and yawning, while a mile distant they are slow-oozing lava. To their left is the eastbound stream, up ahead the static glare of Lincoln. Lights. The world in black and white and red, broken only by an occasional blue flasher strobing the ranger hat of a state policeman. Smokey the Bear's campfire. Westbound 80 is an insomniac world of lights passing lights to the music of the Civilian Band.

"This that Arkansas Traveler, this that Arkansas Traveler, do you copy?"

"How bout that Scorpio Ascending, how bout that Scorpio Ascending, you out there, buddy?"

"This is Chromedome at that 425 marker, who's that circus wagon up ahead? Who's that old boy in the Mrs. Smith's pie-pusher?"

They own the highway at night, the big rigs, slip-streaming in caravans, hopscotching to take turns making the draft, strutting the thousands of dollars they've paid in road taxes on their back ends. The men feel at home out here, they leave their cross-eyed headlights eating whiteline, forget their oily-aired, kidney-jamming cabs to talk out in the black air, to live on the Band.

"This is Roadrunner, westbound at 420, any you eastbound people fill me in on the Smokies up ahead?"

"Ahh, copy you, Roadrunner, she's been clean all the way from that Grand Island town, so motormotor."

(A moving van accelerates.)

"How bout that Roadrunner, this is Overload up to 424, that you behind me?"

(The van's headlights blink up and down.)

"Well come on up, buddy, let's put the hammer down on this thing."

The voices are nasal and tinny, broken by squawks, something human squeezed through wire. A decade of televised astronauts gives them their style and self-importance.

"Ahh, breaker, Overload, we got us a code blue here. There's a four-wheeler coming up fast behind me, might be a Bear wants to give us some green stamps."

"Breaker break, Roadrunner. Good to have you at the back door. We'll hold her back a while, let you check out that four-wheeler."

(The big rigs slow and the passenger car pulls alongside of them.)

"Ahh, negative on that Bear, Overload, it's just a civilian. Fella hasn't heard about that five-five limit."

"10-4 and motormotor."

(Up front now, the car is nearly whooshed off the road when the big rigs blow past. It wavers a moment, then accelerates to try and take them, but can only make it alongside before they speed up. The car falls back, then tries again.)

"Ah, look like we got us a problem, Roadrunner. This uh, Vega—whatever it is, some piece of Detroit shit, wants to play games."

"Looks like it, Overload."

"Don't know what a four-wheeler is doing on the Innerstate this time of night anyhow. Shunt be allowed out with us working people. You want to give me a hand on this, Roadrunner?"

"10-4. I'll be the trapper, you be the sweeper. What we got ahead?"

"There's an exit up to the 402 marker. This fucker gets off the ride at Beaver Crossing."

(The trucks slow and the car passes them, honking, cutting sharp to the inside lane. They let it cruise for a moment, then the lead rig pulls alongside of it and the second closes up behind inches from the car's rear fender. The car tries to run but they stay with it, boxing it, then pushing it faster and faster till the sign appears ahead on the right and the lead truck bulls to the inside, forcing the car to squeal off into the exit ramp.)

"Mission accomplished there, Roadrunner."

"Roger."

The have their own rules, the big rigs, their own road and radio etiquette that is tougher in its way than the Smokies' law. You join the club, you learn the rules, and woe to the man who breaks them.

"All you westbound! All you westbound! Keep your ears peeled up ahead for that you-know-who! He's on the loose again tonight. Ryder P. Moses!"

There is a crowding of channels, a buzzing on the airwaves. Ryder P. Moses!

"Who?"

"Ryder P. Moses! Where you been, trucker?"

"Who is he?"

"Ryder—!"

"—crazy—"

"—weird—"

"—P.—!"

"—dangerous—"

"—probly a cop—"

"—Moses!"

"He's out there tonight!"

"I copied him going eastbound."

"I copied him westbound."

"I copied him standing still on an overpass."

Ryder P. Moses!

On 80 tonight. Out there somewhere. Which set of lights, which channel, is he listening? Does he know we know?

What do we know?

Only that he's been copied on and around 80 every night for a couple weeks now and that he's a terminal case of the heebiejeebs, he's an overdose of strange. He's been getting worse and worse, wilder and wilder, breaking every trucker commandment and getting away with it. Ryder P. Moses, he says, no handle, no Gutslinger or Green Monster or Oklahoma Crude, just Ryder P. Moses. No games with the Smokies, no hide-and-seek, just an open challenge. This is Ryder P. Moses eastbound at 260, going ninety per, he says. Catch me if you can. But the Smokies can't, and it bugs the piss out of them, so they're thick as flies along Nebraska 80, hunting for the crazy son, nailing poor innocent everyday truckers poking at seventy-five, Ryder P. Moses. Memorizes your license, your make, and your handle, then describes you from miles away, when you can't see another light on the entire plain, and tells you he's right behind you, watch out, here he comes right up your ass, watch out watch out! Modulating from what must be an illegal amount of wattage, coming on sometimes with "Ici Radio Canada" and gibbering phony frog over the CB, warning of ten-truck pile-ups and collapsed overpasses that never appear, leading truckers to put the hammer down right into a Smokey with a picture machine till nobody knows who to believe over the Band anymore. Till conversations start with "I am not now nor have I ever been Ryder P. Moses." A truck driver's gremlin that everyone has either heard or heard about, but no one has ever seen.

"Who is this Ryder P. Moses? Int that name familiar?"

"Wunt he that crazy independent got hisself shot up during the Troubles?"

"Wunt he a leg-breaker for the Teamsters?"

"Dint he use to be with P.I.E.?"

"—Allied?"

"—Continental Freightways?"

"—drive a 2500-gallon oil tanker?"

"—run liquor during Prohibition?"

"—run nylons during the War?"

"—run turkeys during Christmas?"

"Int that the guy? Sure it is."

"Short fella."

"Tall guy."

"Scar on his forehead, walks with a limp, left-hand index finger is missing."

"Sure, right, wears a leather jacket."

"—and a down vest."

"—and a lumber jacket and a Hawaiian shirt and a crucifix round his neck."

"Sure, that's the fella, medium height, always dressed in black. Ryder P. Moses."

"Dint he die a couple years back?"

"Sheeit, they aint no such person an never was."

"Ryder P. who?"

"Moses. This is Ryder P. Moses."

"What? Who said that?!"

"I did. Good evening, gentlemen."

Fingers fumble for volume knobs and squelch controls, conversations are dropped and attention turned. The voice is deep and emphatic.

"I'm Ryder P. Moses and I can outhaul, outhonk, outclutch any leadfoot this side of truckers' heaven. I'm half Mack, half Peterbilt, and half Sherman don't-tread-on-me tank. I drink fifty gallons of propane for breakfast and fart pure poison. I got steel mesh teeth, a chrome-plated nose, and three feet of stick on the floor. I'm the Paul mother-lovin Bunyan of the Interstate system and I don't care who knows it. I'm Ryder P. Moses and all you people are driving on *my* goddamn road. Don't you spit, don't you litter, don't you pee on the pavement. Just mind your p's and q's and we won't have any trouble."

Trucks pull alongside each other, the drivers peering across suspiciously, then both wave hands over head to deny guilt. They change channels and check each other out—handle, company, destination. They gang up on other loners and demand identification, challenge each other with trivia as if the intruder were a Martian or a Nazi spy. What's the capital of Tennessee, Tennessee Stomper? How far from Laramie to Cheyenne town, Casper Kid? Who won the '38 World Series, Truckin Poppa?

Small convoys form, grow larger, posses ranging eastbound and westbound on I-80. Only the CB can prove that the enemy is not among them, not the neighboring pair of taillights, the row of red up top like Orion's belt. He scares them for a moment, this Ryder P. Moses, scares them out of the air and back into their jarring hotboxes, back to work. But he thrills them a little, too.

"You still there, fellas? Good. It's question and answer period. Answer me this: do you know where your wife or loved one is right now? I mean *really know* for sure? You been gone a long time fellas, and you know how they are. Weak before Temptation. That's why we love em, that's how we get next to em in the first place, int it, fellas? There's just no telling *what* they're up to, is there? How bout that Alabama Rebel, you know where that little girl of yours is right now? What she's gettin herself into? This minute? And you there, Overload, how come the old lady's always so tired when you pull in late at night? What's she done to be so fagged out? She aint been haulin freight all day like you have. Or has she? I tell you fellas, take a tip from old Ryder P., you can't ever be certain of a *thing* in this world. You out here ridin the Interstate, somebody's likely back home riding that little girl. I mean just *think* about it, think about the way she looks, the faces she makes, the way she starts to smell, the things she says. The *noises* she makes. Now picture them shoes under the bed, aint they a little too big? Since when did you wear size twelves? Buddy, I hate to break it to you but maybe she's right now giving it, giving those faces and that smell and those noises, giving it all to some other guy.

"Some size twelve.

"You know how they are, those women, you see them in the truck stops pouring coffee. All those Billie Raes and Bobbie Sues, those Debbies and Annettes, those ass-twitching little things you marry and try to keep in a house. You know how they are. They're not built for one man, fellas, it's a fact of nature. I just want you to think about that for a while, chew on it, remember the last time you saw your woman and figure how long it'll be before you see her again. Think on it, fellas."

And, over the cursing and threats of truckers flooding his channel he begins to sing—

In the phone booth—at the truck stop
All alone,
I listen to the constant ringing—of your phone.
I'd try the bars and hangouts where
You might be found,
But I don't dare,
You might be there,
You're slippin round.

They curse and threaten but none of them turn him off. And some do think on it. Think as they have so many times before, distrusting with or without evidence, hundred-mile stretches of loneliness and paranoia. How can they know for sure their woman is any different from what they believe all women they meet to be—willing, hot, eager for action? Game in season. What *does* she do, all that riding time?

> I imagine—as I'm hauling
> Back this load.
> You waiting for me—at the finish
> Of the road.
> But as I wait for your hello
> There's not a sound.
> I start to weep,
> You're not asleep,
> You're slippin round.

The truckers overcrowd the channel in their rush to copy him, producing only a squarking complaint, something like a chorus of "Old MacDonald" sung from fifty fathoms deep. Finally the voice of Sweetpea comes through the jam and the others defer to her, as they always do. They have almost all seen her at one time or another, at some table in the Truckers Only section of this or that pit stop, and know she is a regular old gal, handsome looking in a country sort of way and able to field a joke and toss it back. Not so brassy as Colorado Hooker, not so butch as Flatbed Mama, you'd let that Sweetpea carry your load any old day.

"How bout that Ryder P. Moses, how bout that Ryder P. Moses, you out there, sugar? You like to modulate with a me a little bit?"

The truckers listen, envying the crazy son for this bit of female attention.

"Ryder P.? This is that Sweetpea moving along about that 390 mark, do you copy me?"

"Ah, yes, the Grande Dame of the Open Road! How's everything with Your Highness tonight?"

"Oh, passable, Mr. Moses, passable. But you don't sound none too good yourself, if you don't mind my saying. I mean we're just worried *sick* about you. You sound a little—over*strained?*"

"*Au contraire,* Madam, *au contraire.*"

She's got him, she has. You catch more flies with honey than with vinegar.

"Now tell me, honey, when's the last time you had yourself any sleep?"

"Sleep? *Sleep* she says! Who sleeps?"

"Why just *ev*rybody, Mr. Moses. It's a natural fact."

"That, Madam, is where you are mistaken. Sleep is obsolete, a thing of the bygone ages. It's been synthesized, chemically duplicated and sold at your corner apothecary. You can load up on it before a long trip—"

"Now I just don't know *what* you're talkin bout."

"Insensibility, Madam, stupor. The gift of Morpheus."

"Fun is fun, Ryder P. Moses, but you just not making *sense*. We are *not* amused. And we all getting a little bit *tired* of all your prankin around. And we—"

"Tired, did you say? Depressed? Overweight? Got that rundown feeling? Miles to go before you sleep? Friends and neighbors I got just the thing for you, a miracle of modern pharmacology! Vim and vigor, zip and zest, bright eyes and bushy tails—all these can be *yours,* neighbor, relief is just a swallow away! A couple of Co-Pilots in the morning orange juice, Purple Hearts for lunch, a mouthful of Coast-to-Coast for the wee hours of the night, and you'll droop no more. Ladies and gents, the best cure for time and distance is Speed. And we're all familiar with that, aren't we folks? We've all popped a little pep in our day, haven't we? Puts you on top of the world and clears your sinuses to boot. Wire yourself home with a little methamphetamine sulfate, melts in your mind, not in your mouth. No chocolate mess. Step right up and get on the ride, pay no heed to that man with the eight-ball eyes! Start with a little propadrine maybe, from the little woman's medicine cabinet? Clear up that stuffy nose? Then work your way up to the full-tilt boogie, twelve-plus grams of Crystal a day! It kind of grows on you, doesn't it, neighbor! Start eating that Sleep and you won't want to eat anything else. You know all about it, don't you, brothers and sisters of the Civilian Band, you've all been on that roller coaster. The only way to fly."

"Now Ryder, you just calm—"

"Benzedrine, Dexedrine,
We got the stash!"

he chants like a high-school cheerleader.

"Another thousand miles
Before the crash."

"Mr. Moses, you can't—"

"Coffee and aspirin,
No-Doz, Meth.
Spasms, hypertension,
Narcolepsy, death.
"Alpha, methyl,
Phenyl too,
Ethyl-amine's good for you!

"Cause when you're up you're up,
An when you're down you're down,
But when you're up behind Crystal
You're upside down!"

The airwaves crackle with annoyance. Singing on the CB! Sassing their woman, their Sweetpea, with drug talk and four-syllable words!

"—man's crazy—"

"—s' got to go—"

"—FCC ever hears—"

"—fix his wagon—"

"—like to catch—"

"—hophead—"

"—pill-poppin—"

"—weird talkin—"

"—turn him *off!*"

"Now boys," modulates Sweetpea, cooing soft and smooth, "I'm sure we can talk this whole thing out. Ryder P., honey, whoever you are, you must be runnin out of *fuel*. I mean you been going at it for *days* now, flittin round this Innerstate never coming to light. Must be just all *out* by now, aren't you?"

"I'm going strong, little lady, I got a bottle full of energy left and a thermos of Maxwell House to wash them down with."

"I don't mean *that*, Mr. Moses, I mean fuel *awl*. Int your tanks a little low? Must be runnin pert near empty, aren't you?"

"Madam, you have a point."

"Well if you don't fuel up pretty soon, you just gon be out of *luck*, Mister, they isn't but one more place westbound between here and that Grand Island town. Now Imo pull in that Bosselman's up ahead, fill this old hog of mine up. Wynch you just join me, I'll buy you a cup of coffee and we'll have us a little chitchat? That truck you got, whatever it is, can't run on no *pills*."

"Madam, it's a date. I got five or six miles to do and then it's Bosselman's for me and Old Paint here. Yes indeedy."

The other channels come alive. Bosselman's, on the

westbound, he's coming down! That Sweetpea could talk tears from a statue, an oyster from its shell. Ryder P. Moses in person, hotdamn!

They barrel onto the off-ramp, eastbound and westbound, full tanks and empty, a steady caravan of light bleeding off the main artery, leaving only scattered four-wheelers to carry on. They line up behind the diner in rows, twin stacks belching, all ears.

"This is that Ryder P. Moses, this is that Ryder P. Moses, in the parking lot at Bosselman's. Meet you in the coffee shop, Sweetpea."

Cab doors swing open and they vault down onto the gravel, some kind of reverse Grand Prix start, with men trotting away from their machines to the diner. They stampede at the door and mill suspiciously. Is that him, is that him? Faces begin to connect with handles remembered from some previous nighttime break. Hey, there's old Roadrunner, Roadrunner, this is Arkansas Traveler, I known him from before, he aint it, who's that over there? Overload, you say? You was up on I-29 the other night, north of Council Bluffs, wunt you? What you mean no, I had you on for pert near a half hour! You were where? Who says? Roadrunner, how could you talk to him on Nebraska 83 when I'm talking to him on I-29? Overload, somebody been takin your name in vain. What's that? You modulated with me yesterday from Rawlins? Buddy, I'm out of that Davenport town last evening, I'm *west*bound. Clutch Cargo, the one and only, always was and always will be. You're kidding! The name-droppin snake! Fellas we got to get to the bottom of this, but quick.

It begins to be clear, as they form into groups of three or four who can vouch for each other, that this Ryder P. Moses works in mysterious ways. That his voice, strained through capacitors and diodes, can pass for any of theirs, that he knows them, handle and style. It's outrageous, it is, it's like stealing mail or wiretapping, like forgery. How long has he gotten away with it, what has he said using their identities, what secrets spilled or discovered? If Ryder P. Moses has been each of them from time to time, what is to stop him from being one of them now? Which old boy among them is running a double life, which has got a glazed look around the eyes, a guilty twitch at the mouth? They file in to find Sweetpea sitting at a booth, alone.

"Boys," she says, "I believe I just been stood up."

They grumble back to their rigs, leaving waitresses with order pads gaping. The civilians in the diner buzz and puzzle—some mass, vigilante threat? Teamster extortion? Paramilitary maneuvers? They didn't like the menu? The trucks roar from the Bosselman's abruptly as they came.

On the Interstate again, they hear the story from Axle Sally. Sally broadcasts from the Husky three miles up on the eastbound side. Seems a cattle truck is pulled up by the pumps there, left idling. The boy doesn't see the driver, all he knows is it's pretty ripe, even for a stock-hauler. Something more than the usual cowshit oozing out from the air spaces. He tries to get a look inside but it's hard to get that close with the smell and all, so he grabs a flashlight and plays it around in back. And what do you think he sees? Dead. Dead for some time from the look of them, ribs showing, legs splayed, a heap of bad meat. Between the time it takes the boy to run in to tell Sally till they get back out to the pumps, whoever it was driving the thing has pumped himself twenty gallons and taken a powder. Then comes the call to Sally's radio, put it on my tab, he says. Ryder P. Moses, westbound.

They can smell it in their minds, the men who have run cattle or have had a stock wagon park beside them in the sleeping lot of some truck stop, the thought of it makes them near sick. Crazy. Stone wild crazy.

"Hello there again, friends and neighbors, this is Ryder P. Moses, the Demon of the Dotted Line, the Houdini of the Highways. Hell on eighteen wheels. Sorry if I inconvenienced anybody with the little change of plans there, but fuel oil was going for two cents a gallon cheaper at the Husky, and I never could pass up a bargain. Funny I didn't see any of you folks there, y'ought to be a little sharper with your consumer affairs. These are hard times, people, don't see how you can afford to let that kind of savings go by. I mean us truckers of all people should see the writing on the wall, the bad news in the dollars and cents department. Do we 'Keep America Moving' or don't we? And you know as well as me, there aint shit moving these days. Poor honest independent don't have a Chinaman's chance, and even Union people are being unsaddled left and right. Hard times, children. Just isn't enough stuff has to get from here to there to keep us in business. Hell, the only way to make it is to carry miscellaneous freight. Get that per-item charge on a full load and you're golden. Miscellaneous—"

(The blue flashers are coming now, zipping by the westbound truckers, sirenless in twos and threes, breaking onto the channel to say don't panic, boys, all we want is the cattle truck. All the trophy we need for tonight is Moses, you just lay back and relax. Oh those Smokies, when they set their minds to a thing they don't hold back, they hump after it full choke and don't spare the horse. Ryder P. Moses, your ass is *grass*. Smokey the Bear on your case and he will douse your fire. Oh yes.)

"—freight. Miscellaneous freight. Think about it, friends and neighbors, brothers and sisters, think about what exactly it is we haul all over God's creation here, about the goods and what they mean. About what they actually mean to you and me and everyone else in this great and good corporate land of ours. Think of what you're hauling right now. Ambergris for Amarillo? Gaskets for Gary? Oil for Ogalalla, submarines for Schenectady? Veal for Vermillion?"

(The Smokies moving up at nearly a hundred per, a shooting stream in the outside lane, for once allied to the truckers.)

"Tomato for Mankato, manna for Tarzana, stew for Kalamazoo, jerky for Albuquerque. Fruit for Butte."

(Outdistancing all the legitimate truckers, the Smokies are a blue pulsing in the sky ahead, the whole night on the blink.)

"Boise potatoes for Pittsburgh pots. Scottsbluff sugar for Tampa tea. Forage and fertilizer. Guns and caskets. Bull semen and hamburger. Sweetcorn, soy, stethoscopes and slide rules. Androids and zinnias. But folks, somehow we always come back empty. Come back less than we went. Diminished. It's a law of nature, it is, a law—"

They come upon it at the 375 marker, a convention of Bears flashing around a cattle truck on the shoulder of the road. What looks to be a boy or a very young man spread-eagled against the side of the cab, a half-dozen official hands probing his hidden regions. The trucks slow, one by one, but there is no room to stop. They roll down their co-pilot windows, but the only smell is the thick electric-blue of too many cops in one place.

"You see im? You see im? Just a kid!"

"—prolly stole it in the first place—"

"—gone crazy on drugs—"

"—fuckin hippie or somethin—"

"—got his ass but good—"

"—know who he is?"

"—know his handle?"

"—seen im before?"

"—the end of him, anyhow."

All order and etiquette gone with the excitement, they chew it over among themselves, who he might be, why he went wrong, what they'll do with him. Curiosity, and already a kind of disappointment. That soon it will be all over, all explained, held under the dull light of police classification, made into just some crackpot kid who took a few too many diet pills to help him through the night. It is hard to believe that the pale, skinny boy frisked in their headlights was who kept them turned around for weeks, who pried his way into their nightmares, who haunted the CB and outran the Smokies. That he could be the one who made the hours between Lincoln and Cheyenne melt into suspense and tension, that he could be—

"Ryder P. Moses, westbound on 80. Where *are* all you people?"

"Who?"

"What?"

"Where?"

"Ryder P. Moses, who else? Out here under that big black sky, all by his lonesome. I sure would preciate some company, Seems like you all dropped out of the running a ways back. Thought I seen some Bear tracks in my rear-view, maybe that's it. Now it's just me an a couple tons of beef. Can't say these steers is much for conversation, though. Nosir, you just can't beat a little palaver with your truckin brothers and sisters on the old CB to pass the time. Do I have a copy out there? Anybody?"

They switch to the channel they agreed on at the Bosselman's, and the word goes on down the line. He's still loose! He's still out there! The strategy is agreed on quickly—silent running. Let him sweat it out alone, talk to himself for a while and haul ass to catch him. It will be a race.

(Coyote, in an empty flatbed, takes the lead.)

"You're probably all wondering why I called you together tonight. Education. I mean to tell you some things you ought to know. Things about life, death, eternity. You know, tricks of the trade. The popular mechanics of the soul. A little exchange of ideas, communication, I-talk-you-listen, right?"

(Up ahead, far ahead, Coyote see taillights. Taillights moving at least as fast as he, almost eight-five in a strong crosswind. He muscles the clutch and puts the hammer down.)

"Friends, it's all a matter of wheels. Cycles. Clock hand always ends up where it started out, sun always dips back under the cornfield, people always plowed back into the ground. Take this beef chain I'm in on. We haul the semen to stud, the calves to rangeland, the one-year-olds to the feedlot, then to the slaughterhouse the packer the supermarket the corner butcher the table of J. Q. Public. J. Q. scarfs it down, puts a little body in his jizz, pumps a baby a year into the wife till his heart fattens and flops, and next thing you know he's pushing up grass on the lone prayree. You always end up less than what you were. The universe itself is shrinking. In cycles."

(Coyote closes to within a hundred yards. It is a cattle truck. He can smell it through his vent. When he tries to come closer it accelerates over a hundred, back end careening over two lanes. Coyote feels himself losing control, eases up. The cattle truck eases too, keeping a steady hundred yards between them. They settle back to eighty per.)

"Engines. You can grease them, oil them, clean their filters and replace their plugs, recharge them, antifreeze and STP them, treat them like a member of the family, but poppa, the miles take their toll, Time and Distance bring us all to rust. We haul engines from Plant A to Plant B to be seeded in bodies, we haul them to the dealers, buy them and waltz around a couple numbers, then drag them to the scrapyard. Junk City, U.S.A., where they break down into the iron ore of a million years from now. Some cycles take longer than others. Everything in this world is a long fall, a coming to rest, and an engine only affects where the landing will be.

"The cure for Time and Distance is Speed. Did you know that if you could travel at the speed of light you'd never age? That if you went faster than it, you would get younger? Think about that one, friends and neighbors, a cycle reversed. What happens when you reach year zero, egg and tadpole time, and keep speeding along? Do you turn into your parents? Put that in your carburetor and slosh it around."

And on he goes, into Relativity, the relationship of matter and energy, into the theory of the universe as a great Mobius strip, a snake swallowing its own tail. Leaving Coyote far behind, though the hundred yards between stays constant. On he goes, into the life of a cell, gerontology, cryogenics, hibernation theory. Through the seven stages of man and beyond, through the history of aging, the literature of immortality.

(Through Grand Island and Kearney, through Lexington and Cozad and Gothenburg, with Coyote at his heels, through a hundred high-speed miles of physics and biology and lunatic-fringe theology.)

"You can beat them, though, all these cycles. Oh yes, I've found the way. Never stop. If you never stop you can outrun them. It's when you lose your momentum that they get you.

"Take Sleep, the old whore. The seducer of the vital spark. Ever look at yourself in the mirror after Sleep has had hold of you, ever check your face out? Eyes pouched, neck lined, mouth puckered, it's all been worked on, cycled. Aged, Wrinkle City. The cycle catches you napping and carries you off a little closer to the ground. Sleep, ladies, when it has you under, those crows come tiptoeing on your face, sinking their tracks into you. Sleep, gents, you wake from her half stiff with urine, stumble out to do an old man's aimless, too-yellow pee. It bloats your prostate, pulls your paunch, plugs your ears, and gauzes your eyes. It sucks you, Sleep, sucks you dry and empty, strains the dream from your mind and the life from your body."

(Reflector posts ripping by, engine complaining, the two of them barreling into Nebraska on the far edge of control.)

"And you people let it have you, you surrender with open arms. Not me. Not Ryder P. Moses. I swallow my sleep in capsules and keep one step ahead. Rest not, rust not. Once you break from the cycle, escape that dull gravity, then, people, you travel in a straight line and there is nothing so pure in this world. The Interstate goes on forever and you never have to get off.

"And it's beautiful. Beautiful. The things a sleeper never sees open up to you. The most beautiful dream is the waking one, the one that never ends. From a straight line you see all the cycles going on without you, night fading in and out, the sun's arch, stars forming and shifting in their signs. The night especially, the blacker the better, your headlights making a ghost of color on the roadside, focusing to climb the white line. You feel like you can ride deeper and deeper into it, that night is a state you never cross, but only get closer and closer to its center. And in the daytime there's the static of cornfields, cornfields, cornfields, flat monotony like a hum in your eye, like you're going so fast it seems you're standing still, that the country is a still life on your windshield."

(It begins to weave gently in front of Coyote now, easing to the far right, nicking the shoulder gravel, straightening for a few miles, then drifting left. Nodding. Coyote hangs back a little further, held at bay by a whiff of danger.)

"Do you know what metaphor is, truckin mamas and poppas? Have you ever met with it in your waking hours? Benzedrine, there's a metaphor for you, and a good one. For sleep. It serves the same purpose but makes you understand better, makes everything clear, opens the way to more metaphor. Friends and neighbors, have you ever seen dinosaurs lumbering past you, the road sizzle like a fuse, night drip down like old blood? I have, people, I've seen things only gods and the grandfather stars have seen, I've seen dead men sit in my cab beside me and living ones melt like wax. When you break through the cycle you're beyond the laws of man, beyond CB manners or Smokies' sirens or statutes of limitations. You're beyond the laws of nature, time, gravity, friction, forget them. The only way to win is never to stop. Never to stop. Never to stop."

The sentences are strung out now, a full minute or two between them.

"The only escape from friction is a vacuum."

(Miles flying under, North Platte glowing vaguely ahead on the horizon, Coyote, dogged, hangs on.)

There is an inexplicable crackling on the wire, as if he were growing distant. There is nothing for miles to interfere between them. "The shortest distance— between two points—ahh—a straight line."

(Two alone on the plain, tunneling Nebraska darkness.)

"Even the earth—is falling. Even—the sun—is burning out."

(The side-to-side drifting more pronounced now, returns to the middle more brief. Coyote strains to pick the voice from electric jam. North Platte's display brightens. Miles pass.)

"Straight—"

There is a very loud crackling now, his speaker open but his words hung, a crackling past the Brady exit, past Maxwell. (Coyote creeping up a bit, then lagging as the stock-hauler picks up speed and begins to slalom for real. Coyote tailing it like a hunter after a gut-ripped animal spilling its last, and louder crackling as it lurches, fishtails, and lurches ahead wheels screaming smoke spewing saved only by the straightness of the road and crackling back when Coyote breaks into the Band yelling Wake up! Wake up! Wake up! pulling horn and flicking lights till the truck ahead steadies, straddling half on half off the right shoulder in direct line with the upspeeding concrete support of an overpass and he speaks. Calm and clear and direct.)

"This is Ryder P. Moses," he says. "Going west. Good night and happy motoring."

(Coyote swerves through the flameout, fights for the road as the sky begins a rain of beef.)

The Richard Nixon Freischütz Rag

Guy Davenport

GUY DAVENPORT was born in Anderson, South Carolina, and teaches at the University of Kentucky. He is the author of two books of stories, *Tatlin!* and *Da Vinci's Bicycle*, and has also published a long poem, *Flowers and Leaves*, three books of translations of early Greek poetry, and one of Greek philosophy, as well as literary studies and essays.

On the Great Ten Thousand Li Wall, begun in the wars of the Spring and Autumn to keep the Mongols who had been camping nearer and nearer the Yan border from riding in hordes on their przhevalskis into the cobbled streets and ginger gardens of the Middle Flower Kingdom, Richard Nixon said:

—I think you would have to conclude that this is a great wall.

Invited by Marshall Yeh Chien-ying to inspect a guard tower on the ramparts, he said:

—We will not climb to the top today.

In the limousine returning to The Forbidden City, he said:

—It is worth coming sixteen thousand miles to see the Wall.

Of the tombs of the Ming emperors, he said:

—It is worth coming to see these, too.

—Chairman Mao says, Marshal Yeh ventured, that the past is past.

The translator had trouble with the sentiment, which lost its pungency in English.

—All over? Richard Nixon asked.

—We have poem, Marshal Yeh said, which I recite.

West wind keen,
Up steep sky
Wild geese cry
For dawn moon,

For cold dawn
White with frost,
When horse neigh,
Bugle call.

Boast not now
This hard pass
Was like iron
Underfoot.

At the top
We see hills
And beyond
The red sun.

Richard Nixon leaned with attention, grinning, to hear the translation from the interpreter, Comrade Tang Wen-sheng, whose English had been learned in Brooklyn, where she spent her childhood.

—That's got to be a good poem, Richard Nixon said.

—Poem by Chairman Mao, Comrade Tang offered.

—He wrote that? Richard Nixon asked. Made it up?

—At hard pass over Mountain Lu, Marshal Yeh said. Long March. February 1935.

—My! but that's interesting, Richard Nixon said. Really, really interesting.

The limousine slid past high slanting walls of The Forbidden City on which posters as large as tennis courts bore writing Richard Nixon could not read. They proclaimed, poster after poster by which the long limousine moved, *Make trouble, fail. Again make trouble, again fail. Imperialist reactionary make trouble and fail until own destruction. Thought of Chairman Mao.*

The limousine stopped at The Dragon Palace. Richard Nixon got out. Guards of the Heroic People's Volunteer Army stood at attention. On a wall inside the courtyard four tall posters caught the eye of Richard Nixon.

—That's Marx, he said, pointing.

—Marx, repeated Marshal Yeh.

—And that's Engels.

—Engels.

—And that's Lenin and that's Stalin.

—Precisely, Marshal Yeh replied.

Richard Nixon went back to the second poster, pointing to it with his gloved hand.

—That's Engels?

—Engels, Marshal Yeh said with a worried, excessively polite look in his eyes.

—We don't see many pictures of Engels in America, Richard Nixon explained.

That man old Toscanelli put up to sailing to the Japans and Cathay westward out from Portugal, the

Genovese Colombo, they have been saying around the Uffizi, has come back across the Atlantic. *Una prova elegantissima!* Benedetto Arithmetic would say. The Aristotelians will be scandalized, *di quale se fanno beffa*. The Platonists will fluff their skirts and freeze the air with their lifted noses. *È una stella il mundo!* But like the moon, forsooth, round as a melon, plump and green. Oh, he could see those *caravelle* butting salt and savage waves, the awful desert of water and desolation of the eye, until the unimaginable shorebirds of Cipongo wheeled around their sails and the red tiles and bamboo *pergole* of Mongol cities came into focus on capes and promontories. Inland, there were roads out to Samarkand, India, Persia, Hungary, Helvetia, and thus back to Tuscany.

He had completed the world journey of the Magi, it occurred to Leonardo as he moved the bucket of grasses that Salai had brought him from Fiesole. They had come from the East, astrologers, and Colombo's sails, in these days of signs wherein every moving thing must declare itself for God or Islam, would have worn the cross, which the philosophers of the Medes did not wait to learn would be forever, until the end of time, the hieroglyph of the baby before whom they laid their gifts in the dark stable. The world was knit by prophecy, by light.

Meadow grass from Fiesole, icosahedra, cogs, gears, plaster, maps, lutes, brushes, an adze, magic squares, pigments, a Roman head Brunelleschi and Donatello brought him from their excavations, the skeleton of a bird: how beautifully the Tuscan light gave him his things again every morning, even if the kite had been in his sleep.

Moments, hours, days. Had man done anything at all?

The old woman had brought the wine and the bread,

the onions. He and Toscanelli, Pythagoreans, ate no meat.

The machine stood against the worktable, the *due rote*, unaccountably outrageous in design. Saccapane the smith was making the chain that would span the two *rote dentate*. You turned the pedals with your feet, which turned the big cog wheel, which pulled the chain forward, cog by cog, causing the smaller wheel to turn the hind *rota*, thereby propelling the whole machine forward. As long as the machine was in motion, the rider would balance beautifully. The forward motion stole away any tendency to fall right or left, as the flow of a river discouraged a boat from wandering.

If only he knew the languages! He could name his machines as Archimedes would have named them, in the ancient words. He called his flying machine the bird, *l'uccello*. Benedetto said that the Greeks would have called it an *ornitottero,* the wings of a bird.

Light with extravagance and precision, mirror of itself *atomo per atomo* from its dash against the abruptness of matter to the jelly of the eye, swarmed from high windows onto the two-wheeled balancing machine. The rider would grasp horns set on the fork in which the front wheel was fixed and thus guide himself with nervous and accurate meticulousness. Suddenly he saw the Sforze going into battle on it, a phalanx of these *duo rote* bearing lancers at full tilt. *Avanti, O Coraggiosi, O!* the trumpet called, *tambureggiandi le bacchette delli tamburi di battaglia.*

The scamp Salai was up and about.

—*Maestro!* he piped. You've made it!

Leonardo picked up the brown boy Salai, shouldered him like a sack of flour, and danced the long, gliding steps of a sarabande.

—*Sì, Cupidello mio, tutto sennonchè manca la catena.*

—And then I can make it go, ride it like a pony?

—Like the wind, like Ezekiel's angel, like the horses of Ancona.

Salai squirmed free and knelt before the strange machine, touching the pedals, the wicker spokes, the saddle, the toothed wheels around which the chain would fit, *i vinci.*

—*Como leone!*

He turned to the basket of flowering grasses, reaching for his silver pencil. Bracts and umbrels fine as a spider's legs! And in the thin green veins ran hairs of water, and down the hairs of water ran light, down into the dark, into the root. Light from the farthest stars flowed through these long leaves. He had seen the prints of leaves from the time of the flood in mountain rocks, and had seen there shells from the sea.

—Maestro, Salai said, when will the chain be ready?

—Chain? Leonardo asked. What chain?

He drew with his left hand a silver eddy of grass. It was grace that he drew, perfection, frail leaves through which moved the whole power of God, and when a May fly lights on a green arc of grass the splendor of that conjunction is no less than San Gabriele touching down upon the great dome at Byzantium, closing the crushed silver and spun glass of his four wings around the golden shaft of his height.

—The chain, Salai said, the chain!

Did man know anything at all?

Before flying to China, Richard Nixon ordered a thousand targets in Laos and Cambodia bombed by squadrons of B-52s. He sent one thousand, one hundred and twenty-five squadrons of bombers to silence the long-range field guns of North Viet Nam along the border of the DMZ. Richard Nixon was pleased with the bombing, knowing that Chairman Mao would be impressed by such power. Dr. Kissinger had recommended the one thousand, one hundred and twenty-five squadrons of bombers to Richard Nixon as something that would impress Chairman Mao. The bombs were falling thick as hail in a summer storm when Richard Nixon set foot on China, grinning. A band played *The March of the Volunteers*. Premier Chou En-lai did not walk forward. Richard Nixon had to walk to where Premier Chou stood grinning. They shook hands.

—We came by way of Guam, Richard Nixon said. It is better that way.

—You have good trip? Premier Chou asked.

—You should know, Richard Nixon said. You are such a traveler.

Richard Nixon rode in a limousine to Taio Yu Tai, outside The Forbidden City. As soon as he got to his room, the telephone rang.

—Who would be calling me in China? he asked.

Dr. Kissinger answered the telephone.

—Yes? he said.

—Excellency Kissinger? a voice asked. You are there?

—We are here, Dr. Kissinger said.

—His Excellency the President Nixon is there?

—Right here, said Dr. Kissinger, taking off his shoes.

—Would His Excellency Nixon come to telephone?

—Sure, said Dr. Kissinger. For you, Dick.

Richard Nixon took the telephone, put it to his ear, and looked at the ceiling, where scarlet dragons swam through clouds of pearl.

—Nixon here, he said.

—Excellency President Nixon there?

—Right here, Richard Nixon said. To who have I the honor of addressing?

—Now you speak with Comrade Secretary Wang.

A new voice came on the line. It said:

—Chairman Mao invite you, now, come to visit him.

—Right now? Richard Nixon asked. We've just got off the plane. We came by way of Guam.

—Now, said the telephone. You come visit. Yes?

—OK, Richard Nixon said. Will do. You coming to pick us up?

The line had gone dead.

—Son of a bitch, Richard Nixon said.

Dr. Kissinger rocked on his heels and grinned from ear to ear.

Roses, buttons, thimbles, lace. The grass grows up to the stones, the road. There are flowers in the grass and flowers on her dress. And buttons down her dress, and lace on the collar and cuffs and hem. And buttons on her shoes. In the Luxembourg she wears a shawl from Segovia and Pablo says she looks like a Spanish woman of the old school, when women were severe and well-bred and kind, and I say that she looks like an officer in the Union Army. We sing "The Trail of the Lonesome Pine," which she plays on the piano, throwing in snatches of "Marching Through Georgia" and "Alexander's Ragtime Band." She has Pumpelly's nose, the hands of a Spanish saint.

In France she wears a yellow hat, in Italy a Panama. Alice, I say, Assisi, the grass of Assisi, and the leaves Sassetta. We walk comfortably over the stones, hearing the bells ring for the nuns and the girls in their school. It is so quiet, she says, being herself quiet to say that it is quiet. Spain is a still life, I say, only Italy is landscape. The birds there, she says. St. Francis, I say. The birds suffer their suffering each in a lifetime, forgetting it as they endure. We remember suffering from years and years ago. Do not talk of old things, she says. There is no time anymore, only now. Not, say I, if you can hear as I can the bugles and see the scarlet flags.

And I could, I can, I always can. The officers sit in their saddles and the guidons with their Victorian numbers and faded reds move to the head of the column. It is an old way with men, it happened at Austerlitz and Sevastopol. The generals are high on their horses, listening to the band, to the shouts of the sergeants. It is glory. When Leo moved out, we trotted around the room like horses, and Basket went around with us. I was the general and Alice was the officer and Basket was the horse, and all together we were Napoleon. We were pickaninnies cakewalking before the elders on a Saturday in Alabama, we were Barnum and Bailey and the Great Rat of Sumatra going a progress to Chantilly to see the lace and the cream.

It is quiet, she says, and I say, Alice, look at the flowers. Yes, she says. Yes, I say. Is it not grand to say *yes* back and forth when we mean something else and she went behind a bush and loosened her stays and camisole and shamelessly stepped out of the frilly heap they made around her buttoned shoes and I said *yes*, here where St. Francis walked, Alice, you do realize, don't you, that the reason we came to Assisi is you are from San Francisco and this is the hometown of St. Francis and she says I am wrapping my underthings in my shawl, do you think anyone will notice?

Red tile, moss, pigeons. We drink wine under the trees, though it is too hot to drink wine. Well, I say, we are here. Yes, she says, we are here, and her eyes jiggle and her smile is that of a handsome officer who has been called to headquarters and seen General Grant and is pleased to please, well-bred that he is.

This is not Fouquet's, I say. Certainly not Fouquet's, she says. I touch her foot with my foot, she touches my foot with her foot. The crickets sing around us, fine as Stravinsky. If Spain is a still life, what is Italy? They came here, I said, the grand old poets, because the women have such eyes. Surely not to see the cats, Alice says. No, I say, not for the cats. Henry James came here for the tone. William might come here and never see the tone. William if he came would take the proportions, and would not look at the cats. A princess and a cart go by, Henry sees the princess and William sees the wheel of the cart how it is in such fine proportion to the tongue and the body.

When you talk, she says, I shiver all over, things flutter around inside. When you smile, I say, I bite into peaches and Casals plays Corelli and my soul is a finch in cherries. Let us talk and smile forever. This is forever, Alice says. It is so quiet. Look at the dust, I say. Would you walk in it barefoot? Another glass of wine, she says, and I will fly over the bell tower. Did you have a rosewood piano in San Francisco? I ask. With a bust of Liszt on it, she says, and a vase of marigolds.

Look at these colors and you can see why Sassetta was Sassetta. Will we go to England again, she says, to sit in the cathedrals? Look at these hills and you will know why St. Francis was St. Francis.

The roses, she says, are very old. They are the roses of Ovid, I say. They are the only roses that are red. If I knew the Latin for red I would say it, if the Latin for rose, I would say it, the Latin for the only red in the oldest rose, I would say it. Were I Ovid, I would give you a rose and say that it is given for your eyes. I would take it, she says. I am glad you would, I say, touching her foot with my foot. Sassetta's rose, Pablo's rose.

Madame Matisse is a gentian, she says, touching my foot with her foot. Are all women flowers, all girls? Henri Rousseau was married to a sunflower, Cézanne to a pear tree.

Alice, I say. Yes, General Grant, she says. Pickaninny, I say. Augustus Caesar, she says. Do you see those pines over there, the ones that look like William McKinley addressing the Republican Party? You mustn't mention McKinley to Pablo, she says, he thinks he has trod on the honor of Spain. He has, I say, that is the American way. But the pines, Alice, the pines. I see them, she says, they have had a hard life. Do you, I say, see the bronze fall of needles beneath them, and know the perfume of rosin and dust and old earth we would smell if we climbed there? The flutter has begun, she says. And now look at the rocks, the cubist rocks, down the hills from the pines, and the red tile of the roofs, and the chickens in the yard there, the baskets. I see all that, she says. And having seen it, Alice? I ask. It is there to see, she says. That is the answer, I say. It is also the question.

Mao sat in his red armchair looking benign and amused. Richard Nixon sank too far into his chair, his elbows as high as his ears. He beamed. He did not see the stacks of journals, the shelves packed with books, the bundles of folders, the writing brushes in jars. He beamed at Mao and at Dr. Kissinger, whom Mao had called a modern Metternich. The reporters had written that down.

The cluttered room was dark. What light there was came from tall windows which gave onto a courtyard as bleak as the playground of a grammar school. The translator said that Chairman Mao had asked about hegemony.

—We're for it, Richard Nixon said.

—Your aides are very young, Chairman Mao said.

—Are they? Richard Nixon asked.

—We must learn from you on that point, Chairman Mao said. Our government is all of old men.

Richard Nixon did not know what to say.

—Old, Chairman Mao said, but here, still here.

—The world is watching us, Richard Nixon said.

—You mean Taiwan, Chairman Mao said.

—No, Richard Nixon said, beaming, the world out there, the whole world. They are watching their TV sets.

Chairman Mao grinned and leaned back in his comfortable armchair.

—Ah so, he said, the world.

Night March

Tim O'Brien

TIM O'BRIEN is a native of Minnesota and a former reporter for the *Washington Post.* He is the author of *Going After Cacciato,* which won the National Book Award in 1979, and two other novels, *Northern Lights* and *If I Die in a Combat Zone.*

The platoon of twenty-six soldiers moved slowly in the dark, single file, not talking. One by one, like sheep in a dream, they passed through the hedgerow, crossed quietly over a meadow and came down to the rice paddy. There they stopped. Their leader knelt down, motioning with his hand, and one by one the others squatted or knelt or sat. For a long time they did not move. Except for the sounds of their breathing, and once a soft, fluid trickle as one of them urinated, the twenty-six men were silent: some of them excited by the adventure, some of them afraid, some of them exhausted from the long night march, some of them looking forward to reaching the sea, where they would be safe. At the rear of the column, Private First Class Paul Berlin lay quietly with his forehead pressed against the black plastic stock of his rifle, his eyes closed. He was pretending. He was pretending he was not in the war, pretending he had not watched Billy Boy Watkins die of a heart attack that afternoon. He was pretending he was a boy again, camping with his father in the midnight summer along the Des Moines River. In the dark, with his eyes pinched shut, he pretended. He pretended that when he opened his eyes, his father would be there by the campfire and they would talk softly about whatever came to mind and then roll into their sleeping bags, and that later they'd wake up and it would be morning and there would not be a war, and that Billy Boy Watkins had not died of a heart attack that afternoon. He pretended he was not a soldier.

In the morning, when they reached the sea, it would be better. The hot afternoon would be forgotten, would not have happened; he would bathe in the sea, and he would forget how frightened he had been on his first day at the war. The second day would be better. He would learn.

There was a sound beside him, a movement, and then a breathed "Hey!" The shadow whispered, "Hey!" and Paul Berlin opened his eyes, shivering, and the shadow whispered, "Hey! We're *moving,* for Chrissake. Get up."

"Okay."

"You sleeping or something?"

"No." He could not make out the soldier's face. With clumsy, concrete hands he clawed for his rifle, found it, found his helmet.

The soldier-shadow grunted. "You got a very lot to learn, buddy. I'd shoot you if I thought you was sleeping. Let's go."

Private First Class Paul Berlin blinked.

Ahead of him, silhouetted against the sky, he saw the string of soldiers beginning to wade into the flat paddy waters, the black outline of their shoulders and weapons and packs. He was comfortable. He did not want to move. But he was afraid, for it was his first night at the war, and he hurried to catch up, stumbling once, scraping his knee and groping; his boots sank into the thick paddy and he smelled it all around him, the fear, and the war. He would tell his mother how it smelled. Of mud and algae, he would tell her, of cattle manure and chlorophyll, decay, breeding mosquitoes and leeches as big as mice, the rich warmth of the waters rising up to his cut knee. He would tell her this, but not how frightened he had been in the afternoon, when Billy Boy died of a heart attack.

Once they reached the sea, things would be better. Their rear would be guarded by five thousand miles of open ocean, and they would swim and dive into the breakers and hunt crayfish and smell the salt, and they would be safe.

Private First Class Paul Berlin followed the shadow of the man in front of him. It was a clear night. Already the Southern Cross was out. And other stars he could not yet name—soon, he thought, soon he would learn their names. And puffy night clouds. There was not yet a moon. Wading through the paddy, his boots made sleepy, sloshing sounds, like a lullaby, and he tried not to think. Though he was afraid, he now knew that fear comes in many degrees and types and peculiar categories, and he knew that his fear now was not so bad as it had been in the hot afternoon, when poor Billy

Boy Watkins got killed by a heart attack. His fear now was diffuse and unfocused—ghosts in the tree line, nighttime fears of a child, a boogieman in the closet that his father would open to show empty, saying, "See? Nothing there, champ. Now you can sleep." In the afternoon it had been different. The fear had been bundled and tight, and he'd been on his hands and knees, crawling like an insect, an ant escaping a giant's footsteps, thinking nothing, brain flopping like wet cement in a mixer, not thinking at all, watching while Billy Boy died.

Now, as he stepped out of the paddy onto a narrow dirt path, now the fear was mostly the fear of being so terribly afraid again.

He tried not to think.

There were tricks he'd learned to keep from thinking. Counting: he counted his steps, concentrating on the numbers, pretending that the steps were dollar bills and that each step through the night made him richer and richer, so that soon he would become a wealthy man, and he kept counting and considered the ways he might spend the money after the war, what he would do, what he would say if asked. He would look his father in the eye and shrug and say, "It was pretty bad at first, but I learned a lot and I got used to it." Then he would tell his father the story of Billy Boy Watkins. A good war story, a story to be passed on. Yes, he would tell the story, but he would never let on how frightened he had been. "Not so bad," he would say instead, making his father proud.

Songs, another trick to stop the thinking: *Where have you gone, Billy Boy, Billy Boy, oh, where have you gone, charming Billy? I have gone to seek a wife, she's the joy of my life, but she's a young thing and cannot leave her mother,* and other songs that he sang in his thoughts as he walked toward the sea. And when he reached the sea he would dig a deep hole in the sand and he would sleep like the high clouds, and he would not be afraid again.

The moon came out. Pale and shrunken to the size of a dime.

The helmet was heavy on his head. In the morning he would adjust the leather binding. He would clean his rifle, too. Though he had been unable to fire it during the hot afternoon, he would carefully clean the breech and barrel and muzzle so that next time he would be ready and not so afraid. In the morning, when they reached the sea, he would begin to make friends among the other soldiers. He would learn their names and laugh at their jokes. Then when the war ended he would have war buddies, and he would write to them now and then to exchange memories.

Walking, sleeping in his walking, he felt better. He watched the moon come higher.

Once they skirted a sleeping village. The smells again—straw, cattle, mildew. The men were quiet. On the far side of the village, deep in the dark smells, a dog barked. The column stopped until the barking died away; then they marched fast away from the village, through a graveyard waxed with conical-shaped burial mounds and tiny altars of clay and stone. The graveyard had a perfumy smell. A nice place to spend the night. The mounds would make fine battlements, and the smells were good and the place was quiet. But they went on, passing through a hedgerow and through another paddy and east toward the sea.

He walked carefully. He remembered what he'd been taught: stay off the center of the path, for that's where the land mines will be planted, where stupid and lazy soldiers like to walk. Stay alert, he'd been taught. Better alert than inert. Ag-ile, mo-bile, hos-tile. Walking, step on step, he wished he'd paid better attention to the training. He could not remember what they'd said about the awful fear, how to stop it, what to say to it. They'd forgotten the lessons in courage, and they hadn't mentioned how Billy Boy Watkins would die of a heart attack, his face turning pale and the veins popping out.

Private First Class Paul Berlin walked carefully.

Stretching ahead like dark beads on a chain, the string of soldiers whose names he did not yet know moved with the silence and slow grace of smoke. Now and again, moonlight reflected off a machine gun or a wristwatch. But mostly the soldiers were quiet and hidden and faraway-seeming in a peaceful night, strangers on a long street, and he felt quite separate from them, as if trailing behind like the caboose on a night train, pulled along by inertia, sleepwalking, and afterthought to the war.

So he walked carefully, counting his steps. When he had counted to three thousand four hundred and fifty, the column stopped.

One by one, the soldiers squatted or knelt down.

The grass along the path was wet. Private First Class Paul Berlin lay back and turned his head so he could lick at the dew with his eyes closed, another trick to forget the war. He might have slept. "I *wasn't* afraid," he was saying, or dreaming, facing his father's stern eyes. "I wasn't afraid," he was saying, coming up on his elbows. A soldier beside him, quietly chewing mint-smelling gum.

"Sleeping again?" the soldier whispered.

"No," said Private First Class Paul Berlin. "Hell no."

The soldier grunted, twisted the cap off his canteen, swallowed, and handed it through the dark. "Take some."

"Thanks."

"You're the new guy."

"Yes." He did not want to admit it, but he said it again. "Yes."

The soldier handed him a stick of gum. "Chew it quiet, okay? Don't blow no bubbles or nothing."

"Thanks. I won't." He could not make out the boy's face in the shadows.

They sat still, and Private First Class Paul Berlin chewed the gum until all the sugars were gone; then the soldier said, "Bad day today, buddy."

Paul Berlin nodded wisely, but he did not speak.

"Don't think it's always so bad," the soldier whispered. "I don't want to scare you. You'll get used to it soon enough, I guess—they been fighting wars a long time, and you get used to it."

"Sure."

"You will."

They were quiet awhile. And the night was quiet, no crickets or birds, and it was hard to imagine it was truly a war. He searched for the soldier's face but could not find it. It did not matter much. Even if he saw the boy's face he would not know the name, and even if he knew the name it would not matter.

"Haven't got the time?" the soldier whispered.

"No."

"Rats . . . Don't matter, really. Goes faster if you don't know the time, anyhow."

"I suppose."

"What's your name, buddy?"

"Paul."

"Nice to meet and greet ya," he said, and in the dark beside the path they shook hands. "Mine's Tony. Everybody calls me Buffalo, though." The soldier's hand was strangely warm and soft, but it was a very big hand. "Sometimes they just call me Buff," he said.

And again they were quiet. They lay in the grass and waited. The moon was very high now and very bright, and they were waiting for cloud cover.

The soldier suddenly snorted.

"What is it?"

"Nothing," he said, but then he snorted again. "A lousy heart attack! A *heart* attack! Can't get over it—old Billy Boy croaking from a lousy heart attack, pow, down he goes. A heart attack—can you believe it?"

It made Private First Class Paul Berlin smile. He couldn't help it.

"Ever hear of such a thing?"

"Not till now," said Paul Berlin, still smiling.

"Me neither," said the soldier in the dark. "Gawd, dying of a heart attack. Didn't know him, did you?"

"No."

"Tough as nails."

"Yeah."

"And what happens? A heart attack. Can you imagine it?"

"Yes," said Private First Class Paul Berlin. "I can imagine it." And he imagined it clearly. He giggled—he couldn't help it. He imagined Billy's father opening the telegram: SORRY TO INFORM YOU THAT YOUR SON BILLY BOY WAS YESTERDAY SCARED TO DEATH IN ACTION IN THE REPUBLIC OF VIETNAM, VALIANTLY SUCCUMBING TO A HEART ATTACK SUFFERED WHILE UNDER ENORMOUS STRESS, AND IT IS WITH GREATEST SYMPATHY THAT . . . He giggled again. He rolled onto his belly, pressed his face into his arms. He was shaking with the giggles.

The big soldier hissed at him to shut up, but he could not stop giggling and remembering the hot afternoon, and poor Billy Boy, and how they'd been drinking Coke from bright-red aluminum cans, and how they'd started on the day's march, and how a little while later poor Billy Boy stepped on the mine, and how it made a tiny little sound—*poof*—and how Billy Boy just stood there with his mouth wide open, looking down, then shaking his head, surprised-looking, and how finally Billy Boy sat down very casually, not saying a word, his foot lying behind him with most of it still in the boot.

Paul Berlin giggled louder—he could not stop.

He bit his arm, trying to stifle it, but remembering: "War's over, Billy," the man had said in consolation, but Billy Boy got scared and started crying and said it was over. "It's all over," he kept saying, scaring himself. "Nonsense," the medic said, Doc Peret, but Billy Boy kept bawling, tightening up, his face going pale and transparent and his veins popping out. Scared stiff. Even when Doc stuck him with morphine, Billy Boy kept crying.

"Shut up!" the big soldier hissed, but Private First Class Paul Berlin could not stop. Giggling and remembering, he covered his mouth. His eyes stung, remembering how it was when Billy Boy died of fright.

"Quiet!"

But he could not stop giggling, the same way Billy Boy could not stop bawling that afternoon.

Afterward Doc Peret had explained: "You see, Billy Boy really died of a heart attack. He was scared he was ready to die—so scared he had himself a heart attack, and that's what really killed him. I seen it before."

So they wrapped Billy Boy in a plastic poncho, his eyes still wide open and scared stiff, and they carried him over the meadow to the paddy; then, when the medevac helicopter arrived, they carried him through the paddy and shoved him aboard; then things were exploding everywhere, people yelling, the heat, and the chopper pulled up and jerked and Billy Boy came tumbling out, falling slowly and then faster, and the paddy water sprayed up as if Billy Boy had just executed a long and dangerous dive, or as if Billy had been killed by a heart attack.

"Shut up, for Chrissake!" the big soldier hissed, but Paul Berlin could not stop giggling, remembering: scared to death.

Later they had waded in after him, probing for Billy with their rifle butts, elegantly and delicately probing for him through the thick waters, singing—some of them—*Where have you gone, Billy Boy, Billy Boy, oh, where have you gone, charming Billy?* They found him. Green and clothes in algae, his eyes open and still scared, dead of a heart attack.

"Quiet!" the soldier screamed, shaking him.

But Private First Class Paul Berlin could not stop. The giggles came from that place deep in his groin, the place that secreted the purple chemicals of fear, and he could not stop. Giggling, lying on his back, he saw the moon move, or the clouds moving across the moon. Wounded in action, dead of fright. A fine war story. He would tell it to his father, how Billy Boy Watkins had been scared to death, never letting on . . . He could not stop. He was afraid, and he could not stop.

The soldier smothered him. He tried to fight back, but he was weak from the giggles, wet in the eyes.

Then the moon was under clouds. The column was moving. He was tired. The soldier helped him up. "Okay now, buddy?"

"Sure."

"You can get killed, laughing that way."

"I know. I know that."

"You got to stay calm, buddy. It's the whole trick,

staying calm." The soldier handed him his rifle. "Half the battle, at least, just staying calm. You'll get better at it. Come on, now."

He turned away, and Private First Class Paul Berlin hurried after him. He was still shivering.

He fell into the pace of the march, began counting again, each step, one and the next. Lightheaded, blank-eyed in the great dark, he lost track of the numbers, which came without sequence, randomly, a jumbled and tumbling and chaotic rush of numbers that ran like fluid through his head. Ahead of him, quiet, the column of soldiers plodded through the ongoing nighttime. He felt better. He would never be so afraid again. It would become a part of history, it would become a funny and sad tale to tell to his father and his friends, who would either believe or not believe, and there would be other stories later. He walked fast. In the morning he would do better. A war story, a good joke. He closed his eyes and walked, and he smelled many things. He smelled the grass and the trees and the clouds of low fog, and soon he could even smell the sea, but he could not stop being afraid.

Separating

John Updike

JOHN UPDIKE was born in Shillington, Pennsylvania, in 1932, and presently lives in Massachusetts. He has published nine novels and four volumes of poetry, as well as six collections of short stories. His last collection, *Problems and Other Stories*, contains "Separating."

The day was fair. Brilliant. All that June the weather had mocked the Maples' internal misery with solid sunlight—golden shafts and cascades of green in which their conversations had wormed unseeing, their sad murmuring selves the only stain in Nature. Usually by this time of the year they had acquired tans; but when they met their elder daughter's plane on her return from a year in England they were almost as pale as she, though Judith was too dazzled by the sunny opulent jumble of her native land to notice. They did not spoil her homecoming by telling her immediately. Wait a few days, let her recover from jet lag, had been one of their formulations, in that string of gray dialogues—over coffee, over cocktails, over Cointreau—that had shaped the strategy of their dissolution, while the earth performed its annual stunt of renewal unnoticed beyond their closed windows. Richard had thought to leave at Easter; Joan had insisted they wait until the four children were at last assembled, with all exams passed and ceremonies attended, and the bauble of summer to console them. So he had drudged away, in love, in dread, repairing screens, getting the mowers sharpened, rolling and patching their new tennis court.

The court, clay, had come through its first winter pitted and windswept bare of redcoat. Years ago the Maples had observed how often, among their friends, divorce followed a dramatic home improvement, as if the marriage were making one last twitchy effort to live; their own worst crisis had come amid the plaster dust and exposed plumbing of a kitchen renovation. Yet, a summer ago, as canary-yellow bulldozers gaily churned a grassy, daisy-dotted knoll into a muddy plateau, and a crew of pigtailed young men raked and tamped clay into a plane, this transformation did not strike them as ominous, but festive in its impudence; their marriage could rend the earth for fun. The next spring, waking each day at dawn to a sliding sensation as if the bed were being tipped, Richard found the barren tennis court, its net and tapes still rolled in the barn, an environment congruous with his mood of purposeful desolation, and the crumbling of handfuls of clay into cracks and holes (dogs had frolicked on the court in a thaw; rivulets had evolved trenches) an activity suitably elemental and interminable. In his sealed heart he hoped the day would never come.

Now it was here. A Friday. Judith was reacclimated; all four children were assembled, before jobs and camps and visits again scattered them. Joan thought they should be told one by one. Richard was for making an announcement at the table. She said, "I think just making an announcement is a cop-out. They'll start quarrelling and playing to each other instead of focussing. They're each individuals, you know, not just some corporate obstacle to your freedom."

"O.K., O.K. I agree." Joan's plan was exact. That evening, they were giving Judith a belated welcome-home dinner, of lobster and champagne. Then, the party over, they, the two of them, who nineteen years before would push her in a baby carriage along Tenth Street to Washington Square, were to walk her out of the house, to the bridge across the salt creek, and tell her, swearing her to secrecy. Then Richard Jr., who was going directly from work to a rock concert in Boston, would be told, either late when he returned on the train or early Saturday morning before he went off to his job; he was seventeen and employed as one of a golf-course maintenance crew. Then the two younger children, John and Margaret, could, as the morning wore on, be informed.

"Mopped up, as it were," Richard said.

"Do you have any better plan? That leaves you the rest of Saturday to answer any questions, pack, and make your wonderful departure."

"No," he said, meaning he had no better plan, and agreed to hers, though it had an edge of false order, a plea for control in the semblance of its achievement, like Joan's long chore lists and financial accountings and, in the days when he first knew her, her too copious lecture notes. Her plan turned one hurdle for him into four—four knife-sharp walls, each with a sheer blind drop on the other side.

All spring he had been morbidly conscious of insides and outsides, of barriers and partitions. He and Joan stood as a thin barrier between the children and the truth. Each moment was a partition, with the past on one side and the future on the other, a future containing this unthinkable *now*. Beyond four knifelike walls a new life for him waited vaguely. His skull cupped a secret, a white face, a face both frightened and soothing, both strange and known, that he wanted to shield from tears, which he felt all about him, solid as the sunlight. So haunted, he had become obsessed with battening down the house against his absence, replacing screens and sash cords, hinges and latches—a Houdini making things snug before his escape.

The lock. He had still to replace a lock on one of the doors of the screened porch. The task, like most such, proved more difficult than he had imagined. The old lock, aluminum frozen by corrosion, had been deliberately rendered obsolete by manufacturers. Three hardware stores had nothing that even approximately matched the mortised hole its removal (surprisingly easy) left. Another hole had to be gouged, with bits too small and saws too big, and the old hole fitted with a block of wood—the chisels dull, the saw rusty, his fingers thick with lack of sleep. The sun poured down, beyond the porch, on a world of neglect. The bushes already needed pruning, the windward side of the house was shedding flakes of paint, rain would get in when he was gone, insects, rot, death. His family, all those he would lose, filtered through the edges of his awareness as he struggled with screw holes, splinters, opaque instructions, minutiae of metal.

Judith sat on the porch, a princess returned from exile. She regaled them with stories of fuel shortages, of bomb scares in the Underground, of Pakistani workmen loudly lusting after her as she walked past on her way to dance school. Joan came and went, in and out of the house, calmer than she should have been, praising his struggles with the lock as if this were one more and not the last of their chain of shared chores. The younger of his sons, John, now at fifteen suddenly, unwittingly handsome, for a few minutes held the rickety screen door while his father clumsily hammered and chiselled, each blow a kind of sob in Richard's ears. His younger daughter having been at a slumber party, slept on the porch hammock through all the noise—heavy and pink, trusting and forsaken. Time, like the sunlight, continued relentlessly; the sunlight slowly slanted. Today was one of the longest days. The lock clicked, worked. He was through. He had a drink; he drank it on the porch, listening to his daughter. "It was so sweet," she was saying, "during the worst of it, how all the butcher's and bakery shops kept open by candlelight. They're all so plucky and cute. From the papers, things sounded so much worse here—people shooting people in gas lines, and everybody freezing."

Richard asked her, "Do you still want to live in England forever?" *Forever:* the concept, now a reality upon him, pressed and scratched at the back of his throat.

"No," Judith confessed, turning her oval face to him, its eyes still childishly far apart, but the lips set as over something succulent and satisfactory. "I was anxious to come home. I'm an American." She was a woman. They had raised her; he and Joan had endured together to raise her, alone of the four. The others had still some raising left in them. Yet it was the thought of telling Judith—the image of her, their first baby, walking between them arm in arm to the bridge—that broke him. The partition between himself and the tears broke. Richard sat down to the celebratory meal with the back of his throat aching; the champagne, the lobster seemed phases of sunshine; he saw them and tasted them through tears. He blinked, swallowed, croakily joked about hay fever. The tears would not stop leaking through; they came not through a hole that could be plugged but through a permeable spot in a membrane, steadily, purely, endlessly, fruitfully. They became, his tears, a shield for himself against these others—their faces, the fact of their assembly, a last time as innocents, at a table where he sat the last time as head. Tears dropped from his nose as he broke the lobster's back; salt flavored his champagne as he sipped it; the raw clench at the back of his throat was delicious. He could not help himself.

His children tried to ignore his tears. Judith, on his right, lit a cigarette, gazed upward in the direction of her too energetic, too sophisticated exhalation; on her other side, John earnestly bent his face to the extraction of the last morsels—legs, tail segments—from the scarlet corpse. Joan, at the opposite end of the table, glanced at him surprised, her reproach displaced by a quick grimace, of forgiveness, or of salute to his superior gift of strategy. Between them, Margaret, no longer called Bean, thirteen and large for her age, gazed from the other side of his pane of tears as if into a shopwindow at something she coveted—at her father, a crystalline heap of splinters and memories. It was not she, however, but John who, in the kitchen, as they cleared the plates and carapaces away, asked Joan the question: "*Why is Daddy crying?*"

Richard heard the question but not the murmured answer. Then he heard Bean cry, "Oh, no-oh!"—the faintly dramatized exclamation of one who had long expected it.

John returned to the table carrying a bowl of salad. He nodded tersely at his father and his lips shaped the conspiratorial words "She told."

"Told what?" Richard asked aloud, insanely.

The boy sat down as if to rebuke his father's distraction with the example of his own good manners and said quietly, "The separation."

Joan and Margaret returned; the child, in Richard's twisted vision, seemed diminished in size, and relieved, relieved to have had the boogeyman at last proved real. He called out to her—the distances at the table had grown immense—"You knew, you always knew," but the clenching at the back of his throat prevented him from making sense of it. From afar he heard Joan talking, levelly, sensibly, reciting what they had prepared: it was a separation for the summer, an experiment. She and Daddy both agreed it would be good for them; they needed space and time to think; they liked each other but did not make each other happy enough, somehow.

Judith, imitating her mother's factual tone, but in her youth off-key, too cool, said, "I think it's silly. You should either live together or get divorced."

Richard's crying, like a wave that has crested and crashed, had become tumultuous; but it was overtopped by another tumult, for John, who had been so reserved, now grew larger and larger at the table. Perhaps his younger sister's being credited with knowing set him off. "Why didn't you *tell* us?" he asked, in a large round voice quite unlike his own. "You should have *told* us you weren't getting along."

Richard was startled into attempting to force words through his ears. "We *do* get along, that's the trouble, so it doesn't show even to us—" "That we do not love each other" was the rest of the sentence; he couldn't finish it.

Joan finished for him, in her style. "And we've always, *especially,* loved our children."

John was not mollified. "What do you care about *us?*" he boomed. "We're just little things you *had.*"

His sisters' laughing forced a laugh from him, which he turned hard and parodistic: "Ha ha *ha*." Richard and Joan realized simultaneously that the child was drunk, on Judith's homecoming champagne. Feeling bound to keep the center of the stage, John took a cigarette from Judith's pack, poked it into his mouth, let it hang from his lower lip, and squinted like a gangster.

"You're not little things we had," Richard called to him. "You're the whole point. But you're grown. Or almost."

The boy was lighting matches. Instead of holding them to his cigarette (for they had never seen him smoke; being "good" had been his way of setting himself apart), he held them to his mother's face, closer and closer, for her to blow out. Then he lit the whole folder—a hiss and then a torch, held against his mother's face. Prismed by his tears, the flame filled Richard's vision; he didn't know how it was extinguished. He heard Margaret say, "Oh stop showing off," and saw John, in response, break the cigarette in two and put the halves entirely into his mouth and chew, sticking out his tongue to display the shreds to his sister.

Joan talked to him, reasoning—a fountain of reason, unintelligible. "Talked about it for years . . . our children must help us . . . Daddy and I both want . . ." As the boy listened, he carefully wadded a paper napkin into the leaves of his salad, fashioned a ball of paper and lettuce, and popped it into his mouth, looking around the table for the expected laughter. None came. Judith said, "Be mature," and dismissed a plume of smoke.

Richard got up from this stifling table and led the boy outside. Though the house was in twilight, the outdoors still brimmed with light, the long waste light of high summer. Both laughing, he supervised John's spitting out the lettuce and paper and tobacco into the pachysandra. He took him by the hand—a square gritty hand, but for its softness a man's. Yet, it held on. They ran together up into the field, past the tennis court. The raw banking left by the bulldozers was dotted with daisies. Past the court and a flat stretch where they used to play family baseball stood a soft green rise glorious in the sun, each weed and species of grass distinct as illumination on parchment. "I'm sorry, so sorry," Richard cried. "You were the only one who ever tried to help me with all the goddam jobs around this place."

Sobbing, safe within his tears and the champagne, John explained, "It's not just the separation, it's the whole crummy year, I *hate* that school, you can't make any friends, the history teacher's a scud."

They sat on the crest of the rise, shaking and warm from their tears but easier in their voices, and Richard tried to focus on the child's sad year—the weekdays long with homework, the weekends spent in his room with model airplanes, while his parents murmured down below, nursing their separation. How selfish, how blind, Richard thought; his eyes felt scoured. He told his son, "We'll think about getting you transferred. Life's too short to be miserable."

They had said what they could, but did not want the moment to heal, and talked on, about the school, about the tennis court, whether it would ever again be as good as it had been that first summer. They walked to inspect it and pressed a few more tapes more firmly down. A little stiltedly, perhaps trying to make too much of the moment, to prolong it, Richard led the boy to the spot in the field where the view was best, of the metallic blue river, the emerald marsh, the scattered islands velvet with shadow in the low light, the white bits of beach far away. "See," he said. "It goes on being beautiful. It'll be here tomorrow."

"I know," John answered, impatiently. The moment had closed.

Back in the house, the others had opened some white wine, the champagne being drunk, and still sat at the table, the three females, gossiping. Where Joan sat had become the head. She turned, showing him a tearless face, and asked, "All right?"

"We're fine," he said, resenting it, though relieved, that the party went on without him.

In bed she explained, "I couldn't cry I guess because I cried so much all spring. It really wasn't fair. It's your idea, and you made it look as though I was kicking you out."

"I'm sorry," he said. "I couldn't stop. I wanted to but couldn't."

"You *didn't* want to. You loved it. You were having your way, making a general announcement."

"I love having it over," he admitted. "God, those kids were great. So brave and funny." John, returned to the house, had settled to a model airplane in his room, and kept shouting down to them, "I'm O.K. No sweat." "And the way," Richard went on, cozy in his relief, "they never questioned the reasons we gave. No thought of a third person. Not even Judith."

"That *was* touching," Joan said.

He gave her a hug. "You were great too. Thank you." Guiltily, he realized he did not feel separated.

"You still have Dickie to do," she told him. These words set before him a black mountain in the darkness; its cold breath, its near weight affected his chest. Of the four children Dickie was most nearly his conscience. Joan did not need to add, "That's one piece of your dirty work I won't do for you."

"I know. I'll do it. You go to sleep."

Within minutes, her breathing slowed, became oblivious and deep. It was quarter to midnight. Dickie's train from the concert would come in at one-fourteen. Richard set the alarm for one. He had slept atrociously for weeks. But whenever he closed his lids some glimpse of the last hours scorched them—Judith exhaling toward the ceiling in a kind of aversion, Bean's mute staring, the sunstruck growth of the field where he and John had rested. The mountain before him moved closer, moved within him; he was huge, momentous. The ache at the back of his throat felt stale. His wife slept as if slain beside him. When, exasperated by his hot lids, his crowded heart, he rose from bed and dressed, she awoke enough to turn over. He told her then, "If I could undo it all, I would."

"Where would you begin?" she asked. There was no place. Giving him courage, she was always giving him courage. He put on shoes without socks in the dark. The children were breathing in their rooms, the downstairs was hollow. In their confusion they had left lights burning. He turned off all but one, the kitchen overhead. The car started. He had hoped it wouldn't. He met only moonlight on the road; it seemed a diaphanous companion, flickering in the leaves along the roadside, haunting his rearview mirror like a pursuer, melting under his headlights. The center of town, not quite deserted, was eerie at this hour. A young cop in uniform kept company with a gang of T-shirted kids on the steps of the bank. Across from the railroad station, several bars kept open. Customers, mostly young, passed in and out of the warm night, savoring summer's novelty. Voices shouted from cars as they passed; an immense conversation seemed in progress. Richard parked and in his weariness put his head on the passenger seat, out of the commotion and wheeling lights. It was as when, in the movies, an assassin grimly carries his mission through the jostle of a carnival—except the movies cannot show the precipitous, palpable slope you cling to within. You cannot climb back down; you can only fall. The synthetic fabric of the car seat, warmed by his cheek, confided to him an ancient, distant scent of vanilla.

A train whistle caused him to lift his head. It was on time; he had hoped it would be late. The slender drawgates descended. The bell of approach tingled happily. The great metal body, horizontally fluted, rocked to a stop, and sleepy teen-agers disembarked, his son among them. Dickie did not show surprise that his father was meeting him at this terrible hour. He sauntered to the car with two friends, both taller than he. He said "Hi" to his father and took the passenger's seat with an exhausted promptness that expressed gratitude. The friends got into the back, and Richard was grateful; a few more minutes' postponement would be won by driving them home.

He asked, "How was the concert?"

"Groovy," one boy said from the back seat.

"It bit," the other said.

"It was O.K.," Dickie said, moderate by nature, so reasonable that in his childhood the unreason of the world had given him headaches, stomachaches, nausea. When the second friend had been dropped off at his dark house, the boy blurted, "Dad, my eyes are killing me with hay fever! I'm out there cutting that mothering grass all day!"

"Do we still have those drops?"

"They didn't do any good last summer."

"They might this." Richard swung a U-turn on the empty street. The drive home took a few minutes. The mountain was here, in his throat. "Richard," he said, and felt the boy, slumped and rubbing his eyes, go tense at his tone, "I didn't come to meet you just to make your life easier. I came because your mother and I have some news for you, and you're a hard man to get ahold of these days. It's sad news."

"That's O.K." The reassurance came out soft, but quick, as if released from the tip of a spring.

Richard had feared that his tears would return and choke him, but the boy's manliness set an example, and his voice issued forth steady and dry. "It's sad news, but it needn't be tragic news, at least for you. It should have no practical effect on your life, though it's bound to have an emotional effect. You'll work at your job, and go back to school in September. Your mother and I are really proud of what you're making of your life; we don't want that to change at all."

"Yeah," the boy said lightly, on the intake of his breath, holding himself up. They turned the corner; the church they went to loomed like a gutted fort. The home of the woman Richard hoped to marry stood across the green. Her bedroom light burned.

"Your mother and I," he said, "have decided to separate. For the summer. Nothing legal, no divorce yet. We want to see how it feels. For some years now, we haven't been doing enough for each other, making each other as happy as we should be. Have you sensed that?"

"No," the boy said. It was an honest, unemotional answer: true or false in a quiz.

Glad for a factual basis, Richard pursued, even garrulously, the details. His apartment across town, his utter accessibility, the split vacation arrangements, the advantages to the children, the added mobility and variety of the summer. Dickie listened, absorbing. "Do the others know?"

Richard described how they had been told.

"How did they take it?"

"The girls pretty calmly. John flipped out; he shouted and ate a cigarette and made a salad out of his napkin and told us how much he hated school."

His brother chuckled. "He did?"

"Yeah. The school issue was more upsetting for him than Mom and me. He seemed to feel better for having exploded."

"He did?" The repetition was the first sign that he was stunned.

"Yes. Dickie, I want to tell you something. This last hour, waiting for your train to get in, has been about the worst of my life. I hate this. *Hate* it. My father would have died before doing it to me." He felt immensely lighter, saying this. He had dumped the mountain on the boy. They were home. Moving swiftly as a shadow, Dickie was out of the car, through the bright kitchen. Richard called after him, "Want a glass of milk or anything?"

"No thanks."

"Want us to call the course tomorrow and say you're too sick to work?"

"No, that's all right." The answer was faint, delivered at the door to his room; Richard listened for the slam of a tantrum. The door closed normally. The sound was sickening.

Joan had sunk into that first deep trough of sleep and was slow to awake. Richard had to repeat, "I told him."

"What did he say?"

"Nothing much. Could you go say good night to him? Please."

She left their room, without putting on a bathrobe. He sluggishly changed back into his pajamas and walked down the hall. Dickie was already in bed, Joan was sitting beside him, and the boy's bedside clock radio was murmuring music. When she stood, an inexplicable light—the moon?—outlined her body through the nightie. Richard sat on the warm place she had indented on the child's narrow mattress. He asked him, "Do you want the radio on like that?"

"It always is."

"Doesn't it keep you awake? It would me."

"No."

"Are you sleepy?"

"Yeah."

"Good. Sure you want to get up and go to work? You've had a big night."

"I want to."

Away at school this winter he had learned for the first time that you can go short of sleep and live. As an infant he had slept with an immobile, sweating intensity that had alarmed his babysitters. As the children aged, he became the first to go to bed, earlier for a time than his younger brother and sister. Even now, he would go slack in the middle of a television show, his sprawled legs hairy and brown. "O.K. Good boy. Dickie, listen. I love you so much, I never knew how much until now. No matter how this works out, I'll always be with you. Really."

Richard bent to kiss an averted face but his son, sinewy, turned and with his wet cheeks embraced him and gave him a kiss, on the lips, passionate as a woman's. In his father's ear he moaned one word, the crucial, intelligent word: "*Why?*"

Why. It was a whistle of wind in a crack, a knife thrust, a window thrown open on emptiness. The white face was gone, the darkness was featureless. Richard had forgotten why.

Last Courtesies

Ella Leffland

Ella Leffland was born in Martinez, California, and graduated from San Jose State College. She has published stories in *Harper's, The Atlantic, Quarterly Review of Literature, Redbook, The New Yorker* and *Epoch*, as well as three novels, *Mrs. Munck, Love Out of Season,* and *Rumors of Peace.*

"Lillian, you're too polite," Vladimir kept telling her. She did not think so. Perhaps she was not one to return shoves in the bus line, but she did fire off censorious glares; and, true, she never yelled at the paper boy who daily flung her *Chronicle* to a rain-soaked fate, but she did beckon him to her door and remind him of his responsibilities. If she was always the last to board the bus, if she continued to dry out the paper on the stove, that was the price she must pay for observing the minimal courtesy the world owed itself if it was not to go under. Civilized she was. Excessively polite, no.

In any case, even if she had wanted to, she could not change at this stage of life. Nor had Aunt Bedelia ever changed in any manner. Not that she really compared herself to her phenomenal aunt, who, when she had died four months ago at the age of ninety-one, was still a captivating woman; no faded great beauty (the family ran to horse faces), but elegant, serenely vivid. Any other old lady who dressed herself in long gowns circa 1910 would have appeared a mere oddity; but under Bedelia's antiquated hairdo sat a brain; in her gnarled, almond-scented fingers lay direction. She spoke of Bach, of the Russian novelists, of her garden and the consolations of nature; never of her arthritis, the fallen ranks of her friends, or the metamorphosis of the neighborhood, which now featured motorcycles roaring alongside tin cans and blackened banana peels. At rare moments a sigh escaped her lips, but who knew if it was for her crippled fingers (she had been a consummate pianist) or a repercussion from the street? It was bad form, ungallant, to put too fine a point on life's discomfitures.

Since Bedelia's death the flat was lonely; lonely yet no longer private, since a supremely kinetic young woman, herself a music lover, had moved in upstairs. With no one to talk to, with thuds and acid rock resounding from above, Lillian drifted (too often, she knew) into the past, fingering its high points. The day, for instance, that Vladimir had entered their lives by way of the Steinway grand (great gleaming relic of better times) which he came to tune. He had burst in, dressed not in a customary suit but in garage mechanic's overalls and rubber thong sandals, a short square man with the large disheveled head of a furious gnome, who embellished his labors with glorious run-throughs of Bach and Scarlatti, but whose speech, though a dark bog of Slavic intonations, was distinctly, undeniably obscene. Aunt Bedelia promptly invited him to dinner the following week. Lillian stood astonished, but reminded herself that her aunt was a sheltered soul unfamiliar with scabrous language, whereas she, Lillian, lived more in the great world, riding the bus every day to the Opera House, where she held the position of switchboard operator (Italian and German required). The following morning at work, in fact, she inquired about Vladimir. Several people there knew of him. A White Russian, he had fled to Prague with his parents in 1917, then fled again twenty years later, eventually settling in San Francisco, where he quickly earned the reputation of an excellent craftsman and a violent crackpot. He abused clients who had no knowledge of their pianos' intestines, and had once been taken to court by an acquaintance whom he had knocked down during a conversation about Wagner. He wrote scorching letters of general advice to the newspapers; with arms like a windmill he confronted mothers who allowed their children to drop potato chips on the sidewalk; he kept a bucket of accumulated urine to throw on dog-walkers who were unwary enough to linger with their squatting beasts beneath his window. He had been institutionalized several times.

That night Lillian informed her aunt that Vladimir was brilliant but unsound.

The old woman raised an eyebrow at this.

"For instance," Lillian pursued, "he is actually known to have struck someone down."

"Why?" Her aunt's voice was clear and melodious, with a faint ring of iron.

"It was during a conversation about Wagner. Apparently he disapproves of Wagner."

Her aunt gave a nod of endorsement.

"The man has even had himself committed, aunt. Several times, when he felt he was getting out of hand."

The old woman pondered this. "It shows foresight," she said at length, "and a sense of social responsibility."

Lillian was silent for a moment. Then she pointed out: "He said unspeakable things here."

"They were mutually exclusive terms."

"Let us call them obscenities, then. You may not have caught them."

The old woman rose from her chair and arranged the long skirt of her dove-gray ensemble. "Lillian, one must know when to turn a deaf ear."

"I am apparently not in the know," Lillian said dryly.

"Perhaps it is an instinct." And suddenly she gave her unique smile, which was quite yellow (for she retained her own ancient teeth) but completely beguiling, and added: "In any case, he is of my own generation, Lillian. That counts for a great deal."

"He can't be more than sixty, aunt."

"It is close enough. Anyway, he is quite wrinkled. Also, he is a man of integrity."

"How can you possibly know that?"

"It is my instinct." And gently touching her niece's cheek, she said goodnight and went to her room, which peacefully overlooked the back garden, away from the street noises.

Undressing in her own smaller room, Lillian reflected, not for the first time, that though it was Bedelia who had remained unwed—Lillian herself having been married and widowed during the war—it was she, Lillian, who felt more the old maid, who seemed more dated, in a stale, fusty way, with her tight 1950s hairdo, her plain wool suits and practical support stockings . . . but then, she led a practical life . . . it was she who was trampled in the bus queue and who sat down to a hectic switchboard, who swept the increasingly filthy sidewalk and dealt with the sullen butcher and careless paper boy—or tried to . . . it seemed she was a middlewoman, a hybrid, too worldly to partake of aunt's immense calm, too seclusive to sharpen herself on the changing ways . . . aunt had sealed herself off in a lofty, gracious world; she lived for it, she would have died for it if it came to that . . . but what could she, Lillian, die for? . . . she fit in nowhere, she thought, climbing into bed, and thirty years from now she would not have aged into the rare creature aunt was—last survivor of a fair, legendary breed, her own crimped hairdo as original as the Edwardian pouf, her boxy suits as awesome as the floor-sweeping gowns—no, she would just be a peculiar old leftover in a room somewhere. For aunt was grande dame, bluestocking, and virgin in one, and they didn't make that kind anymore; they didn't make those eyes anymore, large, hooded, a deep glowing violet. It was a hue that had passed. . . . And she closed her own eyes, of candid, serviceable gray, said the Lord's Prayer, and prepared to act as buffer between her elite relative and the foul-mouthed old refugee.

Aunt Bedelia prepared the dinner herself, taking great pains; then she creaked into her wet garden with an umbrella and picked her finest blooms for a centerpiece; and finally, over the knobbed, arthritic joint of her ring finger, she twisted a magnificent amethyst usually reserved for Christmas, Easter, and Bach's birthday. These touches Lillian expected to be lost on their wild-eyed guest, but Vladimir kissed the festive hand with a cavalier click of his sandals, acknowledged the flowers with a noisy inhalation of his large, hairy nostrils, and ate his food with admirable if strained refinement. During coffee he capsized his cup, but this was only because he and Bedelia were flying from Bavarian spas and Italian sea resorts to music theory, Turgenev, and God knew what else—Lillian could hardly follow—and then, urged by aunt, he jumped from the table, rolled up the sleeves of his overalls, and flung himself into Bach, while aunt, her fingers stiffly moving up and down on her knee, threw back her head and entered some region of flawless joy. At eleven o'clock Vladimir wrestled into his red lumber jacket, expressed his delight with the evening, and slapped down the steps to his infirm 1938 Buick. Not one vulgar word had escaped his lips.

Nor in the seven following years of his friendship with Bedelia was this precedent ever broken. Even the night when some drunk sent an empty pint of muscatel crashing through the window, Vladimir's respect for his hostess was so great that all scurrility was plucked from his wrath. However, when he and Lillian happened to be alone together he slipped right back into the belching, offensive mannerisms for which he was known. She did not mention this to her aunt, who cherished the idea that he was very fond of Lillian.

"You know how he detests opera," the old lady would assure her, "and yet he has never alluded to the fact that you work at the Opera House and hold the form in esteem."

"A magnanimous gesture," Lillian said, smiling.

"For Vladimir, yes."

And after a moment's thought, Lillian had to agree. Her aunt apparently understood Vladimir perfectly, and he her. She wondered if this insight was due to their shared social origins, their bond of elevated interests, or their more baroque twinhood of eccentricity. Whatever it was, the couple thrived, sometimes sitting up till midnight with their sherry and sheet music, sometimes, when the Buick was well, motoring (Bedelia's term) into the countryside and then winding homeward along the darkening sea, in a union of perfect silence, as the old lady put it.

Bedelia died suddenly, with aplomb, under Toscanini's direction. Beethoven's Ninth was on the phonograph; the chorus had just scaled the great peak before its heart-bursting cascade into the finale; aunt threw her head back to savor the moment, and was gone.

The next morning Lillian called Vladimir. He shrieked, he wept, he banged the receiver on the table; and for ten days, helpless and broken, he spent every evening at the home of his departed love while Lillian, herself desolated, tried to soothe him. She felt certain he would never regain the strength to insult his clients again, much less strike anyone to the ground, but gradually he mended, and the coarseness, the irascibility flooded back, much worse than in the past.

For Bedelia's sake—of that Lillian was sure—he forced himself to take an interest in her welfare, which he would express in eruptions of advice whenever he telephoned. "You want to lead a decent life, Lillian, you give them hell! They sell you a bad cut of meat, throw it in the butcher's face! You get shortchanged, make a stink! You're too soft! Give them the finger, Lillian!"

"Yes, of course," she would murmur.

"For your aunt I was a gentleman, but now she's gone, who appreciates? A gentleman is a fool, a gentleman's balls are cut off! I know how to take care of myself, I am in an armored tank! And you should be too. Or find a protector. Get married!"

"Pardon?" she asked.

"Marry!"

"I have no desire to marry, Vladimir."

"Desire! Desire! It's a world for your desires? Think

of your scalp! You need a protector, now Bedelia's gone!"

"Aunt was not my protector," she said patiently.

"Of course she was! And mine too!"

Lillian shifted her weight from one foot to the other and hoped he would soon run down.

"You want to get off the phone, don't you? Why don't you say, Vladimir get the shit off the phone, I'm busy! Don't be a doormat! Practice on me or you'll come to grief! What about that sow upstairs, have you given her hell yet? No, no, of course not! Jesus bleeding Christ, I give up!" And he slammed the receiver down.

Lillian had in fact complained. Allowing her new neighbor time to settle in, she had at first endured—through apparently rugless floorboards—the girl's music, her door slams, her crashing footfall which was a strange combination of scurry and thud, her deep hollow brays of laughter and shrieks of "You're *kidding!*" and "Fan*tas*tic!"—all this usually accompanied by a masculine voice and tread (varying from night to night, Lillian could not help but notice) until finally, in the small hours, directly above Bedelia's room, where Lillian now slept, ears stuffed with cotton, the night was crowned by a wild creaking of bedsprings and the racketing of the headboard against the wall. At last, chancing to meet her tormentor on the front steps (she was not the Amazon her noise indicated, but a small, thin creature nervously chewing gum with staccato snaps), Lillian decided to speak; but before she could, the girl cried: "Hi! I'm Jody—from upstairs?" with a quick, radiant smile that heartened the older woman in a way that the hair and hemline did not. Clad in a tiny, childish dress that barely reached her hip sockets, she might have been a prematurely worn twenty or an adolescent thirty—dark circles hung beneath the eyes and a deep line was etched between them, but the mouth was babyish, sweet, and the cheeks a glowing pink against the unfortunate mane of brassy hair, dark along its uneven part.

Having responded with her own name (the formal first *and* last) Lillian paused a courteous moment, then began: "I'm glad to have this opportunity of meeting you; I've lived in this flat for twenty-four years, you see . . ." But the eyes opposite, heavily outlined with blue pencil, were already wandering under this gratuitous information. Brevity was clearly the password. "The point is"—restoring attention—"I would appreciate it if you turned down your music after ten P.M. There is a ruling."

"It bugs you?" the girl asked, beginning to dig turbulently through a fringed bag, her gum snaps accelerating with the search.

"Well, it's an old building, and of course if you don't have carpets . . ." She waited to be corroborated in this assumption, but now the girl pulled out her house key with fingers whose nails, bitten to the quick, were painted jet black. Fascinated, Lillian tried not to stare. "Not to worry," the girl assured her with the brief, brilliant smile, plunging the key into the door and bounding inside, "I'll cool it."

"There's something else, I'm afraid. When that door is slammed—"

But the finely arched brows rose with preoccupation; the phone was ringing down from the top of the stairs. "I dig, I dig. Look, hon, my phone's ringing." And closing the door softly, she thundered up the stairs.

After that the phonograph was lowered a little before midnight, but nothing else was changed. Lillian finally called the landlord, a paunchy, sweating man whom she rarely saw, and though she subsequently observed him disappearing into his unruly tenant's flat several evenings a week, the visits were apparently useless. And every time she met the girl, she was greeted with an insufferable "Hi! Have a nice day!"

Unfortunately, Lillian had shared some of her vexation with Vladimir, and whenever he dropped by—less to see her, she knew, than to replenish his memories of Bedelia—his wrath grew terrible under the commotion. On his last visit his behavior had frightened her. "Shut up!" he had screamed, shaking his fist at the ceiling. "Shut up, bitch! Whore!"

"Vladimir, please—this language, just because Bedelia's not here."

"Ah, Bedelia, Bedelia," he groaned.

"She wouldn't have tolerated it."

"She wouldn't have tolerated *that!* Hear the laugh—hee haw, hee haw! Braying ass! Bedelia would have pulverized her with a glance! None of this farting around you go in for!" His large head had suffused with red, his hands were shaking at his sides. "Your aunt was a genius at judging people—they should have lined up the whole fucking rotten city for her to judge!"

"It seems to me that you have always appointed yourself as judge," Lillian said, forcing a smile.

"Yah, but Vladimir is demented, you don't forget? He has it down in black and white! Ah, you think I'm unique, Lillian, but I am one of the many! I am in the swim!" He came over to her side and put his flushed head close, his small intense eyes piercing hers.

"You read yesterday about the girl they found in an alley not far from here, cut to small bits? Slash! Rip! Finito! And you ask why? Because the world, it is demented! A murder of such blood not even in the headlines and you ask why? Because it is commonplace ! Who walks safe on his own street? It is why you need a husband!"

Lillian dropped her eyes, wondering for an

embarrassed moment if Vladimir of all people could possibly be hinting at a marital alliance. Suddenly silent, he pulled a wadded handkerchief from his pocket with trembling fingers and wiped his brow. He flicked her a suspicious glance. "Don't look so coy. I'm not in the running. I loathe women—sticky! Full of rubbishy talk!" And once more he threw his head back and began bellowing obscenities at the ceiling.

"It's too much, Vladimir—please! You're not yourself!"

"I *am* myself!"

"Well then, I'm not. I'm tired, I have a splitting headache—"

"You want me to go! Be rude, good! I have better things to do anyway!" And his face still aflame, he struggled into his lumber jacket and flung out the door.

That night her sleep was not only disturbed by the noise, but by her worry over the violence of Vladimir's emotions. At work the next day she reluctantly inquired about her friend, whose antics were usually circulated around the staff but seldom reached her cubicle. For the first time in years, she learned, the weird little Russian had gone right over the edge, flapping newspapers in strangers' faces and ranting about the end of civilization; storming out on tuning jobs and leaving his tools behind, then furiously accusing his clients of stealing them. The opinion was that if he did not commit himself soon, someone else would do it for him.

On the clamorous bus home that night, shoved as usual into the rear, Lillian felt an overwhelming need for Bedelia, for the sound of that clear, well-modulated voice that had always set the world to rights. But she opened her door on silence. She removed her raincoat and sat down in the living room with the damp newspaper. People at work told her she should buy a television set—such a good companion when you lived alone—but she had too long scorned that philistine invention to change now. For that matter, she seldom turned on the radio, and even the newspaper—she ran her eyes over the soggy turmoil of the front page—even the newspaper distressed her. Vladimir was extreme, but he was right: everything was coming apart. Sitting there, she thought she could hear the world's madness—its rudeness, its litter, its murders—beat against the house with the rain. And suddenly she closed her eyes under an intolerable longing for the past: for the peaceful years she had spent in these rooms with Bedelia; and before that, for the face of her young husband, thirty years gone now; and for even earlier days . . . odd, but it never seemed to rain in her youth, the green campus filled the air with dizzying sweetness, she remembered running across the lawns for no reason but that she was twenty and the sun would shine forever. . . .

She gave way to two large tears. Shaken, yet somehow consoled, and at the same time ashamed of her self-indulgence, she went into the kitchen to make dinner. But as she cooked her chop she knew that even this small measure of comfort would be destroyed as soon as her neighbor came banging through the door. Already her neck was tightening against the sound

But there was no noise at all that night, not until 1 A.M. when the steady ring of the telephone pulled her groggily from bed.

"Listen, you'll kill me—it's Jody, I'm across the bay, and I just flashed on maybe I left the stove burners going."

"Who?" Lillian said, rubbing her eyes, "Jody? How did you get my number?"

"The phone book, why? Listen, the whole dump

could catch fire, be a doll and check it out? The back door's unlocked."

Lillian felt a strange little rush of gratitude—that her name given to such seemingly indifferent ears on the steps that day, had been remembered. Then the feeling was replaced by anger; but before she could speak, the girl said, "Listen, hon, thanks a million," and hung up.

Clutching her raincoat around her shoulders, beaming a flashlight before her, Lillian nervously climbed the dark back stairs to her neighbor's door and let herself into the kitchen. Turning on the light, she stood aghast at what she saw: not flames licking the wall, for the burners were off, but grimed linoleum, spilled garbage, a sink of stagnant water. On the puddled table, decorated with a jar of blackened, long-dead daisies, sat a greasy portable television set and a pile of dirty laundry in a litter of cigarette butts, sodden pieces of paper, and the congealed remains of spare ribs. Hesitating, ashamed of her snoopiness, she peered down at the pieces of paper: bills from department stores, including Saks and Magnin's; scattered food stamps; handwritten notes on binder paper, one of which read "Jamie hony theres a piza in the frezzer I love U"—then several big hearts—"Jody." A long brown bug—a cockroach? was crawling across the note, and now she noticed another one climbing over a spare rib. As she stood cringing, she heard rain blowing through an open window somewhere, lashing a shade into frenzies. Going to the bedroom door, which stood ajar, she beamed her flashlight in and switched on the light. Under the window a large puddle was forming on the floor, which was rugless as she had suspected, though half carpeted by strewn clothes. The room was furnished only with a bed whose convulsed, mummy-brown sheets put her in mind of a pesthouse, and a deluxe television set in a rosewood cabinet; but the built-in bookcase was well stocked, and, having shut the window, she ran her eyes over the spines, curious. Many were cheap paperback thrillers, but there was an abundance of great authors: Dostoevski, Dickens, Balzac, Melville. It was odd, she puzzled, that the girl had this taste in literature, yet could not spell the simplest word and had never heard of a comma. As she turned away, her eardrums were shattered by her own scream. A man stood in the doorway.

A boy, actually, she realized through her fright; one of Jody's more outstanding visitors, always dressed in one of those Mexican shawl affairs and a battered derby hat, from under which butter-yellow locks flowed in profusion, everything at the moment dripping with rain. More embarrassed now than frightened—she had never screamed in her life, or stood before a stranger in her nightgown, and neither had Bedelia—she began pulsating with dignity. "I didn't hear anyone come up the stairs," she indicted him.

"Little cat feet, man," he said with a cavernous yawn. "Where's Jody? Who're you?"

She explained her presence, pulling the raincoat more firmly together across her bosom, but unable to do anything about the expanse of flowered flannel below.

"Jody, she'd forget her ass if it wasn't screwed on," the boy said with a second yawn. His eyes were watery and red, and his nose ran. "If you'll excuse me," she said, going past him. He followed her back into the kitchen and suddenly, with a hostlike warmth that greatly surprised her, he asked, "You want some coffee?"

She declined, saying that she must be going.

At this he heaved a deep, disappointed sigh, which again surprised her, and sank like an invalid into a chair. He was a slight youth with neat little features crowded into the center of his face, giving him, despite his woebegone expression, a pert, fledgling look. In Lillian's day he would have been called a "pretty boy." He would not have been her type at all; she had always preferred the lean profile.

"My name's Jamie," he announced suddenly, with a childlike spontaneity beneath the film of languor; and he proffered his hand.

Gingerly, she shook the cold small fingers.

"Hey, really," he entreated. "Stay and rap awhile."

"Rap?"

"Talk, man. Talk to me." And he looked, all at once, so lonely, so forlorn, that even though she was very tired, she felt she must stay a moment longer. Pulling out a chair, she took a temporary, edge-of-the-seat position across the hideous table from him.

He seemed to be gathering his thoughts together. "So what's your bag?" he asked.

She looked at him hopelessly. "My bag?"

"You a housewife? You work?"

"Oh—yes, I work," she said, offended by his bold curiosity, yet grateful against her will to have inspired it.

"What's your name?" he asked.

He was speaking to her as a contemporary; and again, she was both pleased by this and offended by his lack of deference. "Lillian . . . Cronin," she said uncertainly.

"I'm Jamie," he laughed.

"So you mentioned." And thought—Jamie, Jody, the kinds of names you would give pet rabbits. Where were the solid, straightforward names of yesteryear—the Georges and Harolds, the Dorothys and Margarets? What did she have to say to a Jamie in a Mexican shawl and threadbare derby who was now scratching himself all over with little fidgety movements? But she said, breaking the long silence, which he seemed not to notice: "And what is *your* bag, if I may ask?"

He took several moments to answer. "I don't know, man . . . I'm a student of human nature."

"Oh? And where do you study?"

"Not me, man, that's Jody's scene . . . into yoga, alpha waves, the whole bit . . . even studies macramé and World Lit at jay cee . . ."

"Indeed? How interesting. I noticed her books."

"She's a towering intellect." He yawned, his eyes glassy with fatigue. He was scratching himself more slowly now.

"And does she work, as well?" Lillian asked, once more ashamed of her nosiness.

"Work?" he smiled. "Maybe you could call it that. . . ." But his attention was drifting away like smoke. Fumbling with a breadknife, he picked it up and languidly, distantly, speared a cockroach with the point. Then, with the side of the knife, he slowly, methodically, squashed the other one.

Averting her eyes from the massacre, Lillian leaned forward. "I don't mean to sound familiar, but you seem a quiet person. Do you think you might ask Jody to be a little less noisy up here? I've spoken to the landlord, but—" She saw the boy smile again, an odd, rueful smile that made her feel, for some reason, much younger than he. "You see—" she continued, but he was fading from her presence, slowly mashing his bugs to pulp and now dropping the knife to reach over and click on the food-spattered television. Slouched, his eyes bored by what the screen offered, he nevertheless began following an old movie. The conversation appeared to be over.

Lillian rose. She was not accustomed, nor would Bedelia have been, to a chat ending without some mutual amenity. She felt awkward, dismissed. With a cool nod she left him and descended the splashing stairs to her own flat. Such a contrast the youth was of warmth and rudeness . . . and Jody, an illiterate studying Dostoevski at college . . . food stamps lying hugger-mugger with bills from Saks . . . it was impossible to bring it all into focus; she felt rudderless, malfunctioning . . . how peculiar life had become . . . everything mixed up . . . a generation of fragments. . . .

Climbing heavily back into bed, she wondered what Bedelia would have thought of Jody and Jamie. And she remembered how unkempt and disconcerting Vladimir had been, yet how her aunt had quickly penetrated to the valuable core while she, Lillian, fussed on about his bad language. No doubt Bedelia would have been scandalized by the filth upstairs, but she would not have been so narrow-souled as to find fault with spelling mistakes, first names, taste in clothing. . . . Bedelia might not have pulverized Jody with a glance, as Vladimir suggested, but instead seen some delicate tragedy in the worn cherubic features, or been charmed by the girl's invincible buoyancy . . . it was hard to tell with Bedelia, which facet she might consider the significant one . . . she often surprised you . . . it had to do with largeness of spirit. . . .

Whereas she, Lillian, had always to guard against stuffiness. . . . Still, she tried to hold high the torch of goodwill . . . too pompous a simile, of course, but she knew clearly and deeply what she meant . . . so *let* Vladimir rave on at her for refusing to shrink into a knot of hostility; what was Vladimir, after all? Insane. Her eyes opened in the dark as she faced what she had tried to avoid all day: that Vladimir had been wrenched off the tracks by Bedelia's death, and that this time he felt no need to commit himself. Without question it was Lillian's duty to enlighten him. But she winced at the thought . . . such a terrible thing to have to tell someone . . . if only she could turn to Bedelia . . . how sorely she missed her . . . how sorely she missed George's lean young face under his Army cap . . . youth . . . sunlight . . . outside the rain still fell . . . she had only herself, and the dark, unending rain. . . .

"Stop this brooding," she said aloud; if she had only herself, she had better be decent company. And closing her eyes she tried to sleep. But not until a gray watery dawn was breaking did she drop off.

The Opera House telephoned at three minutes past nine. Leaden, taut-nerved, sourly questioning the rewards of her long, exquisite punctuality, she pulled on her clothes, and, with burning eyes and empty stomach, hurried out of the house. At work, though the board was busy, the hours moved with monumental torpor. She felt increasingly unlike herself, hotly brimming over with impatience for all this switchboard blather: calls from New York, Milan; Sutherland with her sore throat, Pavarotti with his tight schedule—did they really think that, if another *Rigoletto* were never given, anyone would notice? She felt an urge to slur this fact into the headphone, as befitted a truant traipsing in at a quarter to ten, as befitted someone with minimally combed hair and crooked seams and, even worse, with the same underwear on that she had worn the day before. As if a slatternly, cynical Lillian whom she didn't recognize had squeezed slyly into prominence, a Lillian who half-considered walking out on the whole tiresome business and indulging in a lavish two-hour lunch downtown—let someone else serve, let someone else be polite.

Sandwiched into the bus aisle that night, she almost smacked an old gentleman who crunched her right instep under his groping heel; and as she creaked into the house with her wet newspaper and saw that a motorcyclist had been picked off on the freeway by a sniper, she had to fight down a lip curl of satisfaction.

Then, reflectively, still in her raincoat, she walked to the end of the hall where an oval mirror hung, and studied her face. It was haggard, flinty, stripped of faith, scraped down to the cold, atavistic bones of retaliation. She had almost walked off her job, almost struck an old man, almost smiled at murder. A feeling of panic shot through her; what were values if they could collapse at the touch of a sleepless night? And she sank the terrible face into her hands; but a ray of rational thought lifted it again. "Almost." Never mind the querulous inner tremble, at each decisive moment her principles had stood fast. Wasn't a person entitled to an occasional fit of petulance? There is such a thing as perspective, she told herself, and in the meantime a great lust for steam and soap had spread through her. She would scrub out the day in a hot bath and in perfect silence, for apparently Jody had not yet returned from across the bay. God willing, the creature would remain away a week.

Afterward, boiled pink, wrapped in her quilted robe, she felt restored to grace. A fine appetite raced through her, along with visions of a tuna casserole which she hurried into the kitchen to prepare, hurrying out again at the summons of the telephone. It was Vladimir, very excited, wanting to drop by. Her first response was one of blushing discomfort: entertain Vladimir in her quilted bathrobe? Her second she articulated: she was bone-tired, she was going to bed right after dinner. But even as she spoke she heard the remorseless door slam of Jody's return, and a violent spasm twisted her features. "Please—next week," she told Vladimir and hung up, clutching her head as tears of rage and exhaustion burst from her eyes. Weeping, she made a tuna sandwich, chewed it without heart, and sank onto her unmade bed. The next morning, still exhausted, she made an emergency appointment with her doctor, and came home that night with a bottle of sleeping pills.

By the end of the week she was sick with artificial sleep, there was an ugly rubber taste in her mouth, her eye sockets felt caked with rust. And it was not only the noise and pills that plagued her: a second neighborhood woman had been slashed to death by the rain man (the newspapers, in their cozy fashion, had thus baptized the slayer). She had taken to beaming her flashlight under the bed before saying the Lord's Prayer; her medicinal sleep crackled with surreal visions; at the sullen butcher's her eyes were morbidly drawn to the meat cleaver; and at work not only had she upset coffee all over her lap, but she disconnected Rudolf Bing himself in the middle of a sentence.

And never any respite from above. She had called the landlord again, without audible results, and informed the Board of Health about the cockroaches; their reply was that they had no jurisdiction over cockroaches. She had stuck several notes under Jody's door pleading with her to quiet down, and had stopped her twice on the steps, receiving the first time some capricious remark, and the second a sigh of "Christ, Lilly, I'm trying. What d'you want?" Lilly! The gall! But she was gratified to see that the gum-snapping face was almost as sallow as her own, the circles under the eyes darker than ever, new lines around the mouth. So youth could crumble, too. Good! Perhaps the girl's insanely late hours were boomeranging, and would soon mash her down in a heap of deathlike stillness (would that Lillian could implement this vision). Or perhaps it was her affair with Jamie that was running her ragged. Ah, the costly trauma of love! Jealousy, misunderstanding—so damaging to the poor nervous system! Or so she had heard . . . she and George had been blessed with rapport . . . but try not to dwell on the past . . . yes, possibly it was Jamie who was lining the girl's face . . . Lillian has seen him a few times since their first meeting, once on the steps—he smiled, was pleasant, remembered her, but had not remembered to zip his fly, and she had hurried on, embarrassed—and twice in the back garden, where on the less drenching days she tended Bedelia's flowers, but without her aunt's emerald-green thumb . . . a rare sunny afternoon, she had been breaking off geraniums; Jody and Jamie lay on the grass in skimpy bathing suits, their thin bodies white, somehow poignant in their delicacy . . . she felt like a great stuffed mattress in her sleeveless dress, soiled hands masculine with age, a stevedore's drop of sweat hanging from her nose . . . could they imagine her once young and tender on her own bed of love? or now, with a man friend? As if everything closed down at fifty-seven, like a bankrupt hotel!—tearing off the head of a geranium—brash presumption of youth! But she saw that they weren't even aware of her, no, they were kissing and rolling about . . . in Bedelia's garden! "Here, what are you doing!" she cried, but in the space of a moment a hostile little flurry had taken place, and now they broke away and lay separately in charged silence, still taking no notice of her as she stood there, heart thumping, fist clenched. She might have been air. Suddenly, sick from the heat, she had plodded inside.

The next time she saw Jamie in the garden was this afternoon when, arriving home from work and changing into a fresh dress for Vladimir's visit, she happened to glance out her bedroom window. Rain sifted down, but the boy was standing still, a melancholy sight, wrapped in a theatrical black cloak, the derby and Mexican shawl apparently having outlived their effectiveness as eyecatchers . . . youth's eternal and imbecile need to shock . . . Jody with her ebony fingernails and silly prepubescent hemlines; and this little would-be Dracula with his golden sausage curls, tragically posed in the fragile mist, though she noticed his hands were untragically busy under the cloak, scratching as usual . . . or . . . the thought was so monstrous that she clutched the curtain . . . he could not be standing in the garden abusing himself; she must be deranged, suffering prurient delusions—she, Lillian Cronin, a decent, clean-minded woman . . . ah God, what was happening, what was happening? It was her raw nerves, her drugged and hanging head, the perpetual din . . . even as she stood there, her persecutor was trying on clothes, dropping shoes, pounding from closet to mirror (for Lillian could by now divine the activity behind each noise) while simultaneously braying into the telephone receiver stuck between chin and shoulder, and sketchily attending the deluxe television set, which blared a hysterical melodrama . . .

Outside, the youth sank onto a tree stump, from which he cast the upstairs window a long bleak look . . . they must have had a lovers' quarrel, and the girl had shut him out; now he brooded in the rain, an exile; or rather a kicked puppy, shivering and staring up with ponderous woe . . . then, eyes dropping, he caught sight of Lillian, and a broad, sunny, candid smile flashed from the dismal countenance . . . odd, jarring, she thought, giving a polite nod and dropping the curtain, especially after his rude imperviousness that hot day on the grass . . . a generation of fragments, she had said so before, though God knew she never objected to a smile (with the exception of Jody's grimace) . . . and walking down the hall away from the noise, she was stopped woodenly by the sound of the girl's doorbell. It was one of the gentlemen callers, who tore up the stairs booming felicitations which were returned with the inevitable shrieks, this commingled din moving into the front room and turning Lillian around in her tracks. With the door closed, the kitchen was comparatively bearable, and it was time to eat anyway. She bought television dinners now, lacking the vigor to cook. She had lost seven pounds, but was not growing svelte, only drawn. Even to turn on the waiting oven was a chore. But slowily she got herself into motion, and at length, pouring out a glass of burgundy to brace herself for Vladimir's visit, she sat down to the steaming, neatly sectioned pap. Afterward, dutifully washing her glass and fork in the sink, she glanced out the window into the rain, falling in sheets now; the garden was dark and she could not be sure, but she thought she saw the youth still sitting on the stump. It was beyond her, why anyone would sit still in a downpour . . . but everything was beyond her, insurmountable . . . and soon Vladimir would arrive . . . the thought was more than she could bear, but she could not defer his visit again, it would be too rude. . . .

He burst in like a cannonball, tearing off his wet lumber jacket, an acrid smell of sweat blooming from his armpits; his jaws were stubbled with white, great bushes sprouted from his nostrils.

"You look terrible!" he roared.

Even though she had at the last moment rubbed lipstick into her pallid cheeks. She gave a deflated nod and gestured toward the relatively quiet kitchen, but he wanted the Bedelia-redolent front room, where he rushed over to the Steinway and lovingly dashed off an arpeggio, only to stagger back with his finger knifed up at the ceiling. "Still the chaos!" he cried.

"Please—" she said raggedly. "No advice, I beg of you."

"No advice? Into your grave they'll drive you, Lillian!" And she watched his finger drop, compassionately it seemed, to point at her slumped bosom with its heart beating so wearily inside. It was a small hand, yet blunt, virile, its back covered with coarse dark hair . . .

what if it reached farther, touched her? . . . But spittle already flying, Vladimir was plunging into a maelstrom of words, obviously saved up for a week. "I wanted to come sooner, why didn't you let me? Look at you, a wreck! Vladimir knew a second one would be cut—he smells blood on the wind! He wants to come and pound on your door, to be with you, but no, he respects your wish for privacy, so he sits every night out front in his auto, watching!" Here he broke off to wipe his lips, while Lillian, pressing hard the swollen, rusty lids of her eyes, accepted the immense duty of guiding him to confinement. "And every night," he roared on, "while Vladimir sits, Bedelia plays 'Komm, Jesu, Komm,' it floats into the street, it is beautiful, beautiful—"

"Ah, Vladimir," broke pityingly from her lips.

Silence. With a clap of restored lucidity his fist struck his forehead. It remained tightly glued there for some time. When it fell away he seemed quite composed.

"I have always regretted," he said crisply, "that you resemble the wrong side of your family. All you have of Bedelia is a most vague hint of her cheekbones." Which he was scrutinizing with his small glittering eyes. Again, nervously, she sensed that he would touch her; but instead, a look of revulsion passed over his features as he stared first at one cheek, then the other. "You've got fucking gunk on! Rouge!"

With effort, she produced a neutral tone. "I'm not used to being stared at, Vladimir."

"Hah, I should think not," he snapped abstractedly, eyes still riveted.

Beast! Vile wretch! But at once she was shamed by her viciousness. From where inside her did it come? And she remembered that terrible day at work when a malign and foreign Lillian had pressed into ascendancy, almost as frightening a character change as the one she was seeing before her now, for Vladimir's peering eyes seemed actually black with hatred. "Stinking whore-rouge," he breathed; then with real pain, he cried: "Have you no thought for Bedelia? You have the blessing of her cheekbones! Respect them! Don't drag them through the gutter! My God, Lillian! My God!"

She said nothing. It seemed the only thing to do.

But now he burst forth again, cheerfully, rubbing his hands together. "Listen to Vladimir. You want a husband, forget the war paint, use what you have. Some intelligence. A good bearing—straighten the shoulders—and cooking talent. Not like Bedelia's, but not bad. Now, Vladimir has been looking around for you—"

"Vladimir," she said through her teeth.

"—and he has found a strong, healthy widower of fifty-two years, a great enjoyer of the opera. He has been advised of your virtues—"

"Vladimir!"

"Of course you understand Vladimir himself is out, Vladimir is a monolith—" A particularly loud thump shuddered the ceiling, and he jumped back yelling, "Shove it, you swine! Lice!"

"Vladimir, I do not want a man!" Lillian snapped.

"Not so! I sense sex boiling around in you!"

Her lips parted; blood rushed into her cheeks to darken the artificial blush. For certain, with the short, potent word, *sex,* his hands would leap on her.

"But you look a thousand years old," he went on. "It hangs in folds, your face. You must get rid of this madhouse upstairs! What have you done so far—not even told the landlord!"

"I *have!*" she cried; and suddenly the thought of confiding in someone loosened a stinging flood of tears from her eyes, and she sank into a chair. "He has come to speak to her . . . time and time again . . . he seems always to be there . . . but nothing changes. . . ."

"Ah, so," said Vladimir, pulling out his gray handkerchief and handing it to her. "The sow screws him."

She grimaced both at the words and the reprehensible cloth, with which she nevertheless dabbed her eyes. "I don't believe that," she said nasally.

"Why not? She's a prostitute. Only to look at her."

"You've seen her?" she asked, slowly raising her eyes. But of course, if he sat outside in his car every night . . .

"I have seen her," he said, revulsion hardening his eyes. "I have seen much. Even a bat-man with the face of a sorrowful kewpie doll. He pines this minute on the front steps."

"That's her boyfriend," Lillian mumured, increasingly chilled by the thought of Vladimir sitting outside all night, spying.

"Boyfriend! A hundred boyfriends she has, each with a roll of bills in his pocket!"

Tensely, she smoothed the hair at her temples. "Forgive me, Vladimir," she said gently, "but you exaggerate. You exaggerate everything, I'm afraid. I must point this out to you, because I think it does you no good. I really—"

"Don't change the subject! We're talking about her, upstairs!"

She was silent for a moment. "The girl is—too free, I suppose, in our eyes. But I'm certain that she isn't what you call her."

"And how do you come to this idiot conclusion?" he asked scornfully.

She lifted her hands in explanation, but they hung helplessly suspended. "Well," she said at last, "I know she reads Dostoevski . . . she takes courses . . . and she cares for that boy in the cape, even if they do have their quarrels . . . and there's a quality of anguish in her face . . ."

"Anguish! I call it the knocked-out look of a female cretin who uses her ass every night to pay the rent. And that pea-brain boyfriend outside, in his secondhand ghoul costume to show how interesting he is! Probably he pops pills and lives off his washer-woman mother, if he hasn't slit her throat in a fit of irritation! It's the type, Lillian! Weak, no vision, no guts! The sewers are vomiting them up by the thousands to mix with us! They surround us! Slop! Shit! Chaos! Listen to that up there! Hee-haw! Call that anguish! Even pleasure? No, I tell you what it is? Empty, hollow noise—like a wheel spun into motion and never stopped again! It's madness! The madness of our times!"

But as he whipped himself on, Lillian felt herself growing diametrically clear and calm, as if the outburst were guiding her blurred character back into focus. When he stopped, she said firmly, "Yes, I understand what you mean about the wheel spinning. There is something pointless about them, something pitiful. But they're not from a sewer. They're people, Vladimir, human beings like ourselves . . ."

"Ah, blanket democracy! What else would you practice but that piss-fart abomination?"

"I practice what Bedelia herself practiced," she replied tartly.

"Ah," he sighed, "the difference between instinct and application. Between a state of grace and a condition of effort. Dear friend Lillian, tolerance is dangerous without insight. And the last generation with insight has passed, with the things it understood. Like the last generation of cobblers and glass stainers. It is fatal to try to carry on a dead art—the world has no use for it! The world will trample you down! Don't think of the past, think of your scalp!"

"No," she stated, rising and swaying with the

lightheadedness that so frequently visited her now. "To live each moment as if you were in danger—it's demeaning. I will not creep around snarling like some four-legged beast. I am a civilized human being. Your attitude shows a lack of proportion, Vladimir; I feel that you really—"

A flash of sinewy hands; her wrists were seized and crushed together with a stab of pain through whose shock she felt a marginal heat of embarrassment, a tingling dismay of abrupt intimacy. Then the very center of her skull was pierced by his shriek. "You *are* in danger! Can't you *see!*" and he thrust his face at hers, disclosing the red veins of his eyes, bits of sleep matted in the lashes, and the immobile, overwhelmed look of someone who has seen the abyss and is seeing it again. Her heart gave the chop of an axe; with a wail she strained back.

His fixed look broke; his eyes grew flaring, kinetic. "One minute the blood is nice and cozy in its veins—the next, slice! and slice! and slice! Red fountains go up—a festival! Worthy of Handel! Oh marvelous, marvelous! The rain man—" Here he broke off to renew his grip as she struggled frantically to pull away. "The rain man, he's in ecstasies! Such founts and spouts, such excitement! Then at last it's all played out, nothing but puddles, and off he trots, he's big success! And it's big city—many many fountains to be had, all red as—as—red as—"

Her laboring wrists were flung aside; her hands slammed against her face and pressed fiercely into the cheeks.

"Vladimir!" she screamed. "It's Lillian—Lillian!"

The flared eyes contracted. He stepped back and stood immobile. Then a self-admonishing hand rose shakily to his face, which had gone the color of pewter.

After a long moment he turned and walked out of the house.

She blundered to the door and locked it behind him, then ran heavily back into the front room where she came to a blank stop, both hands pressed to her chest. Hearing the sound of an engine starting, she wheeled around to the window and pinched back the edge of the shade. Through the rain she saw the big square car jerk and shudder, while its motor rose to a crescendo of whines and abruptly stopped. Vladimir climbed out and started back across the pavement. Her brain finally clicked: the telephone, the police.

With long strides she gained the hall where the telephone stood, and where she now heard the anticipated knock—but mild, rueful, a diminished sound that soon fell away. She moved on haltingly; she would call the police, yes—or a friend from work—or her doctor—someone, anyone, she must talk to someone, and suddenly she stumbled with a cry: it was Vladimir's lumber jacket she had tripped over, still lying on the floor where he had dropped it, his wallet sticking out from the pocket. Outside, the Buick began coughing once more, then it fell silent. A few moments later the shallow, timid knock began again. Without his wallet he could not call a garage, a taxi. It was fifteen-block walk to his house in the rain. If only she could feel Bedelia's presence beside her, look to the expression in the intelligent eyes. Gradually, concentrating on those eyes, she felt an unclenching inside her. She gazed at the door. Behind it Vladimir was Vladimir still. He had spoken with horrifying morbidity, and even hurt her wrists and face, but he was not the rain man. Bedelia would have seen such seeds. He had been trying to warn her tonight of the world's dangers, and in his passion had set off one of his numerous obsessions—

with her fingertip she touched the rouged and aching oval of her cheek. Strange, tortured soul who had stationed himself out in the cold, night after night, to keep her from harm. Bending down, she gathered up the rough, homely jacket; but the knocking had stopped. She went back into the front room and again tweaked aside the shade. He was going away, a small decelerated figure, already drenched. Now he turned the corner and was lost from sight. Depleted, she leaned against the wall.

It might have been a long while that she stood there, that the noise from above masked the sound, but by degrees she became aware of knocking. He must have turned around in the deluge and was now, with what small hope, tapping on the door again. She hesitated, once more summoning the fine violet eyes, the tall brow under its archaic coiffure, which dipped in an affirmative nod. The jacket under her arm, Lillian went into the hall, turned on the porch light, and unlocked the door.

It was not Vladimir who stood there, but Jamie, as wet as if he had crawled from the ocean, his long curls limply clinging to the foolish cape, his neat little features stamped with despair, yet warmed, saved, by the light of greeting in his eyes. Weary, unequal to any visit, she shook her head.

"Jody?" she thought she heard him say, or more likely it was something else—the rain muffled his voice; though she caught an eerie, unnatural tone she now sensed was reflected in the luminous stare. With a sudden feeling of panic she started to slam the door in his face. But she braked herself, knowing that she was overwrought; it was unseemly to use such brusqueness on this lost creature because of her jangled nerves.

So she paused for one haggard, courteous moment to say, "I'm sorry, Jamie, it's late—some other time." And in that moment the shrouded figure crouched, and instantaneously, spasmlike, rushed up against her. She felt a huge but painless blow, followed by a dullness, a stillness deep inside her, and staggering back as he kicked the door shut behind them, she clung to the jamb of the front-room entrance and slowly sank to her knees.

She dimly comprehended the wet cloak brushing her side, but it was the room that held her attention, that filled her whole being. It had grown immense, lofty, and was suffused with violet, overwhelmingly beautiful. But even as she watched, it underwent a rapid wasting, paled to the faint, dead-leaf hue of an old tintype; and now it vanished behind a sheet of black as the knife was wrenched from her body.

The Kugelmass Episode

Woody Allen

WOODY ALLEN was born in Brooklyn, New York on December 1, 1935. He is a comedian, writer, actor, and film director. His writing has appeared primarily in *The New Yorker* and *The New Republic* as well as in two volumes published by Random House.

Kugelmass, a professor of humanities at City College, was unhappily married for the second time. Daphne Kugelmass was an oaf. He also had two dull sons by his first wife, Flo, and was up to his neck in alimony and child support.

"Did I know it would turn out so badly?" Kugelmass whined to his analyst one day. "Daphne had promise. Who suspected she'd let herself go and swell up like a beach ball? Plus she had a few bucks, which is not in itself a healthy reason to marry a person, but it doesn't hurt, with the kind of operating nut I have. You see my point?''

Kugelmass was bald and as hairy as a bear, but he had soul

''I need to meet a new woman,'' he went on. ''I need to have an affair. I may not look the part, but I'm a man who needs romance. I need softness, I need flirtation. I'm not getting younger, so before it's too late I want to make love in Venice, trade quips at '21,' and exchange coy glances over red wine and candlelight. You see what I'm saying?''

Dr. Mandel shifted in his chair and said, ''An affair will solve nothing. You're so unrealistic. Your problems run much deeper.''

''And also this affair must be discreet,'' Kugelmass continued. ''I can't afford a second divorce. Daphne would really sock it to me.''

''Mr. Kugelmass—''

''But it can't be anyone at City College, because Daphne also works there. Not that anyone on the faculty at C.C.N.Y. is any great shakes, but some of those coeds . . .''

''Mr. Kugelmass—''

''Help me. I had a dream last night. I was skipping through a meadow holding a picnic basket and the basket was marked 'Options.' And then I saw there was a hole in the basket.''

''Mr. Kugelmass, the worst thing you could do is act out. You must simply express your feelings here, and together we'll analyze them. You have been in treatment long enough to know there is no overnight cure. After all, I'm an analyst, not a magician.''

''Then perhaps what I need is a magician,'' Kugelmass said, rising from his chair. And with that he terminated his therapy.

A couple of weeks later, while Kugelmass and Daphne were moping around in their apartment one night like two pieces of old furniture, the phone rang.

"I'll get it," Kugelmass said. "Hello."

"Kugelmass?" a voice said. "Kugelmass, this is Persky."

"Who?"

"Persky. Or should I say The Great Persky?"

"Pardon me?"

"I hear you're looking all over town for a magician to bring a little exotica into your life? Yes or no?"

"Sh-h-h," Kugelmass whispered. "Don't hang up. Where are you calling from, Perksy?"

Early the following afternoon, Kugelmass climbed three flights of stairs in a broken-down apartment house in the Bushwick section of Brooklyn. Peering through the darkness of the hall, he found the door he was looking for and pressed the bell. I'm going to regret this, he thought to himslef.

Seconds later, he was greeted by a short, thin, waxy-looking man.

"You're Persky the Great?" Kugelmass said.

"The Great Persky. You want a tea?"

"No, I want romance. I want music. I want love and beauty."

"But not tea, eh? Amazing.O.K., sit down."

Persky went to the back room, and Kugelmass heard the sounds of boxes and furniture being moved around. Persky reappeared, pushing before him a large object on squeaky roller-skate wheels. He removed some old silk handkerchiefs that were lying on its top and blew away a bit of dust. It was a cheap-looking Chinese cabinet, badly lacquered.

"Persky," Kugelmass said, "what's your scam?"

"Pay attention," Persky said. "This is some beautiful effect. I developed it for a Knights of Pythias date last year, but the booking fell through. Get into the cabinet."

"Why, so you can stick it full of swords or something?"

"You see any swords?"

Kugelmass made a face and, grunting, climbed into the cabinet. He couldn't help noticing a couple of ugly rhinestones glued onto the raw plywood just in front of his face. "If this is a joke," he said.

"Some joke. Now, here's the point. If I throw any novel into this cabinet with you, shut the doors, and tap it three times, you will find yourself projected into that book."

Kugelmass made a grimace of disbelief.

"It's the *emess,*" Persky said. "My hand to God. Not just a novel, either. A short story, a play, a poem. You can meet any of the women created by the world's best writers. Whoever you dreamed of. You could carry on all you like with a real winner. Then when you've had enough you give a yell, and I'll see you're back here in a split second."

"Persky, are you some kind of outpatient?"

"I'm telling you it's on the level," Persky said.

Kugelmass remained skeptical. "What are you telling me—that this cheesy homemade box can take me on a ride like you're describing?"

"For a double sawbuck."

Kugelmass reached for his wallet. "I'll believe this when I see it," he said.

Persky tucked the bills in his pants pocket and turned toward his bookcase. "So who do you want to meet? Sister Carrie? Hester Prynne? Ophelia? Maybe someone by Saul Bellow? Hey, what about Temple Drake? Although for a man your age she'd be a workout."

"French. I want to have an affair with a French lover."

"Nana?"

"I don't want to have to pay for it."

"What about Natasha in 'War and Peace'?"

"I said French. I know! What about Emma Bovary? That sounds to me perfect."

"You got it, Kugelmass. Give me a holler when you've had enough." Persky tossed in a paperback copy of Flaubert's novel.

"You sure this is safe!" Kugelmass asked as Persky began shutting the cabinet doors.

"Safe. Is anything safe in this crazy world?" Persky rapped three times on the cabinet and then flung open the doors.

Kugelmass was gone. At the same moment, he appeared in the bedroom of Charles and Emma Bovary's house at Yonville. Before him was a beautiful woman, standing alone with her back turned to him as she folded some linen. I can't believe this, thought Kugelmass, staring at the doctor's ravishing wife. This is uncanny. I'm here. It's her.

Emma turned in surprise. "Goodness, you startled me," she said. "Who are you?" She spoke in the same fine English translation as the paperback.

It's simply devastating, he thought. Then, realizing that it was he whom she had addressed, he said, "Excuse me. I'm Sidney Kugelmass. I'm from City College. A professor of humanities. C.C.N.Y.? Uptown. I—oh, boy!"

Emma Bovary smiled flirtatiously and said, "Would you like a drink? A glass of wine, perhaps?"

She is beautiful, Kugelmass thought. What a contrast with the troglodyte who shared his bed! He felt a sudden impulse to take this vision into his arms and tell her she was the kind of woman he had dreamed of all his life.

"Yes, some wine," he said hoarsely. "White. No, red. No, white. Make it white."

"Charles is out for the day," Emma said, her voice full of playful implication.

After the wine, they went for a stroll in the lovely French countryside. "I've always dreamed that some mysterious stranger would appear and rescue me from the monotony of this crass rural existence," Emma said, clasping his hand. They passed a small church. "I love what you have on," she murmured. "I've never seen anything like it around here. It's so . . . so modern."

"It's called a leisure suit," he said romantically. "It was marked down." Suddenly he kissed her. For the next hour they reclined under a tree and whispered together and told each other deeply meaningful things with their eyes. Then Kugelmass sat up. He just remembered he had to meet Daphne at Bloomingdale's. "I must go," he told her. "But don't worry, I'll be back."

"I hope so," Emma said.

He embraced her passionately, and the two walked back to the house. He held Emma's face cupped in his palms, kissed her again, and yelled, "O.K., Persky! I got to be at Bloomingdale's by three-thirty."

There was an audible pop, and Kugelmass was back in Brooklyn.

"So? Did I lie?" Persky asked triumphantly.

"Look, Persky, I'm right now late to meet the ball and chain at Lexington Avenue, but when can I go again? Tomorrow?"

"My pleasure. Just bring a twenty. And don't mention this to anybody."

"Yeah. I'm going to call Rupert Murdoch."

Kugelmass hailed a cab and sped off to the city. His

heart danced on point. I am in love, he thought, I am the possessor of a wonderful secret. What he didn't realize was that at this very moment students in various classrooms across the country were saying to their teachers, "Who is this character on page 100? A bald Jew is kissing Madame Bovary?" A teacher in Sioux Falls, South Dakota, sighed and thought, Jesus, these kids, with their pot and acid. What goes through their minds!

Daphne Kugelmass was in the bathroom-accessories department at Bloomingdale's when Kugelmass arrived breathlessly. "Where've you been?" she snapped. "It's four-thirty."

"I got held up in traffic," Kugelmass said.

Kugelmass visited Persky the next day, and in a few minutes was again passed magically to Yonville. Emma couldn't hide her excitement at seeing him. The two spent hours together, laughing and talking about their different backgrounds. Before Kugelmass left, they made love. "My God, I'm doing it with Madame Bovary!" Kugelmass whispered to himself. "Me, who failed freshman English."

As the months passed, Kugelmass saw Persky many times and developed a close and passionate relationship with Emma Bovary. "Make sure and always get me into the book before page 120," Kugelmass said to the magician one day. "I always have to meet her before she hooks up with this Rodolphe character."

"Why?" Persky asked. "You can't beat his time?"

"Beat his time. He's landed gentry. Those guys have nothing better to do than flirt and ride horses. To me, he's one of those faces you see in the pages of *Women's Wear Daily*. With the Helmut Berger hairdo. But to her he's hot stuff."

"And her husband suspects nothing?"

"He's out of his depth. He's a lacklustre little paramedic who's thrown in his lot with a jitterbug. He's ready to go to sleep by ten, and she's putting on her dancing shoes. Oh, well . . . See you later."

And once again Kugelmass entered the cabinet and passed instantly to the Bovary estate at Yonville. "How you doing, cupcake?" he said to Emma.

"Oh, Kugelmass," Emma sighed. "What I have to put up with. Last night at dinner, Mr. Personality dropped off to sleep in the middle of the dessert course. I'm pouring my heart out about Maxim's and the ballet, and out of the blue I hear snoring."

"It's O.K., darling. I'm here now," Kugelmass said, embracing her. I've earned this, he thought, smelling Emma's French perfume and burying his nose in her hair. I've suffered enough. I've paid enough analysts. I've searched till I'm weary. She's young and nubile, and I'm here a few pages after Léon and just before Rodolphe. By showing up during the correct chapters, I've got the situation knocked.

Emma, to be sure, was just as happy as Kugelmass. She had been starved for excitement, and his tales of Broadway night life, of fast cars and Hollywood and TV stars, enthralled the young French beauty.

"Tell me again about O.J. Simpson," she implored that evening, as she and Kugelmass strolled past Abbé Bournisien's church.

"What can I say? The man is great. He sets all kinds of rushing records. Such moves. They can't touch him."

"And the Academy Awards?" Emma said wistfully. "I'd give anything to win one."

"First you've got to be nominated."

"I know. You explained it. But I'm convinced I can act. Of course, I'd want to take a class or two. With Strasberg maybe. Then, if I had the right agent—"

"We'll see, we'll see. I'll speak to Persky."

That night, safely returned to Persky's flat, Kugelmass brought up the idea of having Emma visit him in the big city.

"Let me think about it," Persky said. "Maybe I could work it. Stranger things have happened." Of course, neither of them could think of one.

"Where the hell do you go all the time?" Daphne Kugelmass barked at her husband as he returned home late that evening. "You got a chippie stashed somewhere?"

"Yeah, sure, I'm just the type," Kugelmass said wearily. "I was with Leonard Popkin. We were discussing Socialist agriculture in Poland. You know Popkin. He's a freak on the subject."

"Well, you've been very odd lately," Daphne said. "Distant. Just don't forget about my father's birthday. On Saturday?"

"Oh sure, sure," Kugelmass said, heading for the bathroom.

"My whole family will be there. We can see the twins. And Cousin Hamish. You should be more polite to Cousin Hamish—he likes you."

"Right, the twins," Kugelmass said, closing the bathroom door and shutting out the sound of his wife's voice. He leaned against it and took a deep breath. In a few hours, he told himself, he would be back in Yonville again, back with his beloved. And this time, if all went well, he would bring Emma back with him.

At three-fifteen the following afternoon, Persky worked his wizardry again. Kugelmass appeared before Emma, smiling and eager. The two spent a few hours at Yonville with Binet and then remounted the Bovary carriage. Following Persky's instructions, they held each other tightly, closed their eyes, and counted to ten.

When they opened them, the carriage was just drawing up at the side door of the Plaza Hotel, where Kugelmass had optimistically reserved a suite earlier in the day.

"I love it! It's everything I dreamed it would be," Emma said as she swirled joyously around the bedroom, surveying the city from their window. "There's F.A.O. Schwarz. And there's Central Park, and the Sherry in which one? Oh, there—I see. It's too divine."

On the bed there were boxes from Halston and Saint Laurent. Emma unwrapped a package and held up a pair of black velvet pants against her perfect body.

"The slacks suit is by Ralph Lauren," Kugelmass said. "You'll look like a million bucks in it. Come on, sugar, give us a kiss."

"I've never been so happy!" Emma squealed as she stood before the mirror. "Let's go out on the town. I want to see 'Chorus Line' and the Guggenheim and this Jack Nicholson character you always talk about. Are any of his flicks showing?"

"I cannot get my mind around this," a Stanford professor said. "First a strange character named Kugelmass, and now she's gone from the book. Well, I guess the mark of a classic is that you can reread it a thousand times and always find something new."

The lovers passed a blissful weekend. Kugelmass had told Daphne he would be away at a symposium in Boston and would return Monday. Savoring each moment, he and Emma went to the movies, had dinner in Chinatown, passed two hours at a discothèque, and went to bed with a TV movie. They slept till noon on Sunday, visited SoHo, and ogled celebrities at Elaine's. They had caviar and champagne in their suite on Sunday night and talked until dawn. That morning, in the cab taking them to Persky's apartment, Kugelmass thought, It was hectic, but worth it. I can't bring her here too often, but now and then it will be a charming contrast with Yonville.

At Persky's, Emma climbed into the cabinet, arranged her new boxes of clothes neatly around her, and kissed Kugelmass fondly. "My place next time," she said with a wink. Persky rapped three times on the cabinet. Nothing happened.

"Hmm," Persky said, scratching his head. He rapped again, but still no magic. "Something must be wrong," he mumbled.

"Persky, you're joking!" Kugelmass cried. "How can it not work?"

"Relax, relax. Are you still in the box, Emma?"

"Yes."

Persky, rapped again—harder this time.

"I'm still here, Persky."

"I know, darling. Sit tight."

"Persky, we *have* to get her back," Kugelmass whispered. "I'm a married man, and I have a class in three hours. I'm not prepared for anything more than a cautious affair at this point."

"I can't understand it," Persky muttered. "It's such a reliable little trick."

But he could do nothing. "It's going to take a little while," he said to Kugelmass. "I'm going to have to strip it down. I'll call you later."

Kugelmass bundled Emma into a cab and took her back to the Plaza. He barely made it to his class on time. He was on the phone all day, to Persky and to his mistress. The magician told him it might be several days before he got to the bottom of the trouble.

"How was the symposium?" Daphne asked him that night.

"Fine, fine," he said, lighting the filter end of a cigarette.

"What's wrong? You're as tense as a cat."

"Me? Ha, that's a laugh. I'm as calm as a summer night. I'm just going to take a walk." He eased out the door, hailed a cab, and flew to the Plaza.

"This is no good," Emma said. "Charles will miss me."

"Bear with me, sugar," Kugelmass said. He was pale and sweaty. He kissed her again, raced to the elevators, yelled at Persky over a pay phone in the Plaza lobby, and just made it home before midnight.

"According to Popkin, barley prices in Kraków have not been this stable since 1971," he said to Daphne, and smiled wanly as he climbed into bed.

The whole week went by like that. On Friday night, Kugelmass told Daphne there was another symposium he had to catch, this one in Syracuse. He hurried back to the Plaza, but the second weekend there was nothing like the first. "Get me back into the novel or marry me," Emma told Kugelmass. "Meanwhile, I want to get a job or go to class, because watching TV all day is the pits."

"Fine. We can use the money," Kugelmass said. "You consume twice your weight in room service."

"I met an off-Broadway producer in Central Park yesterday, and he said I might be right for a project he's doing," Emma said.

"Who is this clown?" Kugelmass asked.

"He's not a clown. He's sensitive and kind and cute. His name's Jeff Something-or-Other, and he's up for a Tony."

Later that afternoon, Kugelmass showed up at Persky's drunk.

"Relax," Persky told him. "You'll get a coronary."

"Relax. The man says relax. I've got a fictional character stashed in a hotel room, and I think my wife is having me tailed by a private shamus."

"O.K., O.K. We know there's a problem." Persky

crawled under the cabinet and started banging on something with a large wrench.

"I'm like a wild animal," Kugelmass went on. "I'm sneaking around town, and Emma and I have had it up to here with each other. Not to mention a hotel tab that reads like the defense budget."

"So what should I do? This is the world of magic," Persky said. "It's all nuance."

"Nuance, my foot. I'm pouring Dom Pérignon and black eggs into this little mouse, plus her wardrobe, plus she's enrolled at the Neighborhood Playhouse and suddenly needs professional photos. Also, Persky, Professor Fivish Kopkind, who teaches Comp Lit and who has always been jealous of me, has identified me as the sporadically appearing character in the Flaubert book. He's threatened to go to Daphne. I see ruin and alimony, jail. For adultery with Madame Bovary, my wife will reduce me to beggary."

"What do you want me to say? I'm working on it night and day. As far as your personal anxiety goes, that I can't help you with. I'm a magician, not an analyst."

By Sunday afternoon, Emma had locked herself in the bathroom and refused to respond to Kugelmass's entreaties. Kugelmass stared out the window at the Wollman Rink and contemplated suicide. Too bad this a low floor, he thought, or I'd do it right now. Maybe if I ran away to Europe and started life over . . . Maybe I could sell the *International Herald Tribune*, like those young girls used to.

The phone rang. Kugelmass lifted it to his ear mechanically.

"Bring her over," Persky said. "I think I got the bugs out of it."

Kugelmass's heart leaped. "You're serious?" he said. "You got it licked?"

"It was something in the transmission. Go figure."

"Persky, you're a genius. We'll be there in a minute. Less than a minute."

Again the lovers hurried to the magician's apartment, and again Emma Bovary climbed into the cabinet with her boxes. This time there was no kiss. Persky shut the doors, took a deep breath, and tapped the box three times. There was the reassuring popping noise, and when Persky peered inside, the box was empty. Madame Bovary was back in her novel. Kugelmass heaved a great sigh of relief and pumped the magician's hand.

"It's over," he said. "I learned my lesson. I'll never cheat again, I swear it." He pumped Persky's hand again and made a mental note to send him a necktie.

Three weeks later, at the end of a beautiful spring afternoon, Persky answered his doorbell. It was Kugelmass, with a sheepish expression on his face.

"O.K., Kugelmass," the magician said. "Where to this time?"

"It's just this once," Kugelmass said. "The weather is so lovely, and I'm not getting any younger. Listen, you've read 'Portnoy's Complaint'? Remember The Monkey?"

"The price is now twenty-five dollars, because the cost of living is up, but I'll start you off with one freebie, due to all the trouble I caused you."

"You're good people," Kugelmass said, combing his few remaining hairs as he climbed into the cabinet again. "This'll work all right?"

"I hope. But I haven't tried it much since all that unpleasantness."

"Sex and romance," Kugelmass said from inside the box. "What we go through for a pretty face."

Persky tossed in a copy of "Portnoy's Complaint" and rapped three times on the box. This time, instead of a popping noise there was a dull explosion, followed by a series of crackling noises and a shower of sparks. Persky leaped back, was seized by a heart attack, and dropped dead. The cabinet burst into flames, and eventually the entire house burned down.

Kugelmass, unaware of this catastrophe, had his own problems. He had not been thrust into "Portnoy's Complaint," or into any other novel, for that matter. He had been projected into an old textbook, "Remedial Spanish," and was running for his life over a barren, rocky terrain as the word "*tener*" ("to have")—a large and hairy irregular verb—raced after him on its spindly legs.

The Schreuderspitze

Mark Helprin

MARK HELPRIN is the author of *A Dove of the East, and Other Stories; Refiner's Fire;* and *Ellis Island and Other Stories.* He is a frequent contributor to *The New Yorker.* He has served in the British Merchant Navy, the Israeli Infantry, and the Israeli Air Force. Since writing *The Schreuderspitze,* he has become proficient in Alpine mountaineering.

In Munich are many men who look like weasels. Whether by genetic accident, meticulous crossbreeding, an early and puzzling migration, coincidence, or a reason that we do not know, they exist in great numbers. Remarkably, they accentuate this unfortunate tendency be wearing mustaches, Alpine hats, and tweed. A man who resembles a rodent should never wear tweed.

One of these men, a commercial photographer named

Franzen, had cause to be exceedingly happy. "Herr Wallich has disappeared," he said to Huebner, his supplier of paper and chemicals. "You needn't bother to send him bills. Just send them to the police. The police, you realize, were here on two separate occasions!"

"If the two occasions on which the police have been here had not been separate, Herr Franzen, they would have been here only once."

"What do you mean? Don't toy with me. I have no time for semantics. In view of the fact that I knew Wallich at school, and professionally, they sought my opinion on his disappearance. They wrote down everything I said, but I do not think that they will find him. He left his studio on the Neuhausstrasse just as it was when he was working, and the landlord has put a lien on the equipment. Let me tell you that he had some fine equipment—very fine. But he was not such a great photographer. He didn't have that killer's instinct. He was clearly not a hunter. His canine teeth were poorly developed; not like these," said Franzen, baring his canine teeth in a smile which made him look like an idiot with a mouth of miniature castle towers.

"But I am curious about Wallich."

"So is everyone. So is everyone. This is my theory. Wallich was never any good at school. At best, he did only middling well. And it was not because he had hidden passions, or a special genius for some field outside the curriculum. He tried hard but found it difficult to grasp several subjects; for him mathematics and physics were pure torture.

"As you know, he was not wealthy, and although he was a nice-looking fellow, he was terribly short. That inflicted upon him great scars—his confidence, I mean, because he had none. He could do things only gently. If he had to fight, he would fail. He was weak.

"For example, I will use the time when he and I were competing for the Heller account. This job meant a lot of money, and I was not about to lose. I went to the library and read all I could about turbine engines. What a bore! I took photographs of turbine blades and such things, and seeded them throughout my portfolio to make Herr Heller think that I had always been interested in turbines. Of course, I had not even known what they were. I thought that they were an Oriental hat. And now that I know them, I detest them.

"Naturally, I won. But do you know how Wallich approached the competition? He had some foolish ideas about mother-of-pearl nautiluses and other seashells. He wanted to know how shapes of things mechanical were echoes of shapes in nature. All very fine, but Herr Heller pointed out that if the public were to see photographs of mother-of-pearl shells contrasted with photographs of his engines, his engines would come out the worse. Wallich's photographs were very beautiful—the tones of white and silver were exceptional—but they were his undoing. In the end, he said, 'Perhaps, Herr Heller, you are right,' and lost the contract just like that.

"The thing that saved him was the prize for that picture he took in the Black Forest. You couldn't pick up a magazine in Germany and not see it. He obtained so many accounts that he began to do very well. But he was just not commercially-minded. He told me himself that he took only those assignments which pleased him. Mind you, his business volume was only about two-thirds of mine.

"My theory is that he could not take the competition, and the demands of his various clients. After his wife and son were killed in the motorcar crash, he dropped assignments one after another. I suppose he thought that as a bachelor he could live like a bohemian, on very little money, and therefore did not have to work more than half the time. I'm not saying that this was wrong. (Those accounts came to me.) But it was another instance of his weakness and lassitude.

"My theory is that he has probably gone to South America, or thrown himself off a bridge—because he saw that there was no future for him if he were always to take pictures of shells and things. And he was weak. The weak can never face themselves, and so cannot see the practical side of the world, how things are laid out, and what sacrifices are required to survive and prosper. It is only in fairy tales that they rise to triumph."

Wallich could not afford to get to South America. He certainly would not have thrown himself off a bridge. He was excessively neat and orderly, and the prospect of some poor fireman handling a swollen bloated body resounding with flies deterred him forever from such nonsense.

Perhaps if he had been a Gypsy he would have taken to the road. But he was no Gypsy, and had not the talent, skill, or taste for life outside Bavaria. Only once had he been away, to Paris. It was their honeymoon, when he and his wife did not need Paris or any city. They went by train and stayed for a week at a hotel by the Quai Voltaire. They walked in the gardens all day long, and in the May evenings they went to concerts where they heard the perfect music of their own country. Though they were away for just a week, and read the German papers, and went to a corner of the Luxembourg Gardens where there were pines and wildflowers like those in the greenbelt around Munich, this music made them sick for home. They returned two days early and never left again except for July and August, which each year they spent in the Black Forest, at a cabin inherited from her parents.

He dared not go back to that cabin. It was set like a trap. Were he to enter he would be enfiladed by the sight of their son's pictures and toys, his little boots and miniature fishing rod, and by her comb lying at the exact angle she had left it when she had last brushed her hair, and by the sweet smell of her clothing. No, someday he would have to burn the cabin. He dared not sell, for strangers then would handle roughly all those things which meant so much to him that he could not even gaze upon them. He left the little cabin to stand empty, perhaps the object of an occasional hiker's curiosity, or recipient of cheerful postcards from friends travelling or at the beach for the summer—friends who had not heard.

He sought instead a town far enough from Munich so that he would not encounter anything familiar, a place where he would be unrecognized and yet a place not entirely strange, where he would have to undergo no savage adjustments, where he could buy a Munich paper.

A search of the map brought his flying eye always southward to the borderlands, to Alpine country remarkable for the steepness of the brown contours, the depth of the valleys, and the paucity of settled places. Those few depicted towns appeared to be clean and well placed on high overlooks. Unlike the cities to the north—circles which clustered together on the flatlands or along rivers, like colonies of bacteria—the cities of the Alps stood alone, *in extremis,* near the border. Though he dared not cross the border, he thought perhaps to venture near its edge, to see what he would see. These isolated towns in the Alps promised shining clear air and deep-green trees. Perhaps they were above the tree line. In a number of cases it looked that way—

and the circles were far from resembling clusters of bacteria. They seemed like untethered balloons.

He chose a town for its ridiculous name, reasoning that few of his friends would desire to travel to such a place. The world bypasses badly named towns as easily as it abandons ungainly children. It was called Garmisch-Partenkirchen. At the station in Munich, they did not even inscribe the full name on his ticket, writing merely "Garmisch-P."

"Do you live there?" the railroad agent had asked.

"No," answered Wallich.

"Are you visiting relatives, or going on business, or going to ski?"

"No."

"Then perhaps you are making a mistake. To go in October is not wise, if you do not ski. As unbelievable as it may seem, they have had much snow. Why go now?"

"I am a mountain climber," answered Wallich.

"In winter?" The railway agent was used to flushing out lies, and when little fat Austrian boys just old enough for adult tickets would bend their knees at his window as if at confession and say in squeaky voices, "Half fare to Salzburg!," he pounced upon them as if he were a leopard and they juicy ptarmigan or baby roebuck.

"Yes, in the winter," Wallich said. "Good mountain climbers thrive in difficult conditions. The more ice, the more storm, the greater the accomplishment. I am accumulating various winter records. In January, I go to America, where I will ascend their highest mountain, Mt. Independence, four thousand metres." He blushed so hard that the railway agent followed suit. Then Wallich backed away, insensibly mortified.

A mountain climber! He would close his eyes in fear when looking through Swiss calendars. He had not the stamina to rush up the stairs to his studio. He had failed miserably at sports. He was not a mountain climber, and had never even dreamed of being one.

Yet when his train pulled out of the vault of lacy ironwork and late-afternoon shadow, its steam exhalations were like those of a man puffing up a high meadow, speeding to reach the rock and ice, and Wallich felt as if he were embarking upon an ordeal of the type men experience on the precipitous rock walls of great cloud-swirled peaks. Why was he going to Garmisch-Partenkirchen anyway, if not for an ordeal through which to right himself? He was pulled so far over on one side by the death of his family, he was so bent and crippled by the pain of it, that he was going to Garmisch-Partenkirchen to suffer a parallel ordeal through which he would balance what had befallen him.

How wrong his parents and friends had been when they had offered help as his business faltered. A sensible, graceful man will have symmetry. He remembered the time at youth camp when a stream had changed course away from a once gushing sluice and the younger boys had had to carry buckets of water up a small hill, to fill a cistern. The skinny little boys had struggled up the hill. Their counsellor, sitting comfortably in the shade, would not let them go two to a bucket. At first they had tried to carry the pails in front of them, but this was nearly impossible. Then they surreptitiously spilled half the water on the way up, until the counsellor took up position at the cistern and inspected each cargo. It had been torture to carry the heavy bucket in one aching hand. Wallich finally decided to take two buckets. Though it was agony, it was a better agony than the one he had had, because he had retrieved his balance, could look ahead, and, by carrying a double burden, had strengthened himself and made the job that much shorter. Soon, all the boys carried two buckets. The cistern was filled in no time, and they had a victory over their surprised counsellor.

So, he thought as the train shuttled through chill half-harvested fields, I will be a hermit in Garmisch-Partenkirchen. I will know no one. I will be alone. I may even begin to climb mountains. Perhaps I will lose fingers and toes, and on the way gather a set of wounds which will allow me some peace.

He sensed the change of landscape before he actually came upon it. Then they began to climb, and the engine sweated steam from steel to carry the lumbering cars up terrifying grades on either side of which blue pines stood angled against the mountainside. They reached a level stretch which made the train curve like a dragon and led it through deep tunnels, and they sped along as if on a summer excursion, with views of valleys so distant that in them whole forests sat upon their meadows like birthmarks, and streams were little more than the grain in leather.

Wallich opened his window and leaned out, watching ahead for tunnels. The air was thick and cold. It was full of sunshine and greenery, and it flowed past as if it were a mountain river. When he pulled back, his cheeks were red and his face pounded from the frigid air. He was alone in the compartment. By the time the lights came on he had decided upon the course of an ideal. He was to become a mountain climber, after all—and in a singularly difficult, dangerous, and satisfying way.

A porter said in passing the compartment, "The dining car is open, sir." Service to the Alps was famed. Even though his journey was no more than two hours, he had arranged to eat on the train, and had paid for and ordered a meal to which he looked forward in pleasant anticipation, especially because he had selected French strawberries in cream for dessert. But then he saw his body in the gently lit half mirror. He was soft from a lifetime of near-happiness. The sight of his face in the blond light of the mirror made him decide to begin preparing for the mountains that very evening. The porter ate the strawberries.

Of the many ways to attempt an ordeal perhaps the most graceful and attractive is the Alpine. It is far more satisfying than Oriental starvation and abnegation precisely because the European ideal is to commit difficult acts amid richness and overflowing beauty. For that reason, the Alpine is as well the most demanding. It is hard to deny oneself, to pare oneself down, at the heart and base of a civilization so full.

Wallich rode to Garmisch-Partenkirchen in a thunder of proud Alps. The trees were tall and lively, the air crystalline, and radiating beams spoke through the train window from one glowing range to another. A world of high ice laughed. And yet ranks of competing images assaulted him. He had gasped at the sight of Bremen, a port stuffed with iron ships gushing wheat steam from their whistles as they prepared to sail. In the mountain dryness, he remembered humid ports from which these massive ships crossed a colorful world, bringing back on laden decks a catalogue of stuffs and curiosities.

Golden images of the north plains struck from the left. The salt-white plains nearly floated above the sea. All this was in Germany, though Germany was just a small part of the world, removed almost entirely from the deep source of things—from the high lakes where explorers touched the silvers which caught the world's images, from the Sahara where they found the fine glass which bent the light.

Arriving at Garmisch-Partenkirchen in the dark, he could hear bells chiming and water rushing. Cool currents of air flowed from the direction of this white tumbling sound. It was winter. He hailed a horse-drawn sledge and piled his baggage in the back. "Hotel Aufburg," he said authoritatively.

"Hotel Aufburg?" asked the driver.

"Yes, Hotel Aufburg. There is such a place, isn't there? It hasn't closed, has it?"

"No, sir, it hasn't closed." The driver touched his horse with the whip. The horse walked twenty feet and was reined to a stop. "Here we are," the driver said. "I trust you've had a pleasant journey. Time passes quickly up here in the mountains."

The sign for the hotel was so large and well lit that the street in front of it shone as in daylight. The driver was guffawing to himself; the little guffaws rumbled about in him like subterranean thunder. He could not wait to tell the other drivers.

Wallich did nothing properly in Garmisch-Partenkirchen. But it was a piece of luck that he felt too awkward and ill at ease to sit alone in restaurants while, nearby, families and lovers had self-centered raucous meals, sometimes even bursting into song. Winter took over the town and covered it in stiff white ice. The unresilient cold, the troikas jingling through the streets, the frequent snowfalls encouraged winter fat. But because Wallich ate cold food in his room or stopped occasionally at a counter for a steaming bowl of soup, he became a shadow.

The starvation was pleasant. It made him sleepy and its constant physical presence gave him companionship. He sat for hours watching the snow, feeling as if he were part of it, as if the diminution of his body were great progress, as if such lightening would lessen his sorrow and bring him to the high rim of things he had not seen before, things which would help him and show him what to do and make him proud just for coming upon them.

He began to exercise. Several times a day the hotel

manager knocked like a woodpecker at Wallich's door. The angrier the manager, the faster the knocks. If he were really angry he spoke so rapidly that he sounded like a speeded-up record. "Herr Wallich, I must ask you on behalf of the other guests to stop immediately all the thumping and vibration! This is a quiet hotel, in a quiet town, in a quiet tourist region. Please!" Then the manager would bow and quickly withdraw.

Eventually they threw Wallich out, but not before he had spent October and November in concentrated maniacal pursuit of physical strength. He had started with five each, every waking hour, of pushups, pull-ups, sit-ups, toe-touches, and leg-raises. The pull-ups were deadly—he did one every twelve minutes. The thumping and bumping came from five minutes of running in place. At the end of the first day, the pain in his chest was so intense that he was certain he was not long for the world. The second day was worse. And so it went, until after ten days there was no pain at all. The weight he abandoned helped a great deal to expand his physical prowess. He was, after all, in his middle twenties, and had never eaten to excess. Nor did he smoke or drink, except for champagne at weddings and municipal celebrations. In fact, he had always had rather ascetic tendencies, and had thought it fitting to have spent his life in Munich—"Home of Monks."

By his fifteenth day in Garmisch-Partenkirchen he had increased his schedule to fifteen apiece of the exercises each hour, which meant, for example, that he did a pull-up every four minutes whenever he was awake. Late at night he ran aimlessly about the deserted streets for an hour or more, even though it sometimes snowed. Two policemen who huddled over a brazier in their tiny booth simply looked at one another and pointed to their heads, twirling their fingers and rolling their eyes every time he passed by. On the last day of

November, he moved up the valley to a little village called Altenburg-St. Peter.

There it was worse in some ways and better in others. Altenburg-St. Peter was so tiny that no stranger could enter unobserved, and so still that no one could do anything without the knowledge of the entire community. Children stared at Wallich on the street. This made him walk on the little lanes and approach his few destinations from the rear, which led housewives to speculate that he was a burglar. There were few merchants, and, because they were cousins, they could with little effort determine exactly what Wallich ate. When one week they were positive that he had consumed only four bowls of soup, a pound of cheese, a pound of smoked meat, a quart of yogurt, and two loaves of bread, they were incredulous. They themselves ate this much in a day. They wondered how Wallich survived on so little. Finally they came up with an answer. He received packages from Munich several times a week and in these packages was food, they thought—and probably very great delicacies. Then as the winter got harder and the snows covered everything they stopped wondering about him. They did not see him as he ran out of his lodgings at midnight, and the snow muffled his tread. He ran up the road toward the Schreuderspitze, first for a kilometre, then two, then five, then ten, then twenty—when finally he had to stop because he had begun slipping in just before the farmers arose and would have seen him.

By the end of February the packages had ceased arriving, and he was a changed man. No one would have mistaken him for what he had been. In five months he had become lean and strong. He did two hundred and fifty sequential pushups at least four times a day. For the sheer pleasure of it, he would do a hundred and fifty pushups on his fingertips. Every day he did a hundred pull-ups in a row. His midnight run, sometimes in snow which had accumulated up to his knees, was four hours long.

The packages had contained only books on climbing, and equipment. At first the books had been terribly discouraging. Every elementary text had bold warnings in red or green ink: "It is extremely dangerous to attempt genuine ascents without proper training. This volume should be used in conjunction with a certified course on climbing, or with the advice of a registered guide. A book itself will not do!"

One manual had in bright-red ink, on the very last page: "Go back, you fool! Certain death awaits you!" Wallich imagined that, as the books said, there were many things he could not learn except by human example, and many mistakes he might make in interpreting the manuals, which would go uncorrected save for the critique of living practitioners. But it didn't matter. He was determined to learn for himself and accomplish his task alone. Besides, since the accident he had become a recluse, and could hardly speak. The thought of enrolling in a climbing school full of young people from all parts of the country paralyzed him. How could he reconcile his task with their enthusiasm? For them it was recreation, perhaps something aesthetic or spiritual, a way to meet new friends. For him it was one tight channel through which he would either burst on to a new life, or in which he would die.

Studying carefully, he soon worked his way to advanced treatises for those who had spent years in the Alps. He understood these well enough, having quickly learned the terminologies and the humor and the faults of those who write about the mountains. He was even convinced that he knew the spirit in which the treatises had been written, for though he had never climbed, he had only to look out his window to see high white mountains about which blue sky swirled like a banner. He felt that in seeing them he was one of them, and was greatly encouraged when he read in a French mountaineer's memoirs: "After years in the mountains, I learned to look upon a given range and feel as if I were the last peak in the line. Thus I felt the music of the empty spaces enwrapping me, and I became not an intruder on the cliffs, dangling only to drop away, but an equal in transit. I seldom looked at my own body but only at the mountains, and my eyes felt like the eyes of the mountains."

He lavished nearly all his dwindling money on fine equipment. He calculated that after his purchases he would have enough to live on through September. Then he would have nothing. He had expended large sums on the best tools, and he spent the intervals between his hours of reading and exercise holding and studying the shiny carabiners, pitons, slings, chocks, hammers, ice pitons, axes, étriers, crampons, ropes, and specialized hardware that he had either ordered or constructed himself from plans in the advanced books.

It was insane, he knew, to funnel all his preparation into a few months of agony and then without any experience whatever throw himself alone onto a Class VI ascent—the seldom climbed *Westgebirgsausläufer* of the Schreuderspitze. Not having driven one piton, he was going to attempt a five-day climb up the nearly sheer western counterfront. Even in late June, he would spend a third of his time on ice. But the sight of the ice in March, shining like a faraway sword over the cold and absolute distance, drove him on. He had long passed censure. Had anyone known what he was doing and tried to dissuade him, he would have told him to go to hell, and resumed preparations with the confidence of someone taken up by a new religion.

For he had always believed in great deeds, in fairy

tales, in echoing trumpet lands, in wonders and wondrous accomplishments. But even as a boy he had never considered that such things would fall to him. As a good city child he had known that these adventures were not necessary. But suddenly he was alone and the things which occurred to him were great warlike deeds. His energy and discipline were boundless, as full and overflowing as a lake in the mountains. Like the heroes of his youth, he would try to approach the high cord of ruby light and bend it to his will, until he could feel rolling thunder. The small things, the gentle things, the good things he loved, and the flow of love itself were dead for him and would always be, unless he could liberate them in a crucible of high drama.

It took him many months to think these things, and though they might not seem consistent, they were so for him, and he often spent hours alone on a sunny snow-covered meadow, his elbows on his knees, imagining great deeds in the mountains, as he stared at the massive needle of the Schreuderspitze, at the hint of rich lands beyond, and at the tiny village where he had taken up position opposite the mountain.

Toward the end of May he had been walking through Altenburg-St. Peter and seen his reflection in a store window—a storm had arisen suddenly and made the glass as silver-black as the clouds. He had not liked what he had seen. His face had become too hard and too lean. There was not enough gentleness. He feared immediately for the success of his venture if only because he knew well that unmitigated extremes are a great cause of failure. And he was tired of his painful regimen.

He bought a large Telefunken radio, in one fell swoop wiping out his funds for August and September. He felt as if he were paying for the privilege of music with portions of his life and body. But it was well worth it. When the storekeeper offered to deliver the heavy console, Wallich declined politely, picked up the cabinet himself, hoisted it on his back, and walked out of the store bent under it as in classic illustrations for physics textbooks throughout the industrialized world. He did not put it down once. The storekeeper summoned his associate and they bet and counterbet on whether Wallich "would" or "would not," as he moved slowly up the steep hill, up the steps, around the white switchbacks, onto a grassy slope, and then finally up the precipitous stairs to the balcony outside his room. "How can he have done that?" they asked. "He is a small man, and the radio must weigh at least thirty kilos." The storekeeper trotted out with a catalogue. "It weighs fifty-five kilograms!" he said. "Fifty-five kilograms!," and they wondered what had made Wallich so strong.

Once, Wallich had taken his little son (a tiny, skeptical, silent child who had a riotous giggle which could last for an hour) to see the inflation of a great gas dirigible. It had been a disappointment, for a dirigible is rigid and maintains always the same shape. He had expected to see the silver of its sides expand into ribbed cliffs which would float over them on the green field and amaze his son. Now that silver rising, the sail-like expansion, the great crescendo of a glimmering weightless mass, finally reached him alone in his room, too late but well received, when Berlin station played the Beethoven Violin Concerto, its first five timpanic D's like grace before a feast. After those notes, the music lifted him, and he riveted his gaze on the dark shapes of the mountains, where a lightning storm raged. The radio crackled after each near or distant flash, but it was as if the music had been designed for it. Wallich looked at the yellow light within a softly glowing numbered panel. It flickered gently, and he could hear cracks and flashes in the music as he saw them delineated across darkness. They looked and sounded like the bent riverine limbs of dead trees hanging majestically over rocky outcrops, destined to fall, but enjoying their grand suspension nonetheless. The music travelled effortlessly on anarchic beams, passed high over the plains, passed high the forests, seeding them plentifully, and came upon the Alps like waves which finally strike the shore after thousands of miles in open sea. It charged upward, mating with the electric storm, separating, and delivering.

To Wallich—alone in the mountains, surviving amid the dark massifs and clear air—came the closeted, nasal, cosmopolitan voice of the radio commentator. It was good to know that there was something other than the purity and magnificence of his mountains, that far to the north the balance reverted to less than moral catastrophe and death, and much stock was set in things of extraordinary inconsequence. Wallich could not help laughing when he thought of the formally dressed audience at the symphony, how they squirmed in their seats and heated the bottoms of their trousers and capes, how relieved and delighted they would be to step out into the cool evening and go to a restaurant. In the morning they would arise and take pleasure from the sweep of the drapes as sun danced by, from the gold rim around a white china cup. For them it was always too hot or too cold. But they certainly had their delights, about which sometimes he would think. How often he still dreamed, asleep or awake, of the smooth color plates opulating under his hands in tanks of developer and of the fresh film which smelled like bread and then was entombed in black cylinders to develop. How he longed sometimes for the precise machinery of his cameras. The very word "*Kamera*" was as dark and hollow as this night in the mountains when, reviewing the pleasures of faraway Berlin, he sat in perfect health and equanimity upon a wicker-weave seat in a bare white room. The only light was from the yellow dial, the sudden lightning flashes, and the faint blue of the sky beyond the hills. And all was quiet but for the music and the thunder and the static curling about the music like weak and lost memories which arise to harry even indomitable perfections.

A month before the ascent, he awaited arrival of a good climbing rope. He needed from a rope not strength to hold a fall but lightness and length for abseiling. His strategy was to climb with a short self-belay. No one would follow to retrieve his hardware and because it would not always be practical for him to do so himself, in what one of his books called "rhythmic recapitulation," he planned to carry a great deal of metal. If the metal and he reached the summit relatively intact, he could make short work of the descent, abandoning pitons as he abseiled downward.

He would descend in half a day that which had taken five days to climb. He pictured the abseiling, literally a flight down the mountain on the doubled cord of his long rope, and he thought that those hours speeding down the cliffs would be the finest of his life. If the weather were good he would come away from the Schreuderspitze having flown like an eagle.

On the day the rope was due, he went to the railroad station to meet the mail. It was a clear, perfect day. The light was so fine and rich that in its bath everyone felt wise, strong, and content. Wallich sat on the wooden boards of the wide platform, scanning the green meadows and fields for smoke and a coal engine, but the countryside was silent and the valley unmarred by the black woolly chain he sought. In the distance, toward

France and Switzerland, a few cream-and-rose-colored clouds rode the horizon, immobile and high. On far mountainsides innumerable flowers showed in this long view as a slash, or as a patch of color not unlike one flower alone.

He had arrived early, for he had no watch. After some minutes a car drove up and from it emerged a young family. They rushed as if the train were waiting to depart, when down the long trough-like valley it was not even visible. There were two little girls, as beautiful as he had ever seen. The mother, too, was extraordinarily fine. The father was in his early thirties, and he wore gold-rimmed glasses. They seemed like a university family—people who knew how to live sensibly, taking pleasure from proper and beautiful things.

The littler girl was no more than three. Sunburned and rosy, she wore a dress that was shaped like a bell. She dashed about the platform so lightly and tentatively that it was as if Wallich were watching a tiny fish gravityless in a lighted aquarium. Her older sister stood quietly by the mother, who was illumined with consideration and pride for her children. It was apparent that she was overjoyed with the grace of her family. She seemed detached and preoccupied, but in just the right way. The littler girl said in a voice like a child's party horn, "Mummy, I want some peanuts!"

It was so ridiculous that this child should share the appetite of elephants that the mother smiled. "Peanuts will make you thirsty, Gretl. Wait until we get to Garmisch-Partenkirchen. Then we'll have lunch in the buffet."

"When will we get to Garmisch-Partenkirchen?"

"At two."

"Two?"

"Yes, at two."

"At two?"

"Gretl!"

The father looked alternately at the mountains and at his wife and children. He seemed confident and steadfast. In the distance black smoke appeared in thick billows. The father pointed at it. "There's our train," he said.

"Where?" asked Gretl, looking in the wrong direction. The father picked her up and turned her head with his hand, aiming her gaze down the shimmering valley. When she saw the train she started, and her eyes opened wide in pleasure.

"Ah . . . there it is," said the father. As the train pulled into the station the young girls were filled with excitement. Amid the noise they entered a compartment and were swallowed up in the steam. The train pulled out.

Wallich stood on the empty platform, unwrapping his rope. It was a rope, quite a nice rope, but it did not make him as happy as he had expected it would.

Little can match the silhouette of mountains by night. The great mass becomes far more mysterious when its face is darkened, when its sweeping lines roll steeply into valleys and peaks and long impossible ridges, when behind the void a concoction of rare silver leaps up to trace the hills—the pressure of collected starlight. That night, in conjunction with the long draughts of music he had become used to taking, he began to dream his dreams. They did not frighten him—he was beyond fear, too strong for fear, too played out. They did not even puzzle him, for they unfolded like the chapters in a brilliant nineteenth-century history. The rich explanations filled him for days afterward. He was amazed, and did not understand why these perfect dreams suddenly came to him. Surely they did not arise from within. He had never had the world so beautifully portrayed, had never seen as clearly and in such sure, gentle steps, had never risen so high and so smoothly in unfolding enlightenment, and he had seldom felt so well looked after. And yet, there was no visible presence. But it was as if the mountains and valleys were filled with loving families of which he was part.

Upon his return from the railroad platform, a storm had come suddenly from beyond the southern ridge. Though it had been warm and clear that day, he had seen from the sunny meadow before his house that a white storm billowed in higher and higher curves, pushing itself over the summits, finally to fall like an air avalanche on the valley. It snowed on the heights. The sun continued to strike the opaque frost and high clouds. It did not snow in the valley. The shock troops of the storm remained at the highest elevations, and only worn gray veterans came below—misty clouds and rain on cold wet air. Ragged clouds moved across the mountainsides and meadows, watering the trees and sometimes catching in low places. Even so, the air in the meadow was still horn-clear.

In his room that night Wallich rocked back and forth on the wicker chair (it was not a rocker and he knew that using it as such was to number its days). That night's crackling infusion from Berlin, rising warmly from the faintly lit dial, was Beethoven's Eighth. The familiar commentator, nicknamed by Wallich Mälzels Metronom because of his even monotone, discoursed upon the background of the work.

"For many years," he said, "no one except Beethoven liked this symphony. Beethoven's opinions, however—even regarding his own creations—are equal at least to the collective pronouncements of all the musicologists and critics alive in the West during any hundred-year period. Conscious of the merits of the F-Major Symphony, he resolutely determined to redeem and . . . ah . . . the conductor has arrived. He steps to the podium. We begin."

Wallich retired that night in perfect tranquillity but awoke at five in the morning soaked in his own sweat, his fists clenched, a terrible pain in his chest, and breathing heavily as if he had been running. In the dim unattended light of the early-morning storm, he lay with eyes wide open. His pulse subsided, but he was like an animal in a cave, like a creature who has just escaped an organized hunt. It was as if the whole village had come armed and in search of him, had by some miracle decided that he was not in, and had left to comb the wet woods. He had been dreaming, and he saw his dream in its exact form. It was, first, an emerald. Cut into an octagon with two long sides, it was shaped rather like the plaque at the bottom of a painting. Events within this emerald were circular and never-ending.

They were in Munich. Air and sun were refined as on the station platform in the mountains. He was standing at a streetcar stop with his wife and his two daughters, though he knew perfectly well in the dream that these two daughters were meant to be his son. A streetcar arrived in complete silence. Clouds of people began to embark. They were dressed and muffled in heavy clothing of dull blue and gray. To his surprise, his wife moved toward the door of the streetcar and started to board, the daughters trailing after her. He could not see her feet, and she moved in a glide. Though at first paralyzed, as in the instant before a crash, he did manage to bound after her. As she stepped onto the first step and was about to grasp a chrome pole within the doorway, he made for her arm and caught it.

He pulled her back and spun her around, all very gently. Her presence before him was so intense that it was as if he were trapped under the weight of a fallen beam. She, too, wore a winter coat, but it was slim and perfectly tailored. He remembered the perfect geometry of the lapels. Not on earth had such angles ever been seen. The coat was a most intense liquid emerald color, a living light-infused green. She had always looked best in green, for her hair was like shining gold. He stood before her. He felt her delicacy. Her expression was neutral. "Where are you going?" he asked incredulously.

"I must go," she said.

He put his arms around her. She returned his embrace, and he said, "How can you leave me?"

"I have to," she answered.

And then she stepped onto the first step of the streetcar, and onto the second step, and she was enfolded into darkness.

He awoke, feeling like an invalid. His strength served for naught. He just stared at the clouds lifting higher and higher as the storm cleared. By nightfall the sky was black and gentle, though very cold. He kept thinking back to the emerald. It meant everything to him, for it was the first time he realized that they were really dead. Silence followed. Time passed thickly. He could not have imagined the sequence of dreams to follow, and what they would do to him.

He began to fear sleep, thinking that he would again be subjected to the lucidity of the emerald. But he had run that course and would never do so again except by perfect conscious recollection. The night after he had the dream of the emerald he fell asleep like someone letting go of a cliff edge after many minutes alone without help or hope. He slid into sleep, heart beating wildly. To his surprise, he found himself far indeed from the trolley tracks in Munich.

Instead, he was alone in the center of a sunlit snowfield, walking on the glacier in late June, bound for the summit of the Schreuderspitze. The mass of his equipment sat lightly upon him. He was well drilled in its use and positioning, in the subtleties of placement and rigging. The things he carried seemed part of him, as if he had quickly evolved into a new kind of animal suited for breathtaking travel in the steep heights.

His stride was light and long, like that of a man on the moon. He nearly floated, ever so slightly airborne, over the dazzling glacier. He leaped crevasses, sailing in slow motion against intense white and blue. He passed apple-fresh streams and opalescent melt pools of blue-green water as he progressed toward the Schreuderspitze. Its rocky horn was covered by nearly blue ice from which the wind blew a white corona in sines and cusps twirling about the sky.

Passing the bergschrund, he arrived at the first mass of rock. He turned to look back. There he saw the snowfield and the sun turning above it like a pinwheel, casting out a fog of golden light. He stood alone. The world had been reduced to the beauty of physics and the mystery of light. It had been rendered into a frozen state, a liquid state, a solid state, a gaseous state, mixtures, temperatures, and more varieties of light than fell on the speckled floor of a great cathedral. It was simple, and yet infinitely complex. The sun was warm. There was silence.

For several hours he climbed over great boulders and up a range of rocky escarpments. It grew more and more difficult, and he often had to lay in protection, driving a piton into a crack of the firm granite. His first piton was a surprise. It slowed halfway, and the ringing sound as he hammered grew higher in pitch. Finally, it would go in no farther. He had spent so much time in driving it that he thought it would be as steady as the Bank of England. But when he gave a gentle tug to test its hold, it came right out. This he thought extremely funny. He then remembered that he had either to drive it in all the way, to the eye, or to attach a sling along its shaft as near as possible to the rock. It was a question of avoiding leverage.

He bent carefully to his equipment sling, replaced the used piton, and took up a shorter one. The shorter piton went to its eye in five hammer strokes and he could do nothing to dislodge it. He clipped in and ascended a steep pitch, at the top of which he drove in two pitons, tied in to them, abseiled down to retrieve the first, and ascended quite easily to where he had left off. He made rapid progress over frightening pitches, places no one would dare go without assurance of a bolt in the rock and a line to the bolt—even if the bolt was just a small piece of metal driven in by dint of precariously balanced strength, arm, and Alpine hammer.

Within the sphere of utter concentration easily achieved during difficult ascents, his simple climbing evolved naturally into graceful technique, by which he went up completely vertical rock faces, suspended only by pitons and étriers. The different placements of which he had read and thought repeatedly were employed skillfully and with a proper sense of variety, though it was tempting to stay with one familiar pattern. Pounding metal into rock and hanging from his taut and colorful wires, he breathed hard, he concentrated, and he went up sheer walls.

At one point he came to the end of a subtle hairline crack in an otherwise smooth wall. The rock above was completely solid for a hundred feet. If he went down to the base of the crack he would be nowhere. The only thing to do was to make a swing traverse to a wall more amenable to climbing.

Anchoring two pitons into the rock as solidly as he could, he clipped an oval carabiner on the bottom piton, put a safety line on the top one, and lowered himself about sixty feet down the two ropes. Hanging perpendicular to the wall, he began to walk back and forth across the rock. He moved to and fro, faster and faster, until he was running. Finally he touched only in places and was swinging wildly like a pendulum. He feared that the piton to which he was anchored would not take the strain, and would pull out. But he kept swinging faster, until he gave one final push and, with a pathetic cry, went sailing over a drop which would have made a mountain goat swallow its heart. He caught an outcropping of rock on the other side, and pulled himself to it desperately. He hammered in, retrieved the ropes, glanced at the impassable wall, and began again to ascend.

As he approached great barricades of ice, he looked back. It gave him great pride and satisfaction to see the thousands of feet over which he had struggled. Much of the west counterfort was purely vertical. He could see now just how the glacier was riverine. He could see deep within the Tyrol and over the border to the Swiss lakes. Garmisch-Partenkirchen looked from here like a town on the board of a toy railroad or (if considered only two-dimensionally) like the cross-section of a kidney. Altenburg-St. Peter looked like a ladybug. The sun sent streamers of tan light through the valley, already three-quarters conquered by shadow, and the ice above took fire. Where the ice began, he came to a wide ledge and he stared upward at a sparkling ridge which looked like a great crystal spine. Inside, it was blue and cold.

He awoke, convinced that he had in fact climbed the counterfort. It was a strong feeling, as strong as the reality of the emerald. Sometimes dreams could be so real that they competed with the world, riding at even balance and calling for a decision. Sometimes, he imagined, when they are so real and so important, they easily tip the scale and the world buckles and dreams become real. Crossing the fragile barricades, one enters his dreams, thinking of his life as imagined.

He rejoiced at his bravery in climbing. It had been as real as anything he had ever experienced. He felt the pain, the exhaustion, and the reward, as well as the danger. But he could not wait to return to the mountain and the ice. He longed for evening and the enveloping darkness, believing that he belonged resting under great folds of ice on the wall of the Schreuderspitze. He had no patience with his wicker chair, the bent wood of the windowsill, the clear glass in the window, the green-sided hills he saw curving through it, or his brightly colored equipment hanging from pegs on the white wall.

Two weeks before, on one of the eastward roads from Altenburg-St. Peter—no more than a dirt track—he had seen a child turn and take a well-worn path toward a wood, a meadow, and a stream by which stood a house and a barn. The child walked slowly upward into the forest, disappearing into the dark close, as if he had been taken up by vapor. Wallich had been too far away to hear footsteps, and the last thing he saw was the back of the boy's bright blue-and-white sweater. Returning at dusk, Wallich had expected to see warmly lit windows, and smoke issuing efficiently from the straight chimney. But there were no lights, and there was no smoke. He made his way through the trees and past the meadow only to come upon a small farmhouse with boarded windows and no-trespassing signs tacked on the doors.

It was unsettling when he saw the same child making his way across the upper meadow, a flash of blue and white in the near darkness. Wallich screamed out to him, but he did not hear, and kept walking as if he were deaf or in another world, and he went over the crest of the hill. Wallich ran up the hill. When he reached the top he saw only a wide empty field and not a trace of the boy.

Then in the darkness and purity of the meadows he began to feel that the world had many secrets, that they were shattering even to glimpse or sense, and that they were not necessarily unpleasant. In certain states of light he could see, he could begin to sense, things most miraculous indeed. Although it seemed self-serving, he concluded nonetheless, after a lifetime of adhering to the diffuse principles of a science he did not know, that there was life after death, that the dead rose into a mischievous world of pure light, that something most mysterious lay beyond the enfolding darkness, something wonderful.

This idea had taken hold, and he refined it. For example, listening to the Beethoven symphonies broadcast from Berlin, he began to think that they were like a ladder of mountains, that they surpassed themselves and rose higher and higher until at certain points they seemed to break the warp itself and cross into a heaven of light and the dead. There were signs everywhere of temporal diffusion and mystery. It was as if continents existed, new worlds lying just off the coast, invisible and redolent, waiting for the grasp of one man suddenly to substantiate and light them, changing everything. Perhaps great mountains hundreds of times higher than the Alps would arise in the sea or on the flatlands. They might be purple or gold and shining in many states of refraction and reflection, transparent in places as vast as countries. Someday someone would come back from this place, or someone would by accident discover and illumine its remarkable physics.

He believed that the boy he had seen nearly glowing in the half-darkness of the high meadow had been his son, and that the child had been teasing his father in a way only he could know, that the child had been asking him to follow. Possibly he had come upon great secrets on the other side, and knew that his father would join him soon enough and that then they would laugh about the world.

When he next fell asleep in the silence of a clear windless night in the valley, Wallich was like a man disappearing into the warp of darkness. He wanted to go there, to be taken as far as he could be taken. He was not unlike a sailor who sets sail in the teeth of a great storm, delighted by his own abandon.

Throwing off the last wraps of impure light, he found himself again in the ice world. The word was all-encompassing—*Eiswelt*. There above him the blue spire rocketed upward as far as the eye could see. He touched it with his hand. It was indeed as cold as ice. It was dense and hard, like glass ten feet thick. He had doubted its strength, but its solidity told him it would not flake away and allow him to drop endlessly, far from it.

On ice he found firm holds both with his feet and with his hands, and hardly needed the ice pitons and étriers. For he had crampons tied firmly to his boots, and could spike his toe points into the ice and stand comfortably on a vertical. He proceeded with a surety of footing he had never had on the streets of Munich. Each step bolted him down to the surface. And in each hand he carried an ice hammer with which he made swinging cutting arcs that engaged the shining stainless-steel pick with the mirrorlike wall.

All the snow had blown away or had melted. There were no traps, no pitfalls, no ambiguities. He progressed toward the summit rapidly, climbing steep ice walls as if he had been going up a ladder. The air became purer and the light more direct. Looking out to right or left, or glancing sometimes over his shoulders, he saw that he was now truly in the world of mountains.

Above the few clouds he could see only equal peaks of ice, and the Schreuderspitze dropping away from him. It was not the world of rock. No longer could he make out individual features in the valley. Green had become a hazy dark blue appropriate to an ocean floor. Whole countries came into view. The landscape was a mass of winding glaciers and great mountains. At that height, all was separated and refined. Soft things vanished, and there remained only the white and the silver.

He did not reach the summit until dark. He did not see the stars because icy clouds covered the Schreuderspitze in a crystalline fog which flowed past, crackling and hissing. He was heartbroken to have come all the way to the summit and then be blinded by masses of clouds. Since he could not descend until light, he decided to stay firmly stationed until he could see clearly. Meanwhile, he lost patience and began to address a presence in the air—casually, not thinking it strange to do so, not thinking twice about talking to the void.

He awoke in his room in early morning, saying, "All these blinding clouds. Why all these blinding clouds?"

Though the air of the valley was as fresh as a flower, he detested it. He pulled the covers over his head and strove for unconsciousness, but he grew too hot and finally gave up, staring at the remnants of dawn light soaking about his room. The day brightened in the way that stage lights come up, suddenly brilliant upon a beam-washed platform. It was early June. He had lost track of the exact date, but he knew that sometime before he had crossed into June. He had lost them in early June. Two years had passed.

He packed his things. Though he had lived like a monk, much had accumulated, and this he put into suitcases, boxes, and bags. He packed his pens, paper, books, a chess set on which he sometimes played against an imaginary opponent named Herr Claub, the beautiful Swiss calendars upon which he had at one time been almost afraid to gaze, cooking equipment no more complex than a soldier's mess kit, his clothing, even the beautifully wrought climbing equipment, for, after all, he had another set, up there in the *Eiswelt*. Only his bedding remained unpacked. It was on the floor in the center of the room, where he slept. He put some banknotes in an envelope—the June rent—and tacked it to the doorpost. The room was empty, white, and it would have echoed had it been slightly larger. He would say something and then listen intently, his eyes flaring like those of a lunatic. He had not eaten in days, and was not disappointed that even the waking world began to seem like a dream.

He went to the pump. He had accustomed himself to bathing in streams so cold that they were too frightened to freeze. Clean and cleanly shaven, he returned to his room. He smelled the sweet pine scent he had brought back on his clothing after hundreds of trips through the woods and forests girdling the greater mountains. Even the bedding was snowy white. He opened the closet and caught a glimpse of himself in the mirror. He was dark from sun and wind; his hair shone; his face had thinned; his eyebrows were now gold and white. For several days he had had only cold pure water. Like soldiers who come from training toughened and healthy, he had about him the air of a small child. He noticed a certain wildness in the eye, and he lay on the hard floor, as was his habit, in perfect comfort. He thought nothing. He felt nothing. He wished nothing.

Time passed as if he could compress and cancel it.

Early-evening darkness began to make the white walls blue. He heard a crackling fire in the kitchen of the rooms next door, and imagined the shadows dancing there. Then he slept, departing.

On the mountain it was dreadfully cold. He huddled into himself against the wet silver clouds, and yet he smiled, happy to be once again on the summit. He thought of making an igloo, but remembered that he hadn't an ice saw. The wind began to build. If the storm continued, he would die. It would whittle him into a brittle wire, and then he would snap. The best he could do was to dig a trench with his ice hammers. He lay in the trench and closed his sleeves and hooded parka, drawing the shrouds tight. The wind came at him more and more fiercely. One gust was so powerful that it nearly lifted him out of the trench. He put in an ice piton, and attached his harness. Still the wind rose. It was difficult to breathe and nearly impossible to see. Any irregular surface whistled. The eye of the ice piton became a great siren. The zippers on his parka, the harness, the slings and equipment, all gave off musical tones, so that it was as if he were in a place with hundreds of tormented spirits.

The gray air fled past with breathtaking speed. Looking away from the wind, he had the impression of being propelled upward at unimaginable speed. Walls of gray sped by so fast that they glowed. He knew that if he were to look at the wind he would have the sense of hurtling forward in gravityless space.

And so he stared at the wind and its slowly pulsing gray glow. He did not know for how many hours he held that position. The rape of vision caused a host of delusions. He felt great momentum. He travelled until, eardrums throbbing with the sharpness of cold and wind, he was nearly dead, white as a candle, hardly able to breathe.

Then the acceleration ceased and the wind slowed. When, released from the great pressure, he fell back off the edge of the trench, he realized for the first time that he had been stretched tight on his line. He had never been so cold. But the wind was dying and the clouds were no longer a great corridor through which he was propelled. They were, rather, a gentle mist which did not know quite what to do with itself. How would it dissipate? Would it rise to the stars, or would it fall in compression down into the valley below?

It fell; it fell all around him, downward like a lowering curtain. It fell in lines and stripes, always downward as if on signal, by command, in league with a directive force.

At first he saw just a star or two straight on high. But as the mist departed a flood of stars burst through. Roads of them led into infinity. Starry wheels sat in fiery white coronas. Near the horizons were the few separate gentle stars, shining out and turning clearly, as wide and round as planets. The air grew mild and warm. He bathed in it. He trembled. As the air became all clear and the mist drained away completely, he saw something which stunned him.

The Schreuderspitze was far higher than he had thought. It was hundreds of times higher than the mountains represented on the map he had seen in Munich. The Alps were to it not even foothills, not even rills. Below him was the purple earth, and all the great cities lit by sparkling lamps in their millions. It was a clear summer dawn and the weather was excellent, certainly June.

He did not know enough about other cities to make them out from the shapes they cast in light, but his eye seized quite easily upon Munich. He arose from his trench and unbuckled the harness, stepping a few paces higher on the rounded summit. There was Munich, shining and pulsing like a living thing, strung with lines of amber light—light which reverberated as if in crystals, light which played in many dimensions and moved about the course of the city, which was defined by darkness at its edge. He had come above time, above the world. The city of Munich existed before him with all its time compressed. As he watched, its history played out in repeating cycles. Nothing, not one movement, was lost from the crystal. The light of things danced and multiplied, again and again, and yet again. It was all there for him to claim. It was alive, and ever would be.

He knelt on one knee as in paintings he had seen of explorers claiming a coast of the New World. He dared close his eyes in the face of that miracle. He began to concentrate, to fashion according to will with the force of stilled time a vision of those he had loved. In all their bright colors, they began to appear before him.

He awoke as if shot out of a cannon. He went from lying on his back to a completely upright position in an instant, a flash, during which he slammed the floorboards energetically with a clenched fist and cursed the fact that he had returned from such a world. But by the time he stood straight, he was delighted to be doing so. He quickly dressed, packed his bedding, and began to shuttle down to the station and back. In three trips, his luggage was stacked on the platform.

He bought a ticket for Munich, where he had not been in many many long months. He hungered for it, for the city, for the boats on the river, the goods in the shops, newspapers, the pigeons on the square, trees, traffic, even arguments, even Herr Franzen. So much rushed into his mind that he hardly saw his train pull in.

He helped the conductor load his luggage into the baggage car, and he asked, "Will we change at Garmisch-Partenkirchen?"

"No. We go right through, direct to Munich," said the conductor.

"Do me a great favor. Let me ride in the baggage car."

"I can't. It's a violation."

"Please. I've been months in the mountains. I would like to ride alone, for the last time."

The conductor relented, and Wallich sat atop a pile of boxes, looking at the landscape through a Dutch door, the top of which was open. Trees and meadows, sunny and lush in June, sped by. As they descended, the vegetation thickened until he saw along the cinder bed slow-running black rivers, skeins and skeins of thorns darted with the red of early raspberries, and flowers which had sprung up on the paths. The air was warm and caressing—thick and full, like a swaying green sea at the end of August.

They closed on Munich, and the Alps appeared in a sweeping line of white cloud-touched peaks. As they pulled into the great station, as sooty as it had ever been, he remembered that he had climbed the Schreuderspitze, by its most difficult route. He had found freedom from grief in the great and heart-swelling sight he had seen from the summit. He felt its workings and he realized that soon enough he would come once more into the world of light. Soon enough he would be with his wife and son. But until then (and he knew that time would spark ahead), he would open himself to life in the city, return to his former profession, and struggle at his craft.

My Father's Jokes

Patricia Zelver

PATRICIA ZELVER was born in California, and grew up in Medford, Oregon. She has an M.A. from Stanford and now lives in Portola Valley, California, with her husband and two sons. She has published two novels, *The Honey Bunch* and *The Happy Family* and a recent collection *A Man of Middle Age,* a novella, and twelve short stories.

The Horrible Hairy Spider was dangling over Cissy's head.

"Jello, again, this is Jack Benny," said Jack Benny.

Cissy was sitting on the rug—the Peck hooked rug, made by our New England great-grandmother on my mother's side; her golden corkscrew curls spilled down her back. Father sat in his faded sprung armchair. A Ryan armchair. Grand Rapids, Mother called it, which meant that it was not an antique, which meant that it was common. I sat on the Peck Boston rocker; I sat very straight, as if I were hanging my head from a string in order not to grow up to be a hunchback. I was eleven; Cissy, six.

Mother? Mother was down with one of her Spells. She often had these Spells, which had something to do with a New England conscience.

"Thank God I don't have a New England conscience," Father used to say.

Was it a disease? I often wondered. If so, would I inherit it?

The Horrible Hairy Spider (revolting, nearly five inches across; fat rubber body with long hairy legs, fifteen cents) dropped lower; it hung menacingly near Cissy's forehead, just above her large, long-lashed baby-blue eyes. Ryan eyes, like Father's. Father's eyes were choirboy blue. They were uplifted, now, toward Heaven. Father was one, once—a choirboy. There was a photograph of him in a lacy robe, holding a candle snuffer—that same sweet, sly expression in his choirboy eyes. That was before he stopped being Catholic.

"It's the only church if you go to church," he sometimes said. "They know how to do things up right," he said, with a touch of vanity in his voice, which aggravated Mother. There was no one, really, less vain than Father. Why, then, I wondered, was he vain about having once been Catholic, when decent people, according to Mother, would be ashamed?

> He only does it to annoy
> Because he knows it teases

Father loved Mother. On her last birthday he had given her a peek-a-boo blouse and a transparent purple nightie, which hung in her closet, unworn, except when Cissy played Dress Up. Father was also concerned about Mother's Spells. Mother wore her long chestnut hair in a tight bun at the back of her neck. Could it be that she was exerting too much strain upon her scalp? Father asked her. Perhaps, he said, if she let her hair down, let if fall more loosely, it would ease her suffering. His suggestion had no effect. Every year, it seemed, Mother drew her hair tighter; no loose wave nor tendril was permitted to escape. Still, he continued to urge her. Such lovely hair, he said. Hair like yours should be displayed for people to admire.

"Beauty," said Mother, "is as Beauty does."

Father loved Mother, whatever love was. I was not sure. But the absolute token of his affection was that he liked to tease her. Father always teased the people he loved.

He liked to tease Cissy, most of all. He seldom teased me, any more. Did this mean that he loved Cissy more, or did it mean that I had grown too old for most of his jokes? Or, possibly, too dignified? Was love undignified? No. Mother had great dignity, and Mother loved Father.

"We are One," she used to say. "When two people marry, they become One."

Why then did she suffer so? Why did she grieve? Why did she feel that our home, at 43 North Elm, in Norton, was not truly her home, that her marriage had forced her into some sort of awful exile? Why did she never laugh at Father's jokes? It was her pride, her terrible Peck pride. Those were my thoughts, as I watched, with an ill-disguised, adolescent scorn, the descent of the Horrible Hairy Spider.

"Oh yes, they do things up right," Mother said, when Father talked about having been Catholic. "All that mumbo jumbo! It's for people who have nothing else, who want to crawl on their knees in front of the Pope and kiss his feet. Crawl!" she added, with a shudder.

Father's hands were folded, *innocently,* in his lap, in

a kind of prayerful attitude. But I knew what was in them. The Secret Control Ring! I tensed my body for what was about to occur.

Another jerk! The Spider dropped, swayed to and fro, in front of Cissy's eyes. Ryan eyes, like Father's. Cissy shrieked. Oh, that shriek! Even though I had prepared myself, it went through me like an electric shock.

Father? Father was looking at Cissy with a deep concern. What dreadful thing can have happened to this little girl? What had caused her to cry out in such an anguished manner? Was she in some sort of awful peril? Oh me! Oh my! Poor Cissy!

Then Cissy caught on. She got it. If she were in the funny papers, a shimmering light bulb would have appeared over her head.

"Oh, Dad—dee!" cried Cissy. She plucked the Horrible Hairy Spider out of the air and examined it; she giggled; she stared at Father with unabashed admiration. "Oh, Dad—dee," she said again.

Father's eyes lost their innocent look; they twinkled. The little laugh wrinkles around his eyes and mouth erupted. His chest, beneath his old coat sweater, heaved, and chuckles exploded out of his mouth—little "heh, heh, heh's," like the "heh, heh, heh's" in the balloons over funny paper people. Father and Cissy were funny paper people. "Did you see *Father and Cissy* today? Wasn't the Spider *funny?*"

"She's the perfect fall guy, isn't she?" said Father, winking at me, as if I were a co-conspirator.

I refused to be implicated; I did not acknowledge the wink. I was not a funny paper person, could not have been, even if I tried. I was Emily Peck Ryan, more Peck than Ryan, everyone said.

If Justice ruled the World, which I had, by then,

learned it did not, my name would have been Charity Peck Ryan, instead.

> Charity Peck is my name; in peaceful Warren born
> In Sorrow's School my Infant Mind was pierced
> with a Thorn,
> In Wisdom's Ways, I'll spend my Days,
> Humility be with me
> Should Fortune frown or Friends disown,
> Divine Support can't leave me.

That was the verse Great-Great-Grandmother Charity had embroidered on the Sampler at the age of nine, following the death of her father. Above the verse she had stitched three rows of the alphabet and numbers up to ten in different calligraphic design in order to demonstrate her skill at needlework. Below the verse, a tombstone presided over by a Grieving Angel, such as the one in the Peck Plot in the old IOOF cemetery in Metropolis, which the Reverend Gideon Freeland Peck, owner and publisher of *The Democratic Christian Evangelist* ("Southern Oregon's first newspaper," it said on the historical plaque), had copied from the one he remembered in the Warren cemetery.

Below the tombstone were these lines:

> Phineas Peck departed this life at a
> meeting of the Citizens of Warren on
> July the Fourth, 1831, following the
> discharge of a cannon.

"Why would a man step in front of a cannon at a Fourth of July celebration?" asked Father, one Sunday afternoon, as he stood in the parlor of my grandmother's house in Metropolis, five miles from Norton, the house where Mother had grown up and which was known by all the right people and even some of the wrong ones as the Old Peck Place. Father was examining the Sampler on the parlor wall. He gazed innocently at Granny, at Aunt Dee, at Uncle Gideon, at Mother. "Unless," he said, "he was perhaps not quite sober?"

Uncle Gideon, who was mixing Granny's before-dinner martini—the most important thing, perhaps the only thing, he learned at Harvard, Father sometimes said—shook the frosted cocktail shaker more vigorously than usual; Aunt Dee bustled out of the room to see to dinner; Granny, an Abbot, not a Peck, and whose reaction, therefore, did not matter, smiled; Cissy giggled; Mother was silent. A silence fraught with meaning, I thought. I had just learned "fraught." A fraught-with-meaning silence. A silence, meaningfully fraught. This was how so many of Mother's silences were.

"It was only an idle question, to satisfy a point concerning which I have often been curious," said Father.

When I was born, there was already a Charity Peck Ryan, a year older than I, who was now known as Poor Charity; she died, when I was three, of scarlet fever and now lay under the left wing of the angel in Metropolis. Mother's sorrow impaired her delicate Nervous System. Dr. Conroy prescribed warm baths, brisk walks, and no more babies. Both Mother and Father were deeply concerned over Mother's Nervous System; neither would have wilfully disobeyed Dr. Conroy's orders. What had happened? I should never know.

"Where did you come from Baby dear?
Out of the Nowhere into the Here.
Where did you get those eyes so blue?
God gave them to me, as He did you."

This was how mother responded when Cissy asked Where She Came From, at an age when she was too little to comprehend. I knew, of course, that babies were the result of the most intimate physical expression of the deepest spiritual love between one man and one woman. Cissy had been told this, now, too, but Heaven only knew if Cissy "got" it. Heaven only knew what went on in Cissy's head. "Out of the Nowhere into the Here," though hardly a scientific explanation, seemed to me, on the whole, the best explanation for Cissy's existence.

Cissy, by being born in mysterious violation of the Doctor's Orders, had stolen my Rights of Primogeniture, in more ways than one. Being named "Charity," she would inherit the Peck Sampler. Would she spend her days wisely and humbly? Should Fortune frown and Friends disown, would she be able to count on Divine Support? Knowing Cissy, it seemed to me unlikely.

Father and Cissy were a Team. Like Jack Benny and Rochester. Like Edgar Bergen and Charley. Like George Burns and Gracie Allen. John C. Ryan and His Little Daughter, Cissy. John C. Ryan and His Bag of Magical Tricks and Practical Jokes. Little Cissy, the Perfect Fall Guy! Watch her "fall" for all the Tricks, no matter how many times performed.

FATHER: "Adam and Eve and Pinch Me
Went down to the Water to swim
Adam and Eve were drowned-ed
And who do you think was saved?"
CISSY: Pinch Me.
FATHER: (pinches Cissy)
CISSY: (squealing) Oh, Dad—dee!
FATHER: I can row a boat, canoe?
MOTHER: Oh, John, not again.

EMILY:	It's a pun, stupid. A pun on *words*. (One of the lowest forms of humor, despite Shakespeare's use of it, Miss Wilson, her seventh-grade teacher had said.) One of the lowest forms of humor.
Cissy:	Boat! Can-you? I get it! (giggles)
Mother:	Old Mr. Henry died last night in his sleep.
Father:	Mr. Henry is with Barnum and Bailey.
Cissy:	What's Barnum and Bailey?
Emily:	(who knows her History) It was a famous circus, with Buffalo Bill.
Cissy:	Why is Mr. Henry with them?
Emily:	Barnum and Bailey are dead, stupid.
Cissy:	(silence) (giggle) Oh!

Watch Cissy perform, too. A Chip Off the Old Block. Enjoy her Impersonation of Shirley Temple, singing "The Good Ship, Lollypop." A Mimic. A Great Little Trouper. Can really strut her stuff.

MOTHER:	Not now, Cissy. Judge and Mrs. Blair want to talk.
JUDGE BLAIR:	It isn't every day that an old man is entertained by a pretty little girl. Let's hear your song, Sweetheart.

Jack Benny was over. They were playing the Theme Song. Father turned off the Zenith. "I better go look in on poor Mama," he said.

Cissy's response to this was to stand on her head; her dress fell over her shoulders, revealing her pink panties; then she dropped, plop, in a giggling, quivering heap upon the rug.

"When I was a little girl, I always went to bed the moment Jack Benny was over," said Father.

Cissy looked up at Father, blue eyes big. Silence. Then, "Oh, Dad—dee, you were never a little girl!"

Father picked up Cissy and threw her over his shoulder, marched out of the room with a shrieking Cissy, dimpled legs kicking at the air.

I rose and went into the dining room and sat down at the round oak table (Grand Rapids, Ryan) and prepared to begin my seventh-grade Original Research paper.

"Why don't you write about Old Metropolis?" said Miss Emmeline Trowbridge, my friend and head librarian of the Norton Public Library, when I had consulted her about the theme. "After all," she said, "you are a Peck. Your Grandmother and your Uncle Gideon are filled with information. You must pick a particular subject. The journey of your Great-Grandfather from Massachusetts to Metropolis. The Gold Rush. Your Great-Grandfather's Temperance Crusade, the visit of Rutherford B. Hayes—"

I had decided to write about the Railroad. If it had not been for the Railroad, all Pecks would have been rich today. Not that Pecks cared about material wealth, in itself. It was the respect that went with it.

If it had not been for a man named Norton, who bought up one thousand acres of land in the fertile valley below Metropolis, who bribed the S.P.—

"It was flatter land; it was easier to lay track," said Father.

"He *bribed* them," said Mother, said Uncle Gideon, said Aunt Dee.

History, I sometimes thought, consisted as much, if not more, of what did not happen as what did.

Father was a lawyer in a small Oregon town. John C. Ryan, Atty-at-Law, it said in curly gold-leaf letters on the window of the Union Building, where he had his office. He had never finished law school; he had gone to

World War I, instead. After the war, they made a law that veterans who had left college to enlist could get their degree by passing a formal examination. Father traveled to Salem and was interviewed by the Chief Justice. This is the story he liked to tell concerning the interview:

"The Chief Justice asked me a question, which I wasn't able to answer. Then he asked me another question, which I wasn't able to answer. Then he said, " 'You are now admitted to the practice of law in the State of Oregon.' "

Father enjoyed being a lawyer in a small town. He was not ambitious, either for money or fame. You don't have to be if you have the rare privilege of enjoying your work. He was a popular man among people of every social and economic level. He was unassuming, courtly, gentle, genial, honest. He spent little time in court. By temperament, he was a "settler," not a litigator.

Outside of his work and his family, to whom he was devoted, he fished, gardened, and, after age fifty, played gin rummy every Saturday afternoon at the University Club in town. Outside of the Bar Association, this was his only affiliation; he was not a joiner. Once, someone talked him into the Kiwanis Club, because it would be "good for business." He went to one meeting and found it too serious.

He enjoyed his liquor, but drank like a gentleman. He smoked too much; his rumpled clothes were covered with cigarette ash. His other vice—if you can call it that—was his addiction to practical jokes. He kept *The Catalogue of Magical Tricks and Practical Jokes* on top of the toilet tank. The jokes, which he sent away for, were the only things he ever bought for himself, outside of necessities. This story is about my father's jokes.

THE RUBBER POINTED PENCIL
Looks like Lead
Fools and annoys 'em.

MOTHER: This pencil doesn't work, John. This pencil—Is this one of your *jokes*, John? Will you be so kind as to find me a proper pencil, please?

THE FAKE FLY
Sticks to almost any surface.
Put it on your lapel, on the butter dish.
On Mrs. Social Register's lace tablecloth.
Watch 'em try to brush it off.
Confound your hostess.

MISS SINGER: (County Recorder at the Courthouse to Cissy and Emily, who are waiting for Father in her office) Well, if there's anything I can't tolerate, it's a nasty, filthy fly. I tried to brush it off and it wouldn't move. It just—stuck. I should have guessed! He was going all over the courthouse last week with his squirting flower in his buttonhole. Well, we all know your dad! He makes life just a bit brighter for everyone. No, things are never dull when your dad's around!

THE JUMPING SPOON
Greatest Laugh Producer ever invented.
A startling after-dinner trick. The performer places one of the teaspoons to be found on the dinner table into an ordinary drinking glass. In a few seconds, the spoon jumps out of the glass! This is really surprising and funny.

MRS. BLAIR: (wife of Judge Blair) It was really surprising and funny. I couldn't believe my eyes; it just *jumped* out of the glass!

THE LIVE MYSTERY MOUSE

MISS JOST: (Elevator operator in Union Building. To Cissy and Emily) Going to see your dad?

(The elevator is like an iron cage; through the bars of the cage one sees the cables move past as the elevator rises. Miss Jost has fixed up the interior of the cage like a miniature living room. She sits in an old chintz slipper chair; her knees are covered with a multicolored afghan; her knitting is on her lap. Taped to one of the bars is a photograph of her nephew, Carl, who lost an arm in the service of his country; taped to another bar is a postcard—a pretty rural scene of Denmark, where Miss Jost's parents grew up. Above this, a calendar with a photograph of the Norton Valley with the pear blossoms in bloom, courtesy of the Norton Groceteria.)

"Fifth floor, Miss Jost," he says. (Creaking and grinding of chains, as she pulls the wheel.)

Every morning, every noon—"Fifth floor, please." (The Union Building only has two floors.) He fooled me with that mouse of his, last week. "Could that be a *mouse* in your elevator, Miss Jost?" he says. I looked down and let out a frightful scream. "Don't worry, Miss Jost, I'll get the rascal," he says, and he leans down and picks it up and puts it in his pocket. Very solemnlike. Very calm. You would think he was accustomed to picking up mice everyday! Oh, Mr. Ryan, you almost gave me a heart attack! I said. You really shouldn't, Mr. Ryan!—But you know your dad. There's no stopping him. Heaven only knows what he'll think up next!

THE MECHANICAL HAND VIBRATOR
Startle your friends with a "friendly" handshake.

MISS PORTER: (Father's stenographer. To Cissy and Emily) My hand was still tingling in bed that night.

(Miss Porter is Mother's age. An old maid. They knew each other, *slightly*, at Norton High. Miss Porter lives very quietly in the Kingscote Arms, with her widowed mother. She is the only person Emily and Cissy know who lives "downtown." Miss Porter wears too much rouge. She has her dyed hair done once a week at the Fountain of Beauty; every six months she gets a permanent. She plucks her eyebrows to a fine line and dresses in frilly frocks and sheer silk hose.) "It's a pity someone can't tell her how to dress suitable for an office," says Mother. "I'm sure it must give a bad impression when she meets the Public." Miss Porter is short and plump. Her freckled flesh is so soft it looks as if it would dent if you touched her. She has a soft voice and a slight stammer and is extremely meticulous. Since mother doesn't drive—"I don't care to run around like other women," Mother says—she often asks Emily to phone the office and give Miss Porter a shopping list for Father. If Emily says, "One dozen oranges," Miss Porter will say, "What sort of oranges, dear? Does your mother prefer juice oranges or eating oranges?" This is the part of her meticulousness, which, though appropriate for legal stenography, irritates Mother. (Emily is not sure *why*.) "Miss Porter wants to know if you want juice or eating oranges?" Emily says. "Oh, isn't that just like her! Tell her either kind will do!" Mother's cavalier attitude toward oranges, or, perhaps her cavalier attitude toward Miss Porter, imposes a burden on Emily. "You better say *which*," she tells Mother. "Juice, then! Tell her *juice!*—or, *eating*. Tell her eating! Tell her anything you like," "Juice, please," Emily says. Then Miss Porter inquires after Mother's health. "How is your mother feeling today?" she says. Or, "Is your mother feeling better today?" "Yes, better, thank you," says Emily, no matter how Mother is feeling. She senses that it is not proper to go into more personal details, that neither Miss Porter nor Mother would care for that. Mother, in fact, would prefer that Miss Porter not inquire after her health at all.

Mother never phones, herself, if she can avoid it. Having known Miss Porter, *slightly*, in high school, where they called each other by their first names, it is awkward to phone and say, "This is Mrs. Ryan." On the other hand, it will not do to say, "This is Jean." When it is necessary, for one reason or another to call, herself, Mother says, "Is this Vera?" Then she waits for Miss Porter to recognize her voice, which Miss Porter always does. Miss Porter, recognizing Mother's voice, says, "Oh, how are you?" "Very well, thank you. And you?" says Mother. "I can't complain," says Miss Porter, or, "Chipper, I'm always chipper," she says. Then she says, "I bet you'd like to talk to the Boss." "Yes, please, if he's not occupied," says Mother. "I think I can arrange for you to speak to him," says Miss Porter. "I'll just put a little flea in his ear."

(Mother does not care for Miss Porter calling Father, "the Boss," nor does she care for the expression, "a little flea in his ear." But it does solve the awkward social problem for both of them. In all the ten years in which Miss Porter has worked for Father, she has, somehow, managed never to call Mother either Mrs. Ryan, or Jean.)

MISS PORTER: That dreadful vibrator! It sent funny little shivers all through me. (She gives Cissy a box of paperclips to make into a chain; she gives Emily a stack of magazines—*The Elks Magazine*, *Field and Stream*, an old copy of *The Saturday Evening Post*, to entertain them while they wait for Father to drive them home from the dentist's. She opens the drawer of her desk and takes out a small tin box and opens it and offers them hard little white mints called "pastelles.")

CISSY: (listening to the story of the Vibrator, giggles)

EMILY: (finds story embarrassing. Why would Father shake Miss Porter's hand, she wonders. That soft plump freckled hand. Sending little shivers through her soft plump body. Making Miss Porter tingle. She does not want to think of Miss Porter in bed. Tingling. She does not want to think of Miss Porter as having any existence at all, outside of her duties as Father's stenographer. She looks up from the *Post* and scowls at Cissy for giggling. Cissy, she thinks, lacks the Peck's innate good taste and proud reserve.)

"Isn't Miss Porter beautiful?" Cissy said one night, when we were in our beds in the upstairs bedroom we shared at 43 North Elm.

"Beautiful?" I said scornfully. "What could possibly make you think she is beautiful?"

But Cissy was already asleep.

FATHER: (driving our Buick on the way to the Peck House in Metropolis)

As I was driving to Salt Lake
I met a little rattlesnake
I fed it some jellycake
It got a little bellyache.

MOTHER: (in front seat, holding Father's jacket and tie on her lap; flowers, in a Mason jar, for the Peck Plot, at her feet) Tummy, not belly!

CISSY: (sitting between Mother and Father, because she *claims* to get car sick. Giggles.)

FATHER: It got a little tummyache, not a bellyache, after all.

EMILY: (alone in back seat) It says "belly" in the Bible. (She agrees with Mother, but possesses a fund of knowledge she feels obliged to demonstrate.)

MOTHER: The language of the Bible and the language of everyday life are two different things altogether.

FATHER: Your mother is correct, as always. The language of the Bible is not appropriate language for everyday speech.

MOTHER: (ignoring Father) Drive slowly when we go through Metropolis, so Emily can take notes for her theme.

CISSY: My belly feels fun—ny.

Consternation! Should they stop? Let Cissy out? Roll down the window? Buy her some chewing gum? It is decided to drive *fast* through Metropolis and go straight to the Peck Plot, where she can run about among the tombstones in the fresh air. This, of course, takes precedence over Emily's Original Research.

I got an "A" anyhow. "Emily has Literary Tendencies," Mrs. Wilson wrote across my theme, which I brought home to show to Mother and Father. They were both proud of me. The phrase: "Literary Tendencies" was taken up by them, and then by others.

"Emily has Literary Tendencies," people would say. They didn't mean it, I suppose, but they always made "Literary Tendencies" sound as if it were—not so much a disease, maybe, as a kind of morbidity, a lack of normal health. They may have been right. I don't know.

Perhaps it was like the New England Conscience, which as it turned out, I did inherit from Mother.

Certainly, Cissy didn't inherit it. The way she climbed upon gentlemen's laps, for example; climbed up and burrowed in and snuggled down, as if she were some sort of little animal; made a nest and curled up, peacefully, as long as she was being cuddled, patted, stroked—but, should the gentleman reach for a drink or a cigarette, or, simply pause for a moment, the burrowing and squirming began again to remind him of his neglect and did not stop until the neglect was rectified.

"Cissy, don't pester Judge Blair," or, "Cissy, I think Mr. Hefflinger would be happier if you were to get down at once," Mother would say.

"Oh, Cissy's my girl, aren't you, Cissy?"

"It isn't every day an old codger like myself can hold a pretty blonde on his lap."

The pet names she was called. Cissy. Missy Cissy. Cissy-Pie. Later, scrawled upon the Angel—a famous necking spot for the students at Norton High: "Hot Pants Cissy." This was, fortunately, after Mother's breakdown. Aunt Dee took rubbing alcohol and scrubbed it off.

It was Father's fault. He spoiled her. Mother often said so.

THE DOGGIE DOO DOO

Latex. Fantastically realistic imitation.
Nauseating. Put on your hostess's best rug.
Watch her chide poor Fido.

MRS. HEFFLINGER: (mother of Jimmy Hefflinger, with whom Emily is secretly in love, who has invited the Ryan family to visit them at their cabin at the Lake) Oh, no!

FATHER: (innocent expression in choir-blue eyes) Is something the matter, Mil?

MRS. HEFFLINGER: (to Mr. Hefflinger) Carl!

FATHER: Perhaps I can be of assistance?

MRS. HEFFLINGER: No, no, it's all right. I'm sorry, Bingo's made a mess. Where *is* Bingo? Carl? I'll get paper towels—

CISSY: (looks at Doggie Doo Doo; looks at Father. Giggles.)

EMILY: (silent, dying of shame)

MOTHER: John! John, you didn't—!

MR. HEFFLINGER: Well, I guess we better clean it up.

MRS. HEFFLINGER: I'll do it. You men take the girls down to the Lake. They want to go out in the boat. I'm afraid Bingo's been a very naughty dog.

MOTHER: (pale-faced, weakly) John?

FATHER: I, for one, intend to stay and help Milly. (picks up Doggie Doo Doo, puts it casually in pocket)

JIMMY HEFFLINGER: Hey—that's neat. Let's see it!

EMILY: Let's go out in the boat!

CISSY: Show it to Jimmy, Daddy.

MOTHER: John!

MRS. HEFFLINGER: (laughing) Oh, John, it's one of your jokes!

FATHER: You know I never joke, Mil. (takes out Doggie Doo Doo from pocket and hands it, proudly, to Jimmy. Jimmy and Cissy examine Doggie Doo Doo.)

MRS. HEFFLINGER: You certainly fooled me this time.

JIMMY: (turning Doggie Doo Doo over in his hand) Hey, this is great. (to Cissy) Where'd your father get it?

CISSY: (giggling, looking up at Jimmy with big blue eyes) He has this catalogue. (coquettishly) I'll show it to you, sometime. It's got lots of neat stuff. Come on, you promised to take us for a boat ride.

EMILY: (forever shamed, forever unable to forget her shame when she sees Jimmy Hefflinger at school) I don't think I'll go. I brought a book to read. (Jimmy and Cissy run off, down to the dock. Mrs. Hefflinger fixes gin fizzes for the adults. Mother declines hers. She has a sudden headache, perhaps it is the run, perhaps she had better lie down for a time with a cool wet washcloth on her forehead. Father fetches a cool wet washcloth, returns from the bedroom. Emily sits down with her book.)

FATHER: I've been told my—ah—joke—was not in the best of taste.

MRS. HEFFLINGER: Nonsense! You wouldn't be John Ryan without your jokes. I'm going to tell her to come back out here.

FATHER: Better wait a bit, Mil.

MRS. HEFFLINGER: Well, you know best. (looks at Emily) Emily is quite a little bookworm, isn't she?

FATHER: (proudly) Her teacher says she has Literary Tendencies.

SNOW

(7:00 A.M. February morning. Emily is sixteen; Cissy, eleven. Mother, that winter, has "taken to her bed," a phrase of Aunt Dee's, taken up by others. Father sleeps on a cot, in the hallway, in order to be near her in the night. Cissy and Emily are still asleep. Father enters their bedroom)

FATHER: Girls! Wake up! We're going to give Mother a nice surprise.

EMILY: (always an early riser, already awake, sits up, gets out of bed)

CISSY: (burrows under covers. To Father) Go 'way. (Father pulls covers off Cissy's bed. Cissy shrieks. Both girls follow Father, reluctantly, arms across chests, shivering, in their flannel nighties. Father leads them into Mother's room. Mother is lying on her back, eyes open.

She seems to be looking at something beyond, or perhaps through her visitors.)

FATHER: (to Mother) Surprise! Surprise! We have a little surprise for you this morning. (goes to window, peeps behind drawn curtain; faces Mother again) Ready? (clears throat, assumes theatrical stance) Presto chango! (pulls curtain) Snow! (Father twinkles, beams)

MOTHER: (looks at snow, expression does not change; she seems to be looking at something beyond, or perhaps through this sudden Winter Wonderland)

CISSY: (marveling at the magical metamorphosis produced by Father) Oh, Dad—dee!

FATHER: (to Mother, trying again) Now we see it. (draws curtain) Now we don't. (pulls curtain) Presto chango—Snow!

MOTHER: It's very nice, but the light hurts my eyes. Would you mind closing the curtain, again, please, John?

In 1949, I returned from Reed College, to attend my mother's funeral. She had taken, it seemed, too many pills all at once. The funeral was private, but Miss Porter showed up, anyhow. Her sobs spoiled the lovely simplicity of the words from the Book of Common Prayer—the service Uncle Gideon had arranged. I considered her presence in the worst of taste.

After the funeral, Father, Cissy, and I sat in the living room at 43 North Elm. Father was pale, solemn, still. The laugh lines in his face were etched more deeply; perhaps they were no longer laugh lines, anymore. He chain-smoked, dropping ashes on the Peck hooked rug. I fetched an ashtray.

Father said, "Well, I guess Mama is with Barnum and Bailey."

Cissy giggled, then burst into tears. Father wept with

her. I stood, holding the ashtray—apart, alone, dry-eyed. Being more Peck than Ryan, I could neither laugh nor weep.

This story is about my father's jokes. Father joked. Cissy was his Fall Guy. Mother had her pride. I have Literary Tendencies. I am writing this story. Everyone has his or her way of coping.

Rough Strife

Lynne Sharon Schwartz

LYNNE SHARON SCHWARTZ is the author of *Rough Strife*, a novel in which the present story appears in somewhat different form, and of *Balancing Acts*, to be published later this year by Harper and Row. Her short fiction has appeared in *Redbook, Ploughshares, Transatlantic Review, The Chicago Review,* and many other magazines, as well as anthologies; she has done translations from Italian and written numerous reviews for the *Saturday Review*, the Chicago *Tribune, Ms.*, and others. She was born in New York City, where she presently lives and works.

Now let us sport us while we may;
And now, like am'rous birds of prey
. . . tear our pleasure with rough strife
Through the iron gates of life.

—*Andrew Marvell*

Caroline and Ivan finally had a child. Conception stunned them; they didn't think, by now, that it could happen. For years they had tried and failed, till it seemed that a special barren destiny was preordained.

Meanwhile, in the wide spaces of childlessness, they had created activity: their work flourished. Ivan, happy and moderately powerful in a large foundation, helped decide how to distribute money for artistic and social projects. Caroline taught mathematics at a small suburban university. Being a mathematician, she found, conferred a painful private wisdom on her efforts to conceive. In her brain, as Ivan exploded within her, she would involuntarily calculate probabilities; millions of blind sperm and one reluctant egg clustered before her eyes in swiftly transmuting geometric patterns. She lost her grasp of pleasure, forgot what it could feel like without a goal. She had no idea what Ivan might be thinking about, scattered seed money, maybe. Their passion became courteous and automatic until, by attrition, for months they didn't make love—it was too awkward.

One September Sunday morning she was in the shower, watching, through a crack in the curtain, Ivan naked at the washstand. He was shaving, his jaw tilted at an innocently self-satisfied angle. He wasn't aware of being watched, so that a secret quality, an essence of Ivan, exuded in great waves. Caroline could almost see it, a cloudy aura. He stroked his jaw vainly with intense concentration, a self-absorption so contagious that she needed, suddenly, to possess it with him. She stepped out of the shower.

"Ivan."

He turned abruptly, surprised, perhaps even annoyed at the interruption.

"Let's not have a baby any more. Let's just . . . come on." When she placed her wet hand on his back he lifted her easily off her feet with his right arm, the razor still poised in his other, outstretched hand.

"Come on," she insisted. She opened the door and a

draft blew into the small steamy room. She pulled him by the hand toward the bedroom.

Ivan grinned. "You're soaking wet."

"Wet, dry, what's the difference?" It was hard to speak. She began to run, to tease him; he caught her and tossed her onto their disheveled bed and dug his teeth so deep into her shoulder that she thought she would bleed.

Then with disinterest, taken up only in this fresh rushing need for him, weeks later Caroline conceived. Afterwards she liked to say that she had known the moment it happened. It felt different, she told him, like a pin pricking a balloon, but without the shattering noise, without the quick collapse. "Oh, come on," said Ivan. "That's impossible."

But she was a mathematician, after all, and dealt with infinitesimal precise abstractions, and she did know how it had happened. The baby was conceived in strife, one early October night, Indian summer. All day the sun glowed hot and low in the sky, settling an amber torpor on people and things, and the night was the same, only now a dark hot heaviness sunk slowly down. The scent of the still-blooming honeysuckle rose to their bedroom window. Just as she was bending over to kiss him, heavy and quivering with heat like the night, he teased her about something, about a mole on her leg, and in reply she punched him lightly on the shoulder. He grabbed her wrists, and when she began kicking, pinned her feet down with his own. In an instant Ivan lay stretched out on her back like a blanket, smothering her, while she struggled beneath, writhing to escape. It was a silent, sweaty struggle, interrupted with outbursts of wild laughter, shrieks and gasping breaths. She tried biting but, laughing loudly, he evaded her, and she tried scratching the fists that held her down, but she couldn't reach. All her desire was transformed into physical effort, but he was too strong for her. He wanted her to say she gave up, but she refused, and since he wouldn't loosen his grip they lay locked and panting in their static embrace for some time.

"You win," she said at last, but as he rolled off she sneakily jabbed him in the ribs with her elbow.

"Aha!" Ivan shouted, and was ready to begin again, but she quickly distracted him. Once the wrestling was at an end, though, Caroline found her passion dissipated, and her pleasure tinged with resentment. After they made love forcefully, when they were covered with sweat, dripping on each other, she said, "Still, you don't play fair."

"I don't play fair! Look who's talking. Do you want me to give you a handicap?"

"No."

"So?"

"It's not fair, that's all."

Ivan laughed gloatingly and curled up in her arms. She smiled in the dark.

That was the night the baby was conceived, not in high passion but rough strife.

She lay on the table in the doctor's office weeks later. The doctor, whom she had known for a long time, habitually kept up a running conversation while he probed. Today, fretting over his weight problem, he outlined his plans for a new diet. Tensely she watched him, framed and centered by her raised knees, which were still bronzed from summer sun. His other hand was pressing on her stomach. Caroline was nauseated with fear and trembling, afraid of the verdict. It was taking so long, perhaps it was a tumor.

"I'm cutting out all starches," he said. "I've really let myself go lately."

"Good idea." Then she gasped in pain. A final, sickening thrust, and he was out. Relief, and a sore gap where he had been. In a moment, she knew, she would be retching violently.

"Well?"

"Well, Caroline, you hit the jackpot this time."

She felt a smile, a stupid, puppet smile, spread over her face. In the tiny bathroom where she threw up, she saw in the mirror the silly smile looming over her ashen face like a dancer's glowing grimace of labored joy. She smiled through the rest of the visit, through his advice about milk, weight, travel and rest, smiled at herself in the window of the bus, and at her moving image in the fenders of parked cars as she walked home.

Ivan, incredulous over the telephone, came home beaming stupidly just like Caroline, and brought a bottle of champagne. After dinner they drank it and made love.

"Do you think it's all right to do this?" he asked.

"Oh, Ivan, honestly. It's microscopic."

He was in one of his whimsical moods and made terrible jokes that she laughed at with easy indulgence. He said he was going to pay the baby a visit and asked if she had any messages she wanted delivered. He unlocked from her embrace, moved down her body and said he was going to have a look for himself. Clowning, he put his ear between her legs to listen. Whatever amusement she felt soon ebbed away into irritation. She had never thought Ivan would be a doting parent—he was so preoccupied with himself. Finally he stopped his antics as she clasped her arms around him and whispered, "Ivan, you are really too much." He became unusually gentle. Tamed, and she didn't like it, hoped he wouldn't continue that way for months. Pleasure lapped over her with a mild, lackadaisical bitterness, and then when she could be articulate once more she explained patiently, "Ivan, you know, it really is all right. I mean, it's a natural process."

"Well I didn't want to hurt you."

"I'm not sick."

Then, as though her body were admonishing that cool confidence, she did get sick. There were mornings when she awoke with such paralyzing nausea that she had to ask Ivan to bring her a hard roll from the kitchen before she could stir from bed. To move from her awakening position seemed a tremendous risk, as if she might spill out. She rarely threw up—the nausea resembled violent hunger. Something wanted to be filled, not expelled, a perilous vacuum occupying her insides. The crucial act was getting the first few mouthfuls down. Then the solidity and denseness of the hard unbuttered roll stabilized her, like a heavy weight thrown down to anchor a tottering ship. Her head ached. On the mornings when she had no classes she would wander around the house till almost noon clutching the partly eaten roll in her hand like a talisman. Finishing one roll, she quickly went to the breadbox for another; she bought them regularly at the bakery a half dozen at a time. With enough roll inside her she could sometimes manage a half cup of tea, but liquids were risky. They sloshed around inside and made her envision the baby sloshing around too, in its cloudy fluid. By early afternoon she would feel fine. The baby, she imagined, claimed her for the night and was reluctant to give up its hold in the morning: they vied till she conquered. She was willing to yield her sleeping hours to the baby, her dreams even, if necessary, but she wanted the daylight for herself.

The mornings that she taught were agony. Ivan would wake her up early, bring her a roll, and gently prod her out of bed.

"I simply cannot do it," she would say, placing her legs cautiously over the side of the bed.

"Sure you can. Now get up."

"I'll die if I get up."

"You have no choice. You have a job." He was freshly showered and dressed, and his neatness irritated her. He had nothing more to do—the discomfort was all hers. She rose to her feet and swayed.

Ivan looked alarmed. "Do you want me to call and tell them you can't make it?"

"No, no." That frightened her. She needed to hold on to the job, to defend herself against the growing baby. Once she walked into the classroom she would be fine. A Mondrian print hung on the back wall—she could look at that, and it would steady her. With waves of nausea roiling in her chest, she stumbled into the bathroom.

She liked him to wait until she was out of the shower before he left for work, because she anticipated fainting under the impact of the water. Often at the end she forced herself to stand under an ice cold flow, leaning her head way back and letting her short fair hair drip down behind her. Though it was torture, when she emerged she felt more alive.

After the shower had been off a while Ivan would come and open the bathroom door. "Are you O.K. now, Caroline? I've got to go." It made her feel like a child. She would be wrapped in a towel with her hair dripping on the mat, brushing her teeth or rubbing cream into her face. "Yes, thanks for waiting. I guess this'll end soon. They say it's only the first few months."

He kissed her lips, her bare damp shoulder, gave a parting squeeze to her toweled behind, and was gone. She watched him walk down the hall. Ivan was very large. She had always been drawn and aroused by his largeness, by the huge bones and the taut legs that felt as though he had steel rods inside. But now she watched with some trepidation, hoping Ivan wouldn't have a large, inflexible baby.

Very slowly she would put on clothes. Selecting each article seemed a much more demanding task than ever before. Seeing how slow she had become, she allowed herself over an hour, keeping her hard roll nearby as she dressed and prepared her face. All the while, through the stages of dressing, she evaluated her body closely in the full-length mirror, first naked, then in bra and underpants, then with shoes added, and finally with a dress. She was looking for signs, but the baby was invisible. Nothing had changed yet. She was still as she had always been, not quite slim yet somehow appearing small, almost delicate. She used to pride herself on strength. When they moved in she had worked as hard as Ivan, lugging furniture and lifting heavy cartons. He was impressed. Now, of course, she could no longer do that—it took all her strength to move her own weight.

With the profound sensuous narcissism of women past first youth, she admired her still-narrow waist and full breasts. She was especially fond of her shoulders and prominent collarbone, which had a fragile, inviting look. That would all be gone soon, of course, gone soft. Curious about how she would alter, she scanned her face for the pregnant look she knew well from the faces of friends. It was far less a tangible change than a look of transparent vulnerability that took over the face: nearly a pleading look, a beg for help like a message from a powerless invaded country to the rest of the world. Caroline did not see it on her face yet.

From the tenth to the fourteenth week of her pregnancy she slept, with brief intervals of lucidity when she taught her classes. It was a strange dreamy time. The passionate nausea faded, but the lure of the bed was irresistible. In the middle of the day, even, she could pass by the bedroom, glimpse the waiting bed and be overcome by the soft heavy desire to lie down. She fell into a stupor immediately and did not dream. She forgot what it was like to awaken with energy and move through an entire day without lying down once. She forgot the feeling of eyes opened wide without effort. She would have liked to hide this strange, shameful perversity from Ivan, but that was impossible. Ivan kept wanting to go to the movies. Clearly, he was bored with her. Maybe, she imagined, staring up at the bedroom ceiling through slitted eyes, he would become so bored he would abandon her and the baby and she would not be able to support the house alone and she and the baby would end up on the streets in rags, begging. She smiled. That was highly unlikely. Ivan would not be the same Ivan without her.

"You go on, Ivan. I just can't."

Once he said, "I thought I might ask Ruth Forbes to go with me to see the Charlie Chaplin in town. I know she likes him. Would that bother you?"

She was half-asleep, slowly eating a large apple in bed and watching "Medical Center" on television, but she roused herself to answer. "No, of course not." Ruth Forbes was a divorced woman who lived down the block, a casual friend and not Ivan's type at all, too large, loud and depressed. Caroline didn't care if he wanted her company. She didn't care if he held her hand on his knee in the movies as he liked to do, or even if, improbably, he made love to her afterwards in her sloppy house crawling with children. She didn't care about anything except staying nestled in bed.

She made love with him sometimes, in a slow way. She felt no specific desire but didn't want to deny him, she loved him so. Or had, she thought vaguely, when she was alive and strong. Besides, she knew she could sleep right after. Usually there would be a moment when she came alive despite herself, when the reality of his body would strike her all at once with a wistful throb of lust, but mostly she was too tired to see it through, to leap towards it, so she let it subside, merely nodding at it gratefully as a sign of dormant life. She felt sorry for Ivan, but helpless.

Once to her great shame, she fell asleep while he was inside her. He woke her with a pat on her cheek, actually, she realized from the faint sting, a gesture more like a slap than a pat. "Caroline, for Christ's sake, you're sleeping."

"No, no, I'm sorry. I wasn't really sleeping. Oh, Ivan, it's nothing. This will end." She wondered, though.

Moments later she felt his hands on her thighs. His lips were brooding on her stomach, edging, with expertise, lower and lower down. He was murmuring something she couldn't catch. She felt an ache, an irritation. Of course he meant well, Ivan always did. Wryly, she appreciated his intentions. But she couldn't bear that excitement now.

"Please," she said. "Please don't do that."

He was terribly hurt. He said nothing, but leaped away violently and pulled all the blankets around him. She was contrite, shed a few private tears and fell instantly into a dreamless dark.

He wanted to go to a New Year's Eve party some close friends were giving, and naturally he wanted her to come with him. Caroline vowed to herself she would do this for him because she had been giving so little for so long. She planned to get dressed and look very beautiful, as she could still look when she took plenty of time and tried hard enough; she would not drink very much—it was sleep-inducing—and she would not be the one to suggest going home. After sleeping through the day in preparation, she washed her hair, using something she found in the drugstore to heighten the blond flecks. Then she put on a long green velvet dress with gold embroidery, and inserted the gold hoop earrings Ivan bought her some years ago for her twenty-fifth birthday. Before they set out she drank a cup of black coffee. She would have taken No-Doze but she was afraid of drugs, afraid of giving birth to an armless or legless baby who would be a burden and a heartache to them for the rest of their days.

At the party of mostly university people, she chatted with everyone equally, those she knew well and those she had never met. Sociably, she held a filled glass in her hand, taking tiny sips. She and Ivan were not together very much—it was crowded, smoky and loud; people kept moving and encounters were brief—but she knew he was aware of her, could feel his awareness through the milling bodies. He was aware and he was pleased. He deserved more than the somnambulist she had become, and she was pleased to please him. But after a while her legs would not support her for another instant. The skin tingled: soft warning bells rang from every pore. She allowed herself a moment to sit down alone in a small alcove off the living room, where she smoked a cigarette and stared down at her lap, holding her eyes open very wide. Examining the gold and rose-colored embroidery on her dress, Caroline traced the coiled pattern, mathematical and hypnotic, with her index finger. Just as she was happily merging into its intricacies, a man, a stranger, came in, breaking her trance. He was a very young man, twenty-three, maybe, of no apparent interest.

"Hi. I hear you're expecting a baby," he began, and sat down with a distinct air of settling in.

"Yes. That's quite an opening line. How did you know?"

"I know because Linda told me. You know Linda, don't you? I'm her brother."

He began asking about her symptoms. Sleepiness? Apathy? He knew, he had worked in a clinic. Unresponsive, she retorted by inquiring about his taste in music. He sat on a leather hassock opposite Caroline on the couch, and with every inquisitive sentence drew his seat closer till their knees were almost touching. She shifted her weight to avoid him, tucked her feet under her and lit another cigarette, feeling she could lie down and fall into a stupor quite easily. Still, words were coming out of her mouth, she heard them; she hoped they were not encouraging words but she seemed to have very little control over what they were.

"I—" he said. "You see—" He reached out and put his hand over hers. "Pregnant women, like, they really turn me on. I mean, there's a special aura. You're sensational."

She pulled her hand away. "God almighty."

"What's the matter? Honestly, I didn't mean to offend you."

"I really must go." She stood up and stepped around him.

"Could I see you some time?"

"You're seeing me now. Enjoy it."

He ran his eyes over her from head to toe, appraising. "It doesn't show yet."

Gazing down at her body, Caroline stretched the loose velvet dress taut over her stomach. "No, you're right, it doesn't." Then, over her shoulder, as she left their little corner, she tossed, "Fuck you, you pig."

With a surge of energy she downed a quick scotch, found Ivan and tugged at his arm. "Let's dance."

Ivan's blue eyes lightened with shock. At home she could barely walk.

"Yes, let's." He took her in his arms and she buried

her face against his shoulder. But she held her tears back, she would not let him know.

Later she told him about it. It was three-thirty in the morning, they had just made love drunkenly, and Ivan was in high spirits. She knew why—he felt he had her back again. She had held him close and uttered her old sounds, familiar moans and cries like a poignant, nearly-forgotten tune, and Ivan was miraculously restored, his impact once again sensible to eye and ear. He was making her laugh hysterically now, imitating the eccentric professor of art history at the party, an owlish émigré from Bavaria who expounded on the dilemmas of today's youth, all the while pronouncing "youth" as if it rhymed with "mouth." Ivan had also discovered that he pronounced "unique" as if it were "eunuch." Then, sitting up in bed cross-legged, they competed in making up pretentious scholarly sentences that included both "unique" and "youth" mispronounced.

"Speaking of 'yowth,' " Caroline said, "I met a weird one tonight, Linda's brother. A very eunuch yowth, I must say." And giggling, she recounted their conversation. Suddenly at the end she unexpectedly found herself in tears. Shuddering, she flopped over and sobbed into her pillow.

"Caroline," he said tenderly, "please. For heaven's sake, it was just some nut. It was nothing. Don't get all upset over it." He stroked her bare back.

"I can't help it," she wailed. "It made me feel so disgusting."

"You're much too sensitive. Come on." He ran his hand slowly through her hair, over and over.

She pulled the blanket around her. "Enough. I'm going to sleep."

A fews days later, when classes were beginning again for the new semester, she woke early and went immediately to the shower, going through the ritual motions briskly and automatically. She was finished and brushing her teeth when she realized what had happened. There she was on her feet, sturdy, before eight in the morning, planning how she would introduce the topic of the differential calculus to her new students. She stared at her face in the mirror with unaccustomed recognition, her mouth dripping white foam, her dark eyes startled. She was alive. She didn't know how the miracle had happened, nor did she care to explore it. Back in the bedroom she dressed quickly, zipping up a pair of slim rust-colored woollen slacks with satisfaction. It didn't show yet, but soon.

"Ivan, time to get up."

He grunted and opened his eyes. When at last they focused on Caroline leaning over him they burned blue and wide with astonishment. He rubbed a fist across his forehead. "Are you dressed already?"

"Yes. I'm cured."

"What do you mean?"

"I'm not tired any more. I'm slept out. I've come back to life."

"Oh." He moaned and rolled over in one piece like a seal.

"Aren't you getting up?"

"In a little while. I'm so tired. I must sleep for a while." The words were thick and slurred.

"Well!" She was strangely annoyed. Ivan always got up with vigor. "Are you sick?"

"Uh-uh."

After a quick cup of coffee she called out, "Ivan, I'm leaving now. Don't forget to get up." The January air was crisp and exhilarating, and she walked the half mile to the university at a nimble clip, going over her introductory remarks in her head.

Ivan was tired for a week. Caroline wanted to go out

to dinner every evening—she had her appetite back. She had broken through dense earth to fresh air. It was a new year and soon they would have a new baby. But all Ivan wanted to do was stay home and lie on the bed and watch television. It was repellent. Sloth, she pointed out to him more than once, was one of the seven deadly sins. The fifth night she said in exasperation, "What the hell is the matter with you? If you're sick go to a doctor."

"I'm not sick. I'm tired. Can't I be tired too? Leave me alone. I left you alone, didn't I?"

"That was different."

"How?"

"I'm pregnant and you're not, in case you've forgotten."

"How could I forget?"

She said nothing, only cast him an evil look.

One evening soon after Ivan's symptoms disappeared, they sat together on the living-room sofa sharing sections of the newspaper. Ivan had his feet up on the coffee table and Caroline sat diagonally, resting her legs on his. She paused in her reading and touched her stomach.

"Ivan."

"What?"

"It's no use. I'm going to have to buy some maternity clothes."

He put down the paper and stared. "Really?" He seemed distressed.

"Yes."

"Well, don't buy any of those ugly things they wear. Can't you get some of those, you know, sort of Indian things?"

"Yes. That's a good idea. I will."

He picked up the paper again.

"It moves."

"What?"

"I said it moves. The baby."

"It moves?"

She laughed. "Remember Galileo? *Eppure, si muove.*" They had spent years together in Italy in their first youth, in mad love, and visited the birthplace of Galileo. He was a hero to both of them, because his mind remained free and strong though his body succumbed to tyranny.

Ivan laughed too. "*Eppure, si muove.* Let me see." He bent his head down to feel it, then looked up at her, his face full of longing, marvel and envy. In a moment he was scrambling at her clothes in a young eager rush. He wanted to be there, he said. Caroline, taken by surprise, was suspended between laughter and tears. He had her on the floor in silence, and for each it was swift and consuming.

Ivan lay spent in her arms. Caroline, still gasping and clutching him, said, "I could never love it as much as I love you." She wondered, then, hearing her words fall in the still air, whether this would always be true.

Shortly after she began wearing the Indian shirts and dresses, she noticed that Ivan was acting oddly. He stayed late at the office more than ever before, and often brought work home with him. He appeared to have lost interest in the baby, rarely asking how she felt, and when she moaned in bed sometimes, "Oh, I can't get to sleep, it keeps moving around," he responded with a grunt or not at all. He asked her, one warm Sunday in March, if she wanted to go bicycle riding.

"Ivan, I can't go bicycle riding. I mean, look at me."

"Oh, right. Of course."

He seemed to avoid looking at her, and she did look terrible, she had to admit. Even she looked at herself in the mirror as infrequently as possible. She dreaded what she had heard about hair falling out and teeth rotting, but she drank her milk diligently and so far neither of those things had happened. But besides the grotesque belly, her ankles swelled up so that the shape of her own legs was alien. She took diuretics and woke every hour at night to go to the bathroom. Sometimes it was impossible to get back to sleep so she sat up in bed reading. Ivan said, "Can't you turn the light out? You know I can't sleep with the light on."

"But what should I do? I can't sleep at all."

"Read in the living room."

"It's so cold in there at night."

He would turn away irritably. Once he took the blanket and went to sleep in the living room himself.

They liked to go for drives in the country on warm weekends. It seemed to Caroline that he chose the bumpiest, most untended roads and drove them as rashly as possible. Then when they stopped to picnic and he lay back to bask in the sharp April sunlight, she would always need to go and look for a bathroom, or even a clump of trees. At first this amused him, but soon his amusement became sardonic. He pulled in wearily at gas stations where he didn't need gas and waited in the car with folded arms and a sullen expression that made her apologetic about her ludicrous needs. They were growing apart. She could feel the distance between them like a patch of fog, dimming and distorting the relations of objects in space. The baby that lay between them in the dark was pushing them apart.

Sometimes as she lay awake in bed at night, not wanting to read in the cold living room but reluctant to turn on the light (and it was only a small light, she thought bitterly, a small bedside light), Caroline brooded over the horrible deformities the baby might be born with. She was thirty-one years old, not the best age to bear a first child. It could have cerebral palsy, cleft palate, two heads, club foot. She wondered if she could love a baby with a gross defect. She wondered if Ivan would want to put it in an institution, and if there were any decent institutions in their area, and if they would be spending every Sunday afternoon for the rest of their lives visiting the baby and driving home heartbroken in silence. She lived through these visits to the institution in vivid detail till she knew the doctors' and nurses' faces well. And there would come a point when Ivan would refuse to go any more—she knew what he was like, selfish with his time and impatient with futility—and she would have to go alone. She wondered if Ivan ever thought about these things, but with that cold mood of his she was afraid to ask.

One night she was desolate. She couldn't bear the loneliness and the heaviness any more, so she woke him.

"Ivan, please. Talk to me. I'm so lonely."

He sat up abruptly. "What?" He was still asleep. With the dark straight hair hanging down over his lean face he looked boyish and vulnerable. Without knowing why, she felt sorry for him.

"I'm sorry. I know you were sleeping but I—" Here she began to weep. "I just lie here forever in the dark and think awful things and you're so far away, and I just—"

"Oh, Caroline. Oh, God." Now he was wide awake, and took her in his arms.

"You're so far away," she wept. "I don't know what's the matter with you."

"I'm sorry. I know it's hard for you. You're so—everything's so different, that's all."

"But it's still me."

"I know. I know it's stupid of me. I can't—"

She knew what it was. It would never be the same. They sat up all night holding each other, and they talked. Ivan talked more than he had in weeks. He said of course the baby would be perfectly all right, and it would be born at just the right time, too, late June, so she could finish up the term, and they would start their natural childbirth group in two weeks so he could be with her and help her, though of course she would do it easily because she was so competent at everything, and then they would have the summer for the early difficult months, and she would be feeling fine and be ready to go back to work in the fall, and they would find a good person, someone like a grandmother, to come in, and he would try to stagger his schedule so she would not feel overburdened and trapped, and in short everything would be just fine, and they would make love again like they used to and be close again. He said exactly what she needed to hear, while she huddled against him, wrenched with pain to realize that he had known all along the right words to say but hadn't thought to say them till she woke him in desperation. Still, in the dawn she slept contented. She loved him. Every now and then she perceived this like a fact of life, an ancient tropism.

Two weeks later they had one of their horrible quarrels. It happened at a gallery, at the opening of a show by a group of young local artists Ivan had discovered. He had encouraged them to apply to his foundation for money and smoothed the way to their success. Now at their triumphant hour he was to be publicly thanked at a formal dinner. There were too many paintings to look at, too many people to greet, and too many glasses of champagne thrust at Caroline, who was near the end of her eighth month now. She walked around for an hour, then whispered to Ivan, "Listen, I'm sorry but I've got to go. Give me the car keys, will you? I don't feel well."

"What's the matter?"

"I can't stop having to go to the bathroom and my

feet are killing me and my head aches, and the kid is rolling around like a basketball. You stay and enjoy it. You can get a ride with someone. I'll see you later."

"I'll drive you home," he said grimly. "We'll leave."

An awful knot gripped her stomach. The knot was the image of his perverse resistance, the immense trouble coming, all the trouble congealed and solidified and tied up in one moment. Meanwhile they smiled at the passers-by as they whispered ferociously to each other.

"Ivan, I do not want you to take me home. This is your event. Stay. I am leaving. We are separate people."

"If you're as sick as you say you can't drive home alone. You're my wife and I'll take you home."

"Suit yourself," she said sweetly, because the director of the gallery was approaching. "We all know you're much bigger and stronger than I am." And she smiled maliciously.

Ivan waved vaguely at the director, turned and ushered her to the door. Outside he exploded.

"Shit, Caroline! We can't do a fucking thing any more, can we?"

"You can do anything you like. Just give me the keys. I left mine home."

"I will not give you the keys. Get in the car. You're supposed to be sick."

"You big resentful selfish idiot. Jealous of an embryo." She was screaming now. He started the car with a rush that jolted her forward against the dashboard. "I'd be better off driving myself. You'll kill me this way."

"Shut up," he shouted. "I don't want to hear any more."

"I don't care what you want to hear or not hear."

"Shut the hell up or I swear I'll go into a tree. I don't give a shit any more."

It was starting to rain, a soft silent rain that glittered in the drab dusk outside. At exactly the same moment they rolled up their windows. They were sealed in together, Caroline thought, like restless beasts in a cage. The air in the car was dank and stuffy.

When they got home he slammed the door so hard the house shook. Caroline had calmed herself. She sank down in a chair, kicked off her shoes and rubbed her ankles. "Ivan, why don't you go back? It's not too late. These dinners are always late anyway. I'll be O.K."

"I don't want to go any more," he yelled. "The whole thing is spoiled. Our whole lives are spoiled from now on. We were better off before. I thought you had gotten over wanting it. I thought it was a dead issue." He stared at her bulging stomach with such loathing that she was shocked into horrid, lucid perception.

"You disgust me," she said quietly. "Frankly, you always have and probably always will." She didn't know why she said that. It was quite untrue. It was only true that he disgusted her at this moment, yet the rest had rolled out like string from a hidden ball of twine.

"So why did we ever start this in the first place?" he screamed.

She didn't know whether he meant the marriage or the baby, and for an instant she was afraid he might hit her, there was such compressed force in his huge shoulders.

"Get the hell out of here. I don't want to have to look at you."

"I will. I'll go back. I'll take your advice. Call your fucking obstetrician if you need anything. I'm sure he's always glad of an extra feel."

"You ignorant pig. Go on. And don't hurry back.

Find yourself a skinny little art student and give her a big treat."

"I just might." He slammed the door and the house shook again.

He would be back. This was not the first time. Only now she felt no secret excitement, no tremor, no passion that could reshape into lust; she was too heavy and burdened. It would not be easy to make it up—she was in no condition. It would lie between them silently like a dead weight till weeks after the baby was born, till Ivan felt he could reclaim his rightful territory. She knew him too well. Caroline took two aspirins. When she woke at three he was in bed beside her, gripping the blanket in his sleep and breathing heavily. For days afterwards they spoke with strained, subdued courtesy.

They worked diligently in the natural childbirth classes once a week, while at home they giggled over how silly the exercises were, yet Ivan insisted she pant her five minutes each day as instructed. As relaxation training, Ivan was supposed to lift each of her legs and arms three times and drop them, while she remained perfectly limp and passive. From the very start Caroline was excellent at this routine, which they did in bed before going to sleep. A substitute, she thought, yawning. She could make her body so limp and passive her arms and legs bounced on the mattress when they fell. One night for diversion she tried doing it to Ivan, but he couldn't master the technique of passivity.

"Don't do anything, Ivan. I lift the leg and I drop the leg. You do nothing. Do you see? Nothing at all," she smiled.

But that was not possible for him. He tried to be limp but kept working along with her; she could see his muscles, precisely those leg muscles she found so desirable, exerting to lift and drop, lift and drop.

"You can't give yourself up. Don't you feel what

you're doing? You have to let me do it to you. Let me try just your hand, from the wrist. That might be easier."

"No, forget it. Give me back my hand." He smiled and stroked her stomach gently. "What's the difference? I don't have to do it well. You do it very well."

She did it very well indeed when the time came. It was a short labor, less than an hour, very unusual for a first baby, the nurses kept muttering. She breathed intently, beginning with the long slow breaths she had been taught, feeling quite remote from the bustle around her. Then, in a flurry, they raced her down the hall on a wheeled table with a train of white-coated people trotting after, and she thought, panting, No matter what I suffer, soon I will be thin again, I will be more beautiful than ever.

The room was crowded with people, far more people than she would have thought necessary, but the only faces she singled out were Ivan's and the doctor's. The doctor, with a new russet beard and his face a good deal thinner now, was once again framed by her knees, paler than before. Wildly enthusiastic about the proceedings, he yelled, "Terrific, Caroline, terrific," as though they were in a noisy public place. "O.K., start pushing."

They placed her hands on chrome rails along the table. On the left, groping, she found Ivan's hand and held it instead of the rail. She pushed. In surprise she became aware of a great cleavage, like a mountain of granite splitting apart, only it was in her, she realized, and if it kept on going it would go right up to her neck. She gripped Ivan's warm hand, and just as she opened her mouth to roar someone clapped an oxygen mask on her face so the roar reverberated inward on her own ears. She wasn't supposed to roar, the natural childbirth teacher hadn't mentioned anything about that, she was supposed to breathe and push. But as long as no one seemed to take any notice she might as well keep on roaring, it felt so satisfying and necessary. The teacher would never know. She trusted that if she split all the way up to her neck they would sew her up somehow—she was too far gone to worry about that now. Maybe that was why there were so many of them, yes, of course, to put her back together, and maybe they had simply forgotten to tell her about being bisected; or maybe it was a closely guarded secret, like an initiation rite. She gripped Ivan's hand tighter. She was not having too bad a time, she would surely survive, she told herself, captivated by the hellish bestial sounds going from her mouth to her ear; it certainly was what her students would call a peak experience, and how gratifying to hear the doctor exclaim, "Oh, this is one terrific girl! One more, Caroline, give me one more push and send it out. Sock it to me."

She always tried to be obliging, if possible. Now she raised herself on her elbows and, staring straight at him—he too, after all, had been most obliging these long months—gave him with tremendous force the final push he asked for. She had Ivan's hand tightly around the rail, could feel his knuckles bursting, and then all of a sudden the room and the faces were obliterated. A dark thick curtain swiftly wrapped around her and she was left all alone gasping, sucked violently into a windy black hole of pain so explosive she knew it must be death, she was dying fast, like a bomb detonating. It was all right, it was almost over, only she would have liked to see his blue eyes one last time.

From somewhere in the void Ivan's voice shouted in exultation, "It's coming out," and the roaring stopped and at last there was peace and quiet in her ears. The curtain fell away, the world returned. But her eyes kept on burning, as if they had seen something not meant for living eyes to see and return from alive.

"Give it to me," Caroline said, and held it. She saw that every part was in the proper place, and then shut her eyes.

They wheeled her to a room and eased her onto the bed. It was past ten in the morning. She could dimly remember they had been up all night watching a James Cagney movie about prizefighting while they timed her irregular mild contractions. James Cagney went blind from blows given by poisoned gloves in a rigged match, and she wept for him as she held her hands on her stomach and breathed. Neither she nor Ivan had slept or eaten for hours.

"Ivan, there is something I am really dying to have right now."

"Your wish is my command."

She asked for a roast beef on rye with ketchup, and iced tea. "Would you mind? It'll be hours before they serve lunch."

He bought it and stood at the window while she ate ravenously.

"Didn't you get anything for yourself?"

"No, I'm too exhausted to eat." He did, in fact, look terrible. He was sallow; his eyes, usually so radiant, were nearly drained of color, and small downward-curving lines around his mouth recalled his laborious vigil.

"You had a rough night, Ivan. You ought to get some sleep. What's it like outside?"

"What?" Ivan's movements seemed to her extremely purposeless. He was pacing the room with his hands deep in his pockets, going slowly from the foot of the bed to the window and back. Her eyes followed him from the pillow. Every now and then he would stop to peer at Caroline in an unfamiliar way, as if she were a puzzling stranger.

"Ivan, are you O.K.? I meant the weather. What's it doing outside?" It struck her, as she asked, that it was weeks since she had cared to know anything about the outside. That there was an outside, now that she was emptied out, came rushing at her with the most urgent importance, wafting her on a tide of grateful joy.

"Oh," he said vaguely, and came to sit on the edge of her bed. "Well, it's doing something very peculiar outside, as a matter of fact. It's raining but the sun is shining."

She laughed at him. "But haven't you ever seen it do that before?"

"I don't know. I guess so." He opened his mouth and closed it several times. She ate, waiting patiently. Finally he spoke. "You know, Caroline, you really have quite a grip. When you were holding my hand in there, you squeezed it so tight I thought you would break it."

"Oh, come on, that can't be."

"I'm not joking." He massaged his hand absently. Ivan never complained of pain; if anything he understated. But now he held out his right hand and showed her the raw red knuckles and palm, with raised flaming welts forming.

She took his hand. "You're serious. Did I do that? Well, how do you like that?"

"I really thought you'd break my hand. It was killing me." He kept repeating it, not resentfully but dully, as though there were something secreted in the words that he couldn't fathom.

"But why didn't you take it away if it hurt that badly?" She put down her half-eaten sandwich as she saw the pale amazement ripple over his face.

"Oh, no, I couldn't do that. I mean—if that was what

you needed just then—" He looked away, embarrassed. "Listen," he shrugged, not facing her, "we're in a hospital, after all. What better place? They'd fix it for me."

Overwhelmed, Caroline lay back on the pillows. "Oh, Ivan. You would do that?"

"What are you crying for?" he asked gently. "You didn't break it, did you? Almost doesn't count. So what are you crying about. You just had a baby. Don't cry."

And she smiled and thought her heart would burst.

A Silver Dish

Saul Bellow

SAUL BELLOW, born in Lachine, Quebec, Canada, of Russian immigrant parents, grew up in Chicago and has lived there for most of his life. He is the author of *Henderson the Rain King, Herzog, Seize the Day, Humboldt's Gift,* and other books. He received the Nobel Prize in 1976.

What do you do about death—in this case, the death of an old father? If you're a modern person, sixty years of age, and a man who's been around, like Woody Selbst, what do you do? Take this matter of mourning, and take it against a contemporary background. How, against a contemporary background, do you mourn an octogenarian father, nearly blind, his heart enlarged, his lungs filling with fluid, who creeps, stumbles, gives off the odors, the moldiness or gassiness of old men. I *mean!* As Woody put it, be realistic. Think what times these are. The papers daily give it to you—the Lufthansa pilot in Aden is described by the hostages on his knees, begging the Palestinian terrorists not to execute him, but they shoot him through the head. Later they themselves are killed. And still others shoot others, or shoot themselves. That's what you read in the press, see on the tube, mention at dinner. We know now what goes daily through the whole of the human community, like a global death-peristalsis.

Woody, a businessman in South Chicago, was not an ignorant person. He knew more such phrases than you would expect a tile contractor (offices, lobbies, lavatories) to know. The kind of knowledge he had was not the kind for which you get academic degrees. Although Woody had studied for two years in a seminary, preparing to be a minister. Two years of college during the Depression was more than most high-school graduates could afford. After that, in his own vital, picturesque, original way (Morris, his old man, was also, in his days of nature, vital and picturesque) Woody had read up on many subjects, subscribed to *Science* and other magazines that gave real information, and had taken night courses at De Paul and Northwestern in ecology, criminology, existentialism. Also he had travelled extensively in Japan, Mexico, and Africa, and there was an African experience that was especially relevant to mourning. It was this: On a launch near the Murchison Falls in Uganda, he had seen a buffalo calf seized by a crocodile from the bank of the White Nile. There were giraffes along the tropical river, and hippopotamuses, and baboons, and flamingos and other brilliant birds crossing the bright air in the heat of the morning, when the calf, stepping into the river to drink, was grabbed by the hoof and dragged down. The parent buffaloes couldn't figure it out. Under the water the calf still threshed, fought, churned the mud.

Woody, the robust traveller, took this in as he sailed by, and to him it looked as if the parent cattle were asking each other dumbly what had happened. He chose to assume that there was pain in this, he read brute grief into it. On the White Nile, Woody had the impression that he had gone back to the pre-Adamite past, and he brought reflections on this impression home to South Chicago. He brought also a bundle of hashish from Kampala. In this he took a chance with the customs inspectors, banking perhaps on his broad build, frank face, high color. He didn't look like a wrongdoer, a bad guy; he looked like a good guy. But he liked taking chances. Risk was a wonderful stimulus. He threw down his trenchcoat on the customs counter. If the inspectors searched the pockets, he was prepared to say that the coat wasn't his. But he got away with it, and the Thanksgiving turkey was stuffed with hashish. This was much enjoyed. That was practically the last feast at which Pop, who also relished risk or defiance, was present. The hashish Woody had tried to raise in his back yard from the Africa seeds didn't take. But behind his warehouse, where the Lincoln Continental was parked, he kept a patch of marijuana. There was no harm at all in Woody but he didn't like being entirely within the law. It was simply a question of self-respect.

After that Thanksgiving, Pop gradually sank as if he had a slow leak. This went on for some years. In and out of the hospital, he dwindled, his mind wandered, he couldn't even concentrate enough to complain, except in exceptional moments on the Sundays Woody regularly devoted to him. Morris, an amateur who once was taken seriously by Willie Hoppe, the great pro himself, couldn't execute the simplest billiard shots anymore. He could only conceive shots; he began to theorize about impossible three-cushion combinations. Halina, the Polish woman with whom Morris had lived for over forty years as man and wife, was too old herself now to run to the hospital. So Woody had to do it. There was Woody's mother, too—a Christian convert—needing care; she was over eighty and frequently hospitalized. Everybody had diabetes and pleurisy and arthritis and cataracts and cardiac pacemakers. And everybody had lived by the body, but the body was giving out.

There were Woody's two sisters as well, unmarried, in their fifties, very Christian, very straight, still living with Mama in an entirely Christian bungalow. Woody, who took full responsibility for them all, occasionally had to put one of the girls (they had become sick girls) in a mental institution. Nothing severe. The sisters were wonderful women, both of them gorgeous once, but neither of the poor things was playing with a full deck. And all the factions had to be kept separate—Mama, the Christian convert; the fundamentalist sisters; Pop, who read the Yiddish paper as long as he could still see print; Halina, a good Catholic. Woody, the seminary forty years behind him, described himself as an agnostic. Pop had no more religion than you could find in the Yiddish paper, but he made Woody promise to bury him among Jews, and that was where he lay now, in the Hawaiian shirt Woody had bought for him at the tilers' convention in Honolulu. Woody would allow no undertaker's assistant to dress him but came to the parlor and buttoned the stiff into the shirt himself, and the old man went down looking like Ben-Gurion in a simple wooden coffin, sure to rot fast. That was how Woody wanted it all. At the graveside, he had taken off and folded his jacket, rolled up his sleeves on thick freckled biceps, waved back the little tractor standing by, and shovelled the dirt himself. His big face, broad at the bottom, narrowed upward like a Dutch house. And, his small good lower teeth taking hold of the upper lip in his exertion, he performed the final duty of a son. He was very fit, so it must have been emotion, not the shovelling, that made him redden so. After the funeral, he went home with Halina and her son, a decent Polack like his mother, and talented, too—Mitosh played the organ at hockey and basketball games in the Stadium, which took a smart man because it was a rabble-rousing kind of occupation—and they had some drinks and comforted the old girl. Halina was true blue, always one hundred per cent for Morris.

Then for the rest of the week Woody was busy, had jobs to run, office responsibilities, family responsibilities. He lived alone; as did his wife; as did his mistress: everybody in a separate establishment. Since his wife, after fifteen years of separation, had not learned to take care of herself, Woody did her shopping on Fridays, filled her freezer. He had to take her this week to buy shoes. Also, Friday night he always spent with Helen—Helen was his wife de facto. Saturday he did his big weekly shopping. Saturday night he devoted to Mom and his sisters. So he was too busy to attend to his own feelings except, intermittently, to note to himself, "First Thursday in the grave." "First Friday, and fine weather." "First Saturday; he's got to be getting used to it." Under his breath he occasionally said, "Oh, Pop."

But it was Sunday that hit him, when the bells rang all over South Chicago—the Ukrainian, Roman Catholic, Greek, Russian, African-Methodist churches, sounding off one after another. Woody had his offices in his warehouse, and there had built an apartment for himself, very spacious and convenient, in the top story. Because he left every Sunday morning at seven to spend the day with Pop, he had forgotten by how many churches Selbst Tile Company was surrounded. He was still in bed when he heard the bells, and all at once he knew how heartbroken he was. This sudden big heartache in a man of sixty, a practical, physical, healthy-minded, and experienced man, was deeply unpleasant. When he had an unpleasant condition, he believed in taking something for it. So he thought, What shall I take? There were plenty of remedies available. His cellar was stocked with cases of Scotch whiskey, Polish vodka, Armagnac, Moselle, Burgundy. There were also freezers with steaks and with game and with Alaskan king crab. He bought with a broad hand—by the crate and by the dozen. But in the end, when he got out of bed, he took nothing but a cup of coffee. While the kettle was heating, he put on his Japanese judo-style suit and sat down to reflect.

Woody was moved when things were *honest*. Bearing beams were honest, undisguised concrete pillars inside high-rise apartments were honest. It was bad to cover up anything. He hated faking. Stone was honest. Metal was honest. These Sunday bells were very straight. They broke loose, they wagged and rocked, and the vibrations and the banging did something for him—cleansed his insides, purified his blood. A bell was a one-way throat, had only one thing to tell you and simply told it. He listened.

He had had some connections with bells and churches. He was after all something of a Christian. Born a Jew, he was a Jew facially, with a hint of Iroquois or Cherokee, but his mother had been converted more than fifty years ago by her brother-in-law, the Reverend Dr. Kovner. Kovner, a rabbinical student who had left the Hebrew Union College in Cincinnati to become a minister and establish a mission, had given Woody a partly Christian upbringing. Now Pop was on the outs with these fundamentalists. He said that the Jews came to the mission to get coffee, bacon, canned pineapple, day-old bread, and dairy products. And if they had to listen to sermons, that was O.K.—this was the Depression and you couldn't be too particular—but he knew they sold the bacon.

The Gospels said it plainly: "Salvation is from the Jews."

Backing the Reverend Doctor were wealthy fundamentalists, mainly Swedes, eager to speed up the Second Coming by converting all Jews. The foremost of Kovner's backers was Mrs. Skoglund, who had inherited a large dairy business from her late husband. Woody was under her special protection.

Woody was fourteen years of age when Pop took off with Halina, who worked in his shop, leaving his difficult Christian wife and his converted son and his small daughters. He came to Woody in the back yard one spring day and said. "From now on you're the man of the house." Woody was practicing with a golf club, knocking off the heads of dandelions. Pop came into the yard in his good suit, which was too hot for the weather, and when he took off his fedora the skin of his head was marked with a deep ring and the sweat was sprinkled over his scalp—more drops than hairs. He said, "I'm going to move out." Pop was anxious, but he was set to go—determined. "It's no use. I can't live a life like this." Envisioning the life Pop simply *had* to live, his free life, Woody was able to picture him in the billiard parlor, under the "L" tracks in a crap game, or playing poker at Brown and Koppel's upstairs. "You're going to be the man of the house," said Pop. "It's O.K. I put you all on welfare. I just got back from Wabansia Avenue, from the Relief Station." Hence the suit and the hat. "They're sending out a caseworker." Then he said, "You got to lend me money to buy gasoline—the caddie money you saved."

Understanding that Pop couldn't get away without his help, Woody turned over to him all he had earned at the Sunset Ridge Country Club in Winnetka. Pop felt that the valuable life lesson he was transmitting was worth far more than these dollars, and whenever he was conning his boy a sort of high-priest expression came down over his bent nose, his ruddy face. The children, who got their finest ideas at the movies, called him Richard Dix. Later, when the comic strip came out, they said he was Dick Tracy.

As Woody now saw it, under the tumbling bells, he had bankrolled his own desertion. Ha ha! He found this delightful; and especially Pop's attitude of "That'll teach you to trust your father." For this was a demonstration on behalf of real life and free instincts, against religion and hypocrisy. But mainly it was aimed against being a fool, the disgrace of foolishness. Pop had it in for the Reverend Dr. Kovner, not because he was an apostate (Pop couldn't have cared less), but because the mission was a racket (he admitted that the Reverend Doctor was personally honest), but because Dr. Kovner behaved foolishly, spoke like a fool, and acted like a fiddler. He tossed his hair like a Paganini (this was Woody's addition; Pop had never even heard of Paganini). Proof that he was not a spiritual leader was that he converted Jewish women by stealing their hearts. "He works up all those broads," said Pop. "He doesn't even know it himself, I swear he doesn't know how he gets them."

From the other side, Kovner often warned Woody, "Your father is a dangerous person. Of course, you love him; you should love him and forgive him, Voodrow, but you are old enough to understand he is leading a life of wice."

It was all petty stuff: Pop's sinning was on a boy level and therefore made a big impression on a boy. And on Mother. Are wives children, or what? Mother often said, "I hope you put that brute in your prayers. Look what he has done to us. But only pray for him, don't see him." But he saw him all the time. Woodrow was leading a double life, sacred and profane. He accepted Jesus Christ as his personal redeemer. Aunt Rebecca took advantage of this. She made him work. He had to work under Aunt Rebecca. He filled in for the janitor at the mission and settlement house. In winter, he had to feed the coal furnace, and on some nights he slept near the furnace room, on the pool table. He also picked the lock of the storeroom. He took canned pineapple and cut bacon from the flitch with his pocketknife. He crammed himself with uncooked bacon. He had a big frame to fill out.

Only now, sipping Melitta coffee, he asked himself—had he been so hungry? No, he loved being reckless. He was fighting Aunt Rebecca Kovner when he took out his knife and got on a box to reach the bacon. She didn't know, she couldn't prove that Woody, such a frank, strong, positive boy who looked you in the eye, so direct, was a thief also. But he was also a thief. Whenever she looked at him, he knew that she was seeing his father. In the curve of his nose, the movements of his eyes, the thickness of his body, in his healthy face she saw that wicked savage, Morris.

Morris, you see, had been a street boy in Liverpool—Woody's mother and her sister were British by birth. Morris's Polish family, on their way to America, abandoned him in Liverpool because he had an eye infection and they would all have been sent back from Ellis Island. They stopped awhile in England, but his eyes kept running and they ditched him. They slipped away, and he had to make out alone in Liverpool at the age of twelve. Mother came of better people. Pop, who slept in the cellar of her house, fell in love with her. At sixteen, scabbing during a seamen's strike, he shovelled his way across the Atlantic and jumped ship in Brooklyn. He became an American, and

America never knew it. He voted without papers, he drove without a license, he paid no taxes, he cut every corner. Horses, cards, billiards, and women were his lifelong interests, in ascending order. Did he love anyone (he was so busy)? Yes, he loved Halina. He loved his son. To this day, Mother believed that he had loved her most and always wanted to come back. This gave her a chance to act the queen, with her plump wrists and faded Queen Victoria face. "The girls are instructed never to admit him," she said. The Empress of India, speaking.

Bell-battered Woodrow's soul was whirling this Sunday morning, indoors and out, to the past, back to his upper corner of the warehouse, laid out with such originality—the bells coming and going, metal on naked metal, until the bell circle expanded over the whole of steelmaking, oil-refining, power-producing mid-autumn South Chicago, and all its Croatians, Ukrainians, Greeks, Poles, and respectable blacks heading for their churches to hear Mass or to sing hymns.

Woody himself had been a good hymn singer. He still knew the hymns. He had testified, too. He was often sent by Aunt Rebecca to get up and tell a church full of Scandihoovians that he, a Jewish lad, accepted Jesus Christ. For this she paid him fifty cents. She made the disbursement. She was the bookkeeper, fiscal chief, general manager of the mission. The Reverend Doctor didn't know a thing about the operation. What the Doctor supplied was the fervor. He was genuine, a wonderful preacher. And what about Woody himself? He also had fervor. He was drawn to the Reverend Doctor. The Reverend Doctor taught him to lift up his eyes, gave him his higher life. Apart from this higher life, the rest was Chicago—the ways of Chicago, which came so natural that nobody thought to question them. So, for instance, in 1933 (what ancient, ancient times!)

at the Century of Progress World's Fair, when Woody was a coolie and pulled a rickshaw, wearing a peaked straw hat and trotting with powerful, thick legs, while the brawny red farmers—his boozing passengers—were laughing their heads off and pestered him for whores, he, although a freshman at the seminary, saw nothing wrong, when girls asked him to steer a little business their way, in making dates and accepting tips from both sides. He necked in Grant Park with a powerful girl who had to go home quickly to nurse her baby. Smelling of milk, she rode beside him on the streetcar to the West Side, squeezing his rickshaw puller's thigh and wetting her blouse. This was the Roosevelt Road car. Then, in the apartment where she lived with her mother, he couldn't remember that there were any husbands around. What he did remember was the strong milk odor. Without inconsistency, next morning he did New Testament Greek: The light shineth in darkness—*to fos en te skotia fainei*—and the darkness comprehended it not.

And all the while he trotted between the shafts on the fairgrounds he had one idea—nothing to do with these horny giants having a big time in the city: that the goal, the project, the purpose was (and he couldn't explain why he thought so; all evidence was against it), God's idea was that this world should be a love-world, that it should eventually recover and be entirely a world of love. He wouldn't have said this to a soul, for he could see himself how stupid it was—personal and stupid. Nevertheless, there it was at the center of his feelings. And at the same time Aunt Rebecca was right when she said to him, strictly private, close to his ear even, "You're a little crook, like your father."

There was some evidence for this, or what stood for evidence to an impatient person like Rebecca. Woody matured quickly—he had to—but how could you expect a boy of seventeen, he wondered, to interpret the viewpoint, the feelings of a middle-aged woman, and one whose breast had been removed? Morris told him that this happened only to neglected women, and was a sign. Morris said that if titties were not fondled and kissed they got cancer in protest. It was a cry of the flesh. And this had seemed true to Woody. When his imagination tried the theory on the Reverend Doctor, it worked out—he couldn't see the Reverend Doctor behaving in that way to Aunt Rebecca's breasts! Morris's theory kept Woody looking from bosoms to husbands and from husbands to bosoms. He still did that. It's an exceptionally smart man who isn't marked forever by the sexual theories he hears from his father, and Woody wasn't all that smart. He knew this himself. Personally, he had gone far out of his way to do right by women in this regard. What nature demanded. He and Pop were common, thick men, but there's nobody too gross to have ideas of delicacy.

The Reverend Doctor preached, Rebecca preached, rich Mrs. Skoglund preached from Evanston, Mother preached. Pop also was on a soapbox. Everyone was doing it. Up and down Division Street, under every lamp, almost, speakers were giving out: anarchists, Socialists, Stalinists, single-taxers, Zionists, Tolstoyans, vegetarians, and fundamentalist Christian preachers—you name it. A beef, a hope, a way of life or salvation, a protest. How was it that the accumulated gripes of all the ages took off so when transplanted to America?

And that fine Swedish immigrant Aase (Osie, they pronounced it), who had been the Skoglunds' cook and married the eldest son to become his rich, religious widow—she supported the Reverend Doctor. In her time she must have been built like a chorus girl. And women seem to have lost the secret of putting up their hair in the high basketry fence of braid she wore. Aase took Woody under her special protection and paid his tuition at the seminary. And Pop said . . . But on this Sunday, at peace as soon as the bells stopped banging, this velvet autumn day when the grass was finest and thickest, silky green: before the first frost, and the blood in your lungs is redder than summer air can make it and smarts with oxygen, as if the iron in your system was hungry for it, and the chill was sticking it to you in every breath—Pop, six feet under, would never feel this blissful sting again. The last of the bells still had the bright air streaming with vibrations.

On weekends, the institutional vacancy of decades came back to the warehouse and crept under the door of Woody's apartment. It felt as empty on Sundays as churches were during the week. Before each business day, before the trucks and the crews got started, Woody jogged five miles in his Adidas suit. Not on this day still reserved for Pop, however. Although it was tempting to go out and run off the grief. Being alone hit Woody hard this morning. He thought, Me and the world; the world and me. Meaning that there always was some activity to interpose, an errand or a visit, a picture to paint (he was a creative amateur), a massage, a meal—a shield between himself and that troublesome solitude which used the world as its reservoir. But Pop! Last Tuesday, Woody had gotten into the hospital bed with Pop because he kept pulling out the intravenous needles. Nurses stuck them back, and then Woody astonished them all by climbing into bed to hold the struggling old guy in his arms. "Easy, Morris, Morris, go easy." But Pop still groped feebly for the pipes.

When the tolling stopped, Woody didn't notice that a great lake of quiet had come over his kingdom, the

Selbst Tile Warehouse. What he heard and saw was an old red Chicago streetcar, one of those trams the color of a stockyard steer. Cars of this type went out before Pearl Harbor—clumsy, big-bellied, with tough rattan seats and brass grips for the standing passengers. Those cars used to make four stops to the mile, and ran with a wallowing motion. They stank of carbolic or ozone and throbbed when the air compressors were being charged. The conductor had his knotted signal cord to pull, and the motorman beat the foot gong with his mad heel.

Woody recognized himself on the Western Avenue line and riding through a blizzard with his father, both in sheepskins and with hands and faces raw, the snow blowing in from the rear platform when the doors opened and getting into the longitudinal cleats of the floor. There wasn't warmth enough inside to melt it. And Western Avenue was the longest car line in the world, the boosters said, as if it was a thing to brag about. Twenty-three miles long, made by a draftsman with a T-square, lined with factories, storage buildings, machine shops, used-car lots, trolley barns, gas stations, funeral parlors, six-flats, utility buildings, and junk yards, on and on from the prairies on the south to Evanston on the north. Woodrow and his father were going north to Evanston, to Howard Street, and then some, to see Mrs. Skoglund. At the end of the line they would still have about five blocks to hike. The purpose of the trip? To raise money for Pop. Pop had talked him into this. When they found out, Mother and Aunt Rebecca would be furious, and Woody was afraid, but he couldn't help it.

Morris had come and said, "Son, I'm in trouble. It's bad."

"What's bad, Pop?"

"Halina took money from her husband for me and has to put it back before old Bujak misses it. He could kill her."

"What did she do it for?"

"Son, you know how the bookies collect? They send a goon. They'll break my head open."

"Pop! You know I can't take you to Mrs. Skoglund."

"Why not? You're my kid, aren't you? The old broad wants to adopt you, doesn't she? Shouldn't I get something out of it for my trouble? What am I—outside? And what about Halina? She puts her life on the line, but my own kid says no."

"Oh, Bujak wouldn't hurt her."

"Woody, he'd beat her to death."

Bujak? Uniform in color with his dark-gray work clothes, short in the legs, his whole strength in his tool-and-die-maker's forearms and black fingers; and beat-looking—there was Bujak for you. But, according to Pop, there was big, big violence in Bujak, a regular boiling Bessemer inside his narrow chest. Woody could never see the violence in him. Bujak wanted no trouble. If anything, maybe he was afraid that Morris and Halina would gang up on him and kill him, screaming. But Pop was no desperado murderer. And Halina was a calm, serious woman. Bujak kept his savings in the cellar (banks were going out of business). The worst they did was to take some of his money, intending to put it back. As Woody saw him, Bujak was trying to be sensible. He accepted his sorrow. He set minimum requirements for Halina: cook the meals, clean the house, show respect. But at stealing Bujak might have drawn the line, for money was different, money was vital substance. If they stole his savings he might have had to take action, out of respect for the substance, for himself—self-respect. But you couldn't be sure that Pop hadn't invented the bookie, the goon, the theft—the whole thing. He was capable of it, and you'd be a fool not to suspect him. Morris knew that Mother and Aunt Rebecca had told Mrs. Skoglund how wicked he was. They had painted him for her in poster colors—purple for vice, black for his soul, red for Hell flames: a gambler, smoker, drinker, deserter, screwer of women, and athiest. So Pop was determined to reach her. It was risky for everybody. The Reverend Doctor's operating costs were met by Skoglund Dairies. The widow paid Woody's seminary tuition; she bought dresses for the little sisters.

Woody, now sixty, fleshy and big, like a figure for the victory of American materialism, sunk in his lounge chair, the leather of its armrests softer to his fingertips than a woman's skin, was puzzled and, in his depths, disturbed by certain blots within him, blots of light in his brain, a blot combining pain and amusement in his breast (how did *that* get there?). Intense thought puckered the skin between his eyes with a strain bordering on headache. Why had he let Pop have his way? Why did he agree to meet him that day, in the dim rear of the poolroom?

"But what will you tell Mrs. Skoglund?"

"The old broad? Don't worry, there's plenty to tell her, and it's all true. Ain't I trying to save my little laundry-and-cleaning shop? Isn't the bailiff coming for the fixtures next week?" And Pop rehearsed his pitch on the Western Avenue car. He counted on Woody's health and his freshness. Such a straightforward-looking boy was perfect for a con.

Did they still have such winter storms in Chicago as they used to have? Now they somehow seemed less fierce. Blizzards used to come straight down from Ontario, from the Arctic, and drop five feet of snow in an afternoon. Then the rusty green platform cars, with revolving brushes at both ends, came out of the barns to sweep the tracks. Ten or twelve streetcars followed in slow processions, or waited, block after block.

There was a long delay at the gates of Riverview Park, all the amusements covered for the winter, boarded up—the dragon's-back high-rides, the Bobs, the Chute, the Tilt-a-Whirl, all the fun machinery put together by mechanics and electricians, men like Bujak the tool-and-die-maker, good with engines. The blizzard was having it all its own way behind the gates, and you couldn't see far inside; only a few bulbs burned behind the palings. When Woody wiped the vapor from the glass, the wire mesh of the window guards was stuffed solid at eye level with snow. Looking higher, you saw mostly the streaked wind horizontally driving from the north. In the seat ahead, two black coal heavers both in leather Lindbergh flying helmets sat with shovels between their legs, returning from a job. They smelled of sweat, burlap sacking, and coal. Mostly dull with black dust, they also sparkled here and there.

There weren't many riders. People weren't leaving the house. This was a day to sit legs stuck out beside the stove, mummified by both the outdoor and the indoor forces. Only a fellow with an angle, like Pop, would go and buck such weather. A storm like this was out of the compass, and you kept the human scale by having a scheme to raise fifty bucks. Fifty soldiers! Real money in 1933.

"That woman is crazy for you," said Pop.

"She's just a good woman, sweet to all of us."

"Who knows what she's got in mind. You're a husky kid. Not such a kid either."

"She's a religious woman. She really has religion."

"Well, your mother isn't your only parent. She and Rebecca and Kovner aren't going to fill you up with their ideas. I know your mother wants to wipe me out of your life. Unless I take a hand, you won't even understand what life is. Because they don't know—those silly Christers."

"Yes Pop."

"The girls I can't help. They're too young. I'm sorry about them, but I can't do anything. With you it's different."

He wanted me like himself, an American.

They were stalled in the storm, while the cattle-colored car waited to have the trolley reset in the crazy wind, which boomed, tingled, blasted. At Howard Street they would have to walk straight into it, due north.

"You'll do the talking at first," said Pop.

Woody had the makings of a salesman, a pitchman. He was aware of this when he got to his feet in church to testify before fifty or sixty people. Even though Aunt Rebecca made it worth his while, he moved his own heart when he spoke up about his faith. But occasionally, without notice, his heart went away as he spoke religion and he couldn't find it anywhere. In its absence, sincere behavior got him through. He had to rely for delivery on his face, his voice—on behavior. Then his eyes came closer and closer together. And in this approach of eye to eye he felt the strain of hypocrisy. The twisting of his face threatened to betray him. It took everything he had to keep looking honest. So, since he couldn't bear the cynicism of it, he fell back on mischievousness. Mischief was where Pop came in. Pop passed straight through all those divided fields, gap after gap, and arrived at his side, bent-nosed and broad-faced. In regard to Pop, you thought of neither sincerity nor insincerity. Pop was like the man in the song: he wanted what he wanted when he wanted it. Pop was physical; Pop was digestive, circulatory, sexual. If Pop got serious, he talked to you about washing under the arms or in the crotch or of drying between your toes or of cooking supper, of baked beans and fried onions, of draw poker or of a certain horse in the fifth race at Arlington. Pop was elemental. That was why he gave such relief from religion and paradoxes, and things like that. Now Mother *thought* she was spiritual, but Woody knew that she was kidding herself. Oh, yes, in the British accent she never gave up she was always talking to God or about Him—please-God, God-willing, praise-God. But she was a big substantial bread-and-butter, down-to-earth woman, with down-to-earth duties like feeding the girls, protecting, refining, keeping pure the girls. And those two protected doves grew up so overweight, heavy in the hips and thighs, that their poor heads looked long and slim. And mad. Sweet but cuckoo—Paula cheerfully cuckoo, Joanna depressed and having episodes.

"I'll do my best by you, but you have to promise, Pop, not to get me in Dutch with Mrs. Skoglund."

"You worried because I speak bad English? Embarrassed? I have a mockie accent?"

"It's not that. Kovner has a heavy accent, and she doesn't mind."

"Who the hell are those freaks to look down on me? You're practically a man and your dad has a right to expect help from you. He's in a fix. And you bring him to her house because she's big-hearted, and you haven't got anybody else to go to."

"I got you, Pop."

The two coal trimmers stood up at Devon Avenue. One of them wore a woman's coat. Men wore women's clothing in those years, and women men's, when there was no choice. The fur collar was spiky with the wet, and sprinkled with soot. Heavy, they dragged their shovels and got off at the front. The slow car ground on, very slow. It was after four when they reached the end of the line, and somewhere between gray and black, with snow spouting and whirling under the street lamps. In Howard Street, autos were stalled at all angles and abandoned. The sidewalks were blocked. Woody led the way into Evanston, and Pop followed him up the middle of the street in the furrows made earlier by trucks. For four blocks they bucked the wind and then Woody broke through the drifts to the snowbound mansion, where they both had to push the wrought-iron gate because of the drift behind it. Twenty rooms or more in this dignified house and nobody in them but Mrs. Skoglund and her servant Hjordis, also religious.

As Woody and Pop waited, brushing the slush from their sheepskin collars and Pop wiping his big eyebrows with the ends of his scarf, sweating and freezing, the chains began to rattle and Hjordis uncovered the air holes of the glass storm door by turning a wooden bar. Woody called her "monk-faced." You no longer see women like that, who put no female touch on the face. She came plain, as God made her. She said, "Who is it and what do you want?"

"It's Woodrow Selbst. Hjordis? It's Woody."

"You're not expected."

"No, but we're here."

"What do you want?"

"We came to see Mrs. Skoglund."

"What for do you want to see her?"

"Just to tell her we're here."

"I have to tell her what you came for, without calling up first."

"Why don't you say it's Woody with his father, and we wouldn't come in a snowstorm like this if it wasn't important."

The understandable caution of women who live alone. Respectable old-time women, too. There was no such respectability now in those Evanston houses, with their big verandas and deep yards and with a servant like Hjordis, who carried at her belt keys to the pantry and to every closet and every dresser drawer and every padlocked bin in the cellar. And in High Episcopal Christian Science Women's Temperance Evanston no tradespeople rang at the front door. Only invited guests. And here, after a ten-mile grind through the blizzard, came two tramps from the West Side. To this mansion where a Swedish immigrant lady, herself once a cook and now a philanthropic widow, dreamed, snowbound, while frozen lilac twigs clapped at her storm windows, of a new Jerusalem and a Second Coming and a Resurrection and a Last Judgment. To hasten the Second Coming, and all the rest, you had to reach the hearts of these scheming bums arriving in a snowstorm.

Sure, they let us in.

Then in the heat that swam suddenly up to their mufflered chins Pop and Woody felt the blizzard for what it was; their cheeks were frozen slabs. They stood beat, itching, trickling in the front hall that *was* a hall, with a carved newel post staircase and a big stained-glass window at the top. Picturing Jesus with the Samaritan woman. There was a kind of Gentile closeness to the air. Perhaps when he was with Pop, Woody made more Jewish observations than he would otherwise. Although Pop's most Jewish characteristic was that Yiddish was the only language he could read a paper in. Pop was with Polish Halina, and Mother was with Jesus Christ, and Woody ate uncooked bacon from the flitch. Still now and then he had a Jewish impression.

Mrs. Skoglund was the cleanest of women—her fingernails, her white neck, her ears—and Pop's sexual hints to Woody all went wrong because she was so intensely clean, and made Woody think of a waterfall, large as she was, and grandly built. Her bust was big.

Woody's imagination had investigated this. He thought she kept things tied down tight, very tight. But she lifted both arms once to raise a window and there it was, her bust, beside him, the whole unbindable thing. Her hair was like the raffia you had to soak before you could weave with it in a basket class—pale, pale. Pop, as he took his sheepskin off, was in sweaters, no jacket. His darting looks made him seem crooked. Hardest of all for these Selbsts with their bent noses and big, apparently straightforward faces was to look honest. All the signs of dishonesty played over them. Woody had often puzzled about it. Did it go back to the muscles, was it fundamentally a jaw problem—the projecting angles of the jaws? Or was it the angling that went on in the heart? The girls called Pop Dick Tracy, but Dick Tracy was a good guy. Whom could Pop convince? Here, Woody caught a possibility as it flitted by. Precisely because of the way Pop looked, a sensitive person might feel remorse for condemning unfairly or judging unkindly. Just because of a face? Some must have bent over backward. Then he had them. Not Hjordis. She would have put Pop into the street then and there, storm or no storm. Hjordis was religious, but she was wised up, too. She hadn't come over in steerage and worked forty years in Chicago for nothing.

Mrs. Skoglund, Aase (Osie), led the visitors into the front room. This, the biggest room in the house, needed supplementary heating. Because of fifteen-foot ceilings and high windows, Hjordis had kept the parlor stove burning. It was one of those elegant parlor stoves that wore a nickel crown, or mitre, and this mitre, when you moved it aside, automatically raised the hinge of an iron stove lid. That stove lid underneath the crown was all soot and rust, the same as any other stove lid. Into this hole you tipped the scuttle and the anthracite chestnut rattled down. It made a cake or dome of fire visible through the small isinglass frames. It was a pretty room, three-quarters panelled in wood. The stove was plugged into the flue of the marble fireplace, and there were parquet floors and Axminster carpets and cranberry-colored tufted Victorian upholstery, and a kind of Chinese étagère, inside a cabinet, lined with mirrors and containing silver pitchers, trophies won by Skoglund cows, fancy sugar tongs and cut-glass pitchers and goblets. There were Bibles and pictures of Jesus and the Holy Land and that faint Gentile odor, as if things had been rinsed in a weak vinegar solution.

"Mrs. Skoglund, I brought my dad to you. I don't think you ever met him," said Woody.

"Yes, Missus, that's me, Selbst."

Pop stood short but masterful in the sweaters, and his belly sticking out, not soft but hard. He was a man of the hard-bellied type. Nobody intimidated Pop. He never presented himself as a beggar. There wasn't a cringe in him anywhere. He let her see at once by the way he said "Missus" that he was independent and that he knew his way around. He communicated that he was able to handle himself with women. Handsome Mrs. Skoglund, carrying a basket woven out of her own hair, was in her fifties—eight, maybe ten years his senior.

"I asked my son to bring me because I know you do the kid a lot of good. It's natural you should know both of his parents."

"Mrs. Skoglund, my dad is in a tight corner and I don't know anybody else to ask for help."

This was all the preliminary Pop wanted. He took over and told the widow his story about the laundry-and-cleaning business and payments overdue, and explained about the fixtures and the attachment notice, and the bailiff's office and what they were going to do to him; and he said, "I'm a small man trying to make a living."

"You don't support your children," said Mrs. Skoglund.

"That's right," said Hjordis.

"I haven't got it. If I had it, wouldn't I give it? There's bread lines and soup lines all over town. Is it just me? What I have I divvy with. I give the kids. A bad father? You think my son would bring me if I was a bad father into your house? He loves his dad, he trusts his dad, he knows his dad is a good dad. Every time I start a little business going I get wiped out. This one is a good little business, if I could hold on to that little business. Three people work for me, I meet a payroll, and three people will be on the street, too, if I close down. Missus, I can sign a note and pay you in two months. I'm a common man, but I'm a hard worker and a fellow you can trust."

Woody was startled when Pop used the word "trust." It was as if from all four corners a Sousa band blew a blast to warn the entire world. "Crook! This is a crook!" But Mrs. Skoglund, on account of her religious preoccupations, was remote. She heard nothing. Although everybody in this part of the world, unless he was crazy, led a practical life, and you'd have nothing to say to anyone, your neighbors would have nothing to say to you if communications were not of a practical sort, Mrs. Skoglund, with all her money, was unworldly—two-thirds out of this world.

"Give me a chance to show what's in me," said Pop, "and you'll see what I do for my kids."

So Mrs. Skoglund hesitated, and then she said she'd have to go upstairs, she'd have to go to her room and pray on it and ask for guidance—would they sit down and wait. There were two rocking chairs by the stove. Hjordis gave Pop a grim look (a dangerous person) and Woody a blaming one (he brought a dangerous stranger and disrupter to injure two kind Christian ladies). Then she went out with Mrs. Skoglund.

As soon as they left, Pop jumped up from the rocker and said in anger, "What's this with the praying? She has to ask God to lend me fifty bucks?"

Woody said, "It's not you, Pop, it's the way these religious people do."

"No," said Pop. "She'll come back and say that God wouldn't let her."

Woody didn't like that; he thought Pop was being gross and he said, "No, she's sincere. Pop, try to understand; she's emotional, nervous, and sincere, and tries to do right by everybody."

And Pop said, "That servant will talk her out of it. She's a toughie. It's all over her face that we're a couple of chisellers."

"What's the use of us arguing," said Woody. He drew the rocker closer to the stove. His shoes were wet through and would never dry. The blue flames fluttered like a school of fishes in the coal fire. But Pop went over to the Chinese-style cabinet or étagère and tried the handle, and then opened the blade of his penknife and in a second had forced the lock of the curved glass door. He took out a silver dish.

"Pop, what is this?" said Woody.

Pop, cool and level, knew exactly what this was. He relocked the étagère, crossed the carpet, listened. He stuffed the dish under his belt and pushed it down into his trousers. He put the side of his short thick finger to his mouth.

So Woody kept his voice down, but he was all shook up. He went to Pop and took him by the edge of his hand. As he looked into Pop's face, he felt his eyes growing smaller and smaller, as if something were contracting all the skin on his head. They call it hyperventilation when everything feels tight and light and close and dizzy. Hardly breathing, he said, "Put it back, Pop."

Pop said, "It's solid silver; it's worth dough."

"Pop, you said you wouldn't get me in Dutch."

"It's only insurance in case she comes back from praying and tells me no. If she says yes, I'll put it back."

"How?"

"It'll get back. If I don't put it back, you will."

"You picked the lock. I couldn't. I don't know how."

"There's nothing to it."

"We're going to put it back now. Give it here."

"Woody, it's under my fly, inside my underpants, don't make such a noise about nothing."

"Pop, I can't believe this."

"For Cry-99, shut your mouth. If I didn't trust you I wouldn't have let you watch me do it. You don't understand a thing. What's with you?"

"Before they come down, Pop, will you dig that dish out of your long johns."

Pop turned stiff on him. He became absolutely military. He said, "Look, I order you!"

Before he knew it, Woody had jumped his father and begun to wrestle with him. It was outrageous to clutch your own father, to put a heel behind him, to force him to the wall. Pop was taken by surprise and said loudly, "You want Halina killed? Kill her! Go on, you be responsible." He began to resist, angry, and they turned about several times when Woody, with a trick he had learned in a Western movie and used once on the playground, tripped him and they fell to the ground. Woody, who already outweighed the old man by twenty pounds, was on the top. They landed on the floor beside the stove, which stood on a tray of decorated tin to protect the carpet. In this position, pressing Pop's hard belly, Woody recognized that to have wrestled him to the floor counted for nothing. It was impossible to thrust his hand under Pop's belt to recover the dish. And now Pop had turned furious, as a father has every right to be when his son is violent with him, and he freed his hand and hit Woody in the face. He hit him three or four times in mid-face. Then Woody dug his head into Pop's shoulder and held tight only to keep from being struck and began to say in his ear, "Jesus, Pop, for Christ sake remember where you are. Those women will be back!" But Pop brought up his short knee and fought and butted him with his chin and rattled Woody's teeth. Woody thought the old man was about to bite him. And, because he was a seminarian, he thought, "Like an unclean spirit." And held tight. Gradually Pop stopped threshing and struggling. His eyes stuck out and his mouth was open, sullen. Like a stout fish. Woody released him and gave him a hand up. He was then overcome with many many bad feelings of a sort he knew the old man never suffered. Never, never. Pop never had these grovelling emotions. There was his whole superiority. Pop had no such feelings. He was like a horseman from Central Asia, a bandit from China. It was Mother, from Liverpool, who had the refinement, the English manners. It was the preaching Reverend Doctor in his black suit. You have refinements, and all they do is oppress you? The hell with that.

The long door opened and Mrs. Skoglund stepped in, saying, "Did I imagine, or did something shake the house?"

"I was lifting the scuttle to put coal on the fire and it fell out of my hand. I'm sorry I was so clumsy," said Woody.

Pop was too huffy to speak. With his eyes big and sore and the thin hair down over his forehead, you could see by the tightness of his belly how angrily he was fetching his breath, though his mouth was shut.

"I prayed," said Mrs. Skoglund.

"I hope it came out well," said Woody.

"Well, I don't do anything without guidance, but the answer was yes, and I feel right about it now. So if you'll wait I'll go to my office and write a check. I asked Hjordis to bring you a cup of coffee. Coming in such a storm."

And Pop, consistently a terrible little man, as soon as she shut the door said, "A check? Hell with a check. Get me the greenbacks."

"They don't keep money in the house. You can cash it in her bank tomorrow. But if they miss that dish, Pop, they'll stop the check, and then where are you?"

As Pop was reaching below the belt Hjordis brought in the tray. She was very sharp with him. She said, "Is this a place to adjust clothing, Mister? A men's washroom?"

"Well, which way is the toilet, then?" said Pop.

She had served the coffee in the seamiest mugs in the pantry, and she bumped down the tray and led Pop down the corridor, standing guard at the bathroom door so that he shouldn't wander about the house.

Mrs. Skoglund called Woody to her office and after she had given him the folded check said that they should pray together for Morris. So once more he was on his knees, under rows and rows of musty marbled cardboard files, by the glass lamp by the edge of the desk, the shade with flounced edges, like the candy dish. Mrs. Skoglund, in her Scandinavian accent—an emotional contralto—raising her voice to Jesus-uh Christ-uh, as the wind lashed the trees, kicked the side of the house, and drove the snow seething on the windowpanes, to send light-uh, give guidance-uh, put a new heart-uh in Pop's bosom. Woody asked God only to make Pop put the dish back. He kept Mrs. Skoglund on her knees as long as possible. Then he thanked her, shining with candor (as much as he knew how) for her

Christian generosity and he said, "I know that Hjordis has a cousin who works at the Evanston Y.M.C.A. Could she please phone him and try to get us a room tonight so that we don't have to fight the blizzard all the way back? We're almost as close to the Y as to the car line. Maybe the cars have even stopped running."

Suspicious Hjordis, coming when Mrs. Skoglund called to her, was burning now. First they barged in, made themselves at home, asked for money, had to have coffee, probably left gonorrhea on the toilet seat. Hjordis, Woody remembered, was a woman who wiped the doorknobs with rubbing alcohol after guests had left. Nevertheless, she telephoned the Y and got them a room with two cots for six bits.

Pop had plenty of time, therefore, to reopen the étagère, lined with reflecting glass or German silver (something exquisitely delicate and tricky), and as soon as the two Selbsts had said thank you and goodbye and were in mid-street again up to the knees in snow, Woody said, "Well, I covered for you. Is that thing back?"

"Of course it is," said Pop.

They fought their way to the small Y building, shut up in wire grille and resembling a police station—about the same dimensions. It was locked, but they made a racket on the grille, and a small black man let them in and shuffled them upstairs to a cement corridor with low doors. It was like the small mammal house in Lincoln Park. He said there was nothing to eat, so they took off their wet pants, wrapped themselves tightly in the khaki army blankets, and passed out on their cots.

First thing in the morning, they went to the Evanston National Bank and got the fifty dollars. Not without difficulties. The teller went to call Mrs. Skoglund and was absent a long time from the wicket. "Where the hell has he gone," said Pop.

But when the fellow came back he said, "How do you want it?"

Pop said, "Singles." He told Woody, "Bujak stashes it in one-dollar bills."

But by now Woody no longer believed Halina had stolen the old man's money.

Then they went into the street, where the snow-removal crews were at work. The sun shone broad, broad, out of the morning blue, and all Chicago would be releasing itself from the temporary beauty of those vast drifts.

"You shouldn't have jumped me last night, Sonny."

"I know, Pop, but you promised you wouldn't get me in Dutch."

"Well, it's O.K., we can forget it, seeing you stood by me."

Only, Pop had taken the silver dish. Of course he had, and in a few days Mrs. Skoglund and Hjordis knew it, and later in the week they were all waiting for Woody in Kovner's office at the settlement house. The group included the Reverend Dr. Crabbie, head of the seminary, and Woody, who had been flying along, level and smooth, was shot down in flames. He told them he was innocent. Even as he was falling, he warned that they were wronging him. He denied that he or Pop had touched Mrs. Skoglund's property. The missing object—he didn't even know what it was—had probably been misplaced, and they would be very sorry on the day it turned up. After the others were done with him, Dr. Crabbie said until he was able to tell the truth he would be suspended from the seminary, where his work had been unsatisfactory anyway. Aunt Rebecca took him aside and said to him, "You are a little crook, like your father. The door is closed to you here."

To this Pop's comment was "So what, kid?"

"Pop, you shouldn't have done it."

"No? Well, I don't give a care, if you want to know. You can have the dish if you want to go back and square yourself with all those hypocrites."

"I didn't like doing Mrs. Skoglund in the eye, she was so kind to us."

"Kind?"

"Kind."

"Kind has a price tag."

Well, there was no winning such arguments with Pop. But they debated it in various moods and from various elevations and perspectives for forty years and more, as their intimacy changed, developed, matured.

"Why did you do it, Pop? For the money? What did you do with the fifty bucks?" Woody, decades later, asked him that.

"I settled with the bookie, and the rest I put in the business."

"You tried a few more horses."

"I maybe did. But it was a double, Woody. I didn't hurt myself, and at the same time did you a favor."

"It was for me?"

"It was too strange of a life. That life wasn't *you*, Woody. All those women—Kovner was no man, he was an in-between. Suppose they made you a minister? Some Christian minister! First of all, you wouldn't have been able to stand it, and, second, they would throw you out sooner or later."

"Maybe so."

"And you wouldn't have converted the Jews, which was the main thing they wanted."

"And what a time to bother the Jews," Woody said. "At least *I* didn't bug them."

Pop had carried him back to his side of the line, blood of his blood, the same thick body walls, the same coarse grain. Not cut out for a spiritual life. Simply not up to it.

Pop was no worse than Woody, and Woody was no

better than Pop. Pop wanted no relation to theory, and yet he was always pointing Woody toward a position—a jolly, hearty, natural, likable, unprincipled position. If Woody had a weakness, it was to be unselfish. This worked to Pop's advantage, but he criticized Woody for it, nevertheless. "You take too much on yourself," Pop was always saying. And it's true that Woody gave Pop his heart because Pop was so selfish. It's usually the selfish people who are loved the most. They do what you deny yourself, and you love them for it. You give them your heart.

Remembering the pawn ticket for the silver dish, Woody startled himself with a laugh so sudden that it made him cough. Pop said to him after his expulsion from the seminary and banishment from the settlement house, "You want in again? Here's the ticket. I hocked that thing. It wasn't so valuable as I thought."

"What did they give?"

"Twelve-fifty was all I could get. But if you want it you'll have to raise the dough yourself, because I haven't got it anymore."

"You must have been sweating in the bank when the teller went to call Mrs. Skoglund about the check."

"I was a little nervous," said Pop. "But I didn't think they could miss the thing so soon."

That theft was part of Pop's war with Mother. With Mother, and Aunt Rebecca, and the Reverend Doctor. Pop took his stand on realism. Mother represented the forces of religion and hypochondria. In four decades, the fighting never stopped. In the course of time, Mother and the girls turned into welfare personalities and lost their individual outlines. Ah, the poor things, they became dependents and cranks. In the meantime, Woody, the sinful man, was their dutiful and loving son and brother. He maintained the bungalow—this took in roofing, painting, wiring, insulation, air-conditioning—and he paid for heat and light and food, and dressed them all out of Sears, Roebuck and Wieboldt's, and bought them a TV, which they watched as devoutly as they prayed. Paula took courses to learn skills like macramé-making and needlepoint, and sometimes got a little job as recreational worker in a nursing home. But she wasn't steady enough to keep it. Wicked Pop spent most of his life removing stains from people's clothing. He and Halina in the last years ran a Cleanomat in West Rogers Park—a so-so business resembling a laundromat—which gave him leisure for billiards, the horses, rummy and pinochle. Every morning he went behind the partition to check out the filters of the cleaning equipment. He found amusing things that had been thrown into the vats with the clothing—sometimes, when he got lucky, a locket chain or a brooch. And when he had fortified the cleaning fluid, pouring all that blue and pink stuff in from plastic jugs, he read the *Forward* over a second cup of coffee, and went out, leaving Halina in charge. When they needed help with the rent, Woody gave it.

After the new Disney World was opened in Florida, Woody treated all his dependents to a holiday. He sent them down in separate batches, of course. Halina enjoyed this more than anybody else. She couldn't stop talking about the address given by an Abraham Lincoln automaton. "Wonderful, how he stood up and moved his hands, and his mouth. So real! And how beautiful he talked." Of them all, Halina was the soundest, the most human, the most honest. Now that Pop was gone, Woody and Halina's son, Mitosh, the organist at the Stadium, took care of her needs over and above Social Security, splitting expenses. In Pop's opinion, insurance was a racket. He left Halina nothing but some out-of-date equipment.

Woody treated himself, too. Once a year, and sometimes oftener, he left his business to run itself, arranged with the trust department at the bank to take care of his Gang, and went off. He did that in style, imaginatively, expensively. In Japan, he wasted little time on Tokyo. He spent three weeks in Kyoto and stayed at the Tawaraya Inn, dating from the seventeenth century or so. There he slept on the floor, the Japanese way, and bathed in scalding water. He saw the dirtiest strip show on earth, as well as the holy places and the temple gardens. He visited also Istanbul, Jerusalem, Delphi, and went to Burma and Uganda and Kenya on safari, on democratic terms with drivers, Bedouins, bazaar merchants. Open, lavish, familiar, fleshier and fleshier but (he jogged, he lifted weights) still muscular—in his naked person beginning to resemble a Renaissance courtier in full costume—becoming ruddier every year, an outdoor type with freckles on his back and spots across the flaming forehead and the honest nose. In Addis Ababa he took an Ethiopian beauty to his room from the street and washed her, getting into the shower with her to soap her with his broad, kindly hands. In Kenya he taught certain American obscenities to a black woman so that she could shout them out during the act. On the Nile, below Murchison Falls, those fever trees rose huge from the mud, and hippos on the sandbars belched at the passing launch, hostile. One of them danced on his spit of sand, springing from the ground and coming down heavy, on all fours. There, Woody saw the buffalo calf disappear, snatched by the crocodile.

Mother, soon to follow Pop, was being light-headed these days. In company, she spoke of Woody as her boy—"What do you think of my Sonny?"—as though he was ten years old. She was silly with him, her behavior was frivolous, almost flirtatious. She just didn't seem to know the facts. And behind her all the others, like kids at the playground, were waiting their turn to go down the slide; one on each step, and moving toward the top.

Over Woody's residence and place of business there had gathered a pool of silence of the same perimeter as the church bells while they were ringing, and he mourned under it, this melancholy morning of sun and autumn. Doing a life survey, taking a deliberate look at the gross side of his case—of the other side as well, what there was of it. But if this heartache continued, he'd go out and run it off. A three-mile jog—five, if necessary. And you'd think that this jogging was an entirely physical activity, wouldn't you? But there was something else in it. Because, when he was a seminarian, between the shafts of his World's Fair rickshaw, he used to receive, pulling along (capable and stable), his religious experiences while he trotted. Maybe it was all a single experience repeated. He felt truth coming to him from the sun. He received a communication that was also light and warmth. It made him very remote from his horny Wisconsin passengers, those farmers whose whoops and whore-cries he could hardly hear when he was in one of his states. And again out of the flaming of the sun would come to him a secret certainty that the goal set for this earth was that it should be filled with good, saturated with it. After everything preposterous, after dog had eaten dog, after the crocodile death had pulled everyone into his mud. It wouldn't conclude as Mrs. Skoglund, bribing him to round up the Jews and hasten the Second Coming, imagined it but in another way. This was his clumsy intuition. It went no further. Subsequently, he proceeded through life as life seemed to want him to do it.

There remained one thing more this morning, which was explicitly physical, occurring first as a sensation in his arms and against his breast and, from the pressure, passing into him and going into his breast.

It was like this: When he came into the hospital room and saw Pop with the sides of his bed raised, like a crib, and Pop, so very feeble, and writhing, and toothless, like a baby, and the dirt already cast into his face, into the wrinkles—Pop wanted to pluck out the intravenous needles and he was piping his weak death noise. The gauze patches taped over the needles were soiled with dark blood. Then Woody took off his shoes, lowered the side of the bed, and climbed in and held him in his arms to soothe and still him. As if he were Pop's father, he said to him, "Now Pop. Pop." Then it was like the wrestle in Mrs. Skoglund's parlor, when Pop turned angry like an unclean spirit and Woody tried to appease him, and warn him, saying, "Those women will be back!" Beside the coal stove, when Pop hit Woody in the teeth with his head and then became sullen, like a stout fish. But this struggle in the hospital was weak—so weak! In his great pity, Woody held Pop, who was fluttering and shivering. From those people, Pop had told him, you'll never find out what life is, because they don't know what it is. Yes, Pop—well, what is it, Pop? Hard to comprehend that Pop, who was dug in for eighty-three years and had done all he could to stay, should now want nothing but to free himself. How could Woody allow the old man to pull the intravenous needles out? Willful Pop, he wanted what he wanted when he wanted it. But what he wanted at the very last Woody failed to follow, it was such a switch.

After a time, Pop's resistance ended. He subsided and subsided. He rested against his son, his small body curled there. Nurses came and looked. They disapproved, but Woody, who couldn't spare a hand to wave them out, motioned with his head toward the door. Pop, whom Woody thought he had stilled, only had found a better way to get around him. Loss of heat was the way he did it. His heat was leaving him. As can happen with small animals while you hold them in your hand, Woody presently felt him cooling. Then, as Woody did his best to restrain him, and thought he was succeeding, Pop divided himself. And when he was separated from his warmth he slipped into death. And there was his elderly, large, muscular son, still holding and pressing him when there was nothing anymore to press. You could never pin down that self-willed man. When he was ready to make his move, he made it—always on his own terms. And always, always, something up his sleeve. That was how he was.